Mt. Moriah's
Wake

Mt. Moriah's Wake

A Novel

Melissa Norton Carro

SHE WRITES PRESS

Published 2021
Printed in the United States of America
Print ISBN: 978-1-64742-138-0
E-ISBN: 978-1-64742-139-7
Library of Congress Control Number: 2021900675

For information, address:
She Writes Press
1569 Solano Ave #546
Berkeley, CA 94707

She Writes Press is a division of SparkPoint Studio, LLC.

For Gabe—
Best friend, safe haven, North Star

Survival is perhaps the strangest fantasy of them all.

—Eudora Welty, *The Optimist's Daughter*

1

THE BIG SECRET

FOR EVERY PERSON, THERE IS A PLACE.

A magical place—magical if only because it is yours. With smells and tastes and sights so familiar your throat catches. A place that begs recall at the errant spring breeze or the first hint of snow. A backdrop of Christmases and proms, porch swings and avenues. A place like nowhere else. Somewhere called home.

My place was Mt. Moriah.

I swore I would never return. Four years earlier, mere days after college, I had buried my best friend Grace and, with her, my youth. *Be a writer*, someone once told me. And so, still reeling from grief, I had moved to Chicago. There my dreams of being a writer were buried in a cubicle on the twelfth floor of an ad agency. In the Windy City, careful practice erased the last vestige of Southern twang from my voice. Along Michigan Avenue, I learned to run in kitten heels, balancing a Starbucks latte without a spill. And in Chicago I found and lost the love of my life.

I said I would never come back, but a taxi, plane, and rental car later, here I was. No longer the girl who left, just who *was* the woman that returned? Not only did I not know the answer; I didn't know how to find out.

And so I just stood still. With my heels dug into the wild patch of monkey grass bordering the guardrail, I leaned my knees against the cool steel, closed my eyes, and breathed in a hundred aromatic triggers.

The heady scent of wisteria blankets on garden gates. Lemony jasmine vines and wild clematis creeping up fence posts. The Lunch Box's unmistakable perfume of greasy ground chuck. And the cover of morning rain. These were the fragrant reminiscences of my childhood.

My place.

Behind me, the smell of exhaust. My rented Corolla was idling patiently, waiting to drive me the rest of the way into town. I twisted the gold band on my left hand, and my heart raced impatiently. Atop the hill, I knew I would unearth senses long forgotten, intentionally repressed—that I would be reentering a life that seemed a lifetime ago. Returning to feelings and fears I had tried to escape.

With the humidity covering me like a lead blanket, my shoulders bent with the knowledge of what I was here to do. The long road lay ahead, but an unspoken grief—a haunting secret—made me want to retreat. I didn't know quite how to feel on that day in August 2001, and part of me wondered: had I really left home or just moved away?

Squinting up at the unforgiving Southern sky, I inhaled those scents, and just like that I was a young child again.

Pardoning their pun, people said that my aunt Doro came *alive* at funerals. To her, they were the ultimate venue for Southern poise and finesse, sacraments to be savored. In her two decades in Mt. Moriah, there was hardly a funeral that Doro had missed. As she aged, she had the misfortune of witnessing more and more friends and acquaintances become one-way patrons of the Woodbury Street Funeral Parlor.

Where funerals are concerned, the Woodbury Parlor left nothing to be desired: no table without a bursting box of plush tissues, no candle sconce unlit. Every window was adorned with stained glass apostles and complemented by a brocade swag: the preeminent sanctuary for grief.

For Aunt Doro, grief wore a distinctive face. Doro's resounding voice bounced off every indigo padded folding chair. Her laughter fluttered the leaves of the funeral sprays and, some say, rustled the hair of the dead. You see, death for Doro was the living's last and finest affair.

As a young child at my first funeral in Atlanta, I remember Doro leading me to the casket, my black patent Mary Janes trudging as if weighted by cement. I was sure that in that box awaited bone fragments, rotting flesh, and an oversized skull. What I saw instead, as I stole a terrified peek, was the simple, sleeping face of Betty Mahoney.

"She does look lovely, doesn't she?" Doro quipped as we stood together, me awkwardly clinching the hem of my poplin skirt. "I always thought that was the most glorious shade of pink lipstick she wore. Brought out her blue eyes so much."

Even at the tender age of six, I felt like pointing out that nothing could bring out poor Betty Mahoney's eyes that day: They were closed forever. But there was something I could not yet understand. To the funeral goers, Betty was another weary face of death. But to Aunt Doro, she was something else.

"Death is sad only to the living, doll," she told me in her trademark stage whisper as we drifted back into the crowd of mourners. "But to the one who's died, it's the joy of suddenly understanding the Big Secret."

Aunt Doro referred often to the Big Secret and always in whispers. To be precise, there wasn't one secret, but several. The Big Secret was in bread rising, and in a woodpecker's work, and in the fact that her apricot day lilies came up year after year; it was anything that Doro didn't understand—any fragment of the world that touched her and made her wonder.

On that day, however, Doro wasn't referring to birds or breads or blooms. She was speaking of God—the biggest mystery of all.

I wanted to understand the Big Secret, believe in it. Aunt Doro had brought me because Betty Mahoney was our distant cousin. It was time I attended a funeral, Doro told my parents. But to me, Betty was nothing more than my first glimpse of a corpse, my first funeral—and my first opportunity to wrestle with the Big Secret.

Two years later, on March 17, I would attend my second funeral—that of my mother and father. A car crash suddenly, without warning, forced me to take a hard look at the Big Secret.

After a long night stifled in the hospital waiting room and two days holding an inconsolable little girl, Aunt Doro's eyes were small dots of fire that mid-March morning at my parents' funeral. Yet the voice still carried and the laughter, though dampened by tears, was there. For you see, my Aunt Doro was a Southern lady, and she knew the Big Secret.

That day, at my second funeral, I decided the Big Secret was a lie.

It has been eighteen years since my parents died. I've accompanied Doro to other funeral visitations, always positioning myself in the back, nearest the door and as far from the casket as possible. I detest the stale gardenia air and metallic mutter of air conditioning, the hard softness of the chairs. The last funeral I attended was Grace's.

Today I tug open the cumbrous wooden doors and step into the crowd of murmuring guests at Woodbury Parlor. Heavy drapes frame the windows, light in entrapment. Baskets and pots and sprays of flowers stand throughout the room. In another place, they could be so beautiful.

There is an auspicious silence at Woodbury Parlor today: a shadowy rumble of something out of place. Something lost, something absent.

Of course, it is Aunt Doro: She is what's missing.

Tomorrow is her funeral.

2

THE IDES OF MARCH

IT WAS THE IDES OF MARCH, one week into my eighth year. As crocuses and buttercups prematurely dotted the landscape in the Southern spring of 1983, I found myself orphaned by a 1970 blue Impala, driver unknown. Drunk beyond comprehension, he wandered from the scene of the crash, never to be heard from again. As the Impala was stolen, it seems the driver was hiding a host of sins, not the least of which were the murders of Joe and Anna Wilson.

Joe plus Anna: my name. Beyond the name, I was a merger of the two gene pools—a collage of hair color (a blending of chestnut and black) and eye color (hazel). From nose to brow I was my father, but people say my smile was my mother's. Rarely have chromosomes mixed and mingled so well as in my case: fortunate, as fate would have it, as I am the only remnant of the two distinct people who were my parents.

I never thought my name was very glamorous, instead wanting a name that meant something. After my parents' death, it did.

The night of my parents' accident, I was in Jenny Webber's den, playing Monopoly when Jenny's mother stepped into the room and asked Jenny to go to the kitchen. Then Frances Webber took eight steps across the worn dhurrie rug—each step seeming to take an hour. When she reached me, my hand poised over the Chance cards, Mrs. Webber embraced my cheeks with manicured fingers and simply knelt there, her eyes spilling tears onto the game board.

I had just drawn a Get Out of Jail card. The jailbird on the card was laughing at me.

"JoAnna, dear, something horrible has happened . . ."

I have no idea what other words she said. My throat closed and a burning flush of panic numbed my body and mind from further comprehension. I don't remember saying goodbye to Jenny, or climbing onto the front seat with Mrs. Webber, or arriving in the porte-cachère of the hospital. I remember neither the elevator ride nor the skin color of the nurse who took my right hand.

But I do remember the sight of Aunt Doro sitting alone in a cinder box waiting room, her head resting on the chairback. My pulse throbbed inside my head; my hands and feet were rigid. I lacked the energy I needed to move, until Doro spoke.

"The child," she said softly, before lifting her head to see me standing in the doorway. Perhaps she heard my footsteps or sensed my presence. Perhaps the abominable grief she felt reached across the room and locked arms with mine. Whatever the explanation, Doro knew I was there before her eyes saw me, and she simply opened her arms, and I trotted across the floor to be held.

The hug was punctuated by a short kiss on the ear. Doro arose, taking my hand and leading me out of the hospital—away from the nurses and the ambulances, the revolving doors and revolting smells. I wanted to ask where my parents were, where they had been taken. I wanted to know what was next; I wanted to hear all of the awful truth. But on that mild March evening, I could do nothing more than clutch Doro's thick hand and ride the eight miles back to her apartment in stony silence.

That night, almost two hours after Frances Webber's tears had stained the Short Line railroad space, Doro unlocked the studio apartment she rented on the west side of Atlanta, and motioned for me to sit at the tiny kitchen Formica table. She poured a glass of milk, and set the cookie jar in front of me. Waiting for me to act.

I wasn't hungry, not in the least, but I took two cookies and drank all the milk and then asked my question: "What am I going to do?"

Doro didn't answer me right away. She pulled the Murphy bed down from the wall and began rummaging through the corner armoire. She handed me a flannel pajama top, XL, and I began to slip off my clothes. The top hung off my shoulders and arms, of course, but it was soft and warm and perfect. Then she handed me a toothbrush, her own, filled with Colgate, and led me to the brightly lit little bathroom. When I had brushed, Doro sat me on the commode and washed first my nose, then my cheeks, my mouth, my forehead. I had been doing these things for myself for years—but that night I let Doro care for me as if I were three years old again. Time was suspended, and I was ageless.

At some point, Doro changed into her pajamas. With exacting movements, she rolled her hair onto the pink foam curlers—twelve of them—and removed the crimson lipstick that made her face so dramatic. Grabbing my hand once more, she led me to the bed.

All this time, in the back of my mind was the idea that the world would right itself—that my parents would walk through the door and I would be able to breathe again. Yet somehow I knew the world would never change back.

Up had become down.

On the bed, as Doro reached to turn off the light, I grabbed her hand and asked again.

"What am I going to do?"

My eyes were burning now from fresh tears and the panic that had been repressed by cookies and milk and toiletries. Filled with the sudden, urgent sense that I was not home—that I would never be home again—that there *was* no home anymore.

"I want my mom. I want to go home."

Aunt Doro kissed my hand, reached to turn off the light, and crawled under the covers, dragging me with her.

"We are going to cry, sweet girl. We're just going to lie here and cry. We will figure things out tomorrow."

And so we did. Beneath the lavender chenille bedspread, under the yellow cotton sheet, Doro held me against her heavy chest, and we wept. And wept. There was nothing else to say, nothing else to do.

On that night Doro began to take care of me. In my grief, in my terror, she was steady and calm and gave me a sense of control. Before that time, I had seen Doro only at holidays and occasionally on weekends. She was a favorite, eccentric aunt, who blew into a room with a whoosh of ruby lipstick and bright perfume, her visits always brief. "She's always got a hundred irons in the fire," my dad would chuckle after her departure. I didn't know what that meant, but I deduced it had something to do with the little scraps of paper spilling out of Doro's purse.

And so in mid-March 1983, I stepped out of one life and into another. As my parents' only sibling, Doro was the heir of fifteen years of married assets, including me. Christened JoAnna Patrice Wilson, I ceased being the only daughter of Joseph and Anna Wilson on that day and became the only daughter of Dorothea Wilson.

After that first night, Doro packed her bags and moved across town into my parents' house. My mother's coffee cup was on the counter, my dad's scuffed loafers in the den. Walking down the hall, I think I expected my room to be different. Gone. But I opened the door to find my seven stuffed rabbits, one for each Easter. There, where I had left them, were the autograph hound, my oversized teddy bear, Clue, Battleship, Chatty Cathy, all my Barbies, my jeans, my baby-doll pajamas with spots of syrup on them, the new boom box that had been a birthday gift.

I was back in my world but it felt like a stranger's.

In her mid-fifties, an old maid by some accounts, Doro adjusted amazingly to the radical changes brought by life with a child—by life in a house that was not her home. As an adult now, I wonder if Doro was hesitant, scared of the responsibility. Surely she felt the burden, yet it seemed there was never any doubt in her mind that we belonged together.

Doro's pragmatism kept us together throughout the funeral and the aftermath. She learned my routines, grew to understand my needs, and in the days of unmitigated grief, when neither of us knew what to do, we sobbed. We simply held each other and sobbed.

Two weeks later, on Easter Sunday, I awoke to find my Easter basket complete with the eighth bunny, a pale peach fellow with droopy eyes. I knew it was my last gift from my mother. But it was also the first from Doro.

People are always curious about orphans. At age twenty-six, I have been asked the same question repackaged a hundred ways: *Can you remember your parents? Do you look like them? Where were you when you found out?*

A whole host of questions hint at the coveted information: *how does it feel?* In a society hardened to random shootings, addictions, and disease, it is an affirmation of the good in the world that people cannot fathom the grief of a little girl who has lost her parents. People still want to believe in families, and the thought of being orphaned wrings America's collective heart.

So how *does* it feel? Truthfully I have difficulty recalling time before that spring of 1983. That is not to say that I do not remember my parents, but I do so mostly with my senses, through fleeting vignettes. Closing my eyes, I can smell my father's aftershave or my mother's Jean Nate perfume. I can hear the gentle swish-swish of Mom's seersucker robe as she made her way out of my bedroom at night, the scent of Jergens left on my cheek.

I see the flashing lights of our Christmas tree and the muted sea tones of our kitchen tablecloth. I taste the pancakes and bacon, Saturday morning fare. I remember games and giggles and arguments—the same of any family submerged in their daily routine. Unaware of the tragic disruption mounting the front porch.

And although my parents' voices were the first parts of my memory to dim, I recreate them to my own liking. My mother's, I have made less Southern, my father's less scratchy. Like hidden treasures, I take out those voices and put words in their mouths—imagining what they might say to their daughter of twelve or sixteen or twenty-six. In this way, they are not gone.

How does it feel? The grief, the emptiness have been reduced and resized until they are a comfortable blister on all that I am and do. An orphan: it is what I am. But a little girl, happily setting a place for her Care Bears at the dinner table with Mom and Dad? That is who I am too.

Do I feel cheated? Certainly. Especially in the early years. I think people expect orphans to fall apart—to become bitter and hostile. The fact is, I *was* angry—with God and my parents. I cried, often and hard, taking refuge in my stuffed animals and Barbies, creating a make-believe kingdom that no one could enter. Sinking deeper and deeper into books, into writing stories, I was by myself for hours.

All the time, Doro watched. And waited. Perhaps she was waiting for me to fall apart, but I suspect she was instead waiting for me to pull together. Hers was a deep, abiding faith—not only in God, but in man. Even man in the form of an eight-year-old girl with a wet pillow.

Perhaps she knew of a strength I didn't know I had. Or perhaps she put it there. Regardless, when I saw Doro in the hospital waiting room, when she took me home and brushed my teeth and held me, I had no choice but to follow.

It was the end of one life and the beginning of another.

3

SPRINKLERS

INSIDE THE WOODBURY PARLOR, I moved from person to person—or rather, they moved around me.

"You're in Chicago, right?"

"JoAnna, I'm so sorry."

"Doro was the best of us."

After their hugs, people inevitably looked past my shoulder—hoping for a glimpse of, an introduction to, my husband.

"Oh, he had to work unfortunately," I said to the inquiring eyes.

I imagined my husband flipping on the switch in his office and listening to my voice mail. The truth was, I had hoped he would answer his phone—so I could give him the news in person. It would have been the first time we had talked in days. An argument had kept him at his friend's apartment. An argument had stood in the way of his accompanying me to Mt. Moriah.

He had left me, and I didn't know if he was coming back.

So instead I left a brief message: *Doro has died. I'm going to Mt. Moriah. I will be okay. I love you.* I did love him. But I did not want him here.

Doro was not all I came to Mt. Moriah to bury.

At the front of the room, between two ornate wall sconces, was the casket. My feet moved toward it as if in a dream, people parting around me to clear my path. Doro, Doro, Doro. Surely that wasn't her in the casket. Surely this wasn't real. The door would open, and she would appear, those painted lips parted for the laughter to roll out. *Where are you, Doro?* I leaned in and brushed her cheek with my lips. Between her and me were so many memories that no casket could hold them.

And between us the one secret that was now destined to be buried forever.

At Woodbury it seemed I said the right things, smiled at the right times, and responded appropriately. My hands were shaken and my shoulders embraced until I felt almost dizzy. Yet I moved and spoke and smiled and hugged as if in a dream.

At one point, leaning in to kiss Donnie Rapasco, the butcher, instinctively holding my breath against last night's garlic, I caught a glance out the front window. Across the street two little girls were skipping back and forth through a sprinkler. The arc of water captured colors from the late summer sky, and crepe myrtle petals danced at the girls' wet toes. In my head, I heard the voice of my best friend, Grace Collins.

"Oh my gosh, Jo, look."

We were running through the sprinkler cascading Doro's vegetable garden. It was August 1984, the hottest on record since Kennedy. We were racing to see who could run under the spray and not get drenched. But it became too hot for games; what we wanted was to be dowsed.

Then Doro appeared. She watched us, hands on hips for a minute, then slipped off her Kelly green espadrilles, hiked her skirt up, and raced into the spray. She darted through the water five times before stopping in the middle, soaking herself and twirling her torso in a slightly inappropriate sideshow.

"You just don't know how hot that kitchen is!"

Crippled with laughter, Grace and I held each other up.

"Just think, Jo Jo. That'll be you and me one day . . . old ladies dancing in a sprinkler!"

Nodding, I continued to laugh at my crazy aunt.

Oh, Grace, I thought, watching the girls out the Woodbury Parlor window. We will never be old ladies together.

"JoAnna!"

Although she had aged twenty years in the four since I last saw her, I knew the voice and face of Genia Collins instantly. Grace's mother, Genia was a pruney bitter shrew of a woman. She and Grace shared a monogram and strawberry blonde hair and big brown eyes. And nothing else.

I smiled and leaned into the hug she offered. Feeling small sobs starting, I pulled back.

"Dorothea was a good woman," Genia said. Then, brushing my hair out of my eyes, "I wasn't sure you would come."

Not come because Chicago is in another country? Not come because I'm a hateful person? What must Genia think of me.

She went on to explain. "Well it's just that I know you are married and Chicago is a lifetime away."

"Chicago is so far away," Grace said. We were sitting on the edge of Doro's bed, watching as Doro crammed girdles and corsets into her Samsonite. We had turned twelve, and Doro was taking us to Chicago to celebrate. My writer's imagination captivated by big cities, I wrote stories about a girl who lived in Chicago. "Hmmm," Doro mused, reading one of my stories. "I think it's time you see the city you're writing about."

I had packed days before and was counting down the hours. Grace was less convinced. "My mom says it's a lifetime away," said Grace.

Doro stopped packing for a moment and looked at Grace. "Fiddle faddle. Nothing is far when you can get there by plane, Gracie."

"I don't think my mom likes to travel. Anyway, she said I should call every night." Grace chewed on the place where a thumb nail should be. Anxiety was obviously something easily passed on in lactation.

"We will call your mom, Gracie." Doro paused, hands on her hips, surveying her room to inventory how much more could be crammed into her suitcase-that-would-never-close. "But you just remember that life is an adventure . . . and God intends for us to live it!"

"I got a good flight, Mrs. Collins." I pulled my hands from Genia's bird-like palms. "So how are you?"

"I'm alright, considering. Touch of arthritis in my shoulders and a knee replacement last year." She instinctively touched her right kneecap. "But that's nothing next to my heart . . ."

"Your heart? Oh I didn't know there was something—"

"No, no, child. My heart is broken. Seeing you reminds me of my dear Grace . . ." She bit her trembling lip. "A woman just shouldn't outlive everyone she loves."

The tears began then, as befitting the over-active, on cue tear ducts of a Southern lady. Genia's shoulders were hunched as if toting a backpack of stones.

As, indeed, they were.

4

HIGHEST POINT

On the day of Grace Collins' funeral, Mt. Moriah's fifty-day record drought acquiesced to a gentle, soaking rain—a gift for which the farmers and garden clubs had been praying. Yet no one seemed to notice or care, for Mt. Moriah was in shock over Grace's murder. It happened on the Point, Mt. Moriah's highest tabletop of land that made a perfect picnic spot except for the steep climb up to it. Access to the Point was by Windy Hill Road which, aptly named, was a one-mile stretch of asphalt curves with a grade that took your breath away. At the end of Windy Hill Road was a guardrail and the entrance to the Point marked by a wooden sign, erected by the local Boy Scout Troop, with hand carved letters: "Climb Here to the Point." The path to the Point was another mile.

As children, we were not allowed to hike to the Point alone. Several times our Girl Scout Troop had gone on expeditions up there, holding hands buddy style. The view from the top was stunning. Standing at 200 feet, in all directions the vantage point offered you a view of the four corners of Mt. Moriah down in the valley. Deep tree roots served as footholds and one spring the town council installed railroad ties, driven with stakes into the dirt, to provide additional steps. Holding vigil in the center of the grassy meadow was a single birch, its chalky limbs soaring forty feet into the air.

The day Grace died, torn ropes were found at the base of that tree, and toward the edge of the meadow, the police found Grace's body, one shoe missing and one shoe on, red wallet on the ground. Rope burns on her wrists, Grace had obviously broken free, the police noted, because she was found on her back near the edge, a rope dangling around one leg, a single pristine bullet hole in her forehead.

The murder was never solved. There were no witnesses, at least that the town knew of. That such violence could come to a town shaken even by gossip of adultery or bankruptcy was unspeakable. And so most people shuffled in stunned silence into First Methodist Church on that Tuesday in June 1997.

I sat on the back pew, with Doro. I should have been down front, near Grace's mother Genia, but I could not. I remember Doro's hand on my elbow, leading me in, leading me out. During the service I had the unsettling feeling that I was hovering above, watching a play be played out.

As if I were the one dead.

We left almost as quickly as we came in, ignoring friends as they approached us.

"Jo needs to go home and rest. She's in shock," Doro whispered as a mantra to anyone we passed.

I have since regretted that I cannot recall anything said at my best friend's funeral—that I didn't take part in remembering her. And my guilt goes even further than that: The day of the murder I was to accompany Grace on her hike to the Point. I was anxious to tell her about my potential job. After college graduation and months of submitting my resume to advertising agencies in Chicago, I had gone on an interview for an entry-level position. Grace had something she wanted to tell me too.

"I have news, Jo Jo! A big secret, you might say."

"Me too! Want to eat Mexican? Or take a hike?"

"Both!" Grace giggled. "I've been missing you bad!"

I never got the chance to tell Grace about the job prospect. A freelance project I was working on made me call her and cancel. I never told Grace about the job, never heard her news.

Perhaps it was divine intervention, the hand of Fate, or just sublime irony, but on the afternoon we returned from Grace's funeral, the phone rang. I heard Doro answer downstairs, and then her footsteps on the hardwood steps.

"It's the company, Jo. Get the phone."

Lying on my bed, still in my dress and pantyhose, I turned on my side. I knew what the call was. It didn't matter.

"Jo, you're going to take this call. You. Are. Going. To take. This call."

Never had I heard Doro more emphatic. And like a little child, as I had been doing since I was eight, I didn't question Doro. I rose and went to the phone.

"Yes. Yes, ma'am. August tenth. Yes, I understand. Yes. Thank you. Yes. Goodbye." I don't know what my voice sounded like to the people who had just hired me, or if they could detect the tears that were dripping onto the phone. But I do remember Doro's face when I replaced the receiver and said, "Doro, I can't go."

Her face spoke of the agony Doro felt— it said how much she wanted to lock me in my room against the bad forces in the world. Doro's countenance mirrored my own fear and grief—and revealed that she herself couldn't bear the thought of my leaving.

"You're going." There were tears in Doro's eyes, but her thick, soft hands held each of my cheeks firmly. "You have two months. You'll be ready, Jo, and you can do this.

"Go be a writer."

All I could think was that Doro didn't understand—not the fear, not the grief, not the emptiness inside that would never go away. But she was Doro, and she was mine, and she was finally wise enough to say the one thing that could make me go.

"Grace would want you to."

Six weeks later Doro put me on an airplane with two heavy pieces of luggage and two thousand dollars in traveler's checks—amassed from her savings and my part-time job—to use for room and board and to buy a bed and sofa in my first apartment.

She would see me soon, Doro said, and it was something she believed, that I would return for visits and the wounds would be healed, the grief softened.

But she was mistaken. For the fleshy grief in my heart was quickly replaced with hardness. I blamed God for letting Grace die. I blamed Mt. Moriah because the town continued—laundromats operated, banks did transactions, families took vacations—while for me it seemed that time had stopped.

Most of all, I blamed Doro for giving me false courage. For sending me away for my sake. For thinking me strong and not letting me be weak.

As we waited for me to board the plane to Chicago, Doro noted Kenny G's music in the airport. "Oh, that music's so wonderful, don't you think, Jo?"

We had become fans of his music when I was in high school. At that moment my boarding was announced, and I turned away. I didn't look back after the quick perfunctory kiss, nor did I answer her question.

A silly question, really. Didn't Doro understand there was no wonderful music because there was no wonderful any longer.

The music had been silenced.

I think our lives are like tops.

The broadest part of us, the heavy compilation of all we've done and seen and felt— drives the tip on which our lives spin. Too hard a spin, too many revelations, and our top can spin itself off the table edge. Likewise, too small a spin can leave our top warily revolving, traveling nowhere, inhaling the same air it breathed out.

I see people as the tops they are: spinning their lives into a maze of haphazard patterns like Doro, or quietly circling the block, like Genia Collins, waiting resignedly for the force to end.

Yet some tops beat the odds. A top spun vigorously trips and almost bounces, dizzy in its speed, heading certainly toward the edge of the table and the precipice below. Yet it does not fall; rather it seems to bounce back from the edge, only to spin some more.

Then there's the more circumspect top, barely moving, and yet the few inches it travels make it spiral downward. Why, when care was taken? Why is one top drawn to and the other away from the fall?

Why did Grace have to die?

It was the lucky top that made that other high school senior, not your child, collide head-on. It was a lucky top that made the lump in your breast a benign cyst.

And yet do we really believe in luck?

And what of faith?

Are we created and set in motion like millions of tops, bumping into each other, sliding toward the abyss, some of us pulled back and some freefalling into nothingness? Is there no secret formula for avoiding the precipice?

Perhaps this is not a question but rather the answer.

I had never believed in the freefall. Perhaps I got that from Doro. I suspended myself in treaded waters, holding my breath. If I could just keep circling, slowly, gently, all that I am, all that I love, would remain perched high above me. In safe arms I could never see but knew were there. Blindly. Knew. That's what Doro taught me.

And then Grace died, and with her the faith of Doro—the faith of my childhood.

Grace's was a fire dance of joy, and sparks of energy shot from every part of her pirouette. Yet nothing pulled her back from the edge. Nothing saved that shining top from cascading down.

A prayer was screamed, but no one heard.

When Grace died, everything changed for me. I felt completely alone, irrevocably so, it seemed. There was no power above me, and no power within me, to prevent such a fall.

On the day Grace died, so did my faith in the divine. Life became random.

Aboard the plane to Chicago, I stared out at the clouds floating around me. I strained to look up, knowing with complete certainty that there was nothing there. No one there.

Free fallers we are. Freefalling through life.

Four years later, I am steadfast in my disbelief.

5

WIND

CHICAGO IS EXACTLY 423 MILES FROM MT. MORIAH, and each of those seemed significant on the day my flight landed in August 1997. When I deboarded the plane, I knew Chicago would be everything I needed it to be: specifically, not Mt. Moriah. I was twenty-two years old; my best friend had just died; and I sought refuge from my grief and my memories.

I sought refuge from *myself*. From the streaked window of the cab taking me to my hotel in midtown, I looked out at the blend of old mom-and-pop establishments and gold card stores. I took strange comfort in the horns and the voices and the guttural rumbling of the el. And the people: thousands and thousands of faces I didn't know. Who didn't know me. It was anonymity I wanted, and those 400-odd miles erased who I was.

It was up to me who I wanted to be.

My first home in Chicago was a long-term hotel off Wooster Avenue. One of the perks of Sandalwood & Harris Advertising was that new college grads could rent a room for $750 per month, with the price doubling in six months. I had the option of spending less if I took a roommate but alone was what I wanted.

What I was.

"It will give you time to get settled and find an apartment," said Doro in early July, bringing into my room a bevy of heavy plastic coat hangers. Her nervousness for me—and quite possibly for herself when I left—manifested itself in weekly shopping binges. At the bottom of my cavernous suitcase were enough hangers to outfit a family of four.

I checked in at the front desk of the hotel and got the key to Room 504. Riding up in the shaky elevator, I caught a reflection of myself in the mirrored brass above the door. Who was that girl? Not me. Not JoAnna Wilson.

Did she yet exist?

When I arrived, the door was open across the hall where two lanky girls perched on one of the two beds, painting each other's toenails. They introduced themselves as fellow Sandalwood & Harris newbies. They smiled at me and in those smiles I knew we would never be friends. Not really. I read in their eyes and felt in their limp handshakes that they already had a best friend.

"I'm Tiffany. I'm from Milwaukee."

"Megan. Also from Milwaukee."

College roommates, they had set off together for Chicago for their first great life adventure. Working in the accounts division at Sandalwood & Harris, they aspired to become account executives. Or wives. Whichever came first.

While we were making awkward small talk in the hallway, I heard gasps and then giggles coming from the room next to me. Tiffany and Megan read the look on my face and beckoned me closer.

"That's Lori. She's from Cleveland, and so far we've counted four different boyfriends," whispered Megan.

Tiffany, evidently a peacekeeper, chimed in. "But she seems really sweet, just, you know, over-sexed or something."

There was an awkward silence and the girls dismissed me to my unpacking. Two hours later they appeared in my doorway. Their faces and hair had made dramatic transformations.

"We're going to get dinner and then to Tony's. Do you want to come?" Megan paused. "We could wait for you to get ready."

I looked at my Atlanta Braves shirt and my ratty jeans. I wasn't even sure where to start "getting ready."

My skinny window, opaque with grime, revealed a sliver of the Michigan Avenue Bridge. Below, the trees swayed, and I suddenly wanted to be outside.

"Thanks. I'll pass tonight. I think I'll just hang here."

Did I see a shadow of relief pass across their faces? "Okay, then. But tomorrow night you're coming with us." Tiffany picked up a framed picture of me and Grace from the night of our high school graduation. I had set it up on my desk near the door. "She's pretty," she said, and then they were gone.

Yes. She was.

Grace, I thought. *Where are you, Grace?*

The view outside my window, however obscured, beckoned me. I waited until I knew Tiffany and Megan would be out of sight, then grabbed a jacket and my purse, and headed out. I wanted to meet Chicago.

The cleansing wind whipped around my nylon windbreaker as I walked the long blocks to the Michigan Avenue Bridge. The panels were up, and I waited to cross with the hundreds of other people. On the other side was the Chicago Tribune Tower, and I walked around it, running my hands lightly across the limestone. Notre Dame. Great Wall of China. Taj Mahal. Stepping inside, I could only move to the right, because the left side of the great hall was blocked off. Renovations were underway, with inscriptions being added to the walls. The security guard smiled at me. "Afternoon, ma'am. You a tourist?"

"Sort of. Actually, I just moved to Chicago." I looked around, wondering what it might be like to have a job such as his, surrounded by architectural magnificence. "Come back in a few weeks and it should be finished," he said. He motioned with his Coke bottle toward the inscription behind me. "You'll have to wait on Lincoln to be done, but you've got Burnham's quote there." He shook his head and smirked. "No idea in hell who Burnham was."

I read Daniel Burnham's quote and made a note to myself to find out who he was.

"Make no small plans; they have no magic to stir men's blood."

Thanks for the advice, I thought.

Back outside, I let the wind rip through my jacket. Although the air was chilly, the cold was invigorating. It felt good to feel *something*. I half walked, half jogged the twelve blocks to Lake Michigan. By the time I got there, my heart rate was up and I was perspiring. It was late afternoon, the sun sliding behind the clouds. I stood with Lake Michigan in front of me and breathed in the dampness. I watched lovers and children and carefree college students play on the dirty sand. And there, on that late summer day, I vowed I would never return to Mt. Moriah. Tears came to my eyes, and I looked around to see if anyone noticed. No one did. I was invisible.

Mercifully so.

That first night in Room 504, the nightmares that had plagued me all summer found me in Chicago. I saw Grace's face flash in front of me. I sat up, in a cold sweat, and wondered if I had cried out. I could hear talking and laughter from Lori's room. I had met the long-legged Cleveland beauty when I returned from my walk. She had a space between her teeth and teased hair that begged to return to its natural color. She was nice, though, greeting me with a warm smile and suggesting we have lunch or dinner. Or drinks. Whatever. She was flexible.

Indeed she probably was, I thought.

In those early days in Chicago, I awakened from my dreams, drenched despite the oscillating fan I kept pointed at me. As sun was on the brink of rising, I donned my Reeboks and took off walking, toward Lake Michigan. The wind was my silent partner, propelling me along, erasing my dreams, dulling my thoughts.

Grace was constantly on my mind. I saw her at coffee shops, walking on the beach, in elevators. Her phone number would run through my head, and I would make a mental note to tell her about the greasy, juicy pizza I had eaten. But I couldn't. She was not there; she never would be.

I started seeing a psychologist at Doro's insistence. "I've set up an appointment for you your first week," she had said. Knowing nothing about Chicago, she was sure his office was close to my hotel. It was not. "You need to talk to someone."

Dr. Weisz was balding, and his fifth shirt button strained against his stomach. He was without wit, but not unkind. I told him I was walking. A lot. Running a little. I said I kept imagining I saw Grace. I told him I had nightmares and couldn't sleep unless all the lights in my room were on. Even then I saw shadows. I told him I didn't know sometimes whether I wanted to live—but that I was terrified of dying.

"You're grieving," he said, as if revealing something I did not know.

His stoniness, his "how does that make you feel" interjections did not seem helpful to me. It was movement that brought me relief. My daily walks had picked up pace until I was running. My chest burned until I thought it would explode, and the wind slapped my face until I reached that great majestic body of water. Into Lake Michigan I would squall, the wind carrying my screams away as a mother muffles a small child's sobs against her breast.

The wind was my friend.

In an odd kind of way, Dr. Weisz became my friend too. I continued to see him, every two weeks, paying with checks Doro gave me. Although he seldom offered advice, I found myself looking forward to sitting in the plaid chair and gazing at the family photos displayed behind his desk. Dr. Weisz had the ugliest daughters I had ever seen, but his wife was quite stunning.

She's your prize, I thought. I found myself wondering if the daughters were adopted. How could the mother's beautiful genes have no impact on those four girls? I rattled on about my nightmares while I wondered if the screened-in porch in the picture was as serene as it appeared. I wondered if he and his wife had met at Dartmouth, where his diploma said he received his BS. I wondered why he collected antique model cars. I wondered if those top shelves above his credenza ever got dusted.

I wondered if his wife had nightmares. And if he held her when she did.

And then I would leave his office and be back in the wind, back in the Chicago that swelled up around me and lost me in its wake.

I knew that Dr. Weisz was right: I was grieving. But it was more than that. Beyond sorrow, beyond loneliness, what I felt was guilt. Guilt that Grace had been murdered. We had made plans to be walking at the Point together that day. It could have been me. Should it have been me? Every step I made in my new life in Chicago was a step further without Grace. A step further away.

In those nightmares, strangers lunged for me, and I was terrified. I was relieved to awaken, to squint through my dusty window and see the river in the distance. To know I was alive. What Dr. Weisz couldn't understand, didn't know, was that I was conflicted: between my relief in waking from my nightmares and my guilt at knowing Grace never could.

And so, walking and running became the means to tamp down the emotions that threatened to explode inside me. Learning Chicago by foot, I rode the antique elevators at Macy's, watching each floor fall away, the green balconies luring me into their departments. Hosiery. Men's. Bedding. I spent hours trilling my fingertips over the sheets and towels, sitting in the children's department, staring into the giant wooden giraffe whose body held shelves of plush, loving stuffed animals.

I sat under the el and waited for the rumble, sipping coffee and watching the pigeons pick at the trash. I lingered on the plaza in front of the Wrigley Building, watching the people, the boats in the Chicago River. Observing life that I wasn't a part of.

Lori and Megan and Tiffany were friendly to me. We ordered pizza together and tried out restaurants and watched TV. I was grateful for them, but they were not my friends. My sole friend was the wind—my confidant and companion. Only the vigorous lake air knew my name and the secret guilt pressing on my heart.

When I wasn't running against the wind, running with the wind, I was going through the motions of being alive. Eating, showering, flossing my teeth. And working.

Like the wind, work whipped my grief, my guilt, into a hard knot that I swallowed, that remained hidden through the days. Released only when the nightmares came.

Thank goodness for Dr. Weisz. For the wind. And for work.

6

ELEPHANT EARS

"LITTLE THING! JO."

I searched through the crowd in the Woodbury Parlor for that familiar cadence and the head towering well over six feet. I didn't have to look long to find the face that matched the voice.

"Maddy, hi." I clung to his hunched frame, my head nesting against the knot of his tie. The face, the shiny gray hair, the thick venous hands and lumbering shuffle: my beloved Maddy.

"You're a sight for sore eyes, little thing. We were worried your flight might not get here on time."

Holding me at arms' length and running his calloused paw through my bangs, Maddy searched my eyes.

Maddy's full name was Madison Blair, and his was the lyrical drawl of a Southern gentleman. His voice was thick with emotions and his azure eyes moist.

I cleared my throat. "How are my elephant ears, Maddy?" Then I choked on the spot in my throat. I looked up into the second of Maddy's chins and smelled his old man scent: a combination of garden dirt and expired Old Spice— the clarity of the outdoors sweetened by Southern gentility.

Maddy gave my shoulders a tight squeeze. His eyes were still damp, but his voice had gained a chuckle.

"Tall and thriving, no thanks to you." he laughed.

In my mind's photo album, I could see Maddy's billowy elephant ears, swaying in the breeze, his pride and joy.

At least until I got to them.

What became known—and not affectionately—as the "elephant ear incident" took place during the summer after my parents died. It all started early on a Saturday morning, the third week of June 1983, when Doro opened my blinds and blew me out of bed with her billowy voice.

Dazed with sleep, I was surprised that Doro was awake. The unspoken rule around Doro was no talking until 8:30 a.m., until the last drop from the percolator had entered her ample stomach. On that sticky June morning, the clock read 7:10. Yet Doro was alive with activity, obviously fueled by more than caffeine.

"Morning, sunshine! Hurry up, we're going on a road trip, and I want to be there well before lunch." Doro motioned me to move into the bathroom, tossing last evening's clothes at me.

Fifteen minutes later, we were on our way, doughnuts in hand and a thermos of milk for me. I didn't ask questions—simply turned up Billy Joel on the radio and watched the highway markers slip by. Although I was curious where we were going, in my few months with Doro I had developed a conviction that wherever Doro wanted to take me, that's where I should go. I was a passenger in my own life.

Fog rolled across our windshield as we exited at Mt. Moriah, the highest point between Atlanta and Nashville. I had traveled the mountain once before with my parents, on our way to vacation. At that time it had seemed intimidating, unsettling. With Doro, it seemed peaceful, beautiful. I was too taken with the act of climbing to question.

We turned off the highway, passed through the quaint downtown, and then onto Birkham Lane, turning at crumbling stone pillars. We proceeded down the tree lined driveway almost a quarter of a mile until Doro stopped in front of what appeared to be a haunted house.

"Where are we, Doro? What is this place?" My questions came rolling out then, tripping over each other in the air between Doro and me.

"It's our house, Jo. Our new home."

Seeing the dangling gutters, manic ivy, and decades of peeled paint, I waited for a punch line, but I knew Doro was no kidder.

Instead, I saw the sparkle in her eye. "Come on. Let's look it over. Watch out for poison ivy."

A massive porch spanned the front of the house, with peeling cement steps overcome by moss. Doro accidentally pulled the door off its hinges, set it aside, and whispered with a wink, "We don't need a key."

I must say that the interior made the exterior feel palatial. Thick cobwebs clung to massive crown molding, and brocade wallpaper threatened to ensnare us on its way off the walls. We wandered through the rooms, from dining room to parlor to back kitchen, and then up the winding stairs through an array of bedrooms. A ballroom, fifteen feet by thirty feet, extended across one side of the second floor. Heavy wainscoting and ornate dental molding bespoke a different era. I tiptoed so as not to disturb the ghosts that undoubtedly accompanied me. My writer's imagination was on full alert.

After twenty minutes of silence, Doro paused in front of a tall staircase leading into darkness. Her hand dusting the carved ball atop the bannister, she spoke.

"I've been looking for a place like this for some time, Jo. I was about to sign the papers, actually, the week your parents passed away. It needs renovation, of course, but I bought it for a song, and with some sweat equity I intend to make it into a B&B." Then, seeing the blank look on my face: "Bed and breakfast. A country inn. Did you count the bedrooms? The space is incredible." Doro spoke rapidly, as if to convince me.

"We'll move here, you and me, away from the city," she continued. "There's a good school, and the area here is just beautiful. I have enough money saved to live on, and I can fund the renovation from your father's and my inheritance." She reached over and pushed a loose bang out of my left eye.

"Come on. How can you be excited when you haven't even seen your room yet?"

She flipped a switch and the brightened stairway revealed a door at the top. We climbed, the heat rising with us. Beyond that door was nothing short of a sanctuary—at least in my young writer's eyes. The room was small, but with two long slender windows that faced the front lawn. One window looked directly into a gracious willow, and the other down the long winding driveway. The ceiling was sloped, all around, with nooks and crannies that begged for a little girl to sit in them and read and write. And imagine.

I dropped Doro's hand and moved to the window. Clearing a patch of dust, I gazed into the willow and then back around the room, which was surprisingly light and airy. Seeing for the first time with Doro's optimistic eyes, I saw the potential. I envisioned yellow-checked Priscilla curtains, and my dolls lined up on white wicker corner shelves.

"I like it," I said.

"Hello! Anybody there?"

Doro and I jumped at the voice. We hurried down both sets of hardwood stairs and saw a tall, stooped figure in the doorway, his hand on the knob, one foot in and one foot out. Perhaps he too believed in ghosts.

"Hi, I'm Dorothea Wilson. Mr. Browder, the realtor, said I could stop by this morning." Doro proceeded toward the door with her hand outstretched. "I'm buying this lovely old house."

She emphasized the word *lovely*, as if daring the stranger to disagree.

"Oh really? Rip and I had just about given up hope of anybody taking interest in this old place," said the man, shadowing the front sunlight.

Before we could ask who Rip was, up loped a lanky hound whose posture and ruddy complexion closely mirrored his master's. He settled himself against the man's right leg and, as if staking his territory, emitted an imposing fart.

"Rip, really, that ain't polite." In apology, the man continued. "I caught Rip chewing on a dead squirrel yesterday, and it seemed to mess up his intestines bad."

Straightening her spine, Doro was obviously unimpressed. In her world there was no place for dogs, certainly not in her prospective home. Spiders and mice, yes. Flatulent canines, no.

On the other hand, I was delighted. From my earliest memory I had wanted a pet, preferably a dog, the furrier the better. Releasing Doro's hand and holding my breath, I knelt down beside the dog. Reciprocating my friendliness, Rip uncurled a three foot tongue and slurped my face.

"Careful, Jo, the dog may bite." Doro took hold of my shoulder and urged me to my feet.

"Oh no ma'am, he's harmless. Except maybe to squirrels." He chuckled at his own joke.

Then, to me: "Pretty little girls, he likes. Your name's Jo?"

"JoAnna." Straightening, I inserted my tiny hand into his large one. I found myself level with his belt buckle. Craning my head upwards, I could tell—even at their altitude—that his eyes were a brilliant blue.

"I'm Madison Blair. How do you do. Awfully big name so most people just call me Maddy," he said.

"Do you live around here, Mr. Blair?" asked Doro.

"Maddy. No ma'am, I live in town. But Rip and I try to come up here on Saturdays to work on our garden, our elephant ears."

Elephant ears? My bewilderment was obvious. Laughing at my surprise, Maddy continued.

"You haven't seen the garden, then? Come on, I'll show you."

Now it was Doro's turn to be surprised. "Garden?"

Following Maddy's lead, now immensely curious, Doro and I trampled the ivy around the side of the porch encircling the white clapboard house. Pushing our way through overgrown honeysuckle, we saw boxwoods framing a rusted iron gate and through there we tiptoed, as if approaching Eden itself.

Tidy rows of three foot square stones sat, some tilted at angles, wedged out of their upright position by time and weather. Looking closer, I saw on each stone a name and dates.

This was a cemetery, not a garden!

And then Doro's voice broke the silence. "How simply breathtaking!"

Before I could register my complaint that a cemetery was far from a garden, I followed Doro's gaze. Tall, billowy plants encircled the tombstones. They looked like . . . yes, they looked much like ears.

"You can see where they got their name, don't ya, Jo?" Chuckling, Maddy patted one rather roughly, "These are my babies! Elephant ears they're called."

I laughed out loud at the thought of those "ears" flapping in the breeze. Then I saw, below the large plants, an assortment of annuals displaying a circus of color: marigolds, petunias, impatiens, vincas. Looking around the circle of elephant ears, I counted thirty in all. And at each base was the same meticulous symmetry of design, the same juxtaposition of color.

I was so intrigued that I stepped further in and walked up to the first row of stones. As Doro complimented Maddy on his gardening abilities, I shielded my eyes and leaned forward to read a stone. *Donna. March 4, 1908 to January 12, 1919.* Then another. *Timothy. June 29, 1910 to January 23, 1919.* And others: *Marilyn. Joshua. Elizabeth.*

A cold chill ran down my spine. All were children. None had last names.

Maddy and Doro were kneeling beside a row of impatiens, lost in horticulture.

"Are you a gardener then, Mr., uh, Maddy?" asked Doro.

He laughed. "Unpaid! Gardening is something I love—digging in the dirt. Just a pastime. I guess you could call me a Saturday gardener."

On the other hand, I was lost in the world of the dead. Weaving my way in and out of the stones, I read the inscriptions, names and dates screaming in my head. *Dolores. Katherine. Buford.* Fifteen stones in all. Ten children. Five adults. Two tombstones in the last row were the largest of all. *Beloved father. John Buford Lindsay. July 15, 1868 to February 4, 1919. Devoted mother. Martha Dingham Lindsay. September 1, 1874 to March 5, 1919.*

Beloved father. Devoted mother.

Maddy saw me reading the stones and stepped up beside me.

"This was the Lindsays' farm. They had ten children and, together with Martha's mother, Sarah Dingham, they all lived in that grand old house together." Maddy paused to smack a mosquito climbing his elbow. "Influenza must have got 'em in the winter of nineteen nineteen.

"If you look at the dates, the mother was the last to go. Sad to think of her taking care of all those sick children and then dying herself."

Doro nodded her head absently, the Lindsays' tragedy the farthest thing from her mind.

"The Lindsays were quite well off," said Maddy, brushing off the remains of another mosquito victim. "Did you see that ballroom upstairs?"

As Maddy began to reveal details about the Lindsays, one phrase rang in my head.

The mother was the last to go.

The ways of the human mind are strange indeed. Triggers poise like bees on our emotions, ready to inject pain, to break the dam and open the flood-gates of suppressed feelings.

At that moment, with Maddy and Doro seated on a decrepit bench facing out toward the house, my dam burst.

"Can we go home now?" I stammered to Doro. Feeling tears forming in my eyes, I fought them back and announced, "I'm ready to go home."

Yet Doro was far from ready.

"No, honey, I thought we could find the closest restaurant and get a bite to eat. I know you must be hungry after that sugary breakfast." Turning to Maddy, she explained apologetically. "Just donuts. We had to get on the road."

"I'd be happy to treat you and your little girl," said Maddy. "Let me take you to the Lunch Box—best meatloaf in the South."

"Why, that would be lovely, Mr.— Maddy, " said Doro, touching his arm lightly. Then, to me: "Let's go, Jo."

The mother was the last to go. "I want to go home."

Doro's look was one of disbelief. Nowhere in her parenting manual had the word *no* been mentioned. Truly, in the months we had been together, I had never questioned or disagreed. Perhaps I felt so vulnerable that I didn't dare question the one person who stood between me and eternal loneness.

And so, as much as I wanted to be away from those stones, from the stillness that haunted the air around them, I bit my lip and joined Doro and Maddy as they walked back through the garden gate.

"That's a girl." To Maddy, Doro explained, "She's my niece. Her parents passed away rather recently, and she came to live with me. Joy of my life." Her hand rested on the nape of my neck.

"Well, goodness, I'm sure sorry about your folks, Jo." Maddy patted his hip for Rip to follow. "So you're going to be our neighbors?"

"Yes, there's so much potential in the house; I want to turn it into a B&B." Seeing my same blank look echoed on Maddy's face, Doro explained: "Bed and breakfast. A country inn."

"But I had never ventured this far in my other visits here. The garden is just delightful, the way you have designed it."

Just delightful. *The mother was the last to go.* Just *delightful.*

I quickened my steps, eager to be away from those stones, those inscriptions—from the mother who must have worked so hard to save her children and then lost herself.

Suddenly, in front of me, beside me and all around me, was my mother's face. And the voice inside my head spoke to her.

It should have been that way with you, Mommy. You should have stayed with me. You should have been the last to go.

We left Rip with a bone on the front porch and rode in Doro's Taurus, Maddy in the back seat, his lanky legs folded sideways to avoid the cooler on the floorboard. The Lunch Box was less than fifteen minutes away, on a side street in downtown Mt. Moriah. It had obviously once been a modest white frame residence. The front door was open, a screen door policing the hungry horseflies.

I was shocked to see the crowd seated at the tables. At the abandoned house and remote cemetery, it had felt as if no one else lived in Mt. Moriah, yet here they were. Grandmothers taking their grandchildren to lunch. Couples eating with cranky toddlers. Teenagers sharing a banana split.

The three of us slid into a red vinyl booth and ordered quickly. I sat silently, watching the people, wondering where they all lived. When the food arrived, I ate quietly, savoring each bite of my grilled cheese, surprised at my hunger.

Doro and Maddy ate the same thing: barbeque on cornbread, with sweetened iced tea. Maddy and Doro discussed her plans for the house, and I was happy to be forgotten. I wanted no part of the conversation and no part of Doro and her optimism. *Just delightful!*

I pushed thoughts of that cemetery out of my head, and six weeks later a moving van came and packed us up. To my surprise, the van was not empty when it bumped to a halt against the curb in front of my parents' cottage, where a SOLD sign swayed in the wind. The moving van was already two-thirds full.

"I've had furniture in storage for seven years now, Jo," Doro explained. "Ever since your grandparents died and I inherited the furniture. Your dad didn't want it; guess it was all a bit too old-fashioned for your mama.

"It'll give us a good start on the B&B."

The trip up the mountain took three hours, with us following the truck. We arrived in the early August afternoon sun and finished unloading the truck at dusk. Doro, her massive hair piled on top of her head and her *Thriller* t-shirt soaked, called me periodically to get water from the thermos.

"Hydrate, child! You need to drink!"

My face was red and drenched with sweat, for I had been closeted in my attic room, carefully placing my stuffed animals and dolls. The window air conditioner moaned like a hurt animal and rained little droplets of condensation onto the floor below. Doro had bought me a hot pink bean bag chair for under the windows, and I curled up there, extending my hand in anticipation of those gifts of cold relief.

That day, the excitement I felt when I first saw the house had been reduced to a tight pit in my stomach. Perhaps it was fatigue or loneliness or exhaustion. Or maybe it was walking through our house on Magnolia Drive one final time. Probably it was five months of pretending that I didn't miss my parents and knowing that I did.

Hearing an engine start up, I looked out the window to see the moving truck lumbering slowly down the long driveway, passing Madison Blair's work truck. The sky hinted that dusk was coming in the next hour. Soon the front door opened and that unmistakable bass voice bellowed.

"Good evening! Brought you ladies some dinner," Maddy boomed.

Suddenly I was back at home at 145 Magnolia Drive. I was playing Barbies on my bed, and the clock had just turned to six o'clock, and my dad's voice called out from the back door.

"Where are my girls? Daddy's home with pizza!"

It was a memory so strong, so palpable, that I slipped off the bean bag and sat down hard against my tailbone.

"Jo! Come to dinner, honey!"

Although it was Doro's voice echoing up the stairs, it was my mother's voice I heard. Closing my eyes, I saw Mom's airy blouse, white with cherries and a starched Peter Pan collar. I could hear her squeaky sandals and knew, as Mom called for me, that she was pushing silver wire-rimmed frames against the bridge of her nose. I knew the eyes beyond the frames were a deep brown, and that there was a mole on the bottom of her chin that I rubbed as a child as she read me nursery rhymes. I knew the greasy pizza had coated through the bottom of the box and against my dad's tie.

"You're a mess, Joe." My mother would roll her eyes and slip away from my dad as he slapped her backside and kissed her neck. "Do you just dream up laundry for me?"

"Ah, Annie, that spot will never show with all the wild stripes on that tie."

"It's paisley, silly, not stripes." My mom would try not to smile, feigning aggravation. I knew she would take the tie directly to the washer, and I knew that the Spray 'n Wash would be too high for her to reach and she would call for him to help. Like a movie I had watched many times, I saw my parents sitting on the patio after dinner, drinking coffee and smoking Marlboro Lights. I knew he could blow smoke rings and she could not. I knew they didn't think I knew they smoked.

My eyes closed, I basked in the safety of normal, clinging to a memory that would dissipate in an instant.

"Jo! Come down please. Mr. Blair—Maddy has brought us a delicious dinner!"

Faintly wet, my eyes opened and took in the fading light outside, the massive willow swaying in the wind, storm clouds threatening.

"Thank goodness we got everything inside when we did," Doro was saying to Maddy. "JoANNA!"

When the willow shifted, I saw them. Head stones, mere specks from my vantage points, with the elephant ears dancing rhythmically around them. I saw not only the elephant ears, but also my dad's paisley tie, and smelled the pizza. All at once, the knot in my stomach unraveled, and the tears came.

She was the last to go.

I ran down the stairs two at a time, gasping as tears filled my throat. Darting past Doro and Maddy, I tripped over a box and hurled myself against the screen door. Their voices were behind me, but those elephant ears were calling me.

The last to go. Mommy!

I don't know where I thought I was going—only that being in the evening breeze, as the thunder rustled around me, was all I wanted. It was where I thought I could find the voices of my parents, where I thought I could be their little girl again.

Heat lightning flashed against the tombstones, and the waving elephant ears obscured the names. Ridiculous in their pageantry and height, the plants seemed to taunt me. To mock the dead.

And that's when I saw the clippers.

Abandoned by Maddy the day before, alongside his work gloves, the clippers were heavy. There was a soft creaking as I cut the ears, one after the other, down to the ground. My eyes were stinging from hot tears, my lips were covered in snot, and my arms ached with the weight of the blades.

"Jo! JoAnna!" Maddy and Doro were behind me.

When the last elephant ear was down, over six feet of dead stems lying amongst the stones, I dropped both the shears and myself to the ground. No one moved, not me, not Doro, not Maddy.

"Maddy, I just don't know what got into her head. JoAnna!"

Doro's tone was not one I had heard before. It was angry, shaking, and it scared me. Then came Maddy's voice: gentle, strong.

"It's about to storm. We need to get inside. JoAnna, take my hand." Maddy extended a calloused palm.

Years later, that voice is still so soothing to me. On Mt. Moriah it is said that Maddy's voice is Solomon and God and Charlton Heston all wrapped in one.

On that day in the garden, that voice led me inside. It sat me at the table, where with trembling hands Doro unwrapped the casserole dish. Maddy's voice led me upstairs to my bed, because I was too upset to eat. And it told me the story of the elephant ears.

"What did you have against those elephant ears, Jo?" Maddy's eyes were upon me as he kneeled next to my bed. I could not look at him.

"Did you know I've been growing them close to ten years? I reckon that's as much as you've been alive, eh?"

Silence from me. Silence from Doro, poised just inside the door.

"I planted them because my great granddaddy's farm was always full of flowers. My brother and me, we used to play hide and seek in his garden."

Silence.

"I wanted to make a garden like my great granddaddy Lindsay's. This is my house, JoAnna. My great granddaddy's house."

"Maddy, I didn't know." Doro's voice was hushed. "You're the seller?"

I stopped sobbing and looked at Maddy. "They're your family? The children? The mother?" Then the tears started again. "It's so sad. It's not beautiful."

"Is that what's bothered you? Those graves? When I inherited this house 'bout ten years ago, that land was so overgrown you couldn't even see the tombstones.

"I never did anything inside here, didn't have the time and didn't want to live here, but Rip and I love to be outdoors, and I just couldn't stand those graves being lost in the weeds.

"I just figured something beautiful should live next to something so sad. I planted that garden as a memorial. I kinda think that mother and her children would appreciate that. A sign of respect."

Maddy pulled a handkerchief, surprisingly starched and bright white, out of his back pocket and wiped my eyes and nose.

"What you did was disrespectful."

My voice was quiet and wavering. "I'm sorry. Sir."

"Don't apologize to me. Be sorry for those plants. Be sorry to God Almighty, because I reckon it's his nature you ruined."

Looking into Maddy's ocean blue eyes, I felt both sorry and strangely comforted. "Sorry," I whispered faintly again.

Doro spoke. "Maddy, I am sorry for JoAnna. I don't know—"

Maddy held his hand up to silence her as he continued to hold me in his gaze. "Guess we don't need to know. Guess she knows what was on her heart.

"I accept your apology, JoAnna. And now I'm going to go eat some chicken casserole that the best cook in First Methodist Church made. And you need to come eat some too. Because tomorrow you're going to need your strength.

"Tomorrow you and I are going to replant those ears."

The next day we did. And every year after, we weeded the garden together, spending hours bent over the soil, grimy paths of sweat streaked across our cheeks.

Today the elephant ears reign eight feet high over the Lindsay graves and over a little girl's rage.

7

PREACHER MAN

So BEGAN MY LIFE ON MT. MORIAH—much like the life of anyone who has lived in a small town. A cleaning crew had come before us, and by the time we had been in the house for four days, there was some semblance of order. I spent the morning hours playing in my room, setting up my stuffed animals and books and lounging on the bean bag beneath the dripping air conditioner. Whether she was giving me space to adjust or just needed time on her own, Doro never intruded my morning solitude. After lunch, however, I was hers. We placed and rearranged and dusted and swept. Maddy and Rip stopped by regularly—the flatulent canine and the fastidious old maid exchanging grimaces.

On the Friday that ended our first week in Mt. Moriah, Maddy's truck sputtered to a stop in front of the porch. Doro was sweeping—her wide sundress providing both airflow and a peep show to anyone bold enough to glance.

"Why, Maddy, look at you. Why the coat and tie?"

We were accustomed to seeing Maddy in his jeans and work shirt, thick boots caked with mud, and his bald spot covered by a Braves cap. But Maddy was sporting a black suit, cufflinks, and thinning hair that had been dippy-dooed into submission back across his steep brow.

"I clean up real good sometimes. When I have to," Maddy grinned, handing Doro a basket of squash and tomatoes he had harvested the day before. "I'm on my way to a funeral, actually, but I wanted to stop by and invite you lovely ladies to church this Sunday."

"Well, my goodness, I guess we do need to find a church to go to here. Jo's father and I were raised Episcopalian."

On my parents' cherry dresser was a silver framed photograph of Doro and Joseph Wilson as little children standing under a gothic portico. Grinning for the camera, Doro was wearing a smocked white eyelet dress with starched petticoat, and my dad looked as somber as his black suit. One glimpse at the photograph told you that little boy was itching to be back in his jeans.

The truth was that I didn't feel Episcopalian. My parents and I were devout "Chr-Easters," attending only at Christmas and Easter.

"Oh, it's not that I don't believe, Jo," said my dad one Christmas Eve as he struggled with his tie. "It's just that I have never felt comfortable in stuffy sanctuaries.

"After all, God created golf courses, right? So who's to say you can't be just as close to him on the twelfth tee?"

Maddy was giving Doro directions to the First United Methodist Church in Mt. Moriah. With only two stoplights in the town, the directions seemed unnecessary. We had seen the spire soaring into the clouds. The tin roof made the church seem as if on fire.

"Methodist's all we've got here, but we're not so different from Episcopalians—except no alcohol. You'll be having Holy Communion with grape juice, not wine," said Maddy.

"Well, we'd be delighted to come, and thank you for thinking of us," said Doro.

With a squeeze of my nose, Maddy was off to his funeral, and we were back to our cleaning.

The following Sunday, Doro and I were almost late to the eleven o'clock service. Doro wore a starched peach linen suit, a broad brimmed wicker hat and three inch white pumps that disguised her shortness.

The rest of the week Mt. Moriah had seemed so small, so quiet, but at the First Methodist Church on Sunday there were cars parked in every direction on the sweeping lawn. The church was a white clapboard structure with a narrow, red front door that required harsh tugs. The choir was already processing when we slipped into the third row from the back. I was fumbling with my bulletin when I glimpsed the pastor's robe sweeping past. And then his eyes. Unmistakably, unforgettably blue.

Just as I heard the distinctive bass voice singing *O for a Thousand Tongues to Sing*, I felt the pastor reach out and tweak my nose.

Pastor Madison Blair.

> *He speaks, and, list'ning to His voice,*
> *New life the dead receive,*
> *The mournful, broken hearts rejoice,*
> *The humble poor believe.*

The notes bounced off the baby grand piano and seemed to mirror the light streaming in from the short stained glass windows.

Later, as we knelt at the Communion rail, I watched Maddy move along. When he reached us, his eyes were upon mine as he whispered the grace. "Jesus' bread, broken for you. The blood of our Savior, shed for you, Jo."

As he issued a small prayer releasing us from the Lord's Table, he smiled at Doro.

Afterwards, we gathered with the rest of the congregation on the lawn while Maddy—Brother Blair as we learned he was called—made the rounds, shaking hands and slapping backs. When he came up to us, Doro's face still showed her surprise.

"Why, Reverend Blair—"

"Maddy."

"You are a man full of surprises. I just never . . ." Doro's voice trailed off, speechless for once.

Maddy chuckled. "Not accustomed to seeing a man of the cloth with dirty nails, eh? Well ma'am, I can assure you I scrubbed them before serving the Lord's Supper," said Maddy, holding up his huge calloused hands to show off the obviously clean nails. "I reckon those whiskey-palian priests might not have a hankering for gardening like I do," he grinned.

Doro's face registered the surprise we both felt. We didn't know what to think of the man who fixed up old houses and dug vegetable gardens and knew about elephant ears. And Jesus Christ.

"Say, wait a minute. Let me introduce you to someone."

Excusing himself, he called over two men, somewhere in their twenties, obviously brothers and obviously a bit hung over from the night before.

"Jack and George Russell. Two of the best workers you'll ever know. They need some work, and you need some strong backs. A perfect match."

Doro shook their hands somewhat reluctantly. They offered to come by after church to look at the Lindsay House. After they said goodbye, Maddy offered an answer to the question Doro had not asked.

"Hard times have hit a lot of families up here, Miss Doro. George there has a little boy he has to support and a wife that's not around half the time. They both take care of their mother. They dip into the sauce a bit; I won't lie to you. They just need some odd jobs— get 'em caught up, get their minds onto a good honest project and away from the bar."

Gauging Doro's hesitation, Maddy added what Doro was wanting to hear.

"I've known that family since they were knee high to a grasshopper. Finally got them going to church somewhat regular. They won't disappoint me."

About that time, a member of the congregation tapped Maddy on the shoulder, calling him back to the crowd on the steps.

Doro and I were left under the shade of a low hanging magnolia, approached by first one and then another person. The hellos, the how-do-you-dos, the names, all faded into background noise as I breathed in the freshly cut grass, saw sunshine bursting through the colorful glass windows, and felt my skin baking under a cloudless sky.

I could remember my parents' occasional church in Atlanta. The smell of Sunday School. The Sunday morning waffles. The newspaper spread across the sofa between my parents. The sound of dishes clinking in the kitchen as I played Barbies on my bed.

Home.

I closed my eyes and picked Maddy's and Doro's voices out over the hum of unfamiliar noises. In my mind, bright eyelet gingham curtains hung at a window shaded by a willow. Was that home too?

I cannot say I felt either sad or happy. What I felt was calm and secure. And aren't those the first steps toward happiness? Toward home?

8

APRIL THROUGH NOVEMBER

WORD OF DORO'S IMPENDING RENOVATION of the old Lindsay home spread and, at various times in our second week in the house, five neighbors showed up on the doorstep with bowls and dishes and pans—each brimming with a Southern delicacy. To each new face she met, Doro explained her plan for the B&B, the colors she envisioned and her thematic idea for the whole house.

"I love the changing of seasons and months, so I thought I could have one bedroom representing each month. When visitors come, I'll just ask, 'Oh, would you prefer to be in the June room or the November room?'"

Doro was speaking to Libby McAlister, whose look of confusion arose from her knowledge that there were not enough bedrooms.

"We're going to have to throw up some walls," Doro explained, unrolling blueprints onto the dining room table. Also, I'm going to omit December through March. Those are cold, drab months, don't you think? Then, the former maid's quarters, off the kitchen will be mine." Doro smiled brightly. "What do you think?"

Universally, Doro was met with optimism.

"Why it's just what this town needs!"

"I'm going to tell my sister, Miss Wilson. She and her family are always cramped when they stay with us. She'll be thrilled there's somewhere new to stay."

Before long, Doro ceased being Miss Wilson and became simply Doro. That was her way—to meet Doro was to get the feeling that you had known her for

42

years, or rather, that you *wished* you had. Her happy laugh, her bright red smile disappearing over lipstick smeared teeth, her handshake which utilized both of her hands—all of these endeared Doro to Mt. Moriah. Before long, people were imagining that Doro had been born in Mt. Moriah, that she had gone to high school with them, that she had been in Vacation Bible School with them. She simply wove herself into the enduring fabric of their memories.

In the days before wallpaper steamers, Doro and I—with the Russell brothers' assistance—dampened, peeled, and scraped wallpaper that seemed to have a life of its own. Maddy often dropped by unexpectedly, doling out advice.

"Consider me your contractor," he'd chuckle, slapping George or Jack on the back. "You do the work; I'll be the contractor!"

Gradually, with Doro at the design helm, the rooms began to take shape. Downstairs, the library along the back porch was divided into April and May rooms, with a small bath joining them. April had a spring theme—periwinkle drapes, a white chenille coverlet, and tulip wallpaper. May's walls were painted a pale lavender and the large window facing the backyard draped in silver voile sheers: evoking the feeling of standing in a rainstorm. Upstairs, June—on the home's southwest corner—was the only room with a private bath. It became the bridal suite, with organza drapes, and a crystal vase of orchids and lilies on the dresser. The July and August bedrooms spanned the south wing of the house. July had a patriotic theme, with a Wedgewood blue ceiling and red and white star patterned quilt.

To create more bedrooms, walls went up to divide the fifty-foot ballroom spanning the northern side of the house, converting the space to autumn. The September room was painted a pale russet, with a wreath of autumn flowers. A letterman's jacket from the local high school team was framed on the wall. October's room had a wallpaper border of autumn leaves and November a wintry look—with a Tartan plaid down comforter and overstuffed navy chair pulled next to the window. With a fireplace and wall of bookshelves, which Doro kept stocked, November was the room most often requested. Visitors would pass through during a hot, humid summer, and request the "winter room."

For weeks, the only room that lacked an identity was the home's third original bedroom, August.

"What is August to you?" Doro would ask in the grocery, at the post office. Indeed, it seemed a month without definition. One day the *Mt. Moriah Journal*, the town's weekly paper, ran a contest to design a room for August. We ended up with 125 submissions—not a bad rate of return given that Mt. Moriah's population was 2,420, and the paper's circulation was half that.

It was Rhonda Peters' entry that won. A kindergarten teacher, Rhonda said August reminded her of notebook paper and the sand from her family's annual beach trip before school.

"I'll decorate it totally in white!" said Doro. And so it was, with thick white carpet, a coverlet of ivory matelassé on a white iron bed, with white eyelet curtains framing eggshell walls. It became my favorite room. A few years later, Doro added a white ceiling fan, and sometimes, when August was vacant, I would retreat there and read on the tall bed, the whirring fan casting patterns of light on the plaster ceiling.

We had to wait four weeks for the sign—THE INN AT MT. MORIAH—to be made. It was cast in concrete at the base of the driveway off Birkham Road. The day the sign went up, Doro made homemade ice cream on the lawn. The Inn officially began taking guests in the spring of 1984.

It was the early '80s and everyone's minds were on Reagan-omics, Sally Ride, and the US Embassy bombing in Beirut. But for a few weeks that summer, Doro brought Mt. Moriah together, and for years to come she would be credited with defining August.

That first summer in Mt. Moriah, when I wasn't helping Maddy, Doro, and the Russells with the renovations, I was in my attic sanctuary. Maddy built shelves on each side of my windows, and I lined my books along them. I had always liked to read, but since my parents' death, I escaped more and more often into the pages of a good story. While hammers and paintbrushes did their work downstairs, I lay on my beanbag and read. The breeze in the willow outside my room flung sunlight bubbles across my page.

One evening when Doro had invited Maddy to stay for dinner as thanks for all his hard work, she broached the subject of my reading.

"You need to get outside and play more, doll. You keep your nose stuck in a book all the time."

Something flip-flopped in my chest. I suddenly remembered Jenny Webber and Monopoly and all the games we used to play: Those days seemed like a lifetime ago. The truth was that there were few children in Mt. Moriah, and I knew no one. The loneliness that I had hidden in the pages of my beloved books hit me all at once.

Maddy seemed to sense what I was feeling.

"Well, you know, it's not really a child's yard, is it? How about I build you a tree-house?" And then, with his voice lowered, "I love nothing better than reading up in a tree." And, with his voice louder, "Reading will make her even smarter, Doro."

Doro straightened a bit in her chair, perhaps feeling her parenting questioned.

"I guess I never was a big reader. I remember playing outside as a child. We would play from early morning until our parents called us in for dinner, my brother and . . ."

She caught herself. Not only did I not have a brother to play with, but I also didn't have *her* brother as a father anymore. Doro squeezed my hand.

"I'd just like to see you get some fresh air every day, doll. The treehouse is a lovely idea. Maybe I'll even take up reading!

"Besides, it's only one more week until school starts. You'll have lots of friends and be doing plenty of playing then."

My stomach churned again. The prospect of starting in a new school was terrifying to me. I loved Doro, the Inn, and the life we were building. But it wasn't mine. My life was back in an elementary classroom four blocks away from 145 Magnolia Drive. My life was lying in a bed with the whispered voices of my parents drifting around me.

The first day of school at the Woodbury Street Elementary, I threw up my breakfast. Doro had carefully tamed my curls into submission and made me a new dress to wear. It was red gingham with apple patches as pockets. Those apples were drenched with vomit.

"I'm sorry, Aunt Doro." The tears wouldn't stop; they were tears of utter terror. I saw the paint can sitting in the corner of the foyer, ready for the final touch-up of the June room. I wanted to peel wallpaper—with my nails if I had to—pull weeds from the garden, anything to keep from going to school.

I could tell Doro was upset over the dress by the way she said, "It's only a dress." I could tell by the way she gingerly wiped at those apples with soda water after she had taken the dress from my shivering body. "Go find something else to put on, Jo."

I climbed the steps to my attic, wondering if I could fake a fall, break my leg, wondering if having a broken leg for weeks wouldn't be better than going to school.

In my room, I changed clothes, blew my nose and sat on the edge of my bed, staring into the willow. Then there was a knock at the door.

"I came to escort you lovely ladies to Woodbury Elementary," said Maddy, his sunburnt face smelling of Old Spice and his double chins jiggling as he smiled.

He didn't ask why my eyes were red or mention my sniffling. That was the way with Maddy: He knew people, could see beneath their expressions.

"Hey, little thing, I've got something for you. My mother gave it to me the day I was confirmed. It always brought me courage. I thought maybe today you could use some courage—going to a new school and all."

Maddy unfolded his hand and, inside, lay a small silver cross attached to a thin chain.

"God loves you, little thing. You wear this and be brave, and you go learn what He wants you to learn." Maddy's clear blue eyes were level with mine as he knelt in front of me, fastening the chain around my neck with his big clumsy hands. "Today when you need some courage, you just rub that cross."

At that moment Doro appeared in my door, purse in hand. Buoyed by those two, I got in the car, traveled the three miles to school, and got out without crying. I didn't cry at all until we reached the classroom, Doro and I. Then I turned and buried my head in her thick stomach. It was the first time we had been separated since my parents' death. I felt the bile rise in my throat.

"You can do this, Jo. You're going to make friends and your teacher looks so nice and look at all those books. You can do this, sweetie. I'll see you at three o'clock sharp."

A kiss and then she was gone. I was standing in front of Miss Patterson, who looked so young and so beautiful that my tears stopped mid-stream. She took my hand and led me to my table where two tow-headed boys took turns flicking their erasers at each other. In the third seat was a girl with long legs and two blonde braids hanging below her shoulders.

She smiled brightly, revealing no front teeth and big dimples. It was a smile that spoke of friendship to come, a smile that told me I was going to want to get up and come to school every day.

"Hi," she said. "My name is Grace."

Inside my poplin blouse, dangling against my rapidly beating heart, hung Maddy's cross.

9

BIST DU BEI MIR

"Jo, YOU READY TO GO, LITTLE THING?"

Maddy's hand was on my sleeve. How much time had passed for me, lost in my memories? I had seen the familiar faces at Woodbury, shaken hands, exchanged hugs, been properly appreciative of the guests at the visitation. And yet I felt I had moved through the afternoon as if in a dream.

"Gosh, Maddy, I just haven't been here since, well, since . . ."

"I know, little thing, I know. I was thinking about that sweet Grace too."

Suddenly very tired, I was anxious to be in bed. I was disappointed, then, when Maddy asked me to stop by the church with him.

"I just need to check on things for tomorrow, Jo. We'll just be a minute, then we can go have some dinner together. You can leave your rental car here."

We had not been riding for many miles before Maddy asked the question I knew he had been waiting to ask.

"I didn't think you'd be coming alone, little thing. How is that husband of yours?"

I considered my words carefully and then told a boldface lie.

"He's fine, Maddy. He had to work. He wishes he could have come."

I wanted to say more; I needed to say more. I needed to sit with my head resting on Maddy's shoulder and tell him everything—about my marriage, about me. But what I needed more was to sit on Doro's porch and let the tears come. For Doro, for Grace, and for the childhood that had shadowed me all day. To close my eyes and think and remember.

"Jo, I have some ideas about the music—I know some of Doro's favorite hymns, but I'd appreciate your helping me." Holding my hand, Maddy was navigating me up the Chancel stairs of First Methodist Church.

I had not been in this church in four years—since I left Mt. Moriah. It seemed smaller somehow, the stained glass windows narrower. The burgundy carpet had not been changed, I saw, and the kneeling pads at the front had the same telltale juice spots from toddlers trying to take Communion.

"You know Doro and music," Maddy was saying. "I need some help."

Indeed. To this day, I cannot hear beautiful music without thinking of Doro. Not a trained musician herself, Doro had a beautiful soprano voice, and music was her passion. It was how she relaxed, how she woke up, how she celebrated, and how she comforted herself. The Inn was full of music every day—sometimes Vivaldi on a bright spring morning, and Brahms in the evenings when the guests lingered around the parlor, perusing the bookshelves for a good read, or sipping sherry from Doro's grandmother's Waterford.

Doro loved all kinds of music, but especially classical and church hymns. She rarely needed a hymnal to sing in church, for the lyrics were so ingrained in her head. And consequently in mine. Doro sang as she cleaned, sang as she cooked, and her working songs were mostly Methodist hymns from the dilapidated hymnal with pages 222 and 223 sliding out.

Obviously, the music for Doro's funeral warranted careful consideration.

Behind the pulpit, nested in a hole, was the organ that Doro had helped raise money to buy. When we began going to First Methodist, Doro was incredulous that there was no organ, only a baby grand piano, and she set about fundraising for the cause.

It was an uphill battle. Parishioners were content with the piano, with the old hymns and the second octave A that stuck. Doro was not one to be content with the status quo. Madeline Gifford, the twenty-three-year-old grad student in church music at the nearby college, was the temporary choir director and pianist. She also played the organ, thankfully, and was thrilled by Doro's cause.

"I love piano music. But you need an organ to play classical music, and classical belongs in church," Doro told Maddy one summer evening as we ate dinner on the side porch. "Perhaps it's the Episcopalian in me."

Thirteen months later, through ice cream festivals on the lawn of the Inn, Doro's calls to the congregation asking for money, and through a generous donation from Doro herself, First Methodist was able to purchase an organ. To celebrate, Maddy asked Doro and Madeline to plan a concert, with Bach as the headliner. It was the beginning of a classical touch to First Methodist's church services. Now, almost twenty years later, the white country church is known throughout the county for its music.

Such was Doro's impact.

I fingered the plaque atop the organ's mahogany cabinetry. "Dedicated to Dorothea Wilson, lover of music and child of God."

I looked at Maddy. "Well, Maddy, I think there needs to be Bach tomorrow."

Doro was about Bach the way some people are about Elvis. She adored the CD collection I sent her at Christmas recently. Maddy and I teased Doro about her fanaticism.

"Bach is dead, you know, Doro," I said, winking at Maddy. "You can't go to any of his concerts this year!"

In retribution, she would use Toccata and Fugue to blast me out of bed on teenage mornings, when I considered noon too early to rise.

"Yes, I thought of that, but I don't know which Bach," Maddy said.

It didn't require much thought on my part. I knew exactly which one.

One stifling August day, Grace and I were milling around Doro's kitchen, stealing grapes and tapping our newly painted toes on the tile. We were probably ten at the time, and boredom came easily. Doro kept sidestepping us, rolling her eyes at our ennui.

"Your brains are going to turn to mush if you girls don't find something to do."

"We're bored."

"That's obvious. What about a game?"

"Nah." I slumped against the sink.

"Don't say naaaah, say no. And stand up straight." Doro lifted her casseroles up into the cavernous oven, closed the door and set the timer. "Okay girls, come with me."

Our immediate thoughts were that we were going to be put to work. There was always something to do around the Inn—hundreds of things actually—and at that age Grace and I were Doro's unpaid help.

Instead, Doro led us to her bedroom where she commanded us to lie on the floor. It had been a stormy day, so there was only faint light outside. Doro drew her drapes, making the room almost pitch black. Most kids would have questioned if asked to get on the floor, but Grace and I knew better. This was Doro: Something exciting was about to happen.

Doro flipped through her albums until she found the one she wanted. It began its spin on the turntable.

Doro joined us on the floor. We faced up, staring at the cracked plaster ceiling.

"Close your eyes and listen. We're going to take turns telling the story of the music. Wait a minute; I'll go first."

The music was Copeland, and Doro described the square dance she was seeing in her mind. "Lots of bright skirts, swishing together. Everyone's happy. Now wait. The door's opening. Do you hear this part? A tall girl has entered the room. She's alone. She's lonely."

And so we played Doro's game. On her turn, Grace imagined a bird's flight across cloudless skies to Saint-Saëns. The third song on Doro's Classical Collection was Chopin's Prelude, and it was my turn. The writer in me depicted a sultry argument between two lovers. They were leaning against a high balcony, stormy waters below.

"Wow. I just saw a bird. You saw a whole soap opera," Grace giggled.

The next song was Doro's: a Bach piece. Doro listened to almost the whole thing without speaking. We actually suspected she had fallen asleep, so we leaned up on our elbows to look at her. The look on her face was an indescribable marriage of joy and pain.

When the violins began their ascent, Doro raised her finger. "There. This is the part I love. I see a spiral staircase rising into clouds. Everything's lovely and happy. You can see the brightest sun peaking around and through the clouds."

She was quiet for a minute, as a sole violin took us away on a high G. Doro's voice was hushed when she finally spoke.

"I love that song. I hear it, and I see heaven. It's almost as if, when the song's highest note comes, I can see God."

"I know the one, Maddy. Can David Smiley play the violin? It's called *'Bist du bei mir.'* Do you know it?"

He smiled. "I do, little one. It means God is with me."

We looked through the hymnal together and chose two of Doro's favorites. Outside, dusk was setting and the stained glass parables of Jesus were transitioning from day to night.

Maddy's arm was around me as we headed outside. I had been so lost in my own thoughts, my grief, my confusion, that for the first time I thought about the fact that Maddy was not just officiating at Doro's funeral.

He was her widower.

The last vestiges of summer light slipped away as Maddy and I turned between the stone pillars marking the driveway to the Inn. I sat still, taking in the shiny magnolias and Bartlett pears lining the way. Driving into the Inn was truly like retreating from life; perhaps that is why the B&B's regular vacationers loved it.

Although I had been away for years, I could still close my eyes and envision key landmarks on the ten acres. A forty foot oak anchored the center of the lawn, broad limbs twisted and mangled enough to form a perfect platform for the treehouse Maddy built for me and Grace. As a child, I would peer out the sidelights flanking the front door and watch thunderstorms rolling across the lawn; those convoluted limbs became ominous outlines against the flashing white sky—making me tremble with every bolt. As the new morning dawned, however, the oak's leaves would beckon me to the top branches, and I thought them invincible.

A row of forsythia bushes close to the stone wall were glorious flashes of yellow that, in the springtime, would tempt highway passersby. The broad front porch spanned the house, rocking chairs lined up, their wicker backs home to numerous spider webs. On the eastern end hung a white swing— paint peeling and metal chains squeaking. I knew by heart the magnificent vista glimpsed from that swing seat: It had been mine for so many years.

Maddy grabbed my suitcase, and I mounted the back steps. "I'll get the door, Maddy." The Inn's key still hung from my keychain, and I remembered how to pull the door toward me just enough so the key would connect.

And then inside the smell was of Doro: disinfectant peppered with lavender. A smell that spoke of her age, that told you it—and she—would never change.

At age seventy-six, Doro had begun to let some of the upstairs rooms collect dust. She didn't run the B&B full-time anymore; rather she rented the rooms to house friends who came to visit. Many were former customers—people who through the years had stayed at the B&B regularly en route to a real vacation elsewhere. Now the Inn was their final destination.

But the downstairs was still pristine. I moved through the kitchen, lightly touching the counters, noticing how the plants in the greenhouse window were thriving, the basket of spices, little bottles all thrown together. "Anyone who has their spices neatly lined up doesn't really use them!" Doro would say, as she tossed the bottle of thyme into the basket where it nudged the nutmeg out of its place. Doro's "Kiss the Cook" apron was hanging on the back of the pantry door, which I knew, if opened, would reveal a shelf of cookbooks rarely touched. All of Doro's recipes she knew by heart; many had come from my grandmother.

I continued my tour of the house, my prescient eyes leading me by memory. I knew the rosewood glasses would be arranged from tea to wine to water on the top shelf of the cherry corner cabinet. I knew my great-grandmother's cut glass punch bowl would be in the middle of the dining room table, and that the Bavarian plate on the far right of the collection hanging on the side wall had a chip that I had put there.

The parlor's Duncan Fyfe sofa showed no more wear than on the day it was brought to the Inn, and the same burgundy fringed pillows sat on the wing back chairs in the exact spots they had occupied for years and years. The antique card table in the bay window was set with the glass chess set one of the Inn's long-time visitors, turned long-time friend, had brought Doro ten years ago. Above the mantel my grandmother's Bulova Anniversary clock revealed a fictitious time—10:32—just as it had for the fifty years since it had stopped.

Off the kitchen was a short hallway to two doors: one leading to Doro's and Maddy's bedroom and another with knobby pine paneling, that served as the private den. The small television set, the stereo, the comfortable recliners—these were Maddy and Doro's creature comforts at the end of a day's cooking and hosting. The clay piano I made when I was thirteen and taking a summer pottery class sat on top of the television, and the built-in bookshelves were crammed full of paperbacks, some vertical, some sideways. My school pictures—each one from third grade through high school—lined the top shelf, and the small trophy I had won as "most talented writer" in high school was front and center.

I sank onto the worn loveseat and wrapped the cream afghan around my shoulders. Again, the smell of Doro, the smell of home. Years and miles had passed, and yet no time at all. It seemed that home was ever lingering behind my nose, my ears and eyes, patiently waiting to be sensed again.

Exhausted from the day of travel, I nodded off and awoke groggy and confused. Looking around, I spotted a framed photograph of my husband and me, both sporting red "I Love Chicago" t-shirts and standing on the Michigan Avenue Bridge. I had sent it to Doro two years ago.

My eyes focused on the heart that represented the word love in the center of my chest. I remembered the day the photograph was taken. Happiness was beating in *that* Jo's heart. As I sat on Doro's sofa and stared at my smiling face, I sensed I was on the precipice between two worlds: Mt. Moriah on the one hand, Chicago and my husband on the other.

10

BLUE SKY

THE DAY MY NEW BLACK PUMPS squeaked onto the slate lobby of Sandalwood & Harris Advertising, homesickness and insecurity overtook me. Inside awaited a host of unfamiliar faces, a job I didn't know how to do, and a little less than two thousand dollars a month, which sounded like the lottery.

I spend my first weeks at S&H oscillating between the thrill of the city and the desire for something, someone, familiar. I called Doro only twice on her command.

"Try not to call too much. It'll make you more homesick. Be a writer."

I knew she said this while perched on a stool in her cobalt blue and white kitchen. I did not know that she hung up brushing away tears and longing for me to call as soon as possible.

When I got the job offer at S&H, Doro was convinced that the position of copy editor was synonymous with writer. I made myself believe that I was fulfilling my dream of writing. In actuality, though, editing copy meant checking for typographical errors, suggesting stylistic changes, and then being ignored for the most part. I was always invited to Happy Hour though, a Thursday ritual for those of us on the twelfth floor. I explored the world of syrupy umbrella-ed drinks and cold bottles of wine. All of this was new to me, a Methodist girl from the South, and I dove head-first into the godless world of booze and partying.

People speak of drinking to drown your sorrows, but I was drinking to drown my past.

When I wasn't drinking, I was running along the shores of Lake Michigan or shopping. I purchased four suits that could be mixed and matched. New credit cards came, and I celebrated each arrival with another lunch out, another happy hour.

In the long-term hotel on Wooster, I was cocooned. My room had two beds, a small refrigerator and microwave. At night I would leave the television and lights on, as the traffic outside my window and the noisy corridors made me feel safer.

"How are you sleeping, Jo?"

"Fine, Doro. I'm fine."

It was a lie—to Doro and myself. I discovered airplane bottles to keep in the room, and it took several drinks to sink into fitful sleep. Around one in the morning, I would finally close my heavy eyes—only to be plagued by nightmares. I wasn't thinking, much less writing. Walking became an obsession. On weekdays, I relished my route from the el station to work. At one intersection, I walked through a tunnel under the street. At a certain point, halfway down, I could look up and see the Tribune Tower looming above me. On Saturdays, I took long strolls to the Michigan Avenue Bridge, lingering around the Tribune building, resting finally on the steps of the Wrigley. I never tired of watching the bridge rise and the barges pass underneath. I waved below, but they never saw me. I was invisible. Emotionally, intellectually, spiritually.

Happy hours led to dancing. It seemed there were a million men in Chicago who were just my age. Tall. Short. Handsome. Intellectual. With all the walking, I dropped fifteen pounds and found myself being constantly asked to the dance floor. The faster the music, the better. But inevitably the band would start a slow song, and I'd feel an arm around my waist. That's when I would excuse myself to the bathroom—and from there slip into the windy Chicago night. And then home, to my hotel room where I would lie, fully dressed, on top of my bed, the walls spinning in alcoholic splendor.

I would stare at the TV until I drifted into a few hours of fitful sleep. Then my alarm would startle me and up I would be, ready to walk again. Alcohol was my nighttime friend, but caffeine was the gift of the dawn.

During those first few months in Chicago, the days segued into nights, and the chardonnays to coffee, and one barge became another. Being faithless and faceless was exhilarating.

One Wednesday morning, I was almost late to my first creative team meeting. Standing at the Xerox machine, toner smudging my ivory sleeve, a wad of paper tucked under my armpit, I had been digging my nails into the long yellow machine wand marked "B" for fifteen minutes.

"You have to kick it."

The unexpected voice made me lose my grasp on the paper shreds and sit down hard on the floor. He laughed, extending a hand.

"The copy machine is beating you at its own sick game. You have to show it who's boss." Helping me to my feet, the man pushed tortoise wire rims up on his nose, where they promptly slid again.

"And you kick it to show it who's boss?"

"Of course, not. We call Dunn's to come service it." He reached around me for the wall phone.

"Just because of wadded up paper?"

"Want to violate our service contract?" He took a quick glance at my smudged blouse. "You're new; that's why you try to do everything yourself. You haven't yet surrendered to the system . . . oh, yes, hello, client number is 00576. Sandalwood & Harris. Yes, twelfth floor. Uh-huh. Thanks."

He re-cradled the receiver, smiled and extended a hand. "Tom Rivers."

I shook it. "JoAnna Wilson—people call me Jo—and you're right, I'm so new I didn't even know there *is* a system."

"There is a system for everything." He glanced at his watch. "Gotta scoot. My creative team meeting starts in five minutes, and my photos are still down on six. Good to meet you."

"Oh, you're a photographer . . ." my voice trailed off. He was gone. I, too was due at a team meeting. The black wall clock ticked loudly. Just enough time to try to lighten this smudge.

He jolted me when he flung the heavy paneled door open into my chair.

"Jeez! I'm sorry, JoAnna, was it?"

I moved around and smiled nervously. "Jo. It's okay."

He took a seat next to me, unloading three binders of stock photos on the table. Each held dozens of little Post-it Notes, torn in half to be markers. Feeling my eyes upon him, Tom smiled at me again. "I didn't hurt you, did I?"

"No, that's okay." I paused.

His grin revealed the deepest dimples I had ever seen. "Is this your first team meeting with our illustrious creative director?"

I nodded. "Candace is my boss."

He rolled his eyes. "Well, sit back and enjoy the show."

"The show?" Before he could answer, Candace was in the room.

My pulse raced—not only at the thought of the friendly photographer beside me, but at the sight of Candace, in a short salmon suit, the flip chart at the front of the room, the apples in the middle of the table. A creative team meeting! My creative team!

I sat up straight in my chair, ready.

Soon I was slumping, as the director of sales gave a five-minute speech that lasted thirty. Beside me, Tom stifled a yawn and scribbled some words on the margin of a legal pad. Coyly leaning his elbows on the table, he pushed the pad toward me. I bet the notes he passed in fourth grade English were never discovered.

Know why we call her Blue Sky?

He moved the pad back in front of him, scrawling some gibberish at the top, as if taking notes. Then he drew an arrow pointing to Candace.

I subtly shook my head. Tom smiled and wrote.

Just wait.

They were discussing the new Park Hotel in Nashville. S&H was to have a marketing proposal in one week. The meeting was to plot a strategy for introducing the hotel to the marketplace and defeating the other agencies vying for the account.

"Okay, people, let's get down to work," said Adam Vining, the account executive. "We have seven days to draft a plan. Let's focus on our target audience and message. Then we'll brainstorm on media vehicles to reach our constituency.

"I have some data to get us started; this is from the Nashville Chamber of Commerce." A thin file containing every conceivable local travel statistic wafted to the table. "And here is some demographic data from other Park Hotels around the country."

Another Manila folder made its graceful landing next to the first file. Straightening his tie, Adam leaned his knuckles on the table until they were translucent, the cartilage straining with the pressure.

"And now I'll tell you to disregard this research, because all marketing is inherently local. I don't give a rat's ass why San Diego tourists choose the suite concept; I need to know about Nashville tourists. And I need you to tell me." He turned to the salmon suit beside him. "Candace, who is the biggest 'buyer' of suite services?"

Clearing her throat, Candace leaned forward so that her ecru blouse, already plunging, dove further.

"Adam, that is the sixty-four-thousand-dollar question. If we can pinpoint that answer— if we can define our audience, we will have Park Hotel eating out of our hands."

One could picture someone eating out of her hands. Grapes, perhaps. Strawberries dipped in cream.

"The sixty-four-thousand-dollar question, people."

Candace whipped around in her chair, trailing salmon particles in the air.

"George, what is your perception of the average Nashville tourist?" George Winkel, a balding Northern transplant whose belly bumped the table, cleared his throat but Candace's manicured index finger across her lips shushed him before he had a chance to respond. "Let me see the tourist! Let me close my eyes and see them!"

And her eyes did actually close, as we all sat riveted by the raw sexuality she exuded.

George began to paint the picture. Candace swayed in her chair, closing her eyes to imagine. Kim chimed in next, completing the portrait. Mostly country music fans. Moderate disposable income.

Adam took the reins back. "Okay people, we've painted quite a picture of our tourist industry here, thanks to Candace's input . . ."

It struck me, then, and I glanced at Tom Rivers who winked. Candace had not contributed one iota to the composite tourist portrait. All she had done was price the question at over sixty thousand dollars, yet she seemed a catalyst for the brainstorming. From trivial gestures and idioms flowing from her glossy lips, Candace almost made us believe she was a contributor.

"What will draw them in? What is most important?" Adam turned his flip chart paper over and wrote the heading "Message" along the top in neat, precise, OCD handwriting. Again, he turned first to Candace.

"Blue sky, Adam, blue sky . . ."

Adam Vining ate shredded wheat for breakfast, perched at his kitchen counter, one Armani shoe crossed over the other. He lunched on cantaloupe, berries, tofu, and hearts of palm on spinach leaves, while reading *The Wall Street Journal*. He drank mint tea, and usually dined on Thai carryout. Few fat grams passed his lips, his cholesterol was phenomenally low, and he would die of a heart attack before he turned forty-eight.

For him, advertising was not about the money, or the fame of seeing your tag line on billboards that truckers roared by. It was not about the cocktail receptions, or the free Chicago Cubs tickets. It was about the power of thought: the power of thinking first and thinking best. Surely, above Adam's bed were notches not of women he bedded, but of ideas that were his first.

For Candace Herford, advertising was a venue for her trite idioms, a job she could flirt her way through—a place where she could speak and make people actually think she was saying something.

"Tom, how much and how soon?"

I turned to watch Tom discuss the relative merits of stock photos versus a camera shoot.

"There's no comparison, guys. You can smell a stock photo; they reek of nothingness. For only fifty percent more, we can do our own shoot. Get some nice lighting to make it dramatic!"

"But can it be dramatic in, let's say, five days?" Adam pulled a mono-grammed money clip out of his pocket and fingered the twenties and fifties tucked neatly inside. He liked to feel the money: It gave him a sense of security. His credit cards were maxed out, but those bills made him feel potent. He liked us seeing them too.

"Sure, if you want me to ditch the hospital shoot this Thursday. That's going to occupy two days, on top of the head shots you need printed by tomorrow.

It's not doable this week. Let's just show the Park people our portfolio, let them see the quality we do, and figure a custom shoot into the budget."

"Or we could show them a completed concept, with stock photos, and wow them with our ability to get it turned around in such a short time." Adam threw his money clip on top of the calendar in front of him.

"Well, it depends on if you want it done or done right," Tom said.

Adam turned again to the bared bosom beside him. "Comments? Opinions?"

The pink salmon arms stretched behind her head, daring the pearl buttons on Candace's blouse to pop strategically. "Tom makes a good point. But we need to make sure we aren't confusing apples and oranges." Candace's hands came in front of her now, each cuddling a pretend piece of fruit. "Apples?" The right hand went forward. "Or oranges." Left hand.

"We're trying to sell a hotel, Candace, not a fruit basket," Tom said, looking at his watch. "I've got to run to a conference call." Then, looking at Adam: "Sorry. I had this call with my realtor scheduled before this meeting."

Standing and gathering the negative sheets before him, Tom made a last remark. "My opinion stands. I think stock photos will be a tacky entre to a client that wants class. But that's just my opinion."

And with that, he was out of the room. Following him was a searing look from Candace, her labia-colored lids squinting sharply at his departure.

At that first creative team meeting, I was torn between watching Candace's suit swish as her bare leg swung and my fascination with Tom Rivers.

After lunch on my way to the postage meter, I passed Tom's office. His chairback to me, he was shouting into the phone.

"Yes, another one week does matter. My lease is up, remember?" He nervously clicked a ballpoint. "Okay, talk to her. I don't see why I should have to pay for a hotel. Yeah. I know. It's not your fault. Just talk to her, okay?"

Tom slammed the phone in its cradle, and I dropped the forty-two letters I was carrying to the meter.

I dropped to my knees to begin retrieving them and he watched, never offering assistance.

"Let's see, you were standing in my doorway, trying to think of a cute conversation starter, but your hands let you down!" His tone was sarcastic, but his face was smiling.

"No, I was just staring at the mess in here and wondering how you find your desk." Was I flirting?

He grinned. "I don't need a desk—just a tripod."

My turn for conversation. Why was I speechless? He was not even handsome. And yet, those dimples, that thick luscious hair.

"I agreed with you in the creative meeting."

"On what?"

"On whether to use stock or custom photos." Tucking a loose twig of hair behind my ear, I made a mental note to find a hair salon.

"Oh. Well, they're idiots. And they'll do whatever they want anyway. Adam's creativity extends to his tie collection, and Candace's rests in finding lingerie to match her suits."

He noticed my obvious blush.

"Oh don't tell me you didn't notice that little peach number. She showed us from every angle, and I know there's a little matching thong."

I was embarrassed by this line of conversation, but determined not to let it show.

"You know, do you?"

Tom arose and moved closer, so that we were whispering in his doorway.

"No, I haven't had the dubious honor of sleeping with the bitch, but enough around here have. The bras and panties always match.

"I have a friend at Arnold Associates, where our queen creative director was before here. I found out that not only did she do nothing but glorified telemarketing and poster making, but she slept around. And, yes, her lingerie closet is fabulous!"

I had not heard of Arnold Associates but the information begged the question:

"I thought she had a good deal of experience. From my interview . . ."

We headed toward the elevator. Tom reached and pushed the up button.

"That's what she wants you to think, JoAnna! You see, she flirts with women too!" He flashed a hand to the president, who passed by.

"But you notice her remarks, and pretty soon you'll see that every question is answered with either apples and oranges." Tom turned his fingers down, one by one. "Or blue sky. Or sixty-four-thousand-dollar question."

"And I'm to assume she's slept her way to the top?"

Tom was in the elevator now. "Well, not all the way, but things take time, you know. She's a busy girl." He put a hand between the closing doors. "Are you going up?"

I suddenly felt the weight of the envelopes in my hand and felt a bit foolish. "No, I needed to take these to the postage room. I guess I forgot where—"

"You were distracted. I can understand how that happens around me." He winked and then smiled. "Hey, a guy can wish, can't he?"

As the elevator closed, I swallowed hard around my heart that had moved to my throat.

11

TRAIN TRACKS

In SIXTH GRADE, Billy McGuiness tempted fate by straddling the train tracks until he saw the locomotive round the bend. At the last second he would jump out of the way, diving butt-first onto the shoulder. The girls would shriek and the boys would cheer, and red-faced Billy, with perspiration beading up along his hairline, would bow dramatically.

On Friday nights during my first year in Chicago, I was my own Billy McGuiness. With no audience.

I chose Friday's attire carefully because I knew it would see almost eighteen hours before being discarded on the vinyl chair next to my bed. In the advertising agency, half past four on Friday afternoon heralded a level of excitement like a low drumbeat. The twelfth floor, where most of the junior copywriters, account executives, and designers worked, witnessed a steady flow of traffic into the women's room. With each sway of the door came a waft of fragrance and face powder. Tired Friday faces melded into weekend faces of opportunity and adventure.

In those days I drowned my loneliness in superficial conversations with Megans and Tiffanies and Loris. During the week I would follow along down the block to our favorite sandwich shop, to the coffee cart parked in the courtyard, and on Friday afternoons to Tony's Bar. To be honest, they would call me a good friend. I listened to Megan's landlord problems, sympathized with Tiffany's boyfriend's infidelity, and laughed at Lori's stories of her clueless mother back in Cleveland, worried only that Lori's mittens were sufficiently insulated against the Chicago climate.

64

I called them good friends. But did I consider them such? How could I? I had known Grace—the kind of friend who could encourage with a squeeze of the hand, comfort with her eyes, who knew me as surely as if she had nursed me from birth. The Megans and Tiffanies and Loris were mere companions. They were noise, ways to forget.

And forget we did. Tony's Bar was so stereotypical it might have been a movie set. There were hundreds of regulars like us—yuppies in our twenties from Akron and Galveston and Birmingham and Mt. Moriah. In our knock-off Coach purses was enough cash for a small order of nachos, three Happy Hour drinks, and a cab ride home. And at the back of our wallets was a MasterCard, our first, with a 500 dollar limit and a promise to ourselves that we would use it only for emergencies—which a fourth round too often constituted. After a long week of work, of el rides and heels and pantyhose, the first Friday sips at Tony's were like stepping into a warm shower. The mismatched chairs rocked on the unsteady brick floor, the cramped bathroom had no air flow, and the initials carved into the tables bespoke the generations of young would-be exec-utives who had haunted the bar before diamonds and babies and 401Ks set in. Tony's predictability was as intoxicating as its Long Island Teas, served in frosty mason jars which would have both tickled and shocked Doro.

Shoulder to shoulder with Megan and Lori, I learned to drink. By the time my straw started to make a slurping noise against the bottom of the first jar, I had transformed. I was no longer Jo of the mountain, Jo who was Grace's best friend. I was Jo of Chicago. Nameless. Faceless. Faithless.

Fearless—like Billy McGuiness.

Those godless Friday nights at Tony's were invigorating, thrilling. Conversation was bantered about like paper straw wrapper footballs. With each sip the dust-laden flower-petal chandeliers tightened into focus. My friends' smiles revealed crinkles and lines that I had never noticed before. All my senses were heightened, and as they increased, my fear subsided: buried deep inside me like the God of childhood Vacation Bible School.

Halfway through the second Long Island Tea, I would take off my sweater. Earlier a buffer against the Michigan River winds, my cable knit was no longer a necessary defense. There was a flush spreading upward that needed no protection.

The glory of my Friday nights at Tony's was that the buzz extended until Saturday noon. My headache carried me through until Saturday evening, when a different set of Megans and Tiffanies and Loris would invite me to a movie . . . and drinks. And those drinks would carry me through until Sunday afternoon, when I would walk to the corner laundromat, passing hours people watching out the grimy window. Back in the hotel, I ironed my dress pants and readied myself for the work week. There was no time for reflection, no time for grief. I was happy, or so I thought.

At Tony's, when the music switched to oldies, I'd get up with Megan and Lori and start swaying. We were surrounded by men—boys really—who were also trying to get through until Saturday—but in a completely different way. I would often be kissed, lightly, never more passionately, and my eyes stayed wide open. In a crowd of people, I was in control. My buzz shielded me like a thirty eight in my pocket. At least it felt that way to me.

Beads of sweat would travel down my cleavage, and the air from the ceiling fan would perk my nipples. I knew they were visible through the silk, and part of me reveled in this knowledge. It was part of my Russian roulette—my game against fate. I was Billy McGuiness, and every man I tempted led me to the railroad tracks. And when the train rounded the corner, when hands grasped my waist a bit too tightly, I would turn on my wobbly heels, the sweetest of smiles on my face, and excuse myself to the bathroom. In the stall I would slide the lock and, back against the door, fold my arms over my chest and know that I was alive—that the train had derailed.

Until one Friday night in March 1998.

A random snowstorm had immobilized much of the city, and without as many workers in town, Tony's had only a small group. Tiffany had gone home for the weekend, and Lori was home with a stomach bug, so only Megan and I perched on wobbly stools at the bar's end. Two Long Island Teas later, we were approached by two businessmen who were older than the standard Tony's males. They were whiskey drinkers, not the typical beer crowd.

"Wanna dance?" Trying to make himself heard over Led Zeppelin, a corduroy jacket shouted to Megan and cupped her elbow with his hand. He was in his early thirties, a bourbon in one hand and a look in his eye that said it was his third. His companion leaned in to me, and his eyes—really all of his features—were huge to me, my Long Island Tea eyes skewing reality.

"I'm Dave, and you and I are gonna be perfect together. I know these things," said the navy blazer who jiggled his Jack and Coke in his hand. "Let's try the dance floor."

His eyes were captivating: murky brown and impossible to read. Over his head, I saw Megan raise her eyebrows to me. "Hunks!" those brows said.

We danced, swaying to '80s ballads, for what seemed like hours. Dave was an investment banker. His hands moved up and down my back, finally resting on my butt. His wry smile revealed teeth that were as bright as his conversation was dull.

"You work at Sandalwood & Harris? Impressive. My office is just two blocks up, on Wacker. We should have lunch."

Sober Jo told drunk Jo that Dave never intended to have lunch. But drunk Jo was tightrope walking those train tracks.

As Journey began to play, Dave pulled me to him, and I felt his boner against me. With one hand around my waist, the other hand pulled my chin up until I was within range.

"M. R.," Lori had said one Wednesday in the lunchroom. "Make out range. You know when his face gets to that point, it's going to happen. Eighty to one odds."

Two STDs behind her, she would know.

Dave's lips were not the lips of the usual twenty-something crowd. They were hard and demanding and insistent. Like his eyes.

I never closed my eyes when I kissed: I needed to see the train coming. I had surveyed numerous eyelids—the translucent lids with veins, the slight ones that seemed nonexistent until they popped closed. But Dave's were wide open.

He noticed. "You and I are two of a kind, Jill."

"Jo," I whispered, my throat feeling suddenly swollen with panic.

"Yeah, Jo." His lips grazed mine before his teeth bit down, ever so gently, nipping at my lips. "You're a beauty, you know that?"

Ordinarily, I would never consider myself beautiful. Close-set eyes, bushy brown hair that cascaded my small head like a tidal wave. But I also knew my sweater was low-cut, that my breasts were full, and that my tipsy body was dipping back and forth in an intoxicating way.

Hands on his chest, I pushed back and smiled.

"Maybe you're drunk," I teased. "In the light of day, I'm no beauty."

His hands tightened on my waist.

"I guess I need to see you in the light of day then." He cleared his throat. "I'll have to report back on that in the morning."

And that's when the fight or flight reflex kicked in. Time to jump, Billy. Something about the firmness of Dave's hands, the look in his impenetrable eyes. Sober Jo was scared. Tipsy Jo was catching up.

"I think I need to go to the little girl's room," I said, almost in a whisper. Doro's metaphor for restroom was oddly comforting. I was okay: I was about to escape.

"It'll be hard waiting, but I'll wait." The floor bricks seemed more uneven and his hand more clammy as Dave released my fingertips directly into the bathroom.

In the stall, I slid the latch and backed myself up to the door. But my breathing didn't still. The train had come closer than usual.

Squatting over the toilet, my feet navigating the wet floor, I gathered up my short denim skirt and assumed the position. It was drunk Jo who thought it was a good idea to multi-task. As I flipped open my Nokia to dial the cab service, the phone slid out of my hands and into the commode.

"No!" I whispered, teetering in squat mode, praying that the auto flush light would not engage yet. But as I swung around and plunged my hand into the basin, the whoosh came and down my cell phone went, into the sewers of Chicago.

Warm panic teased the back of my throat.

"Settle down," said sober Jo. "You've been here a good ten minutes. He'll be gone. You can slip out the back door and hail a cab. You can do this."

But Dave's was the first face I saw when I rounded the corner from the bathroom. He was directly blocking the back door—my Friday night escape route off the train tracks.

"Jesus, I was about to go in there," he leered at me. "You okay?"

"Yes, I just think I need to head home," I stammered. "I, uh, I need to get up early tomorrow."

"I'm an early riser myself," he slurred, one hand on his crotch. "Come on, we can share a cab."

No, no, no, the scream inside me said. Too close, too close, it yelled.

But I found myself out on the curb, Dave's hand gripping my elbow so hard I was sure there would be marks. His other hand held my chin, and he bent down to kiss me, hard. His breath tasted like whiskey, and I pulled away.

"Thanks but you don't know where I live. I'm not in your direction." Nice, said sober Jo. You didn't give him an address. Good girl.

"What, darling? You live with me." Another kiss, this time with his eyes closed and his nails digging into my chin. "At least tonight you do."

"Let go!" I pushed, hard, against his chest. The train whistle screeching in my ears, I stumbled backwards and off the curb. I sat down hard in the street and saw two Daves over me, grinning.

"Damn girl! You like it rough, huh?"

He extended both arms and pulled me up into them. His lips were on my neck, now, and I was pressed so closely to him that I couldn't breathe.

"Stop!" I was screaming inside. So why did I only hear whimpers? Where was my voice?

"Please stop," I said again, louder. Gone was my bravado, and in its place cold white fear.

And then a voice. Not mine. "I think she asked you to stop."

Dave tightened his grasp on me but lifted his head long enough to smirk.

"And who the hell are you? Get lost dude."

"I'm Jo's ride home," said Tom Rivers. He extended a hand to me. "Ready, Jo?"

"What the hell? Jenny's my date." Dave turned us around and stuck out his hand for a cab.

"Not anymore she's not." Tom stepped forward, far enough to take hold of my free wrist. "Are you coming?"

Four sets of Tom's eyes were on me, and his hand was pulling. His grasp was as firm as Dave's, but soft. Safe. His hand would lead me from the tracks.

I attempted to wriggle free from Dave, but he swung me around until my hand released Tom's. A cab had pulled to the curb.

"Take a hike, loser. Get a new coat and maybe you'll find your own girl.

Julie's mine." Dave started navigating me from behind, hands on each shoulder, toward the idling taxi.

But in three steps—long, gangly strides—Tom stepped between the cab door and us.

"This is not gonna happen. She's coming with me."

There was nothing threatening about Tom. His stature, perhaps, at six foot four, but his lankiness made him fodder for a strong wind, and his long bony fingers said he had never been in a real fight.

But still. Something about the look in Tom Rivers's gray eyes, something about the tone of his voice, sounded ominous. Perhaps I wasn't worth fighting over. Maybe Dave realized there was a Michelle or Lauren or Amy waiting inside.

"What the fuck ever," he said, giving me a slight push toward Tom, who grabbed my hand and pulled me next to him. "Take the bitch."

"She's not a bitch, and her name is not Julie."

Tom looked down at me now, stared at my lip on which I now tasted blood. "My car's this way."

His hand clasped mine tightly as we walked the two blocks to his car. When he reached to open my door, I protested.

"Thank you. Really. But I can make it home from here. I can call a cab and—"

"I'm taking you home, JoAnna." And then, as if he could read my mind, "Not all men are assholes, kiddo. But if you drink that way, you're going to find them every time.

"Now get in the car."

It was a fifteen minute ride to my hotel. Feeling nauseous, I rolled down the Accord window and stuck out my head to feel the wind from the lake. It was thirty degrees, but Tom didn't question. I guess he realized the wind's healing properties.

To break the awkward silence, Tom cleared his throat and spoke. "Can't believe S&H is still using that hotel. Wonder if the rooms have been updated any." He waited for my response.

I attempted a weak smile. "They're not so bad. I have my own room. So that's nice."

"Sweet." And then, "How long are you going to live here?"

"What?" I brought my face back in from the wind, and his came into focus: only one Tom now. And already the beginnings of a dull headache. Realizing what Tom meant, "Oh, I have until August. Then the rate goes up again, and I can't afford it."

"Then what?"

"What? Oh, then . . . I don't know. Maybe I will leave Chicago."

Leave Chicago? Where did that come from?

Tom didn't question. Instead, "Well that would be a shame, Julie."

I glanced and he was smiling, dimples punctuating the kindness on his face.

"Thanks for coming to my rescue—although I really had it under control."

"I'm no hero." Tom grinned, the dimples expanding. "I was praying the whole time the guy wouldn't pummel me. But I do have the big brother thing going on. I have three little sisters. I spent high school patrolling for girls needing rides."

"And tonight, were you just patrolling?"

He smirked. "Hardly. I had to finish up the slide show that Adam's taking on the road tomorrow. I was walking to the parking garage when I saw you.

"No Tony's for me anymore, although I spent quite a few Friday nights in my twenties there."

His twenties? How old was he?

He continued. "Tony's is the place to be when you're new to Chicago and the ad game." He leaned sideways and looked straight into my eyes. "It's the place to be when you want to get laid."

His car pulled to the curb, and I found myself wishing the ride were longer. The next day I would want to remember the conversation.

"Well, thank you. I'm good now."

"Which window?"

"Window?"

"Which window is yours? I'll wait until I see a light go on."

"Oh, you don't have to . . ."

Tom sighed, leaning his head against the seat rest. "Listen, I'm tired, JoAnna. I need my sofa and a beer. But I can't get to those until you tell me which window."

"Fifth floor, fourth window."

I leaned in the open car window after I had closed the door. "Thanks, Tom. I don't think I needed saving, but, well, thanks."

He offered his hand to shake.

"Sometimes when you think you don't need saving, that's exactly what you need, Julie, Jenny, whatever your name is." His hand was warm and safe.

And like home.

Upstairs, I went to the window and saw his Honda idling. I turned on the lamp. A wave of the hand and Tom was gone. I sank down onto the chair, pulling my sweater around me, ready for my Friday night oblivion. Tears came. I tucked my feet up under me, trying to make myself as small as possible. I had dodged the train. I was safe.

That night I dreamt of Tom Rivers and lighted windows.

And train tracks.

12

PAJAMA PARTY

ONE WEDNESDAY NOT LONG AFTERWARD, TOM FOUND ME.

"Hey, the long-term hotel—you said you have a room to yourself?"

I nodded.

"Okay. Listen. I just bought a house—a bungalow with a very stubborn female owner. I close tomorrow, and she wants to stay in it six more days. Meanwhile, my lease is up and my boxes packed. My realtor doesn't think it'll help to fight it—so I guess I'm hotel bound." He paused then continued. "But it's Market week. No rooms within an hour away. So I have a proposition for you."

"What's that?"

"I only need a hotel for one week, right? And you have a private room, right? Two beds, you said?"

I nodded, not believing what I was hearing.

"How about we be roomies? I don't snore, don't eat crackers in bed. Lights don't bother me. You won't know I'm there."

My facial expression made Tom grin.

"I know, it's weird, but I'll pay your hotel bill. It's a good financial deal for you, and it'll really help me out. And if you're worried about what your parents might think, just tell them I'm gay and harmless."

At that my eyes widened. Those dimples, those eyes. That voice. I was distracted for . . . nothing?

Tom smiled, reading my mind. "Yep, but I can be a good friend. So your parents have nothing to worry—"

"My parents are dead." I couldn't say what drew me to Tom, but in his presence, I felt a calm, a security that I had lost. And his would be a voice to fill the loneliness.

"Oh. Sorry and thanks. When did your parents . . . "

"When I was eight. Car crash."

"Jeez, an orphan." Seeing my expression, he hastened to add, "God, I can't imagine—"

"So, um, how do we move you in?"

"So that's a yes? Fabulous. Well, I'm going to leave my stuff in the moving van. It's only six days, and it sucks to pay that, but what can I do?" His name was paged over the loudspeaker. "That would be realtor Don again. Scared I'm going to slime him out of his commission—as if I could."

He headed toward the door and glanced back.

"I'll be over around seven. What's our room number?"

Just as I said Room 504, I saw Rod Cheshire appear at Tom's back. My face turned strawberry as I saw Rod's expression.

"We're going to be roomies," said Tom. "Tell her, Rod, I'm gay as they come."

Rod looked from Tom to me, then nodded. "Yep, that he is."

They were both gone in an instant, and I was left with my hospital brochure, finding split infinitives, dangling modifiers, inverted letters, and wondering what I had just gotten myself into.

Tom knocked at seven o'clock sharp. I opened the door to find him with a jar of peanut butter in one hand and grape jam in the other.

"I make killer pb and j's," he said.

The surprise on my face must have registered.

"Oh, I'm sorry; maybe you had dinner plans. I just kinda wanted to kick back here and watch TV. Do you like old movies?" Laying out tissues on the table, end to end, Tom set the bread carefully on top. He kept talking as he spread. "*Hush . . . Hush, Sweet Charlotte* is on channel thirty at eight."

"I love them, but not without popcorn." Reaching into the dresser drawer, I pulled out the bag of buttery popcorn I had bought.

"Ooh, love cholesterol. Crusts on or off?"

I watched as Tom trimmed the crusts and then cut one sandwich into four precise little triangles. He noticed me watching.

"I've been eating pb and j sandwiches this way since I was little. My mom always cut them that way for me and, well, I guess I'm my mother's son."

"I'll try mine that way too, please."

"Ah, I'm spoiling you." He smiled and extended the sandwich puzzle pieces to me.

It is unlikely I will ever forget that night. The environs were certainly not memorable: the cracked vinyl of the hotel chairs, the laminate table, the cigarette burn in the carpet where I sat. And yet when I close my eyes and travel back to that evening, I breathe in a sense of equilibrium, of serenity.

After nine months alone in Chicago, I found myself talking almost nonstop during those evenings with Tom. I told stories of the Inn, about my college professor who used to attack nodding students with a foghorn, about faint memories I had of my parents, about my desire to write and my fear I would never write anything worth reading.

"Are you bad?"

"At writing? I don't think so. I've been told I'm good."

"Let me be the judge. Tell me a story idea and let me read something you've written." Observing my face, he read my thoughts.

"Yeah, sure, you think I'm just a photographer. Well sometimes the best person to evaluate another creative person's work is someone who works in a different medium." He stifled a belch, the result of the Taco Bell nachos that had been our dessert. "I'll prove my point tomorrow. I'll show you the photos that are part of my portfolio—that are the work I love, not the stuff I do for the agency."

"I don't have any of my short stories or poems here." I stalled. "I mean, they're boxed up."

"So just tell me what they're about. Tell me the theme of one of them. This will be good mental exercise, get you over writer's block."

Arrogance. Yet attractive. But gay—I remembered that. "Did I say I had writer's block?"

"Don't all writers have writer's block? I always see the writers at S&H running around sobbing, 'I'm blocked! I'm blocked!'" His facial expression, the tenor of his voice and his frantic hand motions sent me into a real fit of laughter. Giggles I'd been suppressing all evening finally erupted.

How long had it been since I laughed? I was like someone constipated whose bowels finally move in a near-orgasmic experience.

Tom was channel surfing. "They lied, *Hush . . . Hush, Sweet Charlotte* is not on anywhere!"

"I can tell you how it ends."

"I know, I've seen it at least twenty times."

"Wow, you really do have a passion for old movies."

"Yes and no. Some are better photographed. This one in particular. Sometimes I just freeze frame and stare at the way Bette Davis's face is lighted. Look how far special effects have come, and yet we can't do any better than that today." He sighed and turned off the TV. "I guess you could say I'm into faces. Especially the female face. I like to ogle."

"Well, if you're going to ogle, I guess the face is better than the female body." I blushed as I said it.

"Nope, not the female body. No interest in that."

Tom's was a mischievous grin, and somewhere inside me a question lingered.

"No sweet Charlotte, so you'll just have to regale me with one of your story ideas." He started gathering the trash. A man who cleaned up: What was that stereotype? "Thought I'd let you off the hook, didn't you?"

"Okay, I'll tell you one. I'm writing about an obsessive compulsive woman who is trying to get help through therapy."

"Interesting. What does she do that's obsessive?"

"Well, if she touches something with one hand, she has to touch it with the other. She applies lipstick, wipes it off, then applies it again, wipes it off, and then third time she can keep the lipstick on. And she has to eat things in even numbers."

Tom pondered for a moment before speaking.

"Okay, I get the touching, even the lipstick, but I think the eating thing is unrealistic. No one would go to such trouble."

"And are you a psychologist?"

"Don't get defensive. I'm just giving you my opinion as a potential reader. No one would do that."

"She does."

"What's her name?"

"Jill. Sandra."

"Jillsandra?"

"No, one or the other. I can't decide."

"Okay, so we'll call her JS. She takes a bag of Cheerios to snack on, and she has to count out the number before putting them in the bag."

"Of course not. No one would do that—"

"Excuse me, didn't I just say that?"

"I mean, if you'll let me finish, she eats an even number out of the bag, like in twos."

"Like Noah's Ark. An underlying religious theme for the story!"

Now I knew I was being mocked. But I wanted more.

"Let's turn the tables. Tell me what your private stock photos are about."

"Faces. I told you. I like faces."

"Angry faces? Sad faces? Ugly faces? Male faces?"

He scrunched up his nose. "My sexuality has nothing to do with my professionalism, ma'am. I actually like blank faces."

"Blank—like no expression?"

"Generally, yes."

"So what if you happen upon a subject who accidentally screws up and, say, smiles?"

"I don't use posed subjects for one thing. I like to happen upon people when they don't know I'm there. When they're not paying attention. When they're most vulnerable."

"Have you sent these photos anywhere? Tried to publish them? I saw what you had in your office—they're really good."

"God knows they're a helluva lot more exciting than a woman with two names who eats Cheerios by twos." He pushed his chin from one side to the other, neck bones crackling underneath. "Say, what if she pulls out a Cheerio that has another one stuck to it; does that count as two or one? Wouldn't that mess up her system?"

More giggles. I went to the bathroom, hesitated and then locked the door. I removed my make-up, brushed my teeth, and put on the sweatsuit that I intended for pajamas. When I got back to the room, Tom was changed and in bed, the lights on his side of the room dimmed.

"Hey, I've got an early shoot in the morning and it's past eleven already. I need to turn in. The light won't bother me if you want to read or something."

"No I should try to get to sleep too." I gathered my covers around me and switched off my light. "I enjoyed our conversation, Tom."

No response and I assumed he was asleep. Five minutes later he piped up.

"So what's the crisis?"

"What?"

"In your story. What's Jillsandra's crisis?"

"Well, she's in therapy, as I explained—"

"Yeah, I know, but what's the crisis she's facing?" He pushed himself up on one elbow. I could see light from the window glinting off the tiny bald spot expanding across his crown. "Not that having that Cheerio problem isn't a crisis in and of itself, but she needs a crisis that leads you to a climax that leads you to closure."

"That's been your experience in writing, huh?"

"Touchy, touchy. Never mind. Just think about it. Without a crisis she's just one more neurotic woman in the world!"

"One more!" But there was silence from my roommate. Soon there were soft snores. I closed my eyes and my father's gentle snoring returned to me, comforting somehow. I lay awake for probably another thirty minutes, listening in the darkness to Tom's breathing. Sleep had not come easily to me for months. But on that night it did. Without a sip of alcohol, I slipped into a deep, dreamless sleep.

When I awoke I was alone, but there was a note next to my toothbrush. "Your turn to cook tonight. TR" When I returned to the hotel the next evening, at almost six o'clock, a pizza in one hand and my so-new-it-still-crinkled briefcase in the other, Tom was sprawled across one bed, balancing his checkbook. A smile and a hello, and I wished I was a man: his kind of man.

"Hi, Ward, you're home. And with pizza, huh?" He took the pizza out of my hand and swept the day's newspaper from our little table.

"How was the photo shoot?"

"Miserable, wretched, long, mind-numbing." He paused. "Okay, I'm not the writer so you'll have to help me along with the adjectives."

"How come?"

"Candace. That's why." He was washing his hands. "She had to second guess me on everything, while twisting the client around her little finger. Of course, the client, Ted Bottoms— have you met him? Well, old Teddy hasn't been laid in quite a while, so obviously who's he going to listen to? The hair-flipping pink bra or me?"

"So what did Candace do besides flirt?"

"Well that's pretty much the total agenda. Mostly it was what she *didn't* do. A good account exec should manage the client, be a liaison between the creative person—in this case myself—and corporate jerks who think a good TV spot is one that shows his inarticulate monologue.

"God, I wonder how much longer I can stand this job!"

"Why do you stay if you hate it so much?" There was more than a bit of defensiveness in my tone. I was proud of the company, delighted to have the name Sandalwood & Harris on my resume. Tom responded as if reading my thoughts.

"I'm sorry; you're probably excited about your first job. Big company, nice conference rooms, the whole bit. I remember being so excited by my first paycheck that I taped it to my mirror for a few days so I could savor it." He paused and sighed again. "But that was several jobs ago."

I felt young, stupid, and naive, in that order. And determined not to show it.

"You have the experience—so quit. Go somewhere else."

"Well, if there were any place better to go, I would. Or maybe I wouldn't. The truth is that it's pretty rare for an agency to put a photographer on the payroll. In fact, I talked them into creating the job for me."

The next day I found a black and white photo of an expressionless woman taped to my cubicle. On it, a note. "This is JS, in a crisis over *what*?"

A further delay in closing meant Tom stayed in my hotel room for ten days. During that time, we would come and go almost as siblings—crossing the street to the laundromat, poring over work on the side of the room each of us had designated as our own. Because I preferred to shower at night and Tom in the early morning, and because our start and end times at work were different, it seemed a perfect logical and amenable coexistence. We were careful not to mention the arrangement at work, and actually, except for the Park Hotel account creative meetings, we saw each other rarely at S&H.

There was an unspoken time in the evening when we were both ready for sleep, but it seemed too impersonal to simply climb under the covers and sleep. So Tom would stretch his arms, or I would loudly and firmly close my book, and we would both know that our bedtime ritual had begun.

Tom used the bathroom first and changed into pajamas. Then the bathroom was mine. After a long shower—something never permitted at Doro's Inn for fear of depleting the antique hot water heater—I brushed my teeth, applied my arsenal of creams and lotions, and then got in my bed.

The lights stayed on, then, and the talking began. Sometimes we both fell asleep mid-sentence, while other nights we didn't fall asleep until past 1:00 a.m. The conversation was as effortless as it was endless.

"I've never seen a man who wears pajamas like Dick Van Dyke," I said one night, crunching ice and spitting it back into the plastic hotel cup. "I remember my dad had some that were that same plaid."

"I don't think you mean that as a compliment," Tom said. "But I'll tell you a little secret: these are my dad's pjs. I borrowed them the night I first came here; I thought they'd be a bit more appropriate than what I usually wear to bed."

My imagination wandered.

"And while we're on the 'I've never seen' category, I've never seen a woman who smothered her face in so much cream. It seems like your face would slide off the pillow."

This bantering punctuated the weightier subjects we discussed: parents, college, work, politics. I told Tom about Doro, about Maddy, about my college life and living in the Inn. I mentioned Grace only in passing. I learned from Tom that he had three sisters and a stereotypical American family. In the ironically safe cocoon of a hotel room, I opened up to a man I barely knew.

"My dad really wanted me to become a dentist and join his practice," said Tom, "and I used to think about that when I was a kid. But somewhere along the way I just knew I couldn't go to work every day for the rest of my life and see a bunch of mouths hanging open, waiting for me.

"I think me going into photography was a great disappointment for him—like I was saying his career was boring, which, honestly, it is to me.

"When I had my first gallery show, I sent him prints to hang in his office. I don't know—somehow I thought this would bond us together. You know, I wasn't there to stare into those open mouths, but they could stare at me."

From that time with Tom, I learned that he had never had a serious relationship, never really been in love. When the question came back to me, I told him about my infatuation with Christian Tuck from high school and my college boyfriend named Jake.

In those weeks with Tom, my insomnia vanished, perhaps because of the soothing snores echoing around me. Maybe it was the sense of not feeling all alone in a big city. But most likely it was because I had found what once was mine, what I had lost—that which alcohol and caffeine and wind and walking could not replace. A friend.

13

BROWN EYED GIRL

AFTER TOM CLOSED ON HIS HOUSE and the hotel room was mine again, I saw him very little. The parent company for Park Hotels had put the ad campaign on hold, so there were no creative team meetings for us to attend together. One day, when Tom had been gone for almost five weeks, I visited his office. It was dark, and the sign-in board indicated he was on vacation.

"Looking for Tom?" The voice belonged to Rod Cheshire, the man I often saw leaving for lunch with Tom. Friend? Lover?

"Actually, I had to pick up a contact sheet but it wasn't ready." Lying made me stammer. "I notice he's on vacation."

"Well I wouldn't call it a vacation," Rod smirked. "He went to his parents' house to pick up some furniture for the money-pit, as we've come to affectionately call his new abode."

"Oh? Troubles?"

"Just a few leaks, some bowed drywall, a little crack in the foundation. Nothing major." Rod made an orange X in the "Out to Lunch" column next to his name. "I don't really understand why people are in such a hurry to be homeowners. I say give me an apartment key and no strings."

"It's that American dream thing I guess."

"Yeah, first the house, then the picket fence, then the bride, then Little League. Not for me . . . not yet, anyway. I'm not in any hurry. Are you?"

It was the summer after my sixteenth birthday. Grace and I sat on the porch swing, batting at flies while we dripped popsicle juice onto the pages of Bride *magazines. Amelia Warren and her three bridesmaids had occupied the March,*

82

April, and May rooms for a bachelorette celebration prior to Amelia's wedding in Cincinnati. They had left behind a stack of well-worn magazines, which were like Christmas morning to us. In our heads swirled images of peach taffeta. White lilies. Bryan Adams music at the reception.

"No way. Haven't really thought about it," I lied.

"Too bad. You and Tom would make a good pair."

My disbelief must have registered on my face. "But Tom is gay."

Rod raised first one eyebrow, then the second. "Oh, that joke??" He chuckled. "Someone has pulled one over on you, girl." He turned to walk down the hall, then paused and looked back at me.

"After all, calling someone the 'cutest thing I ever saw' does not exactly sound like he doesn't like the opposite sex, does it?"

To my silent gape, Rod continued. "Yes, he was talking about you."

Peach taffeta. White lilies. Bryan Adams.

Two weeks later, Tom unexpectedly showed up in my cubicle holding a rusty ball flapper in one hand. He sunk into the straight chair and pushed his glasses back on his nose.

"What was that guy's name on Mt. Moriah? Marty?"

"Maddy."

"Right. Well, did Maddy teach you anything about replacing toilets?"

"Nope. Mostly drywall and painting. I'm pretty good at taping and mudding."

"If you're offering your help, I'll take it. But I'm still at the putting-pails-under-leaks stage." He leaned over and picked up the photo on my desk. "Is this your friend Grace with you?"

Age eighteen, graduation night. We were leaning over the rail of Doro's front porch, in caps and gowns, oversized sunglasses, and our two front teeth blackened in with gum wrappers. "Now why do you girls want to be so silly on a big night like this?" Doro had complained, but she was laughing and snapped the picture anyway.

I felt a sudden, sharp pain in my stomach.

"You weren't lying when you said Grace is pretty."

Was, I thought.

"I don't lie," I say coyly. "But it seems you do."

Tom looked up, genuinely perplexed. "I do?"

"About your sexual orientation, I mean."

Smiling, Tom leaned his elbows on the edge of my desk. "You wouldn't have a case in court. What I said, if I remember correctly, was that you should tell your parents I'm gay. I never actually said I was gay. But I do beg for the court's mercy."

"Why'd you lie? Why about that, Tom?"

"Because I thought you'd never go for that hotel arrangement if you knew I'm straight." He cleared his throat, as a rosy color panned his face. "It just didn't seem appropriate; you're an old-fashioned Southern girl . . .

"Is that an insult?" he asked, seeing my reaction. "It wasn't meant to be. I guess you could say I'm old-fashioned, too. I like that about you."

He leaned forward and looked directly into my eyes.

"I like many things about you, not the least of which is the fact you like to tape and mud."

"I didn't say I *liked* to tape and mud; I said I'm good at it."

He stood and turned to leave. "And that, among other things, makes you, JoAnna Wilson, a woman to be cherished."

Cherished. The word hung in the air, suspended above me, soothing me like the gentle rain pelting the tulips lining Doro's front walk.

What was happening to me?

Two days later, we had lunch in the cafeteria and Tom showed me photos of his house. Money pit seemed a bit too complimentary, but then again, I remembered how the Inn looked when Doro and I first saw it. I actually enjoyed hearing about the work. It reminded me of Saturdays when Doro and I first moved to Mt. Moriah—days that would end with a glorious aching that forced you to bed early. I told Tom so.

"Hey, why not relive your childhood then? What are your plans for Saturday?"

Not exactly a romantic invitation, but then again.

"Would I be slave labor or would there be any compensation?"

"The gas grill works. I can offer you a steak dinner with homemade raspberry glazed cheesecake for dessert."

I was duly impressed. "You know how to make homemade cheesecake?"

He grinned. Those dimples that danced their way across a room. "No, McElvay's Grill around the corner from me does."

The next three Saturdays I spent at the "Manor," as Tom had dubbed it. We worked side by side, drywall dust coating our faces so that only the space under our masks was clean. At dusk we would stop for the day, Tom showering first and then starting the grill while I showered.

We talked little as we worked—only grunting as we hoisted the awkward sheets of drywall and dangled our bodies precariously from ladders. Music bounced off the empty walls, and we sang together, loudly and completely off-pitch. Every now and then a question would break the silence. Questions so trivial, yet so comfortable, that they expanded and filled the space between and around us.

"Greatest Elton John song?"

"'Levon.'"

"No way. 'Someone Saved My Life Tonight.' Best Barry Manilow song?"

"Best and Barry. That's what you writers call an oxymoron."

"Why do all men hate Barry? Okay, better looking: Cindy Crawford or Audrey Hepburn?"

"Oh, give me Audrey any day. What about you—Sean Connery or Paul Newman?"

"Neither. Tom Cruise."

"Please, he's a jerk. You can do better."

"Oh, like who would you suggest?"

Tom pushed thick hair out of his eyes, streaking paste across his forehead. That smile again. "I'll have to give that some thought."

Each Saturday I brought clean clothes with me, showered, and changed while Tom made good on his promise of steak. On the fourth Saturday, I stepped out onto the bathmat, the seductive aroma of sirloin wafting up through the vents. I hung my towel and dressed quickly in a knit dress. My drywall clothes I wadded up into a plastic bag. I was almost to the bottom of the steps when I heard Tom's singing along to Van Morrison.

I stopped, memories flooding over me.

"Know what song I want at my wedding, Jo Jo?"

"Hmmm?" We were lying in the twin beds in my room in the Inn during Christmas break our freshman year in high school.

"'Brown Eyed Girl.'" Grace drew herself up on her elbow, her face framed in the path of moonlight outside the window. "You know, for my eyes." She fluttered her doe-like lashes.

"Well, most bands play it."

"No, not for the band to play. For my husband to sing. I want a man to sing 'Brown Eyed Girl' to me." Sighing, Grace sunk back onto the bed. "So romantic."

Hearing the strains of the old song that Grace loved so much, I realized I had spent four self-absorbed weeks without thinking of her. Without missing her? No, that wasn't true. Grace was with me all the time, but the truth was that I had been happy.

I watched Tom scrub potatoes at the sink, his back to me, and my eyes filled with tears. *He should be yours, Grace. Can you hear this?* Of course it was crazy. I could not see Grace and Tom together. Yet suddenly it was as if she were beside me, and I could talk to her.

"Okay, you're not going to believe this, Grace, but I met this guy, and he likes to hear about things I'm writing, and he's kinda cute— not handsome, but cute—and, get ready to be jealous, he started singing 'Brown Eyed Girl.'"

The conversation was there. The words were formed so vividly in my mind, but there was no one to hear them.

About the time I realized I was crying, Tom turned and saw me. As he reached out his arm to touch me—"Jo, what's the matter?"—I backed up. I didn't want to cry, not here, not amidst the jokes and the drywall dust and the last of the Saturday daylight sliding in around the blinds. I didn't want Tom to see me cry—not Tom of the Cheerios and the photographs and the peanut butter. Not Tom of the dimples that lately lingered in my dreams.

Two worlds were colliding, and I had no idea how to be both happy and sad—except to walk away.

But as I started to move toward the door, Tom caught me, his hands on both arms. It was a firm grasp that told me I could not escape, and the nearness of him escalated my tears into deep, rasping sobs. That's when he clutched me tightly against his chest, a minty smell arising from the four chest hairs standing proud guard against his silky little boy skin. The harder I cried, the closer Tom held me, until we both sank onto the hardwood floor. Tom asked no questions; he simply held me as if it's the most natural thing in the world to break into tears after a day of drywalling.

When Tom finally drew me away, gently holding me at arm's length, I offered an explanation.

"That song, 'Brown Eyed Girl', it reminds me of Grace; it was her favorite song." I paused as he dabbed at my eyes with the kitchen towel from his shoulder.

"A Van Morrison fan! I like this girl."

"Tom, I haven't told you everything. About Grace, I mean. I should've said something sooner—it's just that—well, we've been having such a good time, cutting up together.

"Tom, Grace is dead. She was murdered a few months before I started at the agency."

"Jesus," he muttered.

I gave him a few details—the stalker on the mountain, the funeral, Doro's insistence that I come on to Chicago, and my guilt that I wasn't there. My guilt for feeling anything even close to normality, much less happiness.

After I had finished, Tom cleared his throat.

"Tell me more, Jo. Maybe that'll help. Tell me about you and Grace—what you guys used to do up on the mountain. Just talk. I'll listen."

And so I began to tell Tom the story of Mt. Moriah, of me and Grace. He said little, but kept one hand around my shoulder and the other at my knee. Without moving we sat, until the sun finished its descent and the light there in the foyer evaporated into night.

And out on the grill, two fat steaks sizzled and shrunk their way into charcoal oblivion.

14

GRACE

THERE WERE NEVER TWO MORE OPPOSITE FRIENDS than Grace
Collins and myself. While I loved reading and fancied myself a writer, Grace
forced her way through summer reading books and preferred math and
recess. While she agonized over every decision in her life, I typically made up
my mind quickly and moved on.

Even in our appearances, we were at opposite ends of the spectrum. I was
short, petite, and small-chested, constantly being confused for someone much
younger. Grace was tall with a chest so prematurely developed that she was
often mistaken for a college girl when we were barely fourteen. My hair was
thick and dark, in long curls that I continually pushed out of my face. Grace's
hair, strawberry blonde in color, was full but baby fine, and she kept it long
and straight down her back. Her mahogany eyes, large and soulful, radiated
warmth. Grace's feet warranted a size nine, while I was able to buy size five
off the bargain table. My olive skin tanned deeply, like my mother's, while
Grace's face in the summer was constantly sunburnt and freckled—so much
like Doro's that she looked more like Doro's daughter than I did.

"You're going to have skin cancer someday if you don't watch it," Genia
Collins fussed.

During our senior year in college—Grace at the small liberal arts college
near Mt. Moriah and me at the University of Georgia—we took the Myers-
Briggs personality test. It revealed that Grace was a high E and myself a high
I. She was talkative and outgoing while I was shy—perhaps as a defense mech-
anism, because I always felt different from other children. The shortest girl

in the class, the only one who did all the summer reading. The girl with no parents. I was separate, and I reacted by retreating into myself.

It was Grace who first drew me out. We were in third grade, seated next to each other. She asked to borrow a piece of paper, and I gave her one. Then she asked to borrow a pencil, and I gave her that. She continued to ask for things until I got tickled and giggled. She laughed too.

"Knew I could make you laugh. Do you talk?"

"Not much I guess."

"Wanna sit with me at lunch?"

"Okay."

Such is the way friendships are made when you are eight years old and haven't yet added layers of complication to your personality. When someone asks you to be her friend, you say yes, and soon you are on the playground tire swing together. It's that simple. Maybe that's why childhood friendships are the foundation for our lives, why those made before you have all your permanent teeth are more lasting than those made in adulthood.

Our preferred place to play was the Inn. Mrs. Collins, although kind, was also severe. She was a fastidious housekeeper and strict about bedtimes. Doro gave us a certain amount of freedom, and so we came to feel like we owned the grounds of the Inn. In the warm weather, we would be outside from morning until evening, coming in only for Doro's grilled cheese sandwiches.

When we had had enough of the late afternoon sun, we headed for the side porch and brought out one of our favorite games. We could have been Milton Bradley spokespeople. Clue, Monopoly, Battleship—each day it was a different game. We sneaked polish from Doro's bathroom and painted our toenails while inside the sounds of visitors filled the parlor and dining room. The afternoons felt endless, in the way they only can in childhood. As if we had a lifetime of afternoons.

As Doro's weekly bridge games were fodder for gossip, board games were venues for discussion.

"What do you want to be when you grow up, Jo Jo?"

"A writer of books. Maybe mysteries. How about you?"

"I want to be an actress, darling!" Grace could do a great Zsa Zsa Gabor, with the exact mannerisms. "Or maybe a singer."

"What TV family would you most want to have?"

"*The Brady Bunch.* I've always wanted lots of brothers and sisters." From my time in her house, I knew that Grace's constant level of activity and chattiness veiled a sadness from living alone with a stern mother. Her father had left years ago, and she rarely heard from him. I was an only child too, but I lived in an Inn that bustled with activity and people. And I had Doro, who constantly made life interesting. Grace's mother, on the other hand, made precise ham sandwiches cut into triangles and never forgot the fabric softener.

"Which TV family for you, Jo Jo?"

It was an easy question for me.

"Oh, *Family Affair.*" It was our first summer of cable TV at the Inn, and *Family Affair* had just appeared in reruns. I explained to Grace my fascination with big cities like New York and high-rise apartment buildings.

"I don't know; I think a big city would be kinda scary. And there would be no place for dogs to run around." The Collins bred beagles, and there were always two, albeit perfectly groomed, at Grace's side.

"Maybe you could have poodles, like Mr. French's nanny friend on the show. We would live in apartments on the same floor and take your poodles to the park."

Many of our notions of adulthood came from the television programs we watched in reruns. Our husbands would look like Brad on *Petticoat Junction*, and we would sing like Shirley Partridge, and bunk our children down in pink rooms as on *The Brady Bunch.*

And so we would plan our lives as adults, where we would live, what we would do. The stone walls of that side porch stored our dreams and our silly speculations, as the concrete floor absorbed the grape popsicle juice dripping from around our whispered secrets.

If the Inn's side porch was one mainstay of our childhood, the second pew of First Methodist Church was another. We were not permitted to sit anywhere else because there we were next to Genia, and Doro could watch us from the choir loft. Knowing that we were under constant scrutiny, we became quite creative with our note passing. Soon we were able to pry open the offering envelopes with nary a noise, and write long messages while keeping our eyes fixed on Maddy. It was amazing how many words one offering envelope could hold.

In the end, however, we were always caught red-handed.

"What was the sermon about today, girls?" Genia would ask, Doro at her side.

"Which Bible verse did Maddy read?" was Doro's question.

Rarely did we know the answers to these questions. But what Genia and Doro didn't realize—or perhaps they did and that's why they brought us to church every Sunday of our lives—was that it didn't matter whether we heard or understood the sermon. What mattered were the intangibles: the reassurance of seeing the same faces around us week after week. There was a peace in noting, each Sunday, the snagged stockings of Lillian Fry. A security in hearing the compulsive throat clearings—always three at a time, repeated at two-minute intervals—of Nancy Snowden who sat two rows behind us. A delight in the teasings offered us by Ben Bowdoin, our Sunday School teacher for three years straight.

The church was our family. We sensed the sorrows and the joys that the congregation of First Methodist brought to church: the Owens in altar prayer for their child who was terribly ill. The Fosters whose business had failed. Ed and Myrtle Truman who, at age seventy, still held hands throughout the service. Libby Nelson who kept a steadying hand around her eighty year old mother during the hymns.

Perhaps not rooted in theology, these childhood church experiences nonetheless introduced me to a God whom I had not known from the infrequent trips my parents and I took to the huge church in downtown Atlanta. There, religion seemed stilted and removed. At First Methodist in Mt. Moriah, religion seemed to move around and through me.

Although we spent so many Sundays together—so many that at age sixteen we found pencil marks made four years earlier in our pew—I only remember one distinct conversation Grace and I had about religion. It was nine at night; we were twelve and listening to the rain against the window above Grace's brass bed.

"Do you pray, Jo?"

"Yeah, I guess. Sometimes. I mean sometimes I think things and that feels like a prayer. Ya know?"

"Yeah. Do you think prayer works?"

"I dunno. Doesn't it depend on what you pray for?"

"Well, isn't God supposed to have His own reasons for doing things? Isn't that what Mr. Bowdoin was talking about?" Grace asked.

I was silent a long time before I articulated what had always bothered me, what I had always held against God.

"What was His reason for letting my parents die? How could He do that?"

Grace was silent. The kind of best friend silence that says more than words ever could.

Perhaps we talked a bit more that night, or perhaps we fell asleep quickly to the lulling rain. As so many other times in our friendship, I was comforted not by an answer that we had found together, but by a question we shared.

I remember whispering a prayer before drifting off to sleep that night. Or not really a prayer, perhaps, but a question.

"Why?"

It was Christmas Eve 1989 when we discovered Grace's hidden talent. The morning air was bitter, and I shuddered inside my down coat. I followed behind Doro, who was decorating the church window sills with magnolia clippings and verbena berries. She was irritated because the altar guild—already a small group of only four—had deserted her.

"Decorating this whole church myself on a day when I need to be finishing my Christmas baking," she muttered under her breath. Watching me fumble to separate the brittle branches, she hissed, "JoAnna, you're going to have to take off those gloves if you are going to be any help."

"I'm cold and we've been here since the crack of dawn."

"Eight in the morning is hardly the crack of dawn. I'm cold too, but we have to get it done."

The door swung open, and Maddy came in whistling a Christmas carol. On one arm was a pine wreath.

"How are my Christmas angels?"

Doro scowled. "Better if I had someone besides sourpuss here helping me."

"Sounds like there's more than one bah humbug in this sanctuary," Maddy said. "Good thing I brought a reinforcement."

From behind Maddy, Grace stepped out. "Maddy saved me from grocery hell."

Doro didn't smile. "Don't say hell in church, young lady."

"I don't know; I have to agree with Gracie here. It did look a little like the great fiery underground." Maddy chuckled. "Genia had a handful of coupons, and I happened upon them in the soup aisle. Grace asked if she could come along." Maddy chuckled. "No telling how long that woman was going to be there.

"I thought Grace could start assembling the 'Silent Night' candles."

Doro brightened a bit. "Oh that would be great. Gracie, in the storage closet, there is a box of candles and a box of the paper holders to put them into. Some of the candles are left from last year. Make sure none are too short."

"Got it," said Grace, moving down the aisle to the closet behind the chancel. "Can Jo help too?"

I started to put down my greenery but Doro said, "No. I need her here."

Grace caught my eye and shrugged. I smiled in appreciation of her attempt to rescue me.

Maddy hung the wreath above the altar and, stepping down, said, "Did you hear that Lauren Bishop has strep throat?"

I steeled myself for Doro's reaction. Doro's self-proclaimed favorite moment of the year was Lauren Bishop's mezzo soprano voice projecting the first stanza of *Adeste Fideles* in Latin toward the congregation. A child processed with the candlelighter, a single flame lighting the way. On the second stanza the words changed to English, and the choir began to process, but it was that piercing soprano first verse that brought tears to Doro's eyes. Always tired after a season of entertaining, baking, wrapping and decorating, that first stanza was Doro's Christmas.

"What are we going to do? No *Adeste Fideles*?"

Maddy shrugged. "It's not like we have to cancel Christmas. It's just one verse."

Fatigue made Doro overreact. Her jerky hand movements told Maddy and me she was not in the mood to be talked to, and we both preferred her anger and frustration to be taken out on the verbenas rather than us.

An hour later Doro was sniffling. Still silent. I stood shaking in my coat, wishing I could be back on the floor in the cry room—where parents took fussy babies during the service—with Grace, assembling candles. Maddy moved through the Sanctuary, straightening hymnals and transitioning the pulpit paraments from Advent purple to Christmas white.

The three of us heard it at the same time.

A clear soprano voice, pitch perfect, was singing "Away in a Manger." So pure was the tenor that we stopped what we were doing and listened.

"Is that . . ."

"Grace?" asked Maddy.

Maddy and Doro looked inquisitively at me, but I had never heard my best friend sing like that. The three of us tiptoed to the cry room. Peeking in, we saw Grace cross-legged on the floor. Hard at work, her blonde mane shadowing half her face, Grace continued to sing—until she saw us standing in the doorway.

Looking at her basket of candles and then back at our faces, she said, "What's up? Am I doing them wrong?"

Doro moved toward Grace and, kneeling, took her face in both her hands. "Your voice, Gracie. It's an angel's."

Grace blushed.

"Why have we not heard that before," Maddy asked. "Never heard that in all these years."

Grace shrugged. "I don't sing in front of people, I guess. Mostly just when I'm alone."

Doro stood, hands on hips. "Well that ends now. You have to be Lauren Bishop for the Christmas Eve service. You'd do a beautiful job with *Adeste Fideles.*"

Grace laughed, but her smile disappeared when she realized Doro was serious. "Oh I could never sing that. I could never sing in front of all those people." Frantic eyes searched my face. "Jo Jo, you know I never could do that."

"You do have a beautiful voice, Grace."

"Indeed. That's a voice that needs to be heard," said Maddy.

Grace's protests continued, but Doro would not take no for an answer. Maddy finally proposed a compromise. Grace would sing "Away in a Manger" from the back of the church without being seen. Then the choir would process in to "O Come All Ye Faithful."

"I'm not sure she can do it," Genia whispered to Doro before the service.

"Nonsense. I know she can," replied Doro, as she set her purse down in the second row with me. "Genia, that girl needs to go into music. She has real talent."

Genia's lips were pursed. "You can't support yourself as a singer."

I'll never forget that Christmas Eve; I doubt many in Mt. Moriah will. It was the first time Grace's voice was heard. It was to be one of many times, as she developed the confidence to perform in school plays, to sing the National Anthem at basketball games. Hers was a clarity of sound that was simply . . .

"Angelic," I whispered to Grace as she slipped into the second pew beside me at the conclusion of "O Come All Ye Faithful."

"You think?"

"I know."

15

DOORMAN

AFTER THE SATURDAY I TOLD TOM ABOUT GRACE, he left town for a photo shoot an hour away. I found myself oddly restless. I made excuses to ride the elevator down to his floor, where I could walk past and see his darkened office. I had the oddest feeling, then, as if he were a figment of my imagination. Did I dream up those conversations—that night that seemed to last forever where we talked and talked until we could speak no more? Did I imagine the way his hand felt on my back, fingers pressing into my spine, seeming to say, "Tell me more."

One day, I awoke with my first thoughts of him. As I ate breakfast in the hotel cafeteria and walked the ten blocks to the el station, I thought of what Tom was eating, wearing, thinking. That day again I made an excuse to go to the sixth floor. I didn't go into his office. Just seeing him was what I wanted—a glimpse of him, running his fingers through his rich carpet of hair. He glanced up, noticed me, and waved. Then he turned back to his lightboard. No beckoning inside. Why had I trusted a stranger? Why did I imagine there was something there?

I went to the hall bathroom and threw up.

I'm not sure what I expected, but I felt as if I were standing naked in a crowd—as if the feelings I had tried to mask through alcohol and caffeine and work and the sooty streets of Chicago—had been exposed. And cast off. How dare I trust someone.

I returned to my cubicle and sat doodling on the corner of copy that I was supposed to be editing. Tom was fourteen years older; he had a career and a talent that he was using. He had a house and the ability to sleep peacefully at night. I was pretending to be a writer in a city where I had no home. I was a silly girl, crying to the refrain of a song that made everyone else in the world smile.

At lunch that day I bought the *Tribune* and decided to become serious about finding an apartment. And a life. All my paycheck was now going to the hotel off Wooster, and Lori and Megan had long moved on. I had been very frugal during my months in Chicago—counting the free "drywall dinners" Tom made me as investments in my savings account.

Four days later, I stepped into the elevator where Tom and Rod were riding down.

"So when's it going to be finished?" Rod asked.

"I've got a crew coming to finish up all the drywall first of next week. I just had to get it finished; it was driving me crazy. Then I can start painting— something I'm actually pretty good at." He smiled in my direction. "Drywall is just no fun, is it Jo?"

I thought of those Saturdays, the music blaring, the cold beers we drank on the front porch. The conversations and the ease with which I told Tom things—some things I had never told anyone. Even Grace.

"Nope. No fun," I said. He waved a goodbye as the elevator door closed behind them.

Over the next few Saturdays, I went to see twelve different apartments. Each could be categorized in one of four ways: too many cockroaches, too far, too unsafe, or too blah.

I didn't know what I was looking for—just that I wanted it to be mine. To have character. Something with lots of windows and hardwood floors—a place where I could snuggle in an afghan and write. Riding back to the hotel on the el, I remembered the first and only time I had been to Chicago, as a twelve year old—the trip where Chicago cast a web over me and ensnared me with its lights, its activity, its buildings that told stories. Doro had taken Grace and me to celebrate our birthdays. We wore painted nails and small heels that gave us blisters. We dined in a revolving restaurant, and the view of the sparkling lights reinforced my commitment to live in a big city someday.

As we passed through the grand front doorway of the Hancock Tower, smiling to the attendant, Grace whispered.

"Are there only doormen? You never see a door woman."

"Dunno."

"When you move here, you need an apartment with a doorman," said Grace. "Think of all the stories he could overhear and tell you about. Then you could write them down."

"Well, maybe I need to be the doorman."

Grace giggled, that infectious kind of high-pitched giggle that made you laugh with her.

"No way. Then when I came to visit I'd have to just sit in a chair in the lobby all day, watching you."

"But you'd be the famous friend of the first door woman. Maybe we could drag you and your chair to the door to prop it open."

More giggles.

Doro inserted herself between us, holding both our hands.

"You girls are quite possibly the silliest little so and sos I've ever known. Why are you talking about doors?"

We surrendered totally to the giggles then.

Doro was right: We were twelve years old, foolish and silly. Is there any greater happiness than that?

The fourth Saturday I went through the same routine. Again, there was nowhere I wanted to live. Nothing seemed as safely impersonal as the hotel. Perhaps I just wasn't ready to go on with my life.

Doro sounded a bit perturbed in our phone conversation the next day.

"Is it about money, Jo? Do you not think you can afford an apartment?"

It wasn't. Before I left for Chicago, we had sat down at Doro's kitchen table, pad and calculator in hand, and worked out a budget for my two thousand dollar per month salary. The studio apartments I was looking at were around twelve hundred dollars per month. I was managing fine, and told Doro so.

"What about your slush fund? You still have it in savings—for furniture and deposits?"

"Yes."

Silence on her end, then, "Jo, do you want to come home? Is that why you haven't found a place? Is that what this is about?"

I thought of my daily runs along Lake Michigan. I could almost taste the frosted mugs of beer in the Irish pub around the corner and feel the crowd huddled against the wind, waiting for the Michigan Avenue Bridge to lower.

Chicago was now home. I didn't want to go back. I couldn't say that to Doro, but she knew.

"Why don't Maddy and I come help you apartment hunt?"

The thought was tempting, Maddy surveying the caulking and the electrical and the very foundation of every apartment, and Doro planning for window treatments. But I didn't want them to come. I knew they'd see at least twenty apartments that were appealing, and I'd have to explain why I didn't want them. I'd have to find more excuses to stay in the hotel with the noisy corridors that kept me company on my sleepless nights.

"It'll just take some time, Doro. I can do it. I'll talk to you soon."

The truth is that I was running out of excuses. How much longer could I keep running?

On the sixth week of my apartment shopping, a small ad on the bulletin board in the lunch room of Sandalwood & Harris intrigued me:

room for rent in (almost) renovated old house. use of kitchen.
no smokers. quiet landlord: you won't know i'm here. $700/month.

A room in a house. Not unlike a room in a hotel. I could do this; I wouldn't be completely alone. I dialed the number on the ad, fully expecting an old lady to answer.

But it was a man's voice—and not an unfamiliar one.

"Tom?"

"Yes. Who is this? JoAnna?"

"I, uh, didn't expect you to answer. I mean, I didn't know this was you."

"But you called me. Who did you think would answer?"

"No, I mean, I was just . . ."

I heard a doorbell in the background.

"Hey, Jo, I'd like to chat, but someone's here. I'm renting out part of the house. Can I call you later?"

"Only if you tell me if the person at the door looks like someone who likes to watch old movies and is super clean. Because if not, please wait to rent the room until I can get there."

And so it was that I called Doro the next day with my new address: 408 Hudson Street. She was delighted, although a bit skeptical about my sharing a house with a man. She asked if my space had a lock. I started to tell her Tom's gay story but thought better.

"He's a nice man, Doro. Actually we work together."

"Oh! Is he handsome? Is he a writer too?"

"He's a photographer and kinda cute. We've gotten to be friends."

"Define *friends*, doll." Doro always had to dig.

I changed the subject. "You'd approve of the place, Doro. It has wonderful light."

"Hmph. I would hope it has light." She paused for me to chastise her for her sarcasm. "Seriously, Jo, be careful."

Be careful of what? My safety? My virtue? My money?

My heart?

The space was perfect. In the months since I had helped Tom on the house, he had finished the room over the garage. There was, indeed, great light, from a large casement window. The only inaccurate part of the ad was that I surely knew Tom was there.

He helped me place my daybed, dresser, and dinette set—my first purchases from my savings. Doro was delighted to hear about them as well. Real progress, she thought.

But there was no progress on the romantic front, and I'd be kidding myself to deny that I wanted it. I liked Tom's quietness, his steady demeanor, the time he allowed himself before answering questions. I was drawn to his friendship and his utter kindness. And I shivered with the taps on the back as we passed in the kitchen, each of us leading different daily schedules.

Miracle of miracles, once I moved in to Tom's house, I slept. And in the dark. I would lie in bed and hear Tom's footsteps pounding the hardwood floors downstairs. His drafty cottage creaked and settled around me, and I was reminded of my attic bedroom at the Inn. There I would lie beneath the sloped roof and hear Doro talking to guests in the parlor. Noises of the

Inn—doors shutting, radios whirring, dishes clinking—lulled me to sleep with the promise that I was not alone.

One morning, when I had been living there a month, Tom and I were headed out the front at the same time. With a swoop of his hand, he reached to open the door and beckoned me over the threshold.

"Allow me to be your doorman, me lady!"

Doorman. A gentle pang tugged at my stomach. *Oh, Grace. Was I starting a life?*

Without you?

16

DAUGHTERS

I AWOKE ON DORO'S SOFA with a pattern on my cheek and an extra afghan tucked neatly around me. Maddy, I thought. My watch said 3:00 a.m. I got up and peeked in the door next to the kitchen. I saw Maddy's shape on the tall spool bed and heard his dainty snores that had shocked Doro when they moved in together.

"My new husband snores like a little princess," snorted Doro one morning as she flung around biscuit dough. "Not what I had expected from such a big gruff man."

"And my new wife snores like a truck driver," retorted Maddy.

I closed the door and moved to the curved staircase that presided over the foyer. At the second floor, I passed the June, July, and August rooms and, at the end of the grand hallway, obscured in darkness, was the staircase up to my room. I could not go in. Instead, I retreated back down the stairs to sleep in April.

The day after Grace's funeral, I stepped into Doro's room. "Can I move into April?"

"But what about your room?"

"I don't want to be there. It reminds me of . . ."

Doro touched my arm. "I know, doll."

Maddy stood up. He looked from Doro's face to mine and back again.

"When do you want to do this?"

"Now. As soon as possible please." I turned to Doro: "Can you spare the April room?"

She nodded.

"Well I'll be your pack mule, little thing," said Maddy.

Doro held my gaze. "No, Maddy, Jo and I will do it."

It took an afternoon for us to move my clothes from upstairs. I pulled the door to without a backward glance. Shutting the door on my memories—my childhood, my grief. Doro surveyed the April room.

"Feels awfully empty, Jo."

"It feels just right, Doro."

The room was as empty, as blank, as myself.

Although Doro begged me to come home to get married, I instead wed in a courtyard overlooking Lake Michigan. Maddy officiated, and my in-laws, Doro, and a few friends looked on. My dress was short but white; the calla lilies were simple, and afterwards we dined on steak and shrimp. At one point I caught Doro turning the plate over to read the pattern, and when the salads were brought, she looked suspiciously at the arugula.

"It's wilted."

"I think it's supposed to be that way, Doro dear. It's supposed to be," Maddy whispered a little too loudly.

We invited Doro and Maddy to stay a few days, but they left the next morning. "I've got a boat coming this weekend, doll."

In its early days, when the Inn was booked, Doro called it a full house.

"Why that would be a winning hand in poker, Miss Doro. We call that a boat," teased George Russell. "Why don't you play some hands with us? Rev. Maddy has played with us."

Maddy raised his hands in innocence. "Now don't look at me that way, Doro. It was penny ante poker, and I put my profits in the collection plate."

Doro snapped the towel against his back and walked away humming. From then on, she referred to no vacancies as a boat.

Now in the April room, I was surprised to see it looked just like I had left it years before. Without bothering to take off my clothes, I climbed under the covers. The moonlight bathed my bed and tree limbs scratched at the window. I imagined the twin beds two floors up and found myself talking out loud. To no one.

"I can't believe Doro is gone, Grace. It just seemed like she was going to live forever."

I closed my eyes and let the tears come. For Grace. For Doro. For my husband, so many miles away. For the little girl who used to lie in bed and dream of being a writer. Where was she?

I must have fallen asleep, but was startled awake by a soft cry, a mewing. Sitting up in bed, I looked around. Rubbing my eyes, I expected to see my bedroom in Chicago. As my eyes began to focus, I remembered where I was. More mewing and then a low hissing.

Swinging my legs around the side of the bed, I saw the cat. Perched on the green roof outside the windowsill, a large white fur ball glared at me with golden orbs so large that I felt a wave of nausea. I had never liked cats.

Certain I would never be able to sleep as long as the cat was mewing, I banged on the window to scare him off. He simply stared and waited.

I pushed against the window, thinking if only I could get him inside, he would quiet down. Odd, to see a cat at Doro's. She famously despised cats, their fur, their eyes, and I suppose I had adopted her feelings.

"Come on stupid window!" But despite my pushing and tugging, the window was firmly painted shut. The haunting feline eyes followed my every move.

"Shut up, cat!" I lowered the roman shade which I usually kept up, loving the way the moonlight came in. Yet even with the shade drawn, the mewing continued, and the cat's silhouette in the pre-dawn light made my heart race.

"I'm scared of a damned cat, Grace." I turned on my side away from the window and pulled a pillow over my ear.

For the rest of that night, far away from the house on Hudson Street, I was also distanced from sleep. Dreams of hissing cats haunted me, chased me in and out of sleep, until around 6:00 a.m. I awoke covered in sweat.

The cat was gone.

After a quiet breakfast, punctuated by a few pats on the back or hand, Maddy and I cleaned up the few dishes and got ready for the funeral. Thirty minutes later we were on the way to First Methodist. Maddy looked more tired than I had ever seen him.

"You okay, Maddy?" I reached over to wipe away a dab of shaving cream hiding under his ear.

"Reckon I'll have to be, little thing." He turned and smiled. "It sure is good to have you here."

"Tell me what happened, Maddy. I know it was a stroke, but did she . . ." I couldn't ask what I wanted to know. Didn't know that I wanted to know.

Maddy read my mind. "She didn't linger. It was massive and sudden."

Doro. Dead. It didn't seem real. "I had just talked to her last Sunday night. We had an argument, you know, one of our friendly arguments."

"Over a book," Maddy chuckled.

I smiled. "Yep, how did you know?"

Once I had moved to Chicago and the first Thanksgiving passed without my coming home, Doro's phone calls began to have a frantic edge to them.

"I want you to come home, doll."

"It's not home anymore, Doro." I knew I was hurting her. But Mt. Moriah held nothing for me except bitter, horrible memories of loss. Coming home meant accepting the reality of Mt. Moriah without Grace.

The silence at the other end of the phone finally effected feelings of guilt.

"I do love you and Maddy, Doro. I just can't come home. It's not for me anymore. You and Maddy can visit."

And they did. They drove ten hours on Christmas Day, and we stayed in the Radisson Plaza until New Year's. I could tell they were itching to leave.

"I'm not a big city kind of fella, I guess," Maddy said.

For Doro, and for me, the visit only seemed to accentuate the abyss between us, the pain of losing Grace that neither of us could articulate. My guilt at running away to Chicago. Our collective inability to find anything to say to each other that didn't mention Grace.

One day in the spring after I had moved to Chicago, Doro called me at work.

"I'm sorry to bother you. Can you talk?"

Alarmed at the mid-day telephone call, I asked if anything was wrong.

"It's just that I needed to call before four o'clock. That's when the library closes and I need a book."

"What book?"

"That's why I'm calling you. I'm taking up reading, and I need a suggestion on what to read."

"You don't like to read."

"I'm taking it up."

"Seriously, Doro, I am at work. Can we talk another time?"

"Please, Jo. I was thinking about starting a book club."

"You?" I would have been less surprised to hear Doro was starting a fly fishing club.

"Yes, I have some ladies at the church interested, and I thought you could join us."

"From Chicago?"

"Yes. I was hoping you could make some suggestions and help lead the discussion." A pause. "That's what book clubs do—discuss?"

Candace was nearby, waiting to talk to me.

"Sure, Doro, I'll call you later. I've got to go now."

And that was the beginning of our book club. By the end of three months, we were down to a club of two. Nancy Griffiths was diagnosed with kidney cancer and began chemotherapy. Pregnant with her third child, Wanda Gibbons' daughter was put on bed rest, and Wanda had to help care for the toddlers. Savannah Wiley moved with her husband to Texas. Marjorie Simpson's husband left her so she had to take a second job. Eliza Staples was too busy hosting her husband's clients to read, and, as for Lorna Jenkins, she didn't like the books I chose.

So Doro and I continued alone. To say it was a frustrating, futile exercise for me would be no exaggeration. As a lover of literature, I was matched by someone who literally chose books by their cover.

"I couldn't stand that cover. What did it mean?"

"I don't know. I'm not an artist. What do you care about the cover, Doro?"

One Sunday evening of each month was designated as our phone club "meeting." At our June meeting, Doro lamented the next book I had chosen.

"I thought you'd like Eudora Welty. She's a Southern woman like you, Doro."

"What kind of name is Eudora? Like Samantha's mother on *Bewitched*."

"That's *Endora*." I couldn't help but smile, imagining the frown on Doro's wrinkled brow.

"Well maybe there's something else we could read. I'm not too optimistic about *The Optimist's Daughter.*"

"Give it a try. It's great literature." I paused, listening to the pots and pans doing a dance in Doro's kitchen. "Jesus Christ, Doro, you're killing my ears."

"Language, please." Something like cymbals clashing, and then silence. "I'm sorry, but I can't find my quiche plate, and I've got a boat coming for the first time in a long while."

Thirteen days ago, on our Sunday book club meeting, Doro seemed in a hurry to get off.

"I'm just tired, doll, I guess I've done too much. I did finally finish that book though."

"Doesn't sound like you liked it."

"Well it was pretty good. I made some notes when I read—like you suggested." Doro paused. "Hold on. The doorbell's ringing. I think it's Jean Henry here to borrow a platter. Can we talk later in the week?"

"Sure, Doro. I'll talk to you soon."

Yet I would not talk to her soon or ever again. But for some reason I didn't know, before I hung up, I said the words I had said so rarely in the four years I had been gone.

"Love you, Doro."

"Jo, I know today will be hard for you, losing a mother."

"I'm not Doro's daughter, Maddy."

"Not true from where I sit. Seems to me you were lucky enough to have two mothers on earth."

Maddy's face was grim, and I knew I had insulted him. I climbed out of the car and followed him up the side stairs into First Methodist. Genia Collins was already there, straightening the pew hymnals and spritzing the flowers on the altar. As if that made any difference to Doro.

"Bright and early as always," I whispered to Maddy, pointing my eyes in Genia's direction. "Where'd she park her broomstick?"

Maddy gave me the harshest of glares. "Apologize. That's just a wicked thing to say."

The truth was that I saw little good in Genia Collins. Although they had been best friends for years, the differences between Doro and Genia were stark. I was raised by Doro who saw life as an adventure, and Grace was raised by Genia who viewed life as a burden. It was Genia who guilted Grace into going to the nearby college so she could come home frequently. It was Genia who frowned at Grace's aspirations of being a singer—silly girlish fancies, Genia called them. "Be an accountant and make a good living. You can't count on a man; you need to be able to support yourself."

"I'm sorry, Maddy, but Genia did nothing but be over-bearing and over-protective of Grace, and now she's gone! And what good did that do?" I felt my face flush and felt the tears rise. "Why couldn't she have been the mother Grace needed while she was alive?"

Maddy was quiet for a minute, then took my chin in his hand.

"Just do one thing for me, Jo. Watch ol' Genia Collins during the service."

One hour later, First Methodist was filled beyond capacity. Jim Norwalk worked up a sweat setting up folding chairs in the aisles. Beyond the congregation, there were the regular visitors to the Inn, the summer guests, an eclectic crowd of people from all walks of life—all who had had the good fortune to be touched by Dorothea Wilson. I sat in the front row, watching Maddy in the chancel. His hand trembled slightly as he unfolded and refolded the yellow paper where he had jotted his notes. I looked around at the sea of faces—Sunday School teachers, first crushes, the town mayor, old and young, the winds of time having washed over us all.

In the second pew, stage left, sat a woman Doro's age. Her face looked vaguely familiar, but it was the granddaughter at her side I focused on. She was sitting in the pew Grace and I had occupied for many years, watched over by Doro in the choir. Tapping her Mary Janes against the tile floor, the little girl caught my eye and smiled: a wide toothless smile.

I was instantly transported to the week Grace and I met.

On the first day of school, the day that Maddy gave me his cross, I went home with a long list of things to tell Doro. Most of them included Grace. Doro said she would call Grace's mother and ask Grace to come play the next weekend. I counted the days and hours until Saturday morning, when Grace would arrive. We had said little to each other all week, but wherever I sat, she came and sat

next to me, and where she went on the playground, I went also. When it was
time for reading, we both chose "Little House" books. We'd peek over the tops of
the books and smile at each other.

On Saturday morning I was up early and into my orange pedal pushers. I
sat, feet dangling, on the edge of the side porch, kicking the heels of my Keds
against the stone foundation. Finally I saw a car coming up the driveway.

"Is she here?" Doro came out of the kitchen, wiping the last bits of paint
residue off her hands. She was finishing up stencils on the long wall of the butler's pantry. When Grace and her mother Genia reached the front porch, Doro
smiled and extended her hand to the prim woman who was obviously unaccustomed to shaking hands, much less with women who painted.

"I'm Genia Collins. A pleasure to meet you." It was difficult to tell whether
Mrs. Collins' face was naturally pursed, or pinched because the hair was pulled
back too tightly in a severe bun. Genia bore no resemblance to her daughter,
whose freckles bounced off her cheeks and strawberry braids swayed in the
breeze.

Grace and I took our cue to leave. Grace blew a perfunctory kiss in her
mother's direction and we were off into the house, Grace stopping to explore
each room. When she reached the side porch, one of my favorite haunts, she
squealed.

"This is the perfect place to play, JoAnna! Look what I brought."

She pulled from her denim purse two frilly bonnets, one pink, one yellow.

"I'll be Laura and you be Mary." Biting her lip, she paused. "Well, unless you
really want to be Laura, but it's just that—well, she's my favorite."

"That's good because I like Mary. I wouldn't want to be called Half-Pint." We
were birds of a feather, I could already tell.

"Oh, and I would love to be called Half-Pint. I always wanted a daddy to
call me that."

"Why don't you ask your daddy to?"

A shadow moved across Grace's face.

"He's not here. My parents divorced, and Daddy moved away. I haven't seen
him in a long time." She leaned in close and whispered, "Better not mention him
to my mother."

I surprised myself with what I said next.

"I don't have a daddy either. He died. So did my mom." Was that the first time I had said that out loud? "It's just me and my Aunt Doro."

Another shadow, this time of sympathy, crossed the freckles. Grace's rich brown eyes spoke more than her words ever could—those eyes sucked the sadness out of you.

"I think we're alike, don't you? Maybe we're really twins separated at birth. It could be, don't you think?"

"I don't think so. I was born in Atlanta."

"Hmmm. Well, it doesn't matter. We can be twins if we want to be. Do you want to be? Or sisters, like Laura and Mary."

"Okay, Laura."

A delicious grin. "Okay, Mary."

Grace pulled the yellow bonnet over her head, until all that was visible were those two big puppy dog eyes and the wet paint drop freckles. Then she smiled, a toothless smile that told me I had made a friend for life.

It was that smile I saw when I looked at the little girl in the second pew at Doro's funeral.

17

THE SAND BAR

AT TEN O'CLOCK, Lucie Leffler hoisted her bountiful bottom onto the organ bench. The notes of "Great is Thy Faithfulness" bounced off the wooden beams, and sunlight seeped like water through the stained glass windowpanes. Genia Collins was seated next to me, her hand palm up on the seat beside me. I knew she wanted to hold mine. And I also knew that her shyness, her lack of confidence, would prevent her from reaching out. So we sat, shoulder to shoulder, as the organ and the sunlight teased my memories.

Grace and I were fourteen, had just finished up our waitressing shift at the Inn, and were doing dishes. At the guests' dinner had been a newlywed couple eager to get through the meal and to the June room. The young woman, Margot, had indulged Grace with tales of the wedding, from the ceremony music to the cake. Grace could talk of nothing else.

"My mother said weddings should be by candlelight. And she has this ridiculous idea that brides should wear a veil over their faces."

"That's called a blusher. It is very traditional. I kind of prefer to see the bride's face, though," Doro chatted as she moved through the kitchen, stacking the cups and plates that I had dried. Our dishwasher was on the fritz. "I can get by," Doro had smiled to Maddy. "I have two pretty young dishwashers right here!"

"Well I'm sure my mother will make me wear her veil and probably her dress too."

"You should have the wedding you want, Grace," I said. "The wedding's not for your mom."

"Yeah, Jo, you're right." But I knew, not for the first time, that what Grace felt and what she would do were wildly different.

"Well, as long as you're married in front of God, it will be beautiful, my girls," Doro said.

Years later, Tom Rivers told me he wanted to get married in a Catholic church.

"I want to be married in front of God."

I hesitated, my silence speaking for me.

"Do you not believe in God?" he asked.

"Yes, I do. I guess." *No, I don't,* I thought.

"Your religion is something you've never talked about," I told Tom.

"No, it's not something I talk about. But it's part of me—my beliefs are part of me."

And so we married on the courtyard outside a University chapel. When Maddy called upon us to pray, I bowed my head and closed my eyes and imagined the words leaping off the stained-glass windows, taunting us. Tossed back to us from the Nothingness to which they were sent.

Perhaps Tom married in front of God. I married in front of Nothing.

Maddy stood at the pulpit. Had I been so caught up in myself that I hadn't noticed his pallor, his frailty? I couldn't imagine what he was about to say, much less how he would get through it. Although I had not yet seen him shed a tear, the red rims around his eyes said otherwise.

But Maddy had a gift of storytelling and soon had the congregation gently chuckling and smiling over the life of Dorothea Wilson, a woman beyond compare. After five minutes, he paused.

"I want to close with one more story. I think we all can name things that Doro did for us." Clearing his voice, Maddy focused those penetrating blue eyes directly on me. "But lest anyone think Doro had no children, let me tell you this one last story. And you tell me whether she was a mother or not."

Still holding me in his gaze: "This story takes place at a beach—a sandbar, actually."

I tilted my chin up to catch a path of sunlight. I was ten years old and back at that beach, on that sandbar.

Doro and Maddy married two summers after we moved to Mt. Moriah. Although neither of them was typically at a loss for words, telling people about their relationship brought out a stifling shyness. When Maddy announced his proposal to Doro at a church dinner, the Russell brothers and their friends let out a whoop! and immediately started exchanging tens and twenties.

"Why, Rev, we've been betting on when that was going to happen for almost a year now!"

"Yes, thank the Lord that's finally out," said Emmagene Wilder, irritable from her latest case of gout.

Doro blushed—the only sign of embarrassment I ever saw—and simply leaned up and kissed Maddy on the cheek.

They were married three months later on the grounds of First Methodist. Doro insisted on cooking all the reception food herself, stopping a mere two hours before the ceremony to change into a simple white silk sheath.

"I'm dressed, girls. Make me beautiful!" She picked at the beginnings of a run on her panty hose until in frustration she ripped the hose off and prodded sweaty feet into her pumps. Flapping a fan at her cheeks, Doro sat on a wing-back chair and handed Grace and me a small box of powder, mascara, and hair pins. Although flattered to be asked, we ten-year-old ingénues knew even less than Doro about makeup. Doro, who never could stand to be still for very long, finally sighed and grabbed the brush from our hands. "Do me some eye shadow, and I'll do my own hair."

She brushed and teased her hair up into a bun, fastened with mother-of-pearl combs. With a bit too much green shadow on her left eye (Grace's), and a bit too little on the right (mine), Doro powdered her freckled face and nose, smothered her plump lips with fire engine red lipstick, and announced she was ready.

The next morning, Doro, Maddy, and I arose early to head out on the couple's honeymoon.

"Well of course you're going, doll. We're family now!"

"It's a celebration, little thing," Maddy added.

The honeymoon destination was the beach. Neither Doro nor I had been, and that fact was beyond comprehension for Maddy. It might have seemed a logical choice except for the fact that, while I could swim reasonably well, Doro was terrified of the water.

I could not contain my excitement. When I was little, I had a book about mermaids. Every night I begged my father at bedtime to tell me stories of the beach. Supposedly we had vacationed in Daytona when I was a little baby and then again at age three, but I didn't remember it. Still, though, in the deep recesses of my mind I had what I thought was an early memory—a sensation of the bouncing rhythm of waves against me.

In the days of "our" honeymoon, Gulf Shores, Alabama, was not littered with high-rise condominiums. There were few swimming pools; like the cottage we rented, little wood siding houses with big porches faced the beach. We dined on fish Maddy caught, and in the evenings walked the half mile to the pier where barnacles as thick as chocolate sauce hung on the support beams.

Between Doro's obligations to the Inn and Maddy's commitment to the church, we only had five days to be there, and it rained the first four. We spent time playing cards and charades. In the evenings, I took my book out on to the balcony or wrote stories in my pad. I knew enough to give the middle-aged couple their privacy.

On the fifth day, our last full day at the beach, the sun rose high in the sky, and the water was clear, still, and warm.

"Want to come in for a dip, my darling?" Maddy and I had built a two story sand castle, and he used the bucket to dribble sand and water on Doro's burning calves.

"I'm just fine right here, thank you very much." Doro tilted the wide wicker hat that shielded her freckles from multiplying. She brushed off her sandy calves with a motion that told Maddy and me she was a bit sorry the rain had to end.

"Okay, then, little thing, it's you and me I guess."

"Not too far, Maddy," Doro cautioned. "I'm not sure how good a swimmer Jo is."

Maddy leaned over and placed a kiss on the hand that wasn't holding a *Reader's Digest*. "But I am, my dear!"

Off Maddy and I went into the water, flinging spray over each other until the ground sunk and we had to tread water.

"You see that light patch out there, Jo? That's the sandbar. Let's head for that."

Together we swam, turning now and then to look at Doro, dozing under her magazine.

To this day I can think of no better feeling than the openness of the sky and the waves bumping against me. Even when I could feel no ground beneath me, I felt Maddy beside me, his arm reaching out to hoist me up against a crushing wave, his hand always nearby to steady me.

"Here comes a big one, little thing. I'll hold you up." Maddy reached out for me.

But I pulled away from him. "I can ride it, Maddy!"

Moments later it felt as if I had swallowed a gallon of water. I coughed and sputtered into Maddy's shoulder while he gave me firm pats on the back. I looked up, prepared to smile to assuage Doro's fear, but she was still dozing.

"Just a little ways longer, little thing. We're almost at the sandbar."

Before long, my knees bumped the ocean floor, and I was able to stand up. It felt like utter freedom—standing in the middle of the ocean, with miles and miles of water on either side of me.

I laughed out loud. Maddy and I stretched out there on the sandbar, sitting down and sinking our bottoms into the sand. Maddy told me stories about his father and grandfather who took him deep sea fishing. He told me about camping on the sand and sleeping under a million stars.

"I don't think Doro would do that, do you, Maddy?"

He chuckled. "Why, I'd have a better chance getting her to tightrope walk."

The blazing rays beat down on our shoulders, and I submerged myself further on the sandbar, knowing I had not reapplied sunscreen as Doro instructed. After a few minutes, Maddy dove off the side of the sandbar, trying to catch little fish. It was when he was underwater that Doro awoke. At the moment we couldn't quite understand what was going through her head, but in the days to come, Doro explained how my lying on the sandbar looked exactly like I was sinking alone in the deepest part of the ocean, about to drown.

"My child!" she screamed, over and over again.

I heard the screams, saw the wicker hat go flying off, and saw Doro half waddle, half fall, into the ocean of which she was so frightened. Her hefty bosom was partially out of her shirt. Maddy came up for air then, in time to see Doro plunge butt first into a wave that washed on the shore. Not a dexterous person, much less a graceful body, Doro flipped end over end as one wave, then another crashed into her. With each one she would stand and scream.

"My child! I'm coming, JoAnna!"

"Good lord in heaven, what is that woman doing?" cried Maddy. "Stay here, Jo."

Off he set, using broad, strong strokes to cover the distance between the flailing Doro and himself.

Once he reached her, he put one arm under Doro's skinned knees and one arm behind her head. "Breathe, Doro, dear. I've got you."

She was a mess of snot. "The child, Madison. Jo. She's drowning."

"My God, woman, the only one who's drowning is you." The laughter came then, shaking Maddy's mighty shoulders. Still perched on the sandbar, I couldn't help but grin.

Pushing soggy hair out of her eyes, Doro pointed to me. "Look at her! She's drowning, she is!" She strained to wriggle out of Maddy's firm grasp.

"She's on the sandbar, Doro," Maddy swung Doro around in the water, holding her up every time a wave threatened.

Doro looked as incredulous as if told I was boarding a space ship.

"I've never heard of a sandbar. I . . ." Her voice quietened then. "Why didn't you tell me there was a sandbar, Maddy. I was so scared.

"I thought she was drowning," whimpered the Doro who never whimpers. Maddy held her close then, her body beginning to shake in silent sobs.

"I know you did, Doro, but I got you. I got you both." He kissed her forehead. "And you know what else?"

"What?" She sniffed.

"How the tarnation did you manage to hold on to that?"

In a death grip, Doro's left hand still clinched the now soggy June 1985 *Reader's Digest*.

"It was a mother's love, pure and simple," Maddy told the congregation, who were laughing tears at Maddy's depiction of Doro's graceless pirouettes in the water. "Biologically she was an aunt, but the reality was that Doro was a mother. She was a mother to JoAnna, and she was a mother to many."

The last night of the honeymoon we went to a seafood restaurant. A waiter brought me a Shirley Temple cocktail and noticed my Polaroid camera on the edge of the table. He asked if I wanted him to take a picture of me and my parents. I didn't correct him. That picture, although badly faded, remains on Doro's refrigerator.

From my pew, I dabbed my eyes and smiled back at Maddy. Smiling, he lifted one bushy eyebrow toward the tiny figure on my right. Turning, I saw not the pinched, sour face of a woman embittered by life. I saw the gently sobbing grief of a mother. Perhaps Genia didn't know how to love her daughter in the way she wanted to be loved and supported. But there was no denying her love for her daughter. And perhaps I was not to judge.

I put my palm on top of Genia Collins' tiny hand and held it tight.

"It wasn't just today, Jo. There's nary a church service that Genia doesn't cry her way through."

I sighed. I had disliked Genia Collins for so long that it was hard to dredge up any sympathy.

Maddy and I were picking up plates and cups from the Inn. Just as Doro had opened her house many times to grieving families wanting a place to gather after the service, we opened her house for people to come pay their respects.

It was after 7:00 p.m., and the light outside was starting to fade.

"What are you so angry about, little thing?" Maddy held the trash bag for me to toss the Solo cups into.

"I'm not angry, Maddy. I just can't help thinking that if Genia had let Grace go away to school, she wouldn't have . . ."

"Wouldn't have been on that mountain? Who's to say that, little thing?"

"But maybe not!" I dropped the last plate into the black bag and threw myself down on the sofa. "Of course, I guess you'd say that's God's plan, right, Maddy?"

"For Grace to die? For Doro to die? For any of us to die?" Maddy sat down beside me, bringing my head to rest on his chest. "Naw, I reckon the Good Lord wants us to live. I reckon He was as sad about Grace as any of us."

"But I still don't think that's what you're angry about."

What *was* I angry about? The drunk driver who hit my parents? The friend I had lost? Genia Collins for keeping Grace from going away and pursuing her passion? Doro for sending me away to pursue my passion?

"That's about enough thinking for today, little thing. Let's get some sleep," said Maddy, yawning widely. "I'm worn out."

I was tired, too, and my stomach had been flip flopping all day. Too much reception food. I kissed Maddy goodnight and headed to my room.

In the hall bathroom, I opened the cabinet, looking for a bottle of Tums. From the corner of my eye, I saw its tail.

The cat. It had moved from the window near my bed to the window sill above the commode. Its eyes glared at and through me.

"Jesus Christ, I hate cats," I muttered, knocking my hand against the window. "Scram!"

But it stayed where it was, a statue watching over me, the eyes following me. By the time I crawled under the covers, it had moved to the bedroom sill. Then started the low, guttural mewing.

Pillow over my head, I fought back nausea and finally fell off to sleep to fitful nightmares.

The following morning I ran to the bathroom to vomit.

The cat was nowhere to be seen.

18

REX AND SYLVIA

I WAS UP EARLY THE FOLLOWING MORNING. Was it Wednesday? Thursday? The days had run together. I peeked in on Maddy. His bed looked like a fight had taken place, but he was sound asleep and I knew I should let him sleep in. Just as I was gingerly pulling the door to, the phone rang. I leaped across the kitchen to grab it before Maddy awakened.

"Jo?"

Had it only been a few days since I left Chicago? Since I had heard Tom's voice? Yet there it was, the sound of worlds colliding in my ear.

"Hi, Tom."

He cleared his throat. "The funeral was yesterday, right? How was . . . everything?"

"It was nice. It was, well, it was what Doro would have wanted."

"And Maddy? How's he?"

"Okay. Sleeping late, although I think I hear him up now."

The silence was palpable. Ours were the voices of familiar strangers.

"Jo, I would have come with you."

Silence from me. I didn't know how to do this. Didn't know how to be here and there, how to be Doro's daughter and Tom's wife. Didn't know where I wanted to be.

"I know we both said some things." He paused. "I know what I said."

"I . . . I can't talk right now, Tom. Thank you for calling, though."

"That's it?"

"That's what?"

"Exactly. You're going to run and hide?"

My face flushed. I was hardly hiding. Coming back to Mt. Moriah, to my childhood, to the place where Grace died, was one of the toughest things I had ever done. Hiding? I was brave.

"I'm sorry you see it that way, Tom." I knew my voice sounded harsh. And, just as surely as I knew he was running his hands through the thick grey tendrils above his ears, I knew he was hurting. And that I was doing the hurting.

I also knew I loved him.

"I've got to go, Tom. Can we talk later?"

Silence.

"Sure, Jo. Always later."

The line went dead.

I hung the phone up and turned to face Maddy in his rumpled bathrobe.

"Was that Tom?"

"Yes. He asked about you." I donned Doro's apron and began pulling breakfast items out of the refrigerator—bagels, eggs, milk.

"Sounds like he was asking about more than me." Maddy put weathered palms on each side of my face. "Something going on with you two?"

"It's nothing, Maddy. Just a lover's quarrel I suppose." I wriggled free of his hands and lighted the gas stove, catching a glimpse of the refrigerator magnet holding a picture of Doro and Maddy on their wedding day, Grace and me on either side.

Oh, Doro, how did you make it all look so easy? And where are you now?

Maddy and I spent the day at home, both of us quiet and contemplative. There was so much to do—Doro's clothes to collect and donate, casseroles to freeze, but instead we lingered, looking through pictures, sitting on the porch swing.

The next morning I was up early again, preparing breakfast. Maddy broke the silence.

"How long do I get to have you here, little thing?"

"I don't know, Maddy," and I didn't. Oddly enough, I was not in a hurry to return, not sure where I stood with my job. I was still copy editing and proofreading, my dreams of writing becoming smaller and smaller. And then there was the morning queasiness, like a nagging worry at the back of my mind.

"We do need to go to John Barkham's this afternoon to go over Doro's will," Maddy said. "You know, she left the Inn to you."

Nothing could have shocked me more, and my face must have said so.

"What? Why? That makes no sense! Maddy, this was your family's house to begin with. What the hell am I going to do with it?"

Maddy frowned, signaling his contempt at how easily I threw around curse words.

"Doro and I talked about it a few years back," he said. "I can retire comfortably when the time comes. Not sure when that will be, but she wanted— we both want—you to have something here in Mt. Moriah."

"Well, she should have thought about what I might want. I can tell you it's not Mt. Moriah. I want nothing of this place."

I got up then and, sticking my feet into my sneakers, headed for the back door. I felt as if I was drowning, thrashing and gnawing in my own skin.

Pulling open the door, I startled at the figure with his hand poised near the doorbell.

"Jo, I'm so sorry I missed the funeral. I was out of town." The voice belonged to Christian Tuck, the best friend Grace and I ever had.

"Tuck."

Tuck opened his arms, and I leaned into them. They smelled like high school basketball games. Halloween costumes. Dances. And youth. It was the hug of a friendship long ago paused.

"I missed you Jo."

Oh, I had missed him too. Had not thought of him in years, yet missed him every day. Missed his arms and his smile. Missed everything about this handsome man—the man Grace was dating when she was murdered.

In the summers Grace and I would spend many of our days in the culvert beneath the train tracks, the same ones where Billy McGuiness played Evel Knievel. It was cool there and pungent with the tall honeysuckle border. Although the highway was within our line of vision, we were hidden from the world. Eventually we read all of the graffiti inscribed there. Some of it was quite enlightening to two girls on the verge of puberty. Some of the graffiti— albeit much tamer—we put there ourselves.

We would take our portable Sony discmans and thermoses of Doro's tea, so sweet it's a wonder we didn't sink into immediate diabetic comas. Nested against the cool cement, we taunted each other with the secrets we knew about each other.

"Brian Rayburn likes you."

"Gross. He spits when he talks."

"I don't know. He's kinda cute. He's very smart."

Grace rolled her eyes. "Smart? Who cares about smart? What about handsome?"

On and on—a continuous line of conversation to fill the humid afternoons, as the dragonflies buzzed around us and the sun first rose, then sank.

We had been working all summer on a soap opera. It had no title but featured Rex and Sylvia—two of the sexiest names we could dream up. I would write, and Grace would act out my words. Always Sylvia would end up in harm's way—needing an intricate brain, liver, and double-kidney transplant—and Rex would find a way to save her. REM was singing on the radio, the sky was cloudless, Rex and Sylvia were locked in a tight embrace, and all was right with the world.

When we were twelve we decided it was absolutely crucial that we have a secret code language so we could write about people without being discovered. Years later, as I was helping Grace clean out her closet, I found one of our old notes, barely visible for all its crinkles.

The methodology behind the Gra-Jo language, as we called it, was simple. One line stood for each letter, so that ZZ would actually represent F. Obviously, it took a long time for us to decipher each note, but that didn't matter: We had all the time in the world.

One Saturday morning in April 1987, we were unable to go to Club Culvert, as we called it. It had rained for a solid week, and even though the day had dawned with an unusually hot spring sun, the culvert wouldn't dry out for several days.

We did not do mud.

We tried to write about Rex and Sylvia in my room, but even their lust had grown boring to us, so instead we wandered the grounds of the Inn, debating how I could write Grace's English paper for her without the teacher knowing it was me.

"You could spell badly," Grace suggested.

"I wouldn't even know how to spell something wrong. You just see the word, and you know how it's spelled."

Grace wrinkled her freckled nose in mock disgust. "Not all of us do. In fact, I doubt anyone but you sees words. Do you still do that thing where you try to describe something in your mind?"

"Yep. Like right now you don't just have smelly feet—they're aromatic."

Grace stuck out her tongue and lifted one smelly foot up toward my face. Teasing each other constantly, we seldom actually got mad. The night before, Grace had burnt my forehead with the flat iron. I had been trying to straighten my bangs. But, unaccustomed as I was to the iron, I kept dropping it.

"You're a klutz!" Grace had said. Impatient with my attempts, she grabbed it from my hand and did the job herself. Only the wand got too close, and I bore a burn scar.

"I'm sorry, Jo. I'm sorry." Grace was the one crying, not me. "Can you forgive me?"

I was not one to waste an opportunity.

"Yes, but only if you're my slave for tomorrow."

She sighed. "Deal."

And so on this April Saturday it was up to me to decide what to do. I couldn't think of anything, for Rex, Sylvia, or us. I was actually thinking of the book I was reading and wishing it was time for Grace to go home so I could climb into Maddy's hammock and read until the light was gone.

We were sitting near the front gates of the Inn, watching cars go by on the main road. Suddenly we heard a popping noise and then an explosion of orange onto the windshield of a Chevy that was passing. And then, full-throated laughter.

A boy crouched on the other side of the road, with a bucket of oranges that had been dropped by an Osage orange tree. He threw them at the unsuspecting traffic.

"He shouldn't be doing that," I whispered to Grace.

She giggled. "It's kinda funny. Did you see the look on the driver's face?" A pause and then, "Let's freak him out."

"No, Grace." But she had already yelled across the gates. "Hey, we saw that!" Crouched down behind two large boxwoods, we were invisible to him, but we could clearly see the surprise on his face.

"Who said that?" He pivoted 360 degrees, looking for us.

"He's cute, Jo Jo."

"He's okay. I prefer dark hair."

"He has good skin."

"How can you tell from this distance?"

"Wanna bet me? Let's go see."

"No, I don't want to go meet him."

But Grace had already stood up, revealing herself above the shrubbery. She waved, and he waved back.

"Ooh, he has straight teeth too. Let's go meet him."

"Let's don't and say we did." The bright smile was obvious, as were the clear cheeks. Definitely cute. But I was definitely shy.

"Oh come on. Don't be a dud."

And she started across the road.

"Grace. No. Remember, slave for a day?"

She turned back, blonde hair whipping across her face. "You're healed. Deal's off!"

And that was how we met Christian Tuck. Rex and Sylvia were no more.

Christian Tuck moved to Mt. Moriah from Michigan. His father was the new high school football coach at Woodbury Regional High School, his mom a nurse. He had a beautiful older sister and the ability to tie a cherry stem with his tongue in less than thirty seconds.

Grace and I thought he was perfect. He grew to be our best friend, and we became an inseparable threesome.

And now at the door Tuck was standing before me, a stretched-out, tanner version of the boy with the mock oranges.

"Tuck!" Maddy cried, coming from the kitchen where he had taken over breakfast preparation. His bathrobe was hanging open, revealing more than should be. "So good to see you, boy!"

"Hey, Rev." Tuck and Maddy exchanged hugs, and Tuck whispered in Maddy's ear.

"Check the little soldier, sir."

We were sixteen years old and all going to the school Halloween party. Tuck, having just gotten his license, came to pick up Grace and me.

"I don't like the idea of a sixteen year old driving," said Genia, hands on her hips.

"Truth be told, me neither," agreed Doro.

The looks on their faces told Grace and me there was a battle to be had.

"Let them go, you old worry warts," Maddy said.

When Tuck arrived, he received every word of caution that Genia and Doro could muster. He was literally backed into a corner, until Maddy saved the day.

"Okay, enough of that." Maddy took Tuck's arm and led him to the door, motioning for me and Grace to follow. At the door, Maddy extended his hand to shake Tuck's.

"But let me just issue you one word of caution, son. Keep the little soldier in check."

Reddening, Maddy adjusted himself and retied his bathrobe.

"We were just about to have breakfast. Stay and have some with us. Excuse me and I'll go get presentable. Just excuse me."

I smiled at Tuck. "Looks like you've been drafted into breakfast."

"Well I've probably consumed a thousand breakfasts here at the Inn. Highlights of my life actually." Tuck pulled me in for another hug. "I really wanted to be here yesterday, you know."

I had scanned the crowd at the visitation, then again at the church. I wondered where he was. Of all the people I had talked with, Tuck's was the face I longed to see the most, the one I most needed to see. "I know." I pressed my forefingers into the corner of my eyes to stop the tears pooling there. "But you're here now, and I'm so glad to see you."

Over breakfast Tuck updated me on his life. He had just finished law school and was studying for the bar. He was married to a tall willowy brunette named Debra.

"She has big bosoms, Jo," Doro had told me on the phone. "Unnaturally big if you ask me."

Debra and Tuck had an eight month old son, Andy, and lived in Birmingham where Tuck had just graduated from Samford Law School.

"I imagine we'll stay in Birmingham," Tuck said in answer to Maddy's question. "Debra's family is from there and with a baby, it makes a big difference to be near families. We came to Mt. Moriah two weeks ago to spend a month with my parents.

"They're a little jealous that Debra's parents get to see Andy all the time, and I need to be studying for the bar exam, so this is a good place to do it.

"Not much else to do in Mt. Moriah, you know?"

Maddy snickered. "No, I reckon next to the big city there aren't many distractions on the mountain."

"Well not 'til now, anyway." Tuck clasped my hand. "I might have to take some breaks to spend time with my old friend here. How long are you going to be here, Jo?"

"That's the question of the hour," Maddy said, pouring us all a second cup of coffee.

"I guess you have to get back to work, right? And your husband? Tom?"

I had not seen Tuck since the day of Grace's funeral. We had exchanged no letters, no phone calls. Doro told me Tuck asked for my number in Chicago, but I asked her not to give it. I ceased communication with him, like everyone else on Mt. Moriah. I was surprised, then, to hear how much he knew about my life.

"Doro kept me filled in. She and Maddy came to our wedding, and I would call her every month or so," Tuck explained. "Seems she was lonely without you, or . . ."

"Or Grace."

Tuck cleared his throat, and a pall of sadness crossed his face. "Yeah. You know, Doro had all of us running around the Inn for years and then no one."

Morning stretched into lunchtime, and when Doro's grandfather clock struck one o'clock, Tuck rose to his feet. "I need to get back. It's Andy's nap time, and I usually put him down." He continued, voice softer, almost apologetic. "Debra's a little nervous when it comes to the mothering thing.

"But speaking of Debra, she wanted me to invite you to dinner. Saturday night?"

"I, I guess." I looked at Maddy questioningly.

"All we have on the docket is to meet with the lawyer. You know Saturday will be sermon writing time for me."

"Then I'd love to." It was a boldface lie: I had no desire to meet buxom Debra. Time alone with my old friend Tuck was what I wanted. "Can I bring something?"

"No, but don't bring too much of an appetite, either," Tuck warned. "I love my wife, but she's not a cook like Doro. And my parents are out of town for the weekend, so my mom can't bail us out."

"Sounds like an adventure."

"I'll look forward to it, Jo. I hope we can spend some time together while you're here—before you have to head back to work."

A quick hug and Tuck was gone.

Maddy had already started washing the dishes. "I'm gonna need to go work on my sermon a bit, Jo." He paused. "Do you need to check in with your office?"

My office. Chicago. Tom. The look on Tuck's face when he spoke Grace's name.

Tears that I had suppressed for a week threatened to come.

"What is it, little thing?"

"I don't know, Maddy, just emotional I guess," I lied.

How could I tell him what was going on in Chicago. With my marriage, my life.

And so I didn't.

"What time is our appointment at the lawyer's, Maddy?" I wiped my eyes with the dishtowel.

Maddy drew me to him and gave me the kind of hug that was part pastor and part gardener. Part father and part friend.

"3:30. Thought maybe you could buy me an early dinner afterwards with your fancy pants salary."

"No fancy salary here, sorry to disappoint you. But I could probably afford the Lunch Box."

"Well that suits just fine." Maddy looked over his glasses into my eyes. "Sure you're okay?"

"Fine, Maddy." I lied again. Knowing that he knew it was a lie and also knowing that he wouldn't press me.

§

The law offices of Barkham and Wright were one block off Woodbury Avenue, the main thoroughfare in Mt. Moriah. We parallel parked and walked the brick sidewalks hand in hand. Maddy waved at everyone he saw, whether he knew them or not. The customers in Bruno's Barber Shop glanced our way when Bruno waved back. Few were there for haircuts; most were there to shoot the breeze and escape home or work for a few minutes or a few hours. A Japanese American, Bruno moved to Mt. Moriah in the 1950s with his parents. He adopted the name Bruno to try to appear more American and in ironic deference to his petite, wiry frame. In the early '60s, when Bruno bought the barber shop from Leonard Fulstein, some Mt. Moriah residents were wary of Bruno's olive skin and slanted eyes.

"A Jew barber like Leonard makes sense. But has everyone forgotten Pearl Harbor?" Ellard Jasper carried a plug of tobacco in his lip and one of hatred in his heart. But before long Ellard's rants were overshadowed by Bruno's weekly raffles of free haircuts and the lilting violin concertos he played on the steps of his shop when the weather was nice and business was slow.

"Well, you'd never get anything free from a Jew," Ellard spit. "But I still don't trust that little Jap."

Over thirty years had come and gone (during which time Ellard served time for dog fighting), and there was little memory of Bruno ever being anything but a mainstay in the community. In downtown Mt. Moriah, minutes fell languidly into hours, and there was a sense of comfort in the knowledge that the shops opened at 10:00 a.m. and the gas lamps went on nine hours later. Downtown was a place where the mountain residents went to pump gas, buy bread, mail letters, get their feverish child a strep test. A place where you were guaranteed to run into at least ten people you knew. And come away from each errand with a sense that all is as it should be.

Barkham & Wright was tucked away behind a mahogany panel door and up a flight of steps. We were greeted by June Carter. "Not Cash, just Carter!" she smiled at us, smacking her gum ferociously. "Just have a seat and I'll get Mr. Barkham."

John Barkham was younger than I thought, and after a few minutes of exchanging pleasantries, I realized he was a son of the senior Barkham. Just as I was mentally calculating his age, he beat me to the punch.

"Class of 1993 at Woodbury High?" he asked.

"Yes. You too? I'm sorry, I'm terrible with names . . . and faces." I took his outreached hand. On his desk was a picture of a vaguely familiar blonde. Had I had gone to school with her too?

"It's okay. Better to be non-memorable than so memorable that you land in prison!" John was annoyingly cheerful, like the Brighton clad blonde in the wedding photo.

"We were in junior English together. At least until I dropped out of AP. You were some kind of writer." John pulled his cuffs, first one, then another, from under his coat sleeves and adjusted the JC Penney tie on his chest. "You're in Chicago now?"

"Yes, I'm—" What was I doing in Chicago? Not writing the Great American Novel. Drowning my sorrows in Smirnoff and silently cussing the non-adventures of Jillsandra—"writing for an ad agency."

"Wow, impressive. Big city's not for me, but I think it's awfully cool for someone who loves that kind of thing." John looked at Maddy. "Truth is, I need to be able to get in my truck on Friday afternoon and be at the cabin by eight. Guess I'm just a country boy."

Country boy did a thorough job explaining Doro's will. The Inn was three years away from being paid off, but Doro's life insurance covered that. Still held in trust for me—until age thirty—was my parents' life insurance. And so it seemed that I went from being a struggling copy manager in one of the most expensive cities in the US to a young woman of means.

"But what about the Inn?" I said, when the will had been read.

"Well, JoAnna, as it says, Ms. Wilson was very clear that the Inn was to go to you."

"But I don't, I don't want it." I thought I sensed a wince from Maddy, but I continued anyway. "I don't want to live here."

John rubbed his hands through his hair, and I thought of Tom. What would he say? What would he think? Was he even a factor?

"If you don't want to keep the Inn, I suggest you meet with a realtor relatively soon. A parcel of land that size, depending on the condition of the house, may take a while to find a buyer."

I turned to Maddy. "Maddy, don't you want the Inn? You could keep running it or have guests there, or, or something."

"Little thing, I think you mistake me for someone not pushing eighty." Maddy squeezed my hand. "The Inn was Doro's dream, not mine."

The meeting lasted a little over an hour. Doro, it seems, had been a careful planner. She left, in the capable hands of Barkham and Wright, complete details on her affairs, even instructions on thawing her cantankerous deep freeze in the basement.

As we prepared to leave, John took my hand.

"As for myself, I do wish you'd stay, JoAnna. Or at least keep the Inn. This little town is growing older—no offense, Mr. Blair—and it would be nice to see more of our generation back here.

"You might be surprised at what a nice place to live it is."

We walked from the office to the Lunch Box, and although I had eaten numerous times there over the years, I was instantly transported to my eight-year-old self, to that Saturday with Doro and Maddy and the elephant ears and Doro's dreams.

"You understand, don't you?" I asked, stabbing my open-faced roast beef sandwich as Maddy launched greedily into his BLT. "Mt. Moriah is just not my life anymore."

Maddy was quiet for a minute. "It's not just your life to consider, Jo. I know that. There's Tom to consider too. But for whatever was in that crazy head of hers, Doro felt very strongly that you keep the Inn.

"She had big plans for it, you know."

Maddy told me how he came upon Doro in her pajamas early one Saturday morning, sitting at the kitchen table, drawing on a legal pad, a cup of tepid Earl Grey before her. She wanted to convert the massive side porch into a bakery. The porch was rarely used, but was visible from the road below. She thought it might appeal to people who would like to stroll around the grounds and take away a baked good. With fewer overnight guests, Doro saw this as a way to keep the Inn viable.

"And who would do the baking? Had Doro thought of that?"

"Of course, she had, little thing. That was the genius of it." Maddy paused dramatically. "Who makes the best chocolate chess tarts in the world?"

Indeed I knew.

The summer before senior year in high school, I was totally immersed in our class yearbook. I was editor-in-chief, with an emphasis on chief. When it came to fundraising, I had little interest in other people's ideas: I was so sure my idea of a bake sale was the best. Parents were less than enthusiastic. By the end of high school, so many of those mothers had baked their way through elementary, middle, and high school and were ready to retire.

"Goodness, get the kids to bake themselves!" Doro scoffed.

And I did, which yielded us baggies of cookies, brownies, and Rice Krispies treats. The bake sale was to be held July 4, when Doro always hosted a patriotic concert on the lawn. Sweaty toddlers with red, white, and blue pinwheels chased each other, weaving in and out on the lawn of picnic blankets. Couples took turns using each other's stomachs as pillows, sprawled under the vast sky peeking above the hundred year old oaks. Maddy churned homemade ice cream, and two men from church manned the grill. Hamburger and hotdog plates were five dollars each, with the proceeds benefitting First Methodist's mission work.

"Set up your bake sale on the side porch, and I bet you'll make a killing," Doro said.

I recruited Grace and Tuck to help me. They had little interest in the yearbook, but lately had become inseparable, spending time together as I sat in my room, flipping through college catalogs and yearbook page proofs. We were still a trio, yet I felt myself separating.

"Good news, Jo Jo," Grace said as she bounded up the steps early that afternoon. "My mom has made eight dozen chocolate chess tarts for you. She stayed up all night."

Genia's baked goods were legendary.

"Awesome! Where are they?"

"They are in the trunk of Doro's car." She dropped Doro's keys on the table. "Thanks for letting me borrow your car, Doro. Let me get my arms free, and I'll go get them."

"Oh I'll go," I said. "That's so great."

Indeed, the gooey tarts would have been great had I gone then to get them, had I not told Grace I would do it. Had either of us actually gone to retrieve them from the car parked in the ninety-five-degree sun. Had four hours not passed before either of us realized the tarts were not displayed on the table. By the time we rescued them, the tarts had turned to chocolate rivers and the trunk of Doro's car to a fudge factory.

It was Doro who saved the day when Genia arrived to see no tarts on display.

"Genia, you wouldn't believe the good fortune!" Doro shot me and Grace a look that prohibited us from speaking. "Someone bought them all up."

Straightening a bit, Genia smiled, flushed with pride that her delicacies had been a hit.

"Now, girls, come help me in the kitchen."

Out of range of Genia's ears, Doro waggled her finger at us. "I did not lie. I am purchasing that god-awful mess for two hundred dollars. In exchange you, will clean my car and give me an honest day's work this weekend for no charge."

Doro's will stayed on my mind. Maddy and I spent the next two days idling around the Inn in silence. Maddy had his own built-in barometer for assessing what people were feeling, what they needed. He knew what I needed was quiet. Perhaps he thought I would talk when I was ready.

I had been in Mt. Moriah less than a week and although I couldn't see myself staying here, I also couldn't imagine returning to Chicago. I helped Maddy with the tasks he gave me—sorting through Doro's papers, cleaning out the refrigerator—but when he was out or otherwise engaged, I'd sneak out to the lush magnolia on the front lawn. Hunching over, I slipped under its mighty limbs, my bottom on the cool leafy carpet and my back up against the trunk for support. How many afternoons of my childhood I had whiled away in just such a position, the magnolia umbrella eclipsing the sun—my nose stuck in a book or scribbling my stories filled with characters so alive to me I could hear their voices. Characters who, unlike Jillsandra, had birthdays and feelings and whole lifetimes that I knew as intimately as I knew my own.

How I missed the feeling of writing so fluidly that the words formed effortlessly on the pages. How I missed the feeling of escape that came with an afternoon spent writing, being called to dinner by Doro and having to remind myself of who and where I was.

I missed having something to say.

As much time as I spent with Grace, the magnolia was mine alone—a chapel constructed solely for me and my thoughts. It was an old friend that beckoned me alone, that shielded me from myself.

But not from my thoughts.

Tom had called again, twice. Both times he talked to Maddy. It had been weeks since I had seen my husband, and I missed him. I wanted nothing more than to lean into his arms, to have him stroke my hair. But I also knew there was something keeping me from Tom, from surrendering to love that seemed so easy for him: words unsaid and secrets unshared. I had a decision to make, several decisions, and I knew that there, under my magnolia canopy, knees drawn up to my chin, arms tightly wrapped around my calves, eyes closed, barely breathing, I could be the only way that life was bearable.

Invisible.

I fell asleep, tucked up like a little ball, and was awoken by a familiar footstep. Maddy, one hand on his chest, pulled back a limb to peer at me.

"Thought I'd find you here." Maddy rubbed his chest, and his face was one of concern.

"Why are you rubbing your chest?"

"Oh, I think I pulled a muscle, probably hauling a box." Maddy slid his head in between limbs and peered up, seeing the brilliant green awning from my vantage point. "Nice spot. I'd climb in there and sit with you for a spell, but I doubt I'd be able to get up."

"This was my favorite place when I was a child."

"I remember."

Maddy looked up through the foliage and then back at me. "One of my favorite quotes goes, 'Someone is sitting in the shade today, because someone planted a tree a long time ago.'"

I batted away a mosquito. "Let me guess: Paul to the church at Corinth."

Maddy scowled. "You are Biblically illiterate. It was Warren Buffett actually."

Smiling, I pushed back a branch to see him better. "It feels so . . . safe in here."

"And nowhere else?"

Tears pooled in the corners of my eyes. "I don't know, Maddy. I just, I don't know where I belong." I straightened my legs, and made my way out to where Maddy was standing. So tall, he, like the magnolia, blocked the sun. He, like the ancient tree, was a safe refuge.

I peered up into those eyes, aquamarine and warm as gentle ocean waves. "I've made a mess of things, Maddy. I think I've made a real mess of things."

Maddy put his arms around my shoulder. "You need two things, little bit. First, a nice cup of tea. Secondly, you need to tell someone what's going on." He spread his leathered hands on either side of my eyes, wiping away the tears with thick thumbs.

"I don't know where to start."

"Start at the beginning."

And so I did.

19

CARDINALS

How to start at the beginning? Where *was* the beginning for me and Tom? It was hard to remember a time when I didn't feel like I knew Tom for half a lifetime.

I always thought that the day on which I met my husband would be significant, singular, special in some way. Surely there would be an indication of the change that was to come. But that was the stuff of the fairy tales that my father read me as a child. Closing my eyes, I could feel the scruff on Daddy's chin as it rubbed across my forehead. I was back in Daddy's lap, worshipping the picture of Cinderella descending the steps: her gown so white it was almost blue. That's where we get our ideas—as little girls tucked in our fathers' laps. Our lives unfold like a race to the glass slipper—to be saved by the lonely prince.

Instead I met my husband at a Xerox machine, and Tom was no prince. He was not even handsome, but his cuteness, his steady demeanor and intelligence soon consumed my thoughts. Although there may not have been a beacon pointing to a life together, the friendship we forged was undeniable.

Tom and I lived together, but apart, in the house on Hudson Street for nine months. During that time, there were evenings where he would knock on my door, ever the gentleman, offering me a plate of the lasagna he had made. Or I would bring him the *Tribune* I had rescued from the Doberman next door. We passed each other on our way out, on our way in. On days when Tom was going to be in the office, we carpooled. The time passed—minutes, hours—through inane chatter about nothing.

Since moving out of the long-term hotel, I saw the Megans and Loris and Tiffanis infrequently. I had heard that Megan had quit her job and was waiting tables while she tried to find something else. Riding an elevator with Tiffany, I learned that she had left her boyfriend. The next week she was sporting a diamond tennis bracelet.

"How could I not forgive him!" she chortled.

As for me, I spent hours huddled over copy, red pen poised. I had been at Sandalwood & Harris for almost two years, and I was rewarded with a three percent increase. I was not writing, either at home or at work, and I complained to Tom over grilled cheese one Saturday afternoon when I was helping him strip wallpaper from the powder room.

"Jillsandra hasn't done anything?" he asked.

"No. I try to write at night, but I end up staring at the screen until I fall asleep. I've got nothing."

The fact—which I would never reveal to Tom—was that I did have spurts of inspiration; they just didn't occur when I was at the keyboard. Rather, they happened on the Friday evenings I went to Tony's. They happened as I strolled Wabash on Saturday afternoons. They happened as I rode the antique gold flanked elevators at Macy's.

And they happened most often when I drank.

When I wasn't working, I was walking. And when I wasn't walking, I was drinking. Sometimes I drank as I walked, bourbon lacing the Diet Coke in my McDonald's cup. Walking made me feel powerful, and drinking made me invincible.

There was a moment, just after the second glass, when my eyes cleared and everything seemed possible: I could be a writer; I could be happy. I could, I could. Do. Anything.

The liquor's warmth seeped through my brain, and words formed, whole phrases, suspended in the sky above me like cartoon captions. But then there was the subway ride home. And then I changed into pajamas. And brushed my teeth. And by the time I sat down at my computer, the screen lulled me into sleep.

"You need inspiration," Tom suggested over lunch one day.

"Any ideas?"

"Actually, yes. How about if you tag along on my photo shoot this Saturday. I'm shooting a bunch of anorexic, over-priced, empty-noodled models."

"Hmmm, sounds inspiring."

"Now don't be a doubter. If you like people watching, it doesn't get any better than this."

"Sure you're not just out for slave labor help again?"

"So what if I am!" Tom winked. "Holding the aperture meter is a lot less messy than drywalling, and I'll even take you to dinner afterwards."

"Okay, it's a date."

That was June 1999. The next week Tom took me to the Natural History Museum, and we ate ice cream sitting on the steps next to the formidable lions.

Our third date was to a movie and our fourth was to eat Chinese. All Saturdays punctuating the dreary weeks I had to myself. Weeks where I saw Tom hardly at all.

On the fifth Saturday Tom knocked on my door, a box of Puffs in one hand and a nose the color of Santa's.

"No date tonight. I'm sick."

"Gosh you look awful. Bad cold?"

"Yes. Wanna make me chicken soup?"

"Do you need me to make you chicken soup?"

"No, I'll just go to bed. Rain check on our date?"

"Sure." My mind began racing with the long hours I would have to fill. "Tom, can I ask you something?"

He nodded and coughed, mucous obviously rising in his throat.

"What are we doing?"

"You mean that literally or are you being deep?"

"Are we dating?"

He cleared his throat. "I'd say so. If we weren't, I wouldn't be so disappointed about having to cancel tonight. After all, I had big plans."

"Oh?"

"Tonight I was going to kiss you." Tom stuffed a tissue up to his nose. "But there's the phlegm and everything."

"Phlegm can be sexy, on the right man."

"Yeah?"

"No."

"Goodnight, Jo. Next weekend?"

The Saturdays splayed out in front of me like autumn leaves collecting on the vintage lawns in Hyde Park. Having lived in Chicago over fifteen years, Tom knew all the nooks and crannies of the city. Together we saw the city as native and naïf, through a photographer's lens and a writer's eyes. We strolled, sometimes holding hands to jaywalk across the street, at times talking over each other, at times saying nothing at all.

Two things lingered in my mind: Tom's mention of a kiss (that had never happened), and the weekdays that hung on either side of the Saturdays.

One Saturday in November, when the trees had bared and my clothing layers tripled, Tom and I packed a picnic lunch and boarded the purple train.

"I can't believe you haven't seen the universities in this town," he had said a few weeks before.

"Does University of Chicago not count?"

"Okay, that's one. What about Northwestern? You take the purple line until it stops. That's got to speak to the poet in you."

"I'm a non-existent writer, not a poet."

"Tell ya what. Next Saturday we're going to Loyola. Will you pack us a picnic lunch? And wear a heavy windbreaker; the wind is ferocious where we're going."

We descended the steps at the station and headed to Loyola. The sunny day was unseasonably mild and before long I took off my jacket. I pointed out a few good places for us to eat our picnic. I was hungry, and my new sneakers rubbed a blister.

"Just up ahead. We're almost to the chapel." Tom pointed to the spire 400 yards away.

"Ham and cheese in a church?"

"A chapel. Wait until you see what's behind it. Jillsandra will burst with inspiration!"

"How do you know so much about this school?"

"All my sisters went here. Very Catholic family, ya know."

I knew Tom's family lived two hours away, and that he had gone to DePaul, majoring in photography.

"Why not Loyola?"

"No photography." He bit his lips, and a slight smirk escaped. "And I couldn't get in."

He checked his watch. "Good, it's three hours until another service."

Once inside, I took in the candles, flames dancing against the rose glasses in the south transept. I lingered at the votives, whispering to Tom, "I always thought this was a really pretty tradition. But I can't say I completely understand it."

"No candles in the Methodist church?"

"Just two big ones."

"My very Catholic mother always called them vigil candles. They're for you to remember people."

"Dead people."

"Mostly, but some people light them to pray for lost causes." He leaned in close. "Or writer's block."

I struck a match and lit a candle in the back row. Its lone flame flickered in the darkness.

"For Jillsandra?"

"For Grace."

Tom crossed himself, ending with a kiss on his fingertips.

"Come on. Time for lunch."

It was almost 2:30 in the afternoon when, my stomach rumbling and my head full of ghosts and candles, Tom pushed open the Art Deco doors at the back of the chapel. There, 200 feet across the sandstone courtyard, in all its bold, exuberant power, was Lake Michigan—the lake that I had run beside, its wind chapping my cheeks, erasing who I was and where I had been. Suddenly the massive body of water was before me and around me and took my breath away.

We descended two shallow steps, and I slowly crossed the courtyard to the stone wall. The wind from the water stung my eyes, sliced through my sweater, and instantly made me shiver.

"You'll want that jacket back on," Tom advised.

But I didn't. I wanted to feel the frosty air swirling around me. In all my time in Chicago I had not felt this alive.

We returned to the Loyola Chapel courtyard frequently, dubbing it our spot. One Sunday afternoon just before Thanksgiving, we huddled in down parkas on the stone wall. Tom had brought heated seat pads.

"I never heard of such a thing. But I'm not complaining!" My hands gripped a Styrofoam cup of hot cocoa, the steam escaping in the wind.

"My mom's purchase. She's the kind of mom who thinks of everything— kinda drives you crazy, but your butt never gets cold."

We sat silently sipping our cocoa and gazing at the foreboding water and the birds dipping and soaring, again and again, hunting for food. One of the things I had grown to appreciate about Tom was the fact that conversation was not mandatory. Dr. Weisz was constantly asking me, "How are you feeling?" "How was this week?" "Can you rate the grief you feel?" but Tom simply sat beside me, as content with silence as he was with conversation.

He fiddled with his camera, adjusting the lens, focusing on one particularly crazed bird, unrelenting in his water dives.

"The patterns birds fly are so random," I said.

"Hmmm, but they're not."

"I don't mean when they fly in formations; I just mean this guy's crazy dives."

"I still doubt they're random. But then again, I don't believe in random," Tom said.

"What does that mean? Everything has a plan?"

"Yep. Everything."

I set my empty cup on the ledge and stuffed my frozen hands, mittened insufficiently, inside my parka sleeves.

"You can't believe that."

Tom lowered his camera from his face. The dimples appeared as he smiled.

"Can if I want to."

"No, I mean, what about a baby dying? There's a plan for that?"

"Ah, you had to pick the hardest example." Tom pulled his right glove off with his teeth to grab another roll of film. "I can't say God's hand is in a baby dying, but I do think that life moves to a certain rhythm, and things are just part of that.

"I just don't think things happen randomly."

I sat quietly for a moment, then, "And Grace being killed? That was part of a *plan*?"

"You're misunderstanding. You're making a plan the opposite of random."

"And isn't it?"

"No," said Tom. "Grace died because she chose to walk on a mountain, and a deranged psychopath chose to go up there and look for someone to kill."

My heart skipped a beat, and a shudder ran through my body.

"So she asked for it?"

Tom set the camera down, then, and put his hands on my wrists.

"God, no, Jo, that's not what I'm saying at all. But I'm saying there's free will, and I think that certain things are supposed to happen, or certain people are supposed to react to events. And I do think God oversees it all."

"But doesn't save people." I blinked against threatening tears. "He didn't intervene to save Grace."

"He can't save everyone."

"He's God. I mean, if you believe he's God, then why not?"

"I don't know, Jo."

"And doesn't it bother you that you don't know?"

"No, not really. It bothers me more to think everything's random. What the hell is the point of that?" Tom reached over and pushed my hair from my face, tucking it into my hood. "I prefer to focus on the things I know were planned—things like what that bird is doing. Or like us meeting."

"You think we were meant to meet?"

"You don't?"

"I'm all about random," I reminded Tom.

"So we just happened to be in the same creative team meetings. And I just randomly drove by when that jerk was trying to take advantage of you at Tony's. And you just randomly responded to an ad at the house where I live." Tom smiled. "Sorry—your theory doesn't hold water."

The truth was, I had wondered more than once at the serendipity of our friendship. But I couldn't reconcile the good and the bad, the happy coincidences and the evil happenings.

"I bet you believe in happy ever after too, don't you?"

He placed his hand over his heart, dramatically. "Hello, my name is Tom, and I'm an optimist. I do believe in happy."

I giggled. "You're a little nutty."

"But a happy nut."

Tom picked up the camera, stood and aimed it at me. "Laugh again."

"Say something funny."

"I got nothing. Just fake laugh."

"Why?"

"Because your laugh jumps into your eyes, and it's something to behold." Tom pulled me to my feet and positioned my head, chin up, nose pointing toward Lake Michigan. I heard the sound of several clicks.

He looked over the camera lens. "Anybody ever tell you that you have the saddest eyes?"

"Uh, I don't think that's a compliment."

"Sure it is. Mona Lisa had sad eyes."

"Yeah and an ugly face."

Swinging the camera strap onto his shoulder, Tom reached over to tuck more hair inside my hood. "Your eyes are like falling into a deep well, where you can't get out and you can't see where you're going."

He smiled. Those dimples. "Hey, how was that for poetic?"

"You just compared my eyes to drowning."

"Well I do feel a little like I'm drowning when I'm around you." Tom took a step closer. "But it's a good kind of drowning." Another step, his breath now closer. "Are you as cold as I am, Jo?"

I nodded, and he pulled me gently into his arms. Tom's chin was above the top of my head, and he rested his right cheek against my unruly curls, my hood slipping away. His long arms enwrapped me so closely I felt I would disappear. From the cold. From myself.

"You give good hugs," I whispered.

"You're fun to hug. Your hair smells like . . . you."

His cheek rubbed against my hairline, pushing the curls back, until his cheek rested on mine, Tom's lips dangerously close to mine.

My breathing quickened and I pushed against his chest.

"Tom, what are we—"

"Shut up. I'm trying to move in for a kiss."

His lips found mine then and, eyes wide open, I tried to calm my racing mind. *Too close, it shouted. Too close!* Tom's eyes opened and, lips locked, we stared into each other's eyes.

"Jeez, you kiss with your eyes open!"

"I guess."

"You're trembling." Tom rubbed my arms and then pulled me in for a deeper hug, his mouth still hovering near mine. "Are you cold or . . ."

"A little scared."

"Of me?"

"Of this." I had thought of this kiss since the sick Saturday. Tom's face loomed in my daydreams, and I counted the hours until our weekends together when I lost myself in Tom's kindness, his boisterous laugh. Slipping my hand into Tom's, feeling it swallow my own, I felt safe. And now the gentleness of his supple lips sent a shiver down my thighs.

Yet I felt as if I couldn't breathe, and I pushed away.

"I really like you, Tom." I couldn't look into his eyes. "I think I maybe more than like you."

"I maybe more than like you too, Jo." He lifted my chin and pressed a kiss onto my forehead.

"I just need to go really slow."

"I can do slow. As long as you're not scared of me. I couldn't handle that." Tom peered deeply into my eyes, almost as if he could see what stared back at him. Almost. "I'd never hurt you, Jo."

Our Saturdays continued, as did the kisses. And although I wanted them, I felt my body tense as his mouth pressed harder and harder on mine, his hand roving tenderly, slowly.

"Are your eyes open?" he murmured one evening, mid-kiss. We had been watching an old Bette Davis movie on his sofa. "I'm always spooked I'm going to open my eyes and there you're going to be—staring at me."

"I'm sorry."

"It's a control thing, JoAnna," Dr. Weitz had said. "You've experienced a tragedy beyond your control. Perhaps this is one thing you think you can do to show you are in control of your own life."

"It's a, a control thing I think," I stammered.

"Not sure a relationship is something you can control." Tom leaned back against the sofa, his hands interlocked across his chest. "My mysterious Jo. What's deep inside that beautiful head of yours? What have those sad eyes seen?"

I wanted to tell him, but how could I? How could I tell Tom that every time I was in his arms, every time he kissed me, Grace's face lingered near the surface of my consciousness. Grace and her murderer, Grace and the threat of evil in the world. I had the disconcerting feeling that there was something to worry about—something unfinished, unsaid. A nagging fear lingered at the edge of my subconscious.

Time passed and it was time for Christmas and New Year's.

"Are you going home for the holidays?" Tom asked one Saturday evening, his mouth full of Kung Pao takeout.

"No, Doro and Maddy are coming here."

He cocked his head quizzically. "Can't imagine being in the city for Christmas. The holidays are about home-cooked meals and kitchens, and my dad cussing over the shrubbery lights."

I smiled. "That sounds nice actually. Guess I just have a different sense of home."

The truth was I felt like a person without a home. I was two years into my resolve not to return to Mt. Moriah. Both Christmases and Easters, Doro begged. "Come home, doll. Everyone wants to see you." But for me there was no home. Instead, what felt most like home were Tony's mason jars and Tom's navy plaid Goodwill sofa.

Tom put down his plate. "Hey, come home with me for the holidays. My sisters are dying to meet you. Besides, if Y2K is as bad as everyone predicts, it might be our last time together."

Meeting his family. Sitting at a cherry dining table, with sweet potatoes and heavy pewter candlesticks and childhood anecdotes. A table gilded with laughter and the possibility of happiness. A table where ghosts didn't lurk: a happy place.

"I can't, Tom. Can I take a raincheck?"

I did agree to go with him one Saturday in February. Tom and I threw duffle bags in his trunk and inched along highway traffic toward his home in Aurora.

"Tell me more about your family. All I know is you have three sisters and a dad who's a dentist and a mom who's . . ."

"A kindergarten teacher. In all aspects of the word." Tom flashed a dimpled smile. "She'll probably give you coloring sheets."

"So tell me something unique about your family. I've told you a lot about Doro and Maddy."

Tom sat on his horn as a truck cut him off from the merge lane.

"Well, let's see. Probably the most unique thing about us is a little embarrassing." He cleared his throat. "We all share a monogram."

"You mean, like something that's monogrammed?"

"No, the actual monogram."

"Was that planned?"

He pinched my knee. "Yes, of course. You think there is anything slightly random to a name?"

Tom explained how his mother, Tonya Evans, married Thomas Eugene Rivers, thus becoming T.E.R. like her husband. When Tom was given his father's name, the trend began. The Rivers thought their second child couldn't be the only one without the monogram. So she was named Theresa Evans Rivers.

"Wait a second; I'm still processing that your middle name is Eugene."

He snarled. "Not something I share too readily with people. It was my grandfather's name, though, and he was one cool old coot."

"And so the plan continued with your youngest sisters, the twins?"

"Well I'm not sure there was a plan with regards to my mom getting pregnant a third time. You can chalk that one up to random. But when they were born, they couldn't be the only ones left out of the fun."

"And so?"

"Tammy Elizabeth and Tracey Elise."

"Wow. I have to say, that's pretty unique."

I pushed Tom to tell me stories from his childhood. I was anxious about meeting his family, perhaps about the notion of a family in general. Tom's anecdotes were of creek wading and tire swings and Friday night hamburgers and television. Of rowdy Christmas mornings and yellow labs that stole ham off the Easter platter.

"I don't know that I've ever known someone with such a picket fence life."

"We didn't have a picket fence." Tom frowned. "We had an old chain link that the dogs could escape under."

"And the dogs' names? They're both still alive?"

He paused. "I'll tell you if you don't pass judgement."

"Oh my. Really?"

"Yep. Tatum and Tess."

Built in the 1960s, the Rivers' ranch style house had lofty maples flooding the front yard with shade. Dr. Rivers had converted the den at the back of the house to a dining room with a china cupboard tucked in the corner. The walls were putty colored, thick knobby paneling that said, "Stay, linger here."

Tom's sisters were cut from the same mold: all long-legged, thin, with wavy hair in varying shades of brown. Theresa had her father's close-set eyes and her mother's mouth, and the twins, though fraternal, both favored their mother. In their presence, I saw a Tom I had not seen before: a doting brother who lost ten years just by walking through the door.

"Tommy!" squealed Tracy. She was the most rambunctious of the group. At eighteen, she was equal parts woman and little girl. No sooner were we inside than she took a running leap into his arms. They fell together backwards over the sofa.

"Geez, Trace. Give an old man a break!"

Mrs. Rivers—Tonya as she immediately insisted I call her—laughed and pinned her hair back in place. She looked as if she never stopped laughing.

"Let them get it out of their system, JoAnna." Wiping her hand on a red paisley apron, Tonya clasped my hand in both of hers. Behind me the four Rivers children were rough-housing.

"You'd think they were in elementary school."

I couldn't help but smile. The hallway was adorned with school pictures of Tom and his sisters—pictures of dance recitals, baseball team photos. Memories of Easter dresses and Santa laps. I lingered there, looking at the pictures, wondering if my parents' house would have had such a wall.

"They're a pain to dust," Tonya whispered to me. "But truth be told, with the twins in college and Theresa on her own, there are nights that I plant a little kiss on those sweet baby faces as I head off to bed."

Her face radiated contentment, the sweet visage of a life well lived.

"Excuse me. Let me check the pork chops."

Tom's father was the shortest of the family, though he reached 5'9". In him I could see Tom's mannerisms. They both pushed their wire rimmed glasses up on their noses every few minutes. They both held their glasses up to the light before breathing on them and shining them with their shirt tails. And Tom's trademark dimples were on his father's lined cheeks.

"So tell me what you do at that ad agency, JoAnna," Thomas said at dinner, passing the steamed broccoli. I thought of Doro and what I would later tell her about the dinner.

"You mean plain old broccoli. No cheese sauce? Not a broccoli and rice casserole?"

I was no longer in the South where cheese, Campbell's soup, and bread crumbs smothered any vegetable.

I cleared my throat. "My title is copy manager. What I do is proofread and route the copy through the editing process." I caught the eyes of Theresa, Tracy, and Tammy, all staring at me. Theirs were kind, interested eyes that said they had not met many of their brother's girlfriends.

"Sounds like a good gig. And there's room for advancement, I assume." Thomas adjusted his glasses. "Tom said that was what attracted him to that firm."

He swatted at Tonya's hand, reaching to take back part of the lump of butter on the side of his plate. "Forgive my wife, JoAnna. She thinks I'm getting pudgy."

"I said soft, not pudgy. And just in the gut. Just a little less butter and bread—"

"Shrew, thy name is woman!" He gestured with his butter knife.

"Daddy, you just murdered Shakespeare!" Tammy giggled as Tonya reached out to kick Thomas under the table. Obviously theirs was the kind of marriage that had stood the test of years, the kind of relationship that would make Tom believe in plans and destiny.

Thomas was looking at me, with sideways glances at Tom. "Seems a hard business to be profitable at—photography, that is."

I remembered my conversation with Tom and changed the subject. "Well I really want to be a writer, long-term, but you can't support yourself on that."

Theresa's face said it all. "You're kidding—you're a writer? That's awesome."

"Theresa is our reader," said Tonya. "As a child, she worked her way through the whole children's section."

"Mom exaggerates," said Theresa. "Who are your favorite writers?"

She and I lobbed authors' names across the pewter candlesticks.

"This English major talk is a snooze fest for the rest of us." Tom rested his chin on his hand and pretended to snore. An elbow to his side made him sit upright.

"This girl appreciates Updike. Have some respect." Theresa turned her attention back to me, raising her wine glass. "Please excuse my illiterate brother, but let me say I highly approve of his taste in women."

After dinner the family adjourned to the den to watch the Notre Dame-IU basketball game. I stupidly asked which team they were for. Thomas stuck out his arm. "Take a knife and cut me, JoAnna. It'll bleed purple."

"Dad has a statue of the Touchdown Jesus in his office," smirked Tracy.

By ten o'clock, I could not hide my heavy eyelids. The three glasses of wine at dinner had taken their toll. I caught Tom looking at me quizzically when I held my glass up for a third refill. And then again when I caught the edge of the plate upon trying to set my glass down, making a loud clang.

His mother noticed me nodding off. Football was over, Notre Dame had lost, and Theresa was putting on the DVD of *Forest Gump*.

"Heavens, honey, that's a three hour movie. Haven't you seen it enough?"

Unbeknownst to me, Tom and his sisters could quote every line in the movie along with Tom Hanks.

"Some families play cards; we quote movies," Tom said.

"JoAnna, would you like me to show you your room? It looks like you're about ready to turn in."

I looked at Tom who told me with his eyes that he wanted to stay up a bit longer. He reached over and kissed my forehead.

I followed Tonya down the hallway to the end, where black walls and a leopard bedspread met me. "Is this . . . Tom's room?"

"Yes, he went through this phase as a teenager and wanted his walls painted black." She lifted her palms in mock despair. "And, now it would take so much paint to cover up the black."

While I was looking at the wall beside the bed—covered with photos, mostly black and white—Tonya left the room and returned with towels. "Now you make yourself at home and just ask for anything you need. With four women in the house, we surely have everything covered."

Then she looked pointedly at me and said, "Tommy is going to sleep on the living room sofa bed. I know that you two are living together—"

My face immediately flushed. "No, ma'am, we're not . . . uh . . ."

"Well, I know it's a different era than when I was your age. But at any rate, house rules here and that means girlfriends and boyfriends sleep apart." She shrugged and laughed, trying to ease the awkwardness.

"Thank you, Tonya. Your home and your family are wonderful."

Closing the door, I changed into my nightshirt and slid under the covers. The ceiling was a canopy of lights—those iridescent plastic stars that were the design dream of every eight year old. I lay awake for a long time, listening to the faint voices of Tom Hanks and Sally Fields, to the Rivers' children trying to over-talk each other. I tried to imagine the Tom of six, of twelve, of eighteen. What would a child in this home dream about? What would he fear? What would there be to fear?

As the house quieted under the watchful eyes of those majestic maples, I was lulled to sleep with a sense of safety.

"I wanted this, Mama," I whispered to the Anna Wilson who could not hear me.

The next morning the twins headed back to Loyola for a sorority formal. Issuing a word of caution, Tonya gave hugs that said she knew them better than she knew herself. Warm, tight, all-consuming but never stifling hugs.

"Your mom's a good mom," I told Tom.

Without a trace of sarcasm, just pure pleasure on his face, he agreed. "Yeah, she's the best."

That afternoon we went antiquing, leaving Thomas snoring loudly in his recliner, the *Tribune* crumpled against his chest.

We walked along the main street of Aurora, the charming shops beckoning us inside, the prices driving us back out. Theresa and I talked books while Tom and his mom argued over an antique ottoman she wanted to buy him.

"It's low. Doesn't look comfortable."

Tonya sighed. "It's not supposed to be comfortable. It's supposed to look nice."

"Form over function, eh?"

Tonya turned to me. "Help me here, JoAnna. We females need to stick together."

His arm around my shoulder, Tom pulled me next to him. "This girl is hardly your typical female. We became friends over drywalling, and she even knows her way around a table saw."

"I think you just insinuated I'm not a girl," I teased.

Tom leaned down and kissed me full on the lips. "Oh you're a girl alright."

Tonya and Theresa exchanged smiles, and we strolled on.

Something in the window of a corner store caught my eye. On display outside a glass shop was a hand-blown cardinal, the edges a deep scarlet receding into the berry colored body.

"What do you see? Tom asked, his hand on my shoulder.

"I'm looking at that cardinal."

It was Memorial Day, 1990. Tuck, Grace, and I were clearing plates and cups. Doro had hired a jazz quartet to play patriotic music, and they were on their last song. Guests were starting to head back to their rooms, and people from Mt. Moriah who had sprawled beach towels and picnic blankets on the back lawn were saying their goodbyes.

"I have been officially bitten by every stupid mosquito in Mt. Moriah." Tuck alternated slapping his shins and gouging at bites with his nails.

"It's not because you're sweet, Tuck." Grace retied her apron, opening the two dishwashers and surveying her options.

"What's the point of a mosquito anyway? If every animal has a purpose, what the hell is with mosquitos?"

"I can't see much use in cockroaches," I remarked.

"True that." We worked in silence for a minute, then, "If I came back as an animal, I'd be a lion. What about you guys? What would you be?"

"Easy. A golden retriever. Everyone would love me and pat me all day long," I said.

"Eh, too common. Too much fur." Tuck hopped up onto a bar stool and examined a match box. Soon Doro would come in and find him lounging and that wouldn't be a pretty sight.

"Oh, 'cause lions don't have much hair at all," I said.

"Well, yeah, but I'd be in Africa and I'd be used to the fur. It wouldn't bother me." Tuck winked at me. "And I'd be king."

"You're not going to feel like king when Doro finds you up there on your throne." Grace paused from scraping the plates to wipe beads of sweat from her forehead. "Little help here!"

"You seem to be doing okay," Tuck replied, using a clean table knife to scratch his ankle, then dropping it back into the silverware drawer. "So what's your animal, Gracie?"

Grace dried her hands on a towel, then ran it across her face. "Shh, don't tell Doro." She hung the towel back up and, hands on her hips, declared, "A cardinal."

"What the hell kind of obscure animal is that to pick?"

"They are not obscure. They're unusual," she said, resuming her plate scraping. "Besides, I'm a little afraid of flying but if I were a cardinal I wouldn't be. "I'd be free."

I already knew of Grace's obsession with cardinals. Maddy had given her his St. Louis Cardinals baseball cap; she had a deck of cards with cardinals on the front, and a huge stuffed cardinal sat on her bed.

"They mate for life and they are so royal," she said.

"People hate birds. They have to hunt for food and eat worms," said Tuck. "Think of that."

"And people are scared of lions, but they love to watch cardinals fly," retorted Grace. "In your next life, you will have no friends."

"It's beautiful," said Tonya, interrupting my thoughts. "I love cardinals' symbolism, too. Legend has it that when you see a cardinal in the tree, it's a visit from a loved one who has passed." Tonya paused. "I've noticed a couple of times that a cardinal will show up on a tree in the middle of winter, and I wonder if it's a sign from my parents."

"Hello Granddaddy," Theresa whispered to the window.

Tonya cut her a sharp glance. "Make fun if you like but I think it's a lovely idea."

I smiled at this woman whom I liked so much after such a short time. "I do too, Tonya."

You'd love this, Grace, I thought to myself.

And I thought the same thing when, on my birthday, I opened a box to find that glass cardinal with a single carat solitaire resting on its delicate scarlet crest.

20

THE CHRISTMAS GIFT

"SO YOU LOVE ME," I asked when presented with that diamond. It was a rhetorical question, as Tom had told me so more than once in the time since I moved in.

"Apparently, I do." He swept the curls out of my eyes and kissed my forehead, the lightest touch that made me feel so secure. "You mystify me. You're an enigma that I can't get out of my head, and I want to spend my life with you."

A pause. "How's that for a non-writer?"

I was quiet, running the tip of my finger over that lovely gem, holding it up to the light.

"Are you going to say something? Yes and I love you too would be nice."

"You know I love you, Tom." It was not the first time I had said it. And I did love him. He was like a powerful drug, the effects carrying me through the work weeks. We had taken to leaving each other little notes at our desks, so many floors apart. I spent most of my time in the main house, no longer a tenant, more of a co-owner. At the end of the evening, however, I always returned to my room. It's not that I didn't want to sleep with Tom. His kisses made my heart race and my legs tingle. But he seemed to sense my need to move slowly. And the thought of complete intimacy stirred in me a primal fear, long buried.

"It doesn't make sense," I told Dr. Weisz. "I love Tom."

"You are carrying a great amount of fear," he said, resting his chin on folded

hands. "Your friend was brutally murdered, and it's reasonable that you are
slow to trust.

"You're not scared to love, perhaps, but you're scared to love and lose and
that keeps you at arms' distance."

"I am a very patient man," Tom said one night as we came up for air after
an hour of foreplay that left us both breathless. "I know you need to move
slowly. I want you to be sure when you lose your virginity."

Lose my virginity. Is that what he thought? This man who knew me so well
knew me not at all.

All this was running through my mind as I slipped the ring onto my finger
on that blustery day in March.

"I, I'm not sure what kind of wife I'd make, Tom. I'm not sure I'm loveable."

"That's for me to judge, right?"

I smiled. At that moment Grace and Mt. Moriah hovered at the periphery
of my thoughts. *"You're conquering your grief, JoAnna. I think this relationship*
with Tom has helped dissipate the grief, the loss you feel," Dr. Weisz had said.
And although I wasn't sure that the grief wasn't as mammoth as ever—like a
brick under my feather pillow—at that moment, on that evening with Tom,
I made a conscious effort to smile, to say yes. I could be a good wife. I could
make Tom as happy as he made me. I could begin a life that Grace and I had
dreamt of so long ago on my twin beds.

"Yes." I leaned over and kissed Tom with all the tenderness within me.

With my eyes wide open.

In the simplest of ceremonies we wed in the Loyola courtyard in late June,
when whisper soft summer breezes were bringing out the best of Chicago. I
wore my mother's tea-length ivory lace gown, saved for me all these years by
Doro. She arrived with it two weeks early so she could do last minute alter-
ations. Running my fingers over the lace, I imagined I could smell my mother,
that she was touchable. Trying on the dress, turning back and forth in front
of the mirror, brought tears to my eyes and Doro's.

"Anna's daughter has grown up to be a beautiful woman," Doro said.
"Beautiful in and out."

Theresa was my maid of honor, wearing a short pink lace sundress. Joel

Phillippe, Tom's best friend from high school, was his best man, and a handful of our friends from Sandalwood & Harris, as well as some of Tom's childhood friends, were there. Four rows of chairs offered plenty of seating. Beyond Tom, so dapper in his charcoal suit, Lake Michigan lapped the shores—and with each murmuring wave I felt more resolute, more secure. This was happiness.

I could tell that this small, slightly informal affair was not quite what Tonya had imagined for her son. She didn't know I had pushed hard for a justice of the peace.

"I know you're not sure about religion, Jo," said Tom. "But I just can't be married in a courtroom. Can we compromise?"

For him? The man who was nothing but gentle and patient with me?

"Of course. But if we're going to have a pastor perform the ceremony, are you okay with it not being a priest?"

He knew what I was thinking.

"You want Maddy."

"Yes."

"I think that's perfect."

As we sat at their dining table, making the modest plans, Tonya Rivers, who had been nothing but gracious to me, looked as if I was in the witness protection program.

"You don't want to invite anyone from your home? Mount . . ."

"Moriah. And no, just Maddy and Doro."

I knew what she was thinking. What kind of girl has no friends from home? Has no connection with home?

"Leave her alone, Mom. She's very private. She lost her best friend, and home is not home to her right now." I overheard Tom whispering to his mother as I was carrying dishes to the kitchen. Later I asked him if he understood how I felt.

"Honestly, Jo, no I don't. But that doesn't mean I don't accept it. It doesn't mean I don't love you." He kissed my hand. "I know you."

He didn't know me at all.

Tom stuck to his pledge, and we first made love on our wedding night. He moved slowly, gently, pausing to gauge the expression on my face.

This is progress, Dr. Weisz, I thought. *I'm naked and vulnerable and I'm okay.*

Truly, in those first few months as a newlywed, I was happier than I had been since moving to Chicago. Since Grace's death. Since ever? Tom was so steady, his demeanor so kind. With him I could glimpse a future and a happiness that eclipsed the last few years.

In those early days, Tom was a balm to my scarred heart. I could not get enough of him, conversations with him, eating with him, grocery shopping, and cleaning house with him. I threw myself into life as a Mrs. I bought a slipcover for Tom's Goodwill sofa and, then, fearing it was too plain, bought paisley pillows for the top. I planned dinner parties with people from work and called Doro, frantic for recipes I could manage. We spent Saturdays at yard sales, purchasing outdoor lanterns and salad bowls and video tapes and Christmas coffee mugs.

I fired Dr. Weisz. Already I had whittled down my visits to one a month, and I no longer thought them necessary. I was cured. I was happy and told Doro so.

She was cautiously happy about my happiness.

"Come home for a visit, Jo. Everyone here would like to see you and meet Tom."

And there it was, the tiny thorn like a hard pea in my breast.

Instinctively, I made excuses.

"Tom has so many weekend photoshoots," I said. "And, anyway, I'd prefer for you and Maddy to come and have fun in the city."

Tom passed through the room in time to hear my excuse. He brought it up later as we were getting ready for bed.

"You know, I'd love to go see Mt. Moriah and the Inn and meet everyone. And since when do I have weekend shoots? Only two since March."

"It's just better here, Tom," I said. "You'd get bored with the mountain in a day."

"But I want to see where you're from. You've seen where I'm from."

"And you're from a good place," I blurted out before I could think how it sounded. "I'm from a place that is better forgotten."

He frowned before picking up his book. I picked up mine and read the same lines over and over.

"It's important that you return home at some point, JoAnna," Dr. Weisz had said. *"It's important that you go back in order to move on."*

The hell with you, Dr. Weisz, I thought, as I deliberately turned unread pages. *I* have *moved on.*

And I had. Grace was far from my thoughts most of the time.

Best of all, I was writing again. I had set Jillsandra aside and was writing poems. Already I had a binder full—many of them dark but some quite lovely. Often at night I read them silently to myself, soothing myself to sleep on their lilting waves.

I was also lulled to sleep by liquid peace. Two glasses of wine at dinner, followed by a vodka tonic or third glass of wine at bedtime, and my eyes became deliciously heavy.

"Is my wife becoming a lush?" Tom asked, sliding into bed beside me and looping his hand around my waist.

I smiled. "Perhaps."

Tom nuzzled my neck. "Just wondering if our budget needs to include the fifths of vodka you're going through."

"Can my successful photographer not afford it?" I raked my fingernails gently across his back.

Tom leaned up on one elbow and tucked my hair behind my ears. "You okay?"

"Of course. Don't I look okay?"

"You look incredible. I just don't remember you drinking this much when we started dating."

"Other than the time at Tony's."

"Let's don't bring that up."

I pulled him in for a tight embrace. "I'm fine, Tom. I'm happy."

So at what point did I begin to feel as if I could not breathe? As if I was suffocating? Looking back, perhaps our first Christmas was the beginning.

In December I again resisted Tom's and Doro's requests for us to go to Mt. Moriah. As it turned out, we didn't go anywhere. Two days before Christmas the finest of snowflakes began to drift down around noon. By rush hour, six inches were on the roads and traffic was gridlocked. My afternoon meeting was cancelled, but I knew Tom was booked solid until five o'clock in undoubtedly unpleasant meetings with Adam and Candace. I left a message with his assistant that I was taking the train home. Exiting the train, I slid my way down the street and around the corner to our little bungalow, lowering my head as a buffer to the pelting snow. Our house was pitch black, and suddenly an old familiar panic rose in my throat.

I turned and saw no one on the street. Everyone was either, like Tom, still trying to make it home, or locked inside with roaring fires and vegetable soup. I hurried up the steps and inside, flipping on every light. Suddenly I felt so completely alone.

I changed into fuzzy pajamas and padded my way on sock feet through the house that rattled from the wind and groaned with the radiators.

Calm down, Jo. Tom's delayed in traffic. Get a grip, I told myself. Yet I could sense only darkness around me—in the sky enveloping the house, in the emptiness filling the rooms. In my racing heart. I knew Tom was dead in an accident.

I also knew where to find comfort.

On a shelf in my closet I kept a basket of "supplies"—a quart of vodka, a bottle of Merlot, a pint of gin. Tom had made one too many comments about drinking, so I thought it best to keep a stash away from his questions. I also felt the need for something that was mine alone. In the time we had been married, the more I became Mrs. Tom Rivers, the more I wondered where JoAnna Wilson was. It felt deliciously luxurious to have a basket hidden on my shelf. Somehow the secret made me me again.

Three hours later the Merlot was gone and I was asleep on the sofa, Doro's wedding afghan over me. Headlights shone in my eyes, and moments later Tom was inside, stomping snow off his boots.

"Jeez, I thought I'd never get to the turnoff." He draped his hat and down jacket over a chair and flopped down on the end of the sofa, swinging my feet into his lap. "Well you look comfortable. I'm hungry as hell." He sniffed the air like a bloodhound. "But I don't smell anything going."

"I guess dinner is my job?"

Tom frowned. "No," he said slowly, deliberately, "dinner is the job of whoever gets to the house four hours before the other person." He sighed and walked toward the kitchen. "I'll do it. How about an omelet?

"Oh, and I was going to stop, because we're out of wine but no one would let me over so I just kept going."

No sooner had he said it than his eyes fell on the bottle protruding between my hip and the couch cushions.

He pointed. "We had wine? Where?"

"I had it."

"What do you mean *you* had it? Where?"

"I had it on the shelf. It's not a big deal." I struggled to my feet and lost my balance, sitting back down hard.

"It's a big deal to me. Show me where."

"No, sir, I won't." I was on my feet now, pushing past him to the kitchen, grabbing a skillet out of the dish drainer.

Behind me Tom started opening and closing cabinets. Then he grabbed my elbow and turned me to look at him. *Run,* I thought. That silly old feeling in the pit of my stomach. *Run.*

"Our kitchen is not that big, Jo. Where's the stash?"

"It's not a stash, and you're hurting me."

He let go and walked to the coat closet, a sliver of space barely big enough to hold our coats. Then to the guest room and its closet.

"Tom, for God's sake, what's gotten in to you?"

"Into me? I come home to find my wife catatonic on the couch having polished off a bottle of wine that she's evidently been hiding." His hands ran through the sides of his hair. "It's not normal to hide alcohol, Jo."

"I wasn't hiding it. I was keeping it." I walked to our closet and pulled out the basket, realizing how the situation looked as I held the basket in my hands. My voice was quiet and trembling. "I just wanted it for myself. I didn't want to be judged."

Tom surveyed the basket for a full minute before taking it out of my hands. His voice was steely.

"I don't judge you, Jo. You know I don't. But this, this sneaking alcohol—it just feels scary to me."

I was crying, Merlot tears of shame.

"Are we having our first fight?"

"Yes, I think we are."

"I'll keep the basket in the kitchen."

"Thank you."

"Are we okay?"

"We are okay, Jo. Are *you* okay?"

Although I nodded, I wasn't sure. What I did know was that I would get a new basket and a new hiding place.

Despite the way our holidays started, we spent a decadent two days holed up inside while snow buried the world. We slept late and lay around in our pajamas. On Christmas Eve, Tom brought two sleeping bags and blankets in to the living room, situating them under our tiny, rather pitiful spruce.

"Am I missing something?"

"I'm introducing you to a Rivers family tradition," said Tom. "My sisters and I used to lie like this staring up at the lights, speculating on when Santa would come and what gifts he'd bring. Well, actually I knew the truth but being a good brother I kept up the facade. The twins were determined to catch Saint Nick in the act."

"Did it ever work?"

"Once we almost made it. It was probably one in the morning, and the twins were about four. We had fallen asleep and all of a sudden Tracy peed herself. I'm talking a massive pee. Once we all realized we were swimming, we hightailed it to our beds pretty quickly."

"You're banking on me having a big bladder."

Tom winked.

We drank Irish coffees and held hands, the two sleeping bags outstretched to make a bed. We awoke the next morning to an overturned half-empty cup drenching the sleeping bag.

"Well it's not pee," I said.

Tonya and Thomas called early Christmas morning. Then Maddy and Doro. I know Tom wished he was in his home in Aurora, jousting with his sisters and eating his mother's sausage breakfast casserole. As for me, I was home. Mt. Moriah was just a long ago address.

§

Two days after Christmas, the salt trucks had cleared enough that the delivery trucks could get through. On a Saturday morning, a FedEx driver handed me a box at the door. Before I could open it, Tom rushed into the room and grabbed it from my hands.

"That's definitely bigger than a breadbox," I said. Indeed, it was a large flat carton.

"I'm sorry it didn't get here in time for Christmas," Tom called from the kitchen where he was opening the box so I couldn't see. "Doro had to help me with this one."

"Doro?"

He sauntered back into the living room, the mystery box behind his back.

"Yep, it's a little project we worked on together. It's not wrapped but, well, here." And he lay the feather-light box in my outstretched hands.

What could Tom and Doro have been working on together? Inside the box lay an eighteen by twenty four canvas collage of Grace and me over the years. Dressed as sheep for the Christmas pageant. Trick or treating at age nine. On our bikes in the driveway. My eleventh birthday party, her fourteenth. Eating ice cream on the steps with Tuck. In our waitress uniforms at the Inn, sticking our tongues out at the camera. In prom dresses, hands on hips. Arms linked in our caps and gowns. I was looking into the distance; Grace was smiling directly at the camera.

My feet threatened to buckle, and I sat down hard on the sofa. My face must have registered my feelings. Months of relegating Grace to the deepest corners of my mind, of being a Rivers and not a Wilson, months of pushing Mt. Moriah to the farthest reaches of the earth. Gone. I was back in June 1997, and Grace had just died.

"Thank you," I whispered, so quietly I wasn't sure I had uttered it out loud.

"I know how much you miss your friend," Tom said. He looked intently at my eyes, where tears were gathering. "I thought it was a good idea—kinda bring good memories back to you."

"Yes. It's a really sweet idea." I kissed him lightly on the cheek. "I'm going to make breakfast."

But first I carried the canvas to the guest bedroom, where I slid it, photos to the wall, behind the coats and summer clothes. Then I moved to the bathroom, opened my cosmetic bag and took a strong sip of courage.

That night I couldn't sleep. Since Tom and I had been together, my dreams had slid away like the memories that haunted me. Unlike many wives, I liked my husband's snoring. The syncopated rumbles were soothing, a gentle percussion drowning out my own thoughts. Often I would slide my hand under Tom's pillow, knowing his hand would be there. Linking thumbs or whole hands with him, I would fall into peaceful sleep.

But not on that Christmas weekend. The canvas in the closet taunted me like the porcelain clown on Doro's dresser when I was little. I was so frightened of it Doro put it inside the china buffet. But I knew it was there.

My nightmares returned. They would no longer be eluded by newlywed bliss. My dreams knew me for what I was. They alone knew the secret fear that wrapped around my heart like a snake.

Tom stood sentry over my night terrors. Many times he awakened me, holding my wrists so I wouldn't resist him, turning me into his arms as my heart beat wildly in my chest and tears tracked my cheeks. It was her face, Grace's, that I saw in my dreams, her voice that I heard.

"You're safe, Jo," Tom would whisper. "I'm right here. I got you."

Once I was calmer, when the fear had subsided, Tom pushed my damp hair from my eyes and searched my face for an explanation.

"What is it, Jo? What are you scared of?"

"*Confide in him,*" Dr. Weisz had once said. "*Let him help you. It starts with him knowing everything.*"

But instead I forced a smile and said, "I'm fine, Tom."

And believed myself.

Tom brought up the canvas one evening in February. He was packing for a trip and had gone to the guest room to retrieve his suitcase.

"Well now I know where that canvas is. I wondered where you had hidden it."

I sat cross-legged on our bed, fiddling with the gear in his photography bag.

"It's not that I didn't appreciate it."

"But what?" Tom was distant; he always was when he had work on his mind, and he was leaving for a two-week shoot in London. "If you liked it, you would have put it somewhere that you could see it."

"It just brings back so many memories, and I guess they aren't memories I'm ready to remember."

Tom fastened the strap across the top of his clothes and gave the luggage a final stare. "Yep, I think I got it all," he muttered and zipped up the case. Then he sat down beside me.

"Ya know, Jo, looking at the pictures Doro sent me—and she sent me more than just those—it seems like you had a pretty good friend in Grace."

"Did I ever deny she was a good friend?"

"But doesn't it make you happy to see Grace and remember the good times?"

How could I explain? How could I tell him why I not only wanted to hide pictures of Grace from my sight; I wanted to bury the pictures that lingered in my mind. Wanted to forget her and Mt. Moriah and everything that came before Tom.

"Those pictures looked like the kind of childhood I hope our children have."

"Our children?"

He held my hand, gently rubbing my palm with his thumb. "All four of them."

"Four? I'm not sure I ever agreed to having even one." I grabbed both of Tom's hands. "I might as well tell you, the thought of children terrifies me."

"Why? It's the circle of life. It's the way things go on."

Ever the optimist.

"Until they don't. Until something goes wrong. Until parents die and leave their children alone, or until best friends are murdered."

"Jeez, Jo, you can't think like that! What about the millions of families where that doesn't happen?"

"Like yours." The heavy resentment in my voice surprised me.

Tom lay back on the bed and pulled me down, cradling me under his armpit, our legs balanced on the closed suitcase.

"My favorite dog, Trudy . . ." He paused when I raised up to look at him. "I know, I know, the T thing, anyway she died when I was ten. My grandmother died when I was fourteen, and my grandfather died when I was twenty-two. And the thing is I feel like I need to list out these deaths just to keep up with you."

Clearing his throat, Tom continued. "I never lost anyone suddenly—or anyone who wasn't dying age. But I feel like I have to apologize for having a good, ordinary life, and that's not fair."

"Is that what you think?" I said. "That it's a competition?"

"It's like a contest of grief, Jo. It's like because I've never felt your grief you think I don't understand."

"You don't understand."

"Then help me understand."

"You can't understand because your life has been happy—"

"And so was yours, Jo. All those years in Mt. Moriah were happy years—at least it looks that way. Yes, your parents died when you were little and that's rough, but then you lived with this amazing woman and had this amazing friend—"

"Who died."

Tom pulled his arm out from around me and propped himself up on one arm.

"Yes, and that's horrible—beyond horrible—but how can two bad things wipe out all the good?"

"They don't wipe it out. They . . ." I searched for the word. "They muffle it. It's like how can I enjoy being happy when I don't know what comes next?"

"Seriously? You think like this?"

I had gotten up from the bed and was changing into my nightshirt. I wanted this conversation over. I wanted to lie in his arms and have the words end. I wanted a drink.

"Call me crazy."

"Not crazy, just, I don't know . . ." His hands rubbed his temples, a sign of frustration. "Pessimistic."

Tom sat up.

"So let me get this straight. All the time we've been together, all the good times we've had together, you were waiting for something bad to happen?"

"Waiting for the other shoe to drop." Yes, I had been.

"But doesn't the thought of having kids and playing with them and watching them grow up—doesn't that make you happy?" Tom asked.

"And what if they get hurt? What if something happens to them?"

Tom stared at me as if I were from Mars.

"So you see a cute little girl with pigtails swinging and you think, 'bet she's gonna fall out of the swing and hit a rock and die'?"

"You're making fun of me."

His voice softening, Tom stroked my cheek. "So how did you ever let yourself fall in love with me?"

"I couldn't help it," I sniffled. "But it doesn't keep me from worrying about the future."

"Too much worrying about the future and you miss the present," Tom whispered. "Carpe diem and all that."

The summer before our freshman year in high school, Grace and I were running errands in Target with Genia. Grace and I left Genia in the paper goods and wandered through the racks of clothes. Despite having been raised on a limited budget, Grace had very sophisticated taste in clothes. Snobbish taste, according to Doro.

"It doesn't matter the price of the shirt on your back. What matters is the value of what's inside," Doro said more than once.

As for me, I had an allowance that was burning a hole in my pocket. While Grace's allowance was routinely spent within a few days, I hoarded mine and my paycheck from the Inn. Doro had taught me to value shop. Target was my mecca.

"This is cute," I said, holding up a floral romper for Grace to see. She instantly turned her nose up.

"I don't have any clothes from Target," she said.

"I know you don't. You also don't have any money," I reminded her. "Bet you can find something here you like. You just don't try."

She shrugged and wandered off, gingerly touching the clothes as if they were dirty. Despite her many endearing traits, Grace was a bit of a diva.

In a few minutes, Grace came back, grinning and holding something behind her back.

"Jo Jo, you will be proud. I found us matching t-shirts, and I would actually wear mine. Guess what's on it?" She paused for effect. "Your hint is Robin Williams."

Dead Poets Society had come out that summer, and we had seen it twice, both of us snotty messes at the end. Grace pulled her hands from her back and held up two black t-shirts, with the words Carpe Diem across the front.

"I love it. Let's get them." I reached over and checked the price tag. *"See, they're only five dollars. I told you Target is the best."*

Grace rolled her eyes and then, "I'll have to borrow from you. I'm broke."

Carpe diem. Grace.

"I don't want to lose you," I whispered into Tom's chest.

"So maybe you won't. What if we live to be ninety-five, and our biggest problem is where we put our dentures? What if our kid falls off the swing but just needs stitches, or we have a car accident and just have to find money for a new car? What if the worst doesn't happen?"

I wanted to believe in that, in Tom's happy-ever-after.

But there was that canvas in the closet and shadows in my mind.

21

UNRAVELING

Tom's trip to London was the first of a number of trips he took to Europe in the spring of 2001. With more time on my hands, I frequented my old haunts in Chicago: sitting outside the Macy's on State Street, sipping coffee and feeling the rumble of the el overhead. Sitting in the courtyard outside the Wrigley Building, submerged in the sea of business people and students, all intent on their destination. All busy, all oblivious to me. Sitting on the patio of Houlihan's, in the shadow of the Chicago skyline, sipping Long Island iced teas and swapping office gossip with Megan. During that time, I couldn't help feeling as if Tom didn't exist. Perhaps I had imagined the whole relationship.

I tried to spend as much time as possible at work. Candace was dumping more and more projects on me. Now at S&H for over three years, the excitement of editing other people's copy had worn off. On the bottom of each copy proof was a place for my initials. Every time I penned JAR, I felt diminished. Reduced to just three letters when there was so much more of me—so many words unused within me.

At home more poems stacked up—most bordering on the morbid. My book was going nowhere, and I was restless.

One Wednesday morning in mid-June I happened to be on the elevator with Candace.

"How's the newlywed?" She smiled her brown smile and slid her hands down her hips, smoothing out what was already smooth.

"Not so new," I smiled. "It's been a year actually."

"Oh," she said, examining her hair in the mirrored elevator door. "I didn't realize. That's so . . ." she turned to look at me, her smile forcing her eyes into thin slits, "sweet." She touched my elbow lightly so I would be assured of how very sweet she thought our little marriage was.

I could hear Tom's voice in my head. *Assert yourself. Speak up for yourself.*

"Candace, could we talk sometime about my future here at S&H?" As the words came out I noticed a spot of salad dressing that I was wearing on my black blazer. Very professional.

"Why, JoAnna, the sky is the limit, isn't it?" Candace raised her eyebrows in her carefully perfected "I hear you and appreciate you" facial expression.

"Well it's just that I would like to do some copywriting." I paused and cleared my throat, Tom's voice again in my head. "I'm a good writer."

"I didn't know you wanted to write. Yes, we can certainly talk, JoAnna, but what would we do with your job? You're just too valuable in that role!" The elevator door opened and she stepped out. "But call Nicole and ask her to set up a coffee for us. Cheers!"

So I was too valuable to do more than I was doing. I took the train home that night, instead of waiting for Tom. I got off one stop before our house and went to our favorite liquor store, Windy City Liquors, on the corner. An old man named Louis manned the register and smiled at me as I set bottles of Stoli and Merlot on the counter.

"You look like you had a hard day, miss," said Louis, a toothpick hanging from the corner of his mouth and a half-eaten hoagie behind him.

"Yeah, kind of I guess." I saw the electrician handbook open next to the sandwich and pointed to it. "Studying something?"

"Three more months before I can sit for my electrician license," Louis said in a thick Italian accent.

"Good for you. So I won't see you here anymore?"

Louis smirked. "Ha. I doubt that. My wife just had our fifth." He handed me my brown bag. "But at least maybe money won't be so tight. Maybe take a vacation one day."

"Well, enjoy *your* fifth, miss."

"And congratulations on yours," I said, warmed by his joke. Part of

Chicago's allure were the mom and pop shops I passed every day, and the people like Louis who were threads in my life's quilt.

The sun sinking fast, I hurried the three blocks to our house. Living in downtown Chicago two years ago, I felt a false sense of security. I was brazen and daring. But now in the suburbs, I felt alone, vulnerable, scared of my own shadow. Of all shadows.

At home, I flipped on all the lights. Opening the Merlot, I thought about Louis. How many jobs was he working? How many hours of class was he taking each week in addition to a wife and five children at home? How blessed my life is, I thought. Why can't I be happy?

Suddenly my eyes moistened and there was the threat of tears. A sinus infection had plagued me all week. Damn! Had I forgotten to take my antibiotic? More importantly, had I forgotten my birth control pill? No on both counts. I remembered taking them both before breakfast.

I poured myself a glass of wine and turned on the news, telling myself I would anonymously leave a nice tip on the counter for Louis the next time I went into the store. By the time I had finished my fourth glass, Tom came through the door. I had left the bottle in the kitchen so it wouldn't be so obvious that Mr. Merlot had been my couch companion. The only telltale sign was the heaviness of my eyelids. I may have felt professionally dejected but I was also sinking into a delicious sleepiness.

But Tom didn't seem to notice my slightly sedated state or me in general for that matter.

"Guess what?" he said, performing his nightly ritual of stepping out of his shoes, undoing his belt, and untucking his shirttail, letting out a little sigh with each added bit of freedom.

I shrugged.

"The Tommy Hilfiger campaign won an Addy. That means me!" He leaned over and kissed me hard on the lips. "Hmmm, I think I'll have some wine too!" He headed to the kitchen for a glass, then stuck his head back around the corner. "Your husband has won an Addy. Can you believe it?'

I could believe it, actually. Tom's gritty portraits were what made the Tommy Hilfiger campaign so effective.

"Does Candace know yet?"

He sat opposite me on the sofa. "Of course. She called me to her office to tell me. That's why I was late. She and Adam must have felt pretty confident, because they already had a bottle of champagne chilled."

Once he said that I could see the telltale red in his eyes.

"So you drank champagne with them?"

"We had a toast, yes." Tom leaned across the sofa to kiss me. "Then I came home to celebrate with my baby."

Your *baby*? Since when did he call me that?

"Because I talked to Candace today, and she didn't mention it," I said.

"Maybe they hadn't gotten the word yet. Or she wanted me to hear it first." He took a hefty swig of the wine, then stretched out with his head in my lap. "So what did you talk to Candace about? Writing?"

"Yes, I tried to talk to her but I'm not sure how much she heard. She said we'd have coffee, but then said I was too valuable in my current job."

"Well you are the best."

"That's hardly the point, Tom. I could be writing. I *should* be writing."

"Well, and you'll tell her that over coffee." He reached up and played with my curls, dangling over his cheek. "Remind her you are a famous photographer's woman."

His *woman*? As happy as I was for Tom and what it meant for his career, a little voice inside me wondered when I had stopped being JoAnna Wilson, aspiring writer and become JoAnna Rivers. Someone's *woman*. His *baby*.

Tom's eyes were semi-closed, and I could tell sleep was coming soon for both of us.

"Hey, I don't mean to make this all about me, but can I tell you something else?"

I had to smile at his cuteness. "Go ahead."

"We were celebrating something else in Candace's office. We landed the Higgins Properties account. Twenty locations. I'm going to be able to pass off some of the lesser accounts . . ."

Lesser accounts? Was his ego growing before my very eyes?

"Because I'll need to clear my plate. We'll be traveling for most of July, coming back just in time for the Addys on the 28th."

"We?"

"Candace and I. They're using two different contract writers. They'll be meeting us on the road."

"So you and ol' Candy."

"She's the account exec, Jo. She won the account." He sat up and looked at me quizzically. "Are you terribly jealous of the exotic junket I'm going on? Milwaukee? Toledo? Pittsburgh? Shall I continue?"

"When do you leave?"

"Two weeks."

That night, as tired as we both were, we made love. As our bodies moved in a comfortable syncopation, I stared at the ceiling fan. I was there and yet not.

I was already lonely.

I called Nicole and got on Candace's schedule to have coffee on the day in July she and Tom were to leave for the photoshoots. My husband's career is taking off, I thought. At least I can work on mine.

"I don't know what to say to her," I said the night before. Tom had made my favorite pasta but the sight of it was unappetizing. I chased the ziti noodles around the bowl with my fork.

"Tell her you want to write. It doesn't have to be a big speech." Tom was eating at lightning speed. *Where's the fire?* I could hear Doro say.

"It's not that big a deal."

"It's a big deal to me, Tom."

"That's not what I meant. I just mean that I'm sure Candace expects—that every boss expects—that an employee is going to want to do more or move up the ladder. Just tell her you're willing to work hard and that you're a fabulous writer, if she'll give you the chance."

A piece of ziti accidentally sprung from my fork and landed on the floor.

"Yeah, like Candy Cane would know a fabulous writer if it bit her in her perfect ass."

Tom reached with his napkin to retrieve the errant noodle. "Ya know, you might want to stop calling her Candy Cane so you don't accidentally say it to her face."

I leaned my arms on the table, pushing my untouched pasta away.

"Since when did you stop calling her Candy?"

"Since when did you stop eating?"

Truthfully, the pasta smell had triggered bile rising in my throat since Tom set the bowl in front of me.

"I do eat. My stomach's just been bothering me lately. Now what about my question?"

Tom reached over to stab some ziti from my bowl. "Well she still bothers me," he pointed his fork directly at me. "A lot. But I can appreciate that she does have leadership skills. She does land some big name accounts."

"And beds some big name men!" Seeing from his face I had roused his curiosity, I continued. "Paul McMann's wife thinks Candy is sleeping with him. She asked Joyce."

Paul McMann was our CFO and Joyce his loyal administrative assistant, formatting his contracts and reports for twenty years. Two decades of coffee with three creamers, of reminding him of his wife's birthday, and whispering to him when his tie was stained.

"I'm pretty sure old Paul *is* sleeping with Candace. Not my business. Or yours." Tom stood to begin clearing the dishes. "Can we go back to you not eating?"

"Clearly I eat, Tom." I patted my rump. "I just have a little stomach thing."

Tom deposited the dishes in the sink.

"Jo, do you think you could be pregnant?"

What a ridiculous notion. Especially since I had been so careful, not missing a day.

And yet what if?

The thought set my heart racing and brought that bile back into my throat. What if?

The next morning I was waiting outside Candace's office at 10:00 a.m. I knew that she and Tom were heading to the airport at noon. Tom and I had said our goodbyes in the parking garage that morning.

"You'll take care of the tire rotation?"

"Yes and the house and the mail."

He leaned in for a kiss. It was slow and tender. "Seriously, will you be okay with me gone?"

I said, "Why wouldn't I be?" but I was thinking, *No! Don't go! Don't leave me alone!*

The chairs outside Candace's office were an oatmeal damask. A butler's table in between held recent copies of *Time, Newsweek, Forbes,* and *Glamor.* A porcelain lamp cast shadows across the eternally youthful face of Meg Ryan. Looking up from this magazine, suddenly there were a thousand dots, like fleas, in front of my eyes. Nicole, sitting across the waiting area, was spinning.

"JoAnna! Oh my gosh, are you okay?"

I was on the floor, and Nicole was hovering, waving Meg Ryan's face over mine. Miles Brennan had stopped to help. My pencil skirt was hiked up mid-thigh. I sat up and saw that Candace's door was still closed. I felt the familiar bile and thought I was going to vomit. Accepting their arms, I assured them I was alright but asked that they apologize to Candace for me: I needed to go home.

With each lurch of the train, I fought back phlegm, determined to wait until my stop. I longed for my soft yellow pajamas, worn in the knees and missing a button. I longed for a steamy bath.

And, for the first time in years, I longed for Doro. And home.

When I reached our house, emptied my stomach in the toilet, and changed into my pjs, I called Doro. There were no guests in the Inn, so she was heating up leftovers. Maddy was at church, working on his sermon.

"I was sitting here reading," Doro said, and I could picture her navy recliner, at the corner of their bedroom, where a high window delivered a beam of sunlight, speckled through the pines. Closing my eyes, I could smell the meatloaf warming, could see the crepe myrtles breaking out in ruby measles.

"What are you reading?" I crunched on ice—a bad habit that Doro hated.

"You'll crack your teeth, I keep telling you! I'm reading *The Optimist's Daughter.* Have you not started it yet?"

"I read it in college."

"Oh. Well. So far it's a little strange. What's with all those relatives showing up?"

"You have to get through to the end, Doro."

"Ya know, it reminds me of you."

I couldn't imagine what I had in common with Laurel McKelva and said so.

"Hmmm, maybe it's the place. I don't know . . . just some things she says and thinks."

"Write them down in the margins so we can discuss."

"No, no, it's a library book. But I'll use sticky notes. Anyhoo . . ." I heard the thump of the book against the side table. "What's new with you? Have you been back to Dr. Weisz?"

"Jesus, Doro, how can you go from a pleasant book discussion to nagging me? No, I am not going back to Dr. Weisz. Everything is fine. I just have a little stomach bug, and Tom is gone so I thought I'd call. I guess I missed you."

"Well, that is a sound for sore ears. Why don't you come home this week-end? I'll buy you a ticket."

Honestly, the thought of being back at the Inn was tempting—eating fluffy biscuits on Doro's gingham placemats and pulling worn quilts over me as crickets sang outside.

"I can't come home, Doro. I've told you that."

"That's in your head. You can come home and you should. Laurel did."

"I'm not a fictional character."

"Well, you may as well be for all we see you."

"I have to go, Doro. I just wanted to say hello, and that I love you. Make sure you finish that book in two weeks for our club."

"Eh, I'll try. Now what is wrong with your stomach?"

"Just a little virus or something. No big deal." In my mind, however, Tom's question lingered, and I was counting days. Weeks. When was my last period?

I hung up and climbed into bed, although it was barely eight o'clock. As was my custom when I was alone, every light in the house stayed on. Every part of me hurt. I should get up and drink some water, I thought. But I was too achy to move.

Tom's call woke me up.

"Jo, what the hell? Candace said you wiped out outside her office. You okay? Why didn't you call me?"

"Did you just now hear?" Frankly, I had been expecting his call for the last six hours.

"Yes, obviously. If I had heard earlier, I would have called earlier. I'm outside a restaurant now. We're at dinner, and Candace just told me."

"Nice of her."

"Jo, let's focus on you. What's wrong?"

"I think I have a stomach thing. I'm okay. I'm humiliated that I have to reschedule with her."

"All humans get sick."

"Ah, but Candace is not human!"

He chuckled. "I guess if you can make jokes, you're not too bad off."

"I'm okay." There was a lull between us, filled with the noise of restaurant-goers, the whooshes of air as the door opened and closed.

"Well I better get back in. I'll check with you tomorrow. You sure you're okay?"

"Yes."

"Okay, then I better get back in there before they order for me."

"They? Not just you and Candy? Candace?"

"No Todd's here too. You have nothing to worry about; she has the hots for him I think."

Before we hung up, I blurted out what I had told myself I wouldn't say.

"Tom, before you go, I need to tell you something."

"Yes?"

"I think I'm pregnant."

Tom called back the next day and the next and the next. Each time his question was the same: "Did you take the test?"

And every time my answer was no. I ignored the aisle with the home pregnancy tests. I avoided families on the el and changed the channel at every baby food commercial. I worked longer hours, crackers stashed between files in my drawer.

"Damnit, Jo, don't you want to know?" Tom was calling from Philadelphia, six days post my blurting out the possible news.

"I think it's too soon to show up on a test."

"No that's not true. Candace said that certain kits can tell—"

"Wait. You shared this with Candy Cane?"

Busted, he was.

"Yes, but I wanted to talk to someone, and you haven't seemed to want to talk to me. Anyway, both she and my mom—"

"Your *mom*?" My face flushed with anger. "It there anyone you haven't told *my* news to?"

He was silent for a minute, then, "You mean *our* news."

"It's my news right now. It's, it's nobody's news. We don't even know that there's news!"

"So take the test so we know . . . so I can be justified in screaming the news."

And that's when I realized, like a cold towel across the face, that we were at an impasse: He wanted a baby. I didn't.

The next day I made an appointment at Planned Parenthood.

22

WAITING

ON THAT MONDAY IN THE CROWDED WAITING ROOM, I was surprised by the number of young children, most trailing crusty blankets or huddled around the secondhand Lego table in the corner. Walking from the train to the Planned Parenthood office, I slipped my wedding ring off and into my wallet. Why? Did I feel regret? Embarrassment? Guilt that I, a married woman, was contemplating what I was?

After signing in, I sat on the edge of a mustard vinyl chair in the corner. On my left was a middle-aged Hispanic woman and her teenage daughter. The girl sunk in her chair so that she was balancing on her tailbone. She gnawed at her nubby fingernails, which had once sported a plum polish. An "S" pendant hung where cleavage should be, were the girl not flat-chested. I found myself trying to guess her name. Sarah? Susan? Samantha? Evidently I was staring unknowingly, and our eyes locked. She smiled very slightly, telling me with big basset hound eyes that she was more than an initial. In her anemic smile was a story that I would never know.

I was directed to pee in a cup and then sent back to the waiting room. My spot was occupied by a fifty-something wiry woman with tight white curls and freckles that reminded me of Doro. To her left was a black couple who could not have been over seventeen. His basketball shorts hung around his knees, and his right high top Converse dug an imaginary hole in the linoleum, while he played something on his Nintendo DX.

"I'm hungry," I heard the girl whisper. Distractedly, he held up his right arm so she could dig in his jacket pocket. As she did, she revealed a very pregnant belly. Was she five months along? Seven? I couldn't gauge, knowing nothing about pregnancy, babies, or children. She retrieved a package of M&Ms and adjusted herself in her chair, stopping to rub her belly.

"Marco, feel." Grabbing his free hand, she set it on her protruding stomach. He reluctantly moved his eyes from his Nintendo. Hanging in the air between them was an air of expectation, of uncertainty girded by joy. Another story I would never know.

What do they know about raising a baby, I thought and then, just as quickly, *what do I?*

A policewoman with an attractive face and hair a la Suzi Quatro sat down on the other side of me and smiled. "This place is crowded, huh?"

"Yeah, I guess I'm surprised by how crowded."

"At least there were no protestors this early. They usually get started after lunch." She filled the clipboard form out quickly, in perfect seraph script. "Two months ago I was here with my friend, and we had to walk through them.

"It just about killed her. Creepy."

Protestors: I hadn't thought about that. Truly I hadn't thought about choice or non-choice or life at all. It was never something on my perimeter. The cop was still talking.

"That's why I wore my uniform today. Thought it might keep trouble away."

I felt my stomach do its now familiar flip flops and dug in my purse for a packet of Saltines. Watching me, the woman began talking again.

"I'm not sick at all. Weird, right?"

I smiled, not anxious to continue the conversation.

"Ya know, there are more boyfriends and husbands here than usual." She stuck out her hand. "I'm Jane."

"Clarissa." Had I really just said that?

"What's your story—is your man in the picture?"

"Yes, it's just . . . I'm just exploring my options."

"Oh." Her smile faded a bit. "I don't really have those."

How was I supposed to react to that? My body tensed, and I wanted not to be here talking to this woman. To not be anywhere.

"Me and Jared—my husband—have twin three year olds and a ten month old and three jobs between us. His mom lives with us; she don't work, and his daddy done run out on her." She popped a piece of gum in her mouth. "No one told me you can get pregnant when nursing."

"Oh, I, I didn't know that either."

"Now I knew about the antibiotic thing; that's how my friend Justine got knocked up."

"Wait, what about antibiotics?"

"Oh yeah, them with the pill makes it not work."

My sinus infection. Damn!

"Jo Wilson?"

I arose immediately when I heard my name, then remembered the lie I had told. Turning back to Jane, I said, "I'm Clarissa Jo."

She laughed, revealing a tooth missing at the side of her mouth. "Yeah you are," she said.

The frumpy woman who called me back had reddish hair parted by a skunk stripe. It was difficult to gauge her age: one of those women who seems stilted in time. Pinned to the top of her pink scrubs was a name badge (Angie) and a wide button with six laughing children's faces. She directed me to a chair in a room the size of a closet. On one wall was a cross-stitched "Tomorrow is the first day of the rest of your life," and on the other an enormous poster of the female reproductive system, including a uterus with fetus tucked inside. I looked away and asked about her button.

"Are those your kids?"

She kissed her finger, then the button. "Grandkids. I have seven now; this was before the baby was born."

"Wow, you don't look old enough to have grandchildren."

Smiling, she revealed braces on her teeth. "I started young. I was nineteen when my oldest was born. Then I had three more lickety-split."

Her voice revealed a Southern drawl. Alabama perhaps?

She took my blood pressure and temperature. To settle my nerves, I kept talking.

"You have a Southern accent."

She smiled broadly. "And you do too! I'm from Mississippi—about twenty miles South of Jackson."

"How long have you been here?"

She finished making notes on her clipboard and then leaned back in her seat, rubbing knees that obviously ached. "Let's see, my Jimmy got a job driving trucks, and we moved here around '87. All these years and I still haven't gotten used to the winters.

"Now, let's talk about you. Your test results are positive."

"I'm pregnant." Those foreign words echoed against my heart that threatened to pump out of my chest.

"Yes indeed. When was your last period?"

I thought back. "It was around May 20. But I've been on the pill; I never missed a day."

"No days missed? Were you on an antibiotic by chance?"

"Yes, I had never heard about that."

She smiled sweetly. "Most people haven't. At any rate that puts you at about seven weeks. That would make your due date February 24." She scribbled more notes. "Of course, these dates are an estimate." She put the clipboard down and scooted her stool closer. "So I assume you are here to talk about options."

"Yes," I said quietly, then interjecting a "ma'am." I'm not sure why I added that, except that Angie seemed old and wise and so comforting. I could listen to the gentle lilt of her voice all day long. I wanted to climb into her ample lap and have her read me a story. "I mean, I wasn't planning to do anything today."

"Honey, that's not how it works. Today we determine whether you are pregnant, and we send you along with some information. Are you considering termination?"

Hideous word. "Yes, I guess. I mean, that's why people come here right?"

She chewed on her lips and arched her eyebrows dramatically. "Well, if you believe certain politicians, that's all we're here for, but the truth is that termination is a very small part of what we do. Many women come to us because they want to consider other options: adoption, for instance. Or because they're pregnant and need pre-natal care."

She tucked a strand of greying hair behind her ear and continued. "You seem like a professional woman. Let's see . . ." She consulted my paperwork.

"You work for an ad agency? Well that must be nice. I'm sure you have insurance, right?"

To my nod, she said, "You're lucky. So many women don't have it. That's why we're here. A huge part of what we do is screenings. Women who can't afford to get a pap or mammogram somewhere else."

She slid the stool to the drawer underneath the examination table and pulled out some brochures: *Your Baby and You. Caring for Yourself. Understanding Abortion. Adoption Resources.* My eyes clung to the pamphlet on top: *Making the Right Decision for Yourself.*

A lone tear slid down my cheek. "How do I make the right decision?"

She handed me a box of Puffs. "There is a mandatory counseling session that most women find helpful. Beyond that, you have to think about what you want. No one else can tell you that."

"Do most women . . ." I trailed off, unsure of what I intended to ask.

"There are no mosts here, honey. I've seen girls barely thirteen years old who were pregnant with their daddy's baby and refused to terminate. Women who walked in here so beat up by their husbands they could hardly open their eyes. Some choose one path, some another. Yesterday I worked with a woman who has five children under the age of seven. Husband works two jobs and won't let her use birth control. Thinks it's the Lord's plan if she gets pregnant." She cleared her throat. "Her mother brought her here."

Angie patted my knee. "But you know what all those women have in common with you?" When I shook my head, she said, "Nothing. Every woman is different. Every situation is different. That's what the counseling is for."

Both cheeks were now lined with tears, and my throat choked. "I'm married," I whispered, almost as an apology.

"I see," she said. She was quiet for a minute, watching my face contort with the tears. Wise woman that she was, she knew they needed to come. Then, from out of nowhere, "I had an abortion when I was fifteen."

My eyes immediately turned to that button—those laughing children.

"I grew up in rural Mississippi. Kind of place where everyone's up in your business. Boy's name was Chad, and it was in the back seat of his Camaro the night of the state championship. He was three years older, wanting to go to med school.

"I knew it would ruin his life, or so I thought. I knew my daddy would kill me, or so I thought. So I confided in my aunt, and she drove me up to Memphis to the Planned Parenthood office there. Two years later I met Jimmy, and on my eighteenth birthday we got married in the Church of Christ downtown. I started nursing school the next week and had my first baby right before our first anniversary. Jimmy wasn't Chad. He was the right one."

She pulled an appointment card from her pocket. "We'll need to see you back in two weeks, for your counseling session. Set aside a couple of hours to spend with us. We'll be doing a pelvic exam at that time too." She paused. "You can bring your husband if you want."

Tom. In two weeks he would be back. I couldn't imagine him in this place. Right now, I couldn't imagine him at all.

Angie ushered me toward the door. "God bless you, honey. You'll make the right choice. Now give this card to the front desk, and they'll make your appointment."

Two weeks. It must seem an eternity for a scared teenaged girl. I tried to picture the Angie of fifteen, sitting in a Memphis waiting room. I looked at the card in my hand. July 30, it said. Two days after the Addys.

I passed Angie again on my way out.

"Can I ask you one more thing?" She nodded. "Have you ever regretted your decision—the one you made when you were fifteen?"

Angie's smile was weak but warm. Wistful. Wise.

"Sometimes yes. Most days I think it was the right thing." Angie put her hand on my arm. "But I work here because I'm thankful I had a choice. Every woman deserves one."

Out on the street, even though the sun was blazing down, I felt goosebumps on my arm. Not caring who saw, I walked to the trash can in front of me and vomited. I wiped my mouth with the damp Kleenex balled up in my fist and looked up to see the spire of the Loyola chapel, not three blocks away. Onto the small pool of spittle in the trash I tossed all of the brochures except one.

That one I kept.

23

THE ABYSS

"ARE YOU PREGNANT, LITTLE THING? Is that what's on your mind?" Maddy's excitement was obvious. I had omitted the fact that I went to Planned Parenthood, what I was considering. We were walking back to the house, as storm clouds rolled in from the west.

"I think I might be." I could not look Maddy in the eye, nor could I tell him the truth.

"Hot dog!" He picked me up and spun me around, only a half turn, clutching his chest as he set me back down.

"You should get that looked at, Maddy. Might be more than a pulled muscle."

"Nah, you're just getting heavy, little thing." Maddy took his hand off his chest and grabbed mine.

We spent the evening cooking together and watching mindless television, our conversation starting and stopping in little bits.

"Will Tom be happy?"

"He really wants a baby. It's me that doesn't know." We had finished the dishes, and I headed for the sofa, unable to keep my eyes open. "I don't know if I can be a mother, Maddy."

Maddy sunk into the leather recliner. "Ya know, Doro was in her fifties when she became a mother to you." He kicked off his shoes. "What scares you?"

"I don't know, everything. I don't know anything about children. What kind of mother would I be? I just don't know that I'm ready to bring a child into this world."

"Well, you have no option there, do you?" said Maddy. Of course, in his world, there was no "choice," no option. "But you would be a wonderful mother; why would you not be?"

How to explain that motherhood meant surrendering, losing, more of myself—relinquishing any control over my own future.

"Children just weren't part of my plan—not now anyway," I said. "I still want to be a writer."

"Writers don't have children?" Maddy asked. "Maybe children aren't part of your plan, but they're part of God's plan."

"Oh my gosh, you sound like Tom. You and your plans and your God."

I could tell I had struck a chord with Maddy. His eyes flared.

"My God? You mean our God, Jo."

I was quiet, knowing I had offended him. I also knew how I felt.

"I'm not sure I believe anymore, Maddy." I paused to gauge the look on his face. It was one of concern, one that said he was trying hard to listen, to not speak. "Once Grace died, I just—"

He interrupted. "You closed yourself off—from Doro, from me, from everyone."

"Because everyone's lives were going on, and Doro was so insistent that I take that job in Chicago; it was like no one noticed that Grace had been killed, that I . . ." I stopped myself before I entered a conversation I didn't want to have.

"Doro insisted you take that job because she wanted you to move on with your life. Did you know she cried every night because she missed you and worried about you?" Maddy waited for a response that didn't come.

Maddy came over to the sofa and pulled me against him. "Listen, I know you are still grieving the loss of your friend. We all are, but I know you are especially because you were supposed to be on a walk with Grace that day."

His words pierced my soul.

"Maddy, you heard that I had to work—that that's why I wasn't able to walk with Grace?"

"Yes, but it's not your fault. Your being there would not have changed anything."

Maddy was quiet for a moment, then continued.

"But I hate to hear that what happened to Grace took away your faith or made you think this is not a world to bring a baby into," Maddy squeezed my hand. "This is the world that brought you and Tom together. One evil thing doesn't make it a bad world."

I looked up into those beautiful eyes and wanted more than anything to believe. But secret pains constricted my heart, and I could not.

"I don't believe in a God that would let what happen to Grace happen. It doesn't make any sense."

"You're right, it doesn't make any sense. But I still believe. And I suspect that deep down inside, you do too."

We sat there quietly, as the grandfather clock in the hall ticked its way steadily toward bedtime. Past bedtime. I was tired of explaining myself—to Maddy, to Tom. I wanted to close my eyes and be in an all-white apartment overlooking Lake Michigan, a cup of strong coffee in a stoneware mug, my computer before me. I wanted pages piling up in a box, and my agent leaving voice mails on the answering machine. Most of all, I wanted to be able to call Grace and plan a girls' weekend in Chicago.

We sat there so long that we both nodded off—roused by the stroke of eleven on the clock.

"You need sleep, little thing," said Maddy. "You sure you're sleeping okay in the April room?" He paused. "You don't want to sleep up in your old room? I can clean out that old air conditioner."

I wanted no part of my room, the place where Grace and I had shared secrets, learned to dance, and spent the wee hours of the mornings whispering. That room, hovering at the top of the attic stairs, was like the giant canvas in my Chicago closet.

"No, Maddy, I'm good."

He kissed me on the cheek and headed toward his room. Pausing in the door frame, he turned to look at me.

"I love you, little thing. If you are pregnant, Doro would be so happy."

Ringing in my ears, as I started down the hall toward April, were his words. *You were supposed to be with Grace that day.*

I spent the next morning in bed, sleeping until past noon. At some point

Maddy came into the room, set a bagel and cream cheese and a glass of iced tea on my nightstand with a note that he was going to visit someone in the hospital.

Tom's call woke me up around one.

"I've tried to call several times. I've been checking on you with Maddy."

"You don't need to check on me."

Tom cleared his throat. I could tell he was trying to stay calm.

"There was a message on the machine, Jo. You missed your appointment."

"I know."

"What does that mean?"

"It means my aunt died and I left town and missed my appointment."

"But what does it mean . . . for us?"

"I don't know. But I know you left me. I have to go, Tom."

I couldn't tell him that I didn't know myself. All I knew was that I felt completely alone, shut off from my husband, from Maddy. And I was not ready to return to the world—to their questions, to the decisions in front of me.

I just wanted to be swallowed up by magnolia branches: to be invisible.

I nibbled at my bagel, drank the tea, and took my dishes to the kitchen. Passing Doro's corkboard I noticed the calendar. No one had turned the page from July to August.

There at the bottom, screaming at me, was July 30.

Tom returned home the day before the Addys. It was Friday morning, and when he called from O'Hare I was hunched over my cubicle desk, a forty-eight-page annual report before me, my eyes squinting against the columns of numbers.

"There's my girl. I'm home!"

I smiled. His was a voice you had to smile at. "Hi. Sorry I couldn't get you from the airport. I'm really racing against the clock. This proof has to go back to the printer by the end of the day."

"No problem. I'm not much fun, and I think I stink. I'm ready for a shower and a nap."

"There's some leftover pizza in the fridge; I'm afraid there's not much more."

"Okay. You know what I really want?"

I knew.

"Yes, I took the test."

"And?"

"I am pregnant," I whispered.

A scream erupted from the other end of the phone, and I could imagine the look on his face. "Screw that annual report and get home so I can hold my baby." He paused. "Both my babies."

The lump was like a brick in my throat.

"Tom, I gotta go. I'll see you tonight."

"Okay, go be responsible. Hey, but Jo."

"Yes?"

"I love you."

I hung up, tears clouding the profits and losses.

When I got home, just past eight, the sun was low in the sky, and Tom had cleaned the kitchen, done laundry, and showered, his wavy hair still damp.

"Hey."

"Hey back." I moved into his arms and clung tightly. "I missed you," I said, surprising myself with how much I meant it. "It feels like you've been gone forever."

"I know. So ready to be back." He pried my arms from around his waist and looked me up and down. "How are you feeling? You look beautiful!"

"I'm okay . . . just nauseous and tired all the time."

"I brought you a present."

"Oh?"

"Yeah, I was hoping I hadn't bought it in vain since I wouldn't be able to return it." He pulled a small blue bag from his briefcase.

I reached inside and felt a book. He knew there was no shorter path to my heart than a book. I smiled and pulled it out. Immediately, my smile dimmed.

I was holding *What to Expect When You're Expecting*.

That night I feigned fatigue and huddled on my corner of the bed far from Tom's reach. My mind replayed our dinner-time conversation: all focused on babies and birth.

"Let's call my parents. Have you told Doro and Maddy?"

"Lots of pregnancies don't make it to twelve weeks, and I'm not there yet. Let's wait, okay?"

Tom agreed and I silently cursed myself. I was duplicitous, deceitful. The card that said July 30 screamed obscenities at me from my purse. When at last I heard Tom's breathing deepen into a rhythmic snore, I turned and whispered to the back of his t-shirt.

"I need to talk to you."

"Hmmm," he muttered in his sleep.

But my voice was silenced by fear. By cowardice and a desire for privacy. And so we slept together, secrets suspended in the space between us.

The Addys were held in the Sheraton downtown. Tom and I posed for a photographer from the *Tribune*. Although he had never been textbook handsome, Tom looked delicious in his tux. The royal blue sequined dress I borrowed from Lori fit surprisingly well. Her waist was a couple of inches smaller than mine, and I was concerned that mine had expanded in the previous weeks. However, when I stepped on the scale that morning, I was down a couple of pounds— undoubtedly lost to the trash cans in S&H. The blue dress pushed my tender breasts up and cinched my waist, and I felt pretty for the first time in months.

"You're very distracting in that dress," Tom said as we waited in line at the bar. "A gin and tonic and one plain tonic," Tom told the bartender. He handed me my anemic drink with a shrug. "Sorry—hate to drink in front of you."

About fifteen minutes into the program, the Sandalwood & Harris Addy was announced. Tom, Candace, and Adam, along with a couple of other people I didn't know well, were beaming on stage. Tom looked directly at me and winked.

See that, Grace. That's him. That's my heart, I thought. *Grace. Where are you, Grace? I need you!*

Tom returned to his seat. I leaned over and kissed him on the cheek.

"I'm very proud of you," I whispered.

"You are?" He was a little six-year-old boy, wanting my reassurance.

"Very, very proud."

"I'm proud of me too," he whispered sheepishly, his dimples taking twenty years off his age. The award show had already lasted an hour, and I could tell from the program that we had another hour to go. A server came and removed the rubber beef, bloody and barely touched, from in front of me.

"I could ask them for something else," Tom whispered, though we both knew he couldn't.

"No, I'm fine. I ate the potatoes and salad."

"Baby doesn't like his meat rare." Tom pulled my hand to his lips. Had he ever seemed happier?

My face flushed, and I felt hot all over.

"I'm going to the restroom."

"You okay?"

"Yeah, sure. I just want to get some water, and I have to pee."

I gently pushed the heavy door of the ballroom to and walked toward the bathroom. There was a crowd outside—women of assorted ages and sizes, adjusting their dresses, waiting in line to reapply makeup. I felt invisible to their chatter.

In front of me was the bar. I looked around, unsure who or what I was looking for. The only person who could possibly care about my stopping at the bar was floating on his own personal Cloud Nine inside the ballroom.

Sucking in my stomach, as if there were anything to suck in, I requested a vodka tonic from the bartender. It went down in three swallows, and I followed a hunch, circling the ballroom to find a different bartender on the back corridor. Passing fifteen minutes there, I returned to the first bartender who undoubtedly presumed the glass I extended for a refill was the one he had originally handed me.

"You having a nice evening, miss?"

"Oh yes. My husband is the talk of the town. I have a dead end job I'll probably be doing the rest of my life. The person who loved me longer and better than anyone was murdered, and I'm pregnant with a baby I don't want. And my prime rib was bloody."

Such were my thoughts. What I said was: "Could you make it a double please?"

With the third vodka, I felt the familiar sharpening of colors and shapes. The liquor coated not only my throat but my nerves, giving me a false sense of peace. Like everything that could never be right again would be. Once I had taken the last sip I turned and almost bumped against Tom.

"What are you doing?" His voice was shaky, his tone a cocktail of rage, fear and concern. "Are you drinking?"

"I just had . . ." I paused. The vodka was not playing nice with the greens in my stomach. "Tom, I have to . . ." I stepped out of my slingbacks and reached the bathroom in time to retch in the toilet. Mercifully, the bathroom was vacant, and I sunk down onto the toilet seat, the small space spinning around me. I made it to the sink and splashed cold water on my face, my beaded chest.

I looked into the gilded mirror and saw not a professional woman, not an elegant party-goer. I saw the scared little girl going to Woodbury Elementary in the early 1980s. I saw the teenage girl huddled over her composition book, pages filled, pencil digging a crevice in her finger. I saw the girl whacking the elephant ears and dancing at the prom with her best friend.

I saw failure. And remorse. And fear.

"You've got to face this," I whispered to myself as an older woman, three facelifts to her credit, pushed past me toward a stall.

What I had to face was Tom.

He sat on a low bench between the bathrooms. He had removed his tie, and his lanky legs crossed in front of him at the ankle. Those beautiful grey eyes spoke volumes. In one hand was his award. In the other dangled my black heels. Dejected and deserted: them and him. I wanted to bury his head in my chest, to hold him until the look on his face was erased. But I knew I had done something—was about to do something—that was not erasable.

"I'm sorry."

He didn't say a word. Just stared straight ahead—at me? Past me?

"I guess I shouldn't have . . ." Why wasn't he speaking? Where was that giddy smile I had seen on stage? I knew: I had taken it away.

"Did you throw up?" Tom said finally.

"Yes, just a little."

"Are you okay?"

I reached out and took my heels from his hand. "I'm fine. We can go back in." I reached for Tom's hand, but he snapped it back as if mine carried an electric charge.

"Is the valet slip in your purse? It's not in my pocket." His eyes stayed locked with mine.

"Tom, are you mad? I just so wanted a drink. Just a little drink."

He took my hand then, steadying me as I pulled on my left heel. "You scare me, Jo," he whispered. "I don't know what you're thinking. You know you shouldn't be drinking. You have to think about—"

"The baby?" I finished his sentence a bit too ruefully. "It was just a couple of drinks, Tom." I almost lost my balance trying to put on the other shoe. "I'm fine."

"You don't look fine. Here." Taking my purse from me, he stood to let me have the bench. "Let me look for the valet slip." My purse was so tiny that the valet slip was easy to find.

As was the Planned Parenthood appointment card.

The ride home, although only forty minutes, seemed endless. Tom maintained both hands on the wheel, steely gaze straight ahead. Was this the man who had rescued me from Tony's? Pulled me to him when I collapsed in tears at song lyrics? The man beside whom I had agreed to spend the rest of my life on the Loyola courtyard? Why, then, did he seem a stranger? Or perhaps I had become the stranger.

When we reached the house, Tom threw the car into park, turned off the ignition with a jerk, and came around to my door, helping me out. Ever the gentleman.

Even when he hated me.

Inside, Tom moved through the house like a madman, flipping switches—as if to expose me for what I was. I stood behind a wingback chair in the living room, waiting. I was cold sober now, but the bitter taste permeated my stomach, my mouth. My heart.

In Tom's hand was the appointment card. He had not torn, bent, or crumpled it. Perhaps to do so would have made it real. He spoke finally.

"Is this what I think?"

I cleared my throat. "I went to Planned Parenthood a couple of weeks ago—to have the test done. That's when I found out I'm pregnant."

Tom smirked, a chilly, mean chuckle that I did not recognize. "People don't go to that place for a pregnancy test, Jo*Anna*." His emphasis on my name diminished me: I was a child in his eyes. "They go to Walgreen's for that."

"I went for several things. I wanted to find out my options." I grabbed the chair more firmly for support. "I'm not happy about the baby like you are, Tom."

"And so you, what, want an abortion? Is that what this appointment is for?"

"The appointment is for counseling. They make sure you've thought about it . . ."

The smirk again. "Oh, good to know. So have you been thinking about this— what, for several weeks? Were you going to share this with me?"

"I, I wasn't sure how you'd feel. I wasn't sure you'd support my decision."

"*Your* decision? Yours? You mean ours?" He flung the card at me. "That's *our* baby. That means mine too."

"And my body."

He turned and began to pace, like a puppy caged at the shelter. Desperately wanting a home.

"For God's sake, I'm Catholic, Jo."

"And I'm not! You want me to have a baby I don't want? To be a mother if I don't want to be?"

"You don't want children? Not ever?"

"I didn't say that. I don't know. I just know that I'm not ready to be a mother. I can barely . . ." My voice caught in my throat. "I feel like I'm drowning, like I can barely take care of myself."

"And so you would give it up just like that? Because it might be hard?"

"I don't know that I want to bring a child into this world—"

"*This* world? We'd be bringing it into our world, yours and mine. Jo, it's part of us. It continues us."

My voice sounded angry, although I don't think I was. Hurt. Confused. But not angry—not at Tom, never at him. "Tell me you're not going to give me an ancestry speech, Tom. Why do we need a baby to continue, Tom? Why not just us?"

"Because that's the way the world works. It's the way things go on." Calmer now, Tom took my hand, the brocade chair between us. "I want a family. I want to fight about money, and lose sleep when the kids are sick, and be so tired we can't see straight. I want all of that."

"And I'm your incubator?"

The look on his face said I had wounded him.

"You're my wife. I want the baby—with you. I love that I know when you're about to get your period because you slam cabinet doors, and I love that we argue about whether the fruit goes on the counter or in the refrigerator." Dropping my hand, Tom ran his hands through his hair so that little spikes stood up, eavesdropping. "I love the way your hair is so straight when it's wet, but when you wake up, those curls have overtaken you.

"I love that we fantasize about a new refrigerator and can't afford it. I want everything that kids bring—stepping on toys and cleaning poop. I want the whole messy family life."

Then he took my hand back. "But it's all because I want you." Pause. "And I thought you wanted all that too."

What did I want? I wanted my best friend back. I wanted to be a writer, a real writer. I longed to live in a high-rise in downtown Chicago. I wanted someone to take away the fear that haunted me, that paralyzing fear of something evil. Lurking.

"I don't know what I want. I want to be me."

Tom looked at my hand, analyzing its contours like an ancient fossil only recently excavated.

"And you can't be you with me? You can't be you with a baby?"

"I don't know. I just want to have the chance to decide. I want some control over my—"

He grabbed my hand again. "There's no such thing as control, Jo. You of all people should know that. Think of Grace—"

I yanked my hand away. "Grace?" I took a step backward. "You are bringing up Grace?"

"She died and it hurt you. It was something outside your control."

"It *changed* me." My ears filled with tears. "It changed me in ways you don't know, ways you can't possibly know. So don't you dare bring her into this when you . . . when you don't understand."

"Then help me understand, Jo. Tell me what I don't understand. I know you better than anyone, Jo. Talk to me."

My voice was shrill around my sobs. "The person who knew me better than anyone is dead." Then I said what I should never have said, perhaps didn't even mean. "You don't know me at all, Tom."

And with that, Tom stared down at the floor for what seemed an eternity, then left the room. I heard the opening of our closet door, the banging of drawers. When he returned, he had changed clothes and was holding a duffle bag.

"Where are you going?" I was subdued now, regretting words I could not take back. *Stay*, I thought. *I need you*, I pleaded silently.

"I don't know. To Rod's I guess. I can't stay here." Tom waited, atoms of silence splitting the distance between us. I wanted to reach out, ask him to stay, to tell him . . . everything. My mind flashed on Grace's casket lowering into the ground. And with it her secret. And mine.

Yet I said nothing.

"There's a dark place in you, Jo." Unblinking, Tom's eyes focused on my face. "There's a place I can't reach, a place you won't let me in."

"I'm scared," I said finally.

"Scared of what? Of me?"

"Of everything. Of us."

"I think we're pretty great. I like us." He moved closer but didn't touch me. How could part of me want to lean in, press my head onto his shoulder, and the rest of me want to run like the wind.

"We are great. You're great. You're too great. I just don't know what happiness looks like." Tom waited for me to finish, his eyes not moving from mine. "I guess it just seems too good to be true."

When Tom spoke, his voice had grown colder—an iciness I had not heard before.

"Is this the I-don't-know-how-to-be-happy conversation? Is there a pity party to follow?"

I took another step backward, almost toppling the floor lamp behind me. Did he really just say that?

Tom rubbed the back of his neck. Ruffling his hair first this way and that like the nap of a carpet, his hand paced. Then he stopped. *Just hold me*, I thought. *Just stop talking and hold me.*

"Here's the thing, Jo. Sometimes it *is* that simple. It doesn't have to be hard to be happy." He paused, waiting for a response while I picked at a loose fiber in the top of the chair. "My parents have been together almost forty years. Sometimes I think when it's easy it's really love."

Dr. Weisz's voice rang in my head. *"You are going to have to open up to Tom, JoAnna. You're going to have to talk, tell your story. That is the path toward happiness."*

"My parents and Grace . . ." I could say no more. My feelings were locked in a safe at the pit of my heart.

Now Tom's hands pressed on either side of his temples.

"They're dead." His voice was loud now. *Stop,* I thought. *Stop talking. Just hold me.* "It's not fair, and you miss them. I get it. But what does that have to do with you and me?"

His voice calmer now, Tom leaned in and cupped my chin in his right hand.

"What does that have to do with us being happy? What keeps you from being happy?"

If only I could tell him. If only I could tell him the secret that I had tried to bury with drinking and flirting and work and maudlin poems. And perhaps with marriage. The private guilt that surrounded and consumed me. But I could not. Perhaps I didn't trust Tom enough; perhaps I didn't trust myself enough. Maybe giving voice to my fears would make them even more real. Possibly, deep down inside, I was afraid that, once named, those fears would consume me. Destroy Tom's love for me.

And so I had no answer. There was an emotional bridge I couldn't cross, an explanation I couldn't give. A breath I couldn't draw and a feeling I couldn't escape. Was it possible for me to live life without a foot on Billy McGuiness' train tracks?

My voice came out in a whisper.

"I just. Need. Space," I choked out.

Tom's hand fell then, and he stepped back. First one step, then two and three. With each one, his hands spread out in the air.

"Space?"

When I didn't reply, Tom asked the question that would never have occurred to me. "Is there someone else?" His voice warbled like a kindergartener wanting to hear his mother's voice.

"No, of course not. How could you think that?"

"How could I think anything, Jo? How could I think at all? Help me understand, if you want me to *think* something. Otherwise, my mind will continue to run circles. What is this space for?"

I studied the loose fiber on the chair. Unraveling like me, like us. I couldn't answer and instead just shook my head. Ringing in my ears, my silence was the loudest form of self-sabotage.

Tom shrugged, a weary movement that told me he wished he had married someone less complicated, that his love was a little bit diminished, that I was losing him.

In a guttural whisper, equal parts regret and fatigue, Tom hissed, "You're afraid of being happy. Afraid to let me make you happy. And here's the thing. That's something I can't fix. That's something *you* have to fix. You have to wake up and decide to be happy."

I smirked then. "As simple as that, huh?"

Anger now flamed from his eyes.

"Yes, Jo. As simple as that. You have to choose happiness. And you have to choose me."

I said nothing. My head was pounding, and I wanted a drink. I wanted to pull the covers over my head. But most of all, I wanted Tom to hold me and stop talking. It really wasn't him I wanted space from; it was his words, the way he stared at me.

Perhaps if I had told him that, perhaps if I had just asked to be held, his response would have been different. As it was, I pushed him into saying the words I most dreaded.

Tom sighed heavily—a long, empty sigh, devoid of life and air. Then he moved to the door and grabbed his jacket. I knew it was soft and smelled of him. *Don't*, I thought. *Stop him*, I thought.

But I was silent.

"You want space, Jo?" In Tom's voice now was the cool hatred of a man who had been pushed too far, a man who had given everything he had. "Look at me, Jo."

When I finally looked up, he reached for the doorknob.

"I'll give you space," he said. "But I want you to keep your eyes on this door. Because you are about to see the best friggin' thing in your life walk away."

Tom swung open the door and then paused. My body tensed for the slam that was coming, but it didn't. *Say something,* I said to myself. *Stop him.*

Looking straight into my eyes one last time, Tom spoke the words that pierced my soul. "I love you. But I'm walking away."

And with that the door slammed, vibrating the wall and shaking the wedding sampler that Doro had made. Only then did I move, rushing toward the door, throwing my arms against it and sobbing. But I didn't open it. Nor did I know that Tom was on the other side, his head leaning against the door, tears welling in those beautiful grey eyes.

It was just a door. And yet an abyss we could not cross.

After the longest Sunday of my life, Monday came: July 30. I called in sick. It was only a half lie. Tom didn't call to check on me. Still in my pajamas at noon, I kept the appointment card in my pocket: 3:00 p.m. I still wasn't sure if I was going. I didn't want to go alone. I didn't want to *be* alone. But I was. All alone.

At one o'clock, the phone rang and my heart leapt. I answered it on the second ring.

"Tom?"

Silence at the other end, then that sweet familiar voice.

"It's Maddy. Little thing, you need to come home. It's Doro.

"Come home."

24

FROM RAIN TO SUN

THE LAST THING I WANTED TO DO was call Tom. He had walked out. But on that July 30, I knew I had to. Tom's phone went to voice mail.

"Tom, I got a call from Maddy today. Doro died . . ." My voice cracked. "I'm going home, Tom."

And then, before I hung up, before the message cut me off, "Love you."

I took two red eyes and reached Mt. Moriah just as the sun was pushing through the clouds. The day before, Doro pulled twelve Big Boys from the vine, dropped them into her basket, carried the tomatoes to the counter next to the sink. One was still a little green, so Doro set that one on the window sill to ripen. She wiped her forehead with the back of her gardening gloves and then slumped to the floor.

A massive stroke. She never regained consciousness.

Thoughts of Doro interrupted my thoughts constantly, and yet I had not yet cried for her. Four days had passed since I approached her casket, looked in at the face that was as peacefully asleep as Betty Mahoney's. Three days since the ground covered her up, burying my childhood and with it all the secrets that ever existed between Doro and me.

Although on one hand the hours and days seemed to slide aimlessly into the next, I was also keenly aware of the passage of time and distance. I knew that seven days had passed since I saw Tom. Seventy-eight days since my last period.

Six days since July 30.

Three miles to Tuck's house.

It was nearing six o'clock in the evening and the relentless sun was giving up when I reached the Tucks' house that Saturday evening. Christian Tuck's childhood home was at the end of a cul-de-sac in a subdivision, Newman Farms, built on the site of the old Newman estate. I vividly remember Doro and Maddy shaking their heads as the land was cleared in the late '80s.

"All those trees! That's a crying shame." Maddy had said, shaking his head.

On Tuck's front lawn stood the largest oak of all, eighty years in the making. Perhaps because the Tucks demanded it, perhaps because the contractor sensed the wrath of the town, that oak remained. The driveway encircled the oak, so that in summer the front door was obscured. The massive tree slid shade across the pale grey siding and the stone encircling the arched front porch.

How many times had I visited that house and yet, my hand on the brass knocker, it was if for the first time. I turned and looked out to the street, trying to see past the oak, but its broad branches were all I could see. Turning back I saw chubby hands pressed up against the side window.

Tuck pried his son's fingers from the window and swung the door open. "Look, Andy, we have company!"

I handed Tuck a bottle of Chardonnay. I had driven twenty-five miles into the next town to find a liquor store. Grocery stores in Mt. Moriah didn't carry wine, and no one had yet opened a liquor store in the dry Southern town. The wine now seemed out of place, juxtaposed against a man, a toddler, and a half-eaten box of animal crackers.

"Hi, Andy," I said, wishing I had taken Maddy's suggestion of bringing him a gift. Although children were a mystery to me, a bit frightening actually, the little boy in front of me was as intoxicating as any wine, and I could barely take my eyes off him. He had Tuck's hair— so blonde it was almost white, and long eyelashes that curved up and over his blue eyes. And his fingers. So stubby. So . . . perfect.

Tuck balanced Andy, the animal crackers, and the wine and led me into the kitchen. I was back in high school: Beverly Tuck had not changed a thing. The same rose vine wallpaper wrapped around the large kitchen. Ivory cabinets segued to white tile counters, with various fruit tiles punctuating the starkness. Above her planning desk was the huge corkboard her husband had installed when we were in middle school. Recipes, appointment cards, and pictures dotted the landscape so there was barely an inch of cork showing.

"Tuck, are these Sarah's girls?" I asked. Sarah was Tuck's older sister, in college years before us. I did a quick mental calculation that she must be in her thirties now.

"Yep, she has three. Can you believe it? They're in Savannah. Stair steps."

A husky female voice chimed in, "Which makes our Andy the only grand-son and therefore the little prince!" A tall, female version of Andy stepped out from behind the refrigerator. "I'm Debra. It's so nice to finally meet you!"

I wanted to hate her—not only for her breasts and figure but because she had stolen Tuck's heart, and that heart was meant for Grace. Or me. Or both of us.

But the truth was that, try as I might, I couldn't hate Debra: I couldn't even dislike her. All during dinner—which was far more edible than I had been led to expect—she kept food on Andy's highchair tray while Tuck and I told one story after another from high school. Smiling often, she laughed on cue, seeming utterly at peace in her own skin. And with Tuck.

Around 7:30, it was clear Andy had had enough of the dinner. And the day.

"C'mon, little buddy, I think it's time to get in your pjs." Tuck lifted Andy out of his chair while I marveled at the number of accoutrements a baby needed.

Andy leaned and grabbed the corner of my shirt, threatening to pull me to my feet or push himself out of his father's arms.

"You want Aunt Jo Jo to come with us?"

The little boy nodded solemnly, then grinned to reveal three teeth.

"Well, you're a hit," Debra said, not smiling. Did I detect a tinge of jealousy?

I took Andy's finger and walked with Tuck down the hallway. A white crib was set up in the corner of Tuck's old bedroom. Across from it were the walnut desk and dresser with Tuck's football and basketball trophies lined up. Charmingly incongruent were the baby Andy and adolescent Tuck sides of the room.

I pried my finger away and stood behind Tuck as he changed Andy. How could this man who couldn't reliably wear deodorant as a teen be so gentle, so responsible with his son?

"You okay back there?" He turned his head to look at me. My head was turned, my eyes on the trophies and a Michael Jordan poster.

"I don't think I've ever seen a little, you know, boy before."

"Rotten little things. Can get you right between the eyes if you're not careful." Tuck grinned. "That timing I cultivated as an athlete comes in quite handy with diaper duty."

He lay Andy in his crib and started to read *The Napping House*. I knelt beside Andy's crib and watched the hues of the house in the book change from deep blues to sunny yellows as the story progressed through a rainstorm. I found myself lulled by the rhythm of the repetitive words. Andy, sucking on his sippy cup, was transfixed by the story—by the simple way in which life turned rain into sun.

As if.

When the book had been read twice, Tuck put it down and turned on the cassette player. I expected lullabies, but what came out was the theme song from Aladdin.

Tuck winked at me. "Memories, eh?"

In April 1993, A Whole New World was the theme of our senior prom. With only weeks left to put the yearbook to bed, I found the chatter about prom themes annoying.

"It's your senior prom, doll. Aren't you excited?" Doro asked. We were playing Scrabble one Friday night that I boycotted the basketball game, feigning a cold. It was Tuck's final game as a senior and Grace's as a cheerleader. I remember feeling ugly and out of place. A little apartment in Chicago with built-in bookcases where books spilled out in every direction, the lights and drama of the big city. My mind was filled with thoughts of such. And with the University of Georgia, whose campus I had memorized by heart from the brochures.

As much of a loner as I was, as much of a would-be intellectual, I was actually one of the first girls asked to prom. His name was Roger Horton, and we both loved Shakespeare. He had bad acne but a beautiful voice for poetry.

"At least he's tall," said Grace, as we headed toward Tuck's Jeep after school. "At least you have a date!"

Grace's bad mood was obvious.

"Who peed in your Wheaties?" Tuck asked.

"Nobody. Let's just go somewhere." Grace ducked in the back seat, slinging her backpack down beside her.

Tuck and I exchanged glances, then took our spots in his Jeep. I gingerly stepped over a spilled milkshake and placed my feet atop a Doritos bag.

Tuck started the engine but didn't put the car in gear.

"I'm not moving until we get rid of your bad mood."

"I'm just tired of hearing about everyone's prom dates. Why doesn't someone ask me?"

"Good grief, it's just March."

"Jo has a date already. Everyone is pairing up but me." Sinking down in her seat, Grace stuck her bottom lip out. *"I'm ugly."*

"Oh for God's sake, Gracie, you'll get asked," I said. *"Besides, as you pointed out, my date has a pizza face."*

She giggled. *"Yeah, well I'm sorry I said that. At least you have a date."*

Tuck backed out of the parking lot and headed for the new Wendy's. Frosties had become mainstays of our after-school diet. He was conspicuously quiet.

"Who are you taking, Tuck?" I asked.

He shrugged. *"Dunno. Probably a girl."*

"Well that sure narrows it down, Einstein," said Grace. *"What girl?"*

Another shrug. *"Too soon to tell."*

"Why don't you take Grace?"

"Jo! Shut up!" Grace flushed.

Silence from Tuck.

"See, even my best guy friend thinks I'm ugly." Grace set her head back dramatically against the head rest.

"Ah, you're not so bad," said Tuck. He searched for her in his rearview mirror. *"Do you want me to take you?"*

"Really?" Grace brightened up.

"Really. Now you have a date and my mom will get off my back!"

I remember being happy that my two best friends were helping each other out. Now Roger and I would have a fun couple to hang out with.

But my feelings changed when I saw them walk into the gymnasium on that April evening. Neither of them had ever looked better. Grace's cotton candy dress shimmered under the lights. With her long legs and curvy *figure, she was captivating. She and Tuck floated onto the dance floor like royalty, becoming such hours later when they were named Prom King and Queen.*

My arms around Roger's neck, I swayed to the sounds of Bonnie Raitt, but couldn't take my eyes off the couple at the center of the dance floor. Somehow I knew that things were about to change.

"Pssst. Jo!" Tuck was trying to get my attention; I was still at the prom.

We were sitting on the floor by Andy's crib; Tuck's right hand extended through the rails, and Andy's grip on it was gradually loosening.

"How long do we sit like this?" Restless Heart was singing "When She Cries." "What is this mix tape anyway?"

"I call it Class of '93. Best sounds of high school," Tuck whispered, gently removing his hand and tucking a stuffed rat under the snoring boy's armpit. "It usually takes until 'Come Undone' comes on. He was tired tonight." Tuck motioned toward the door, his sock feet tiptoeing carefully.

"You play Duran Duran as a lullaby?" I said when we were out in the hall.

Tuck gently pulled the door to. "Duran Duran. Bon Jovi. Boy needs to learn music."

Back in the kitchen, Debra was just finishing up.

"Debra, I would have helped you. I'm sorry," I said.

"No problem. I know you two want to catch up. Honestly, if you're here, I won't have to endure either the noise of the baseball game or Chris's cussing at his law books." She leaned up and gave Tuck a quick kiss. "My new *People* and I have a date in the bathtub.

"JoAnna, I hope we'll see more of you before you have to head back. It was really, really nice to put a face with the stories."

Once she was gone, Tuck started to pour me a glass of wine. I held my hands up: "I better not. Long drive."

"Fifteen minutes."

Tom's face popped into my subconscious. "I better not."

"Well I'm going to have another beer." He popped the cap off a Bud Lite and led me out to the deck.

"I would think a law student would be into higher brow beers, *Chris*."

"Indeed I am, but I'm also residing in a football coach's house, and Bud was always just fine for Coach T." He settled himself on one of the two chaise lounges. "Yeah, so Debra calls me by my real name."

"Sorry, but I'm not going to be able to get used to that."

"I changed it when I started at Samford. I guess I just wanted to reinvent myself. Ever feel that way?"

"Daily."

"Well, you did that in Chicago, huh? By the way, I was hoping I would get to meet your Tom."

I flinched at Tom's name. It didn't belong here, on this deck where I had spent so many Friday evenings after football games. I changed the subject.

"Remember when we had too many people out here and the deck started shaking like it was about to fall? Coach T was pissed."

"I remember when it did fall, the next summer. You were already off to Georgia by then."

Like it was yesterday, I could remember the night before Doro and Maddy drove me to Georgia. Tuck, Grace, and I had eaten Taco Bell and seen *Sleepless in Seattle*. Tuck had complained throughout the movie and afterwards.

"Yeah, like that happens. Love doesn't work that way."

"Don't be such a guy," I said.

"Yeah, be more like Tom Hanks," Grace said, her arm around his waist. The two were casual with each other, but there was something about the way he looked at her, the way she looked at him.

It made me curious, all these years later.

"When did you and Grace start dating?" I asked, stealing a swig from his bottle. The beer was like water to a desert hiker.

"Wow, no segue there, Jo Jo." Tuck repositioned himself on the chair. I could tell he was a bit uncomfortable with my question.

"You don't have to answer."

"No, no, I'll answer. I have to say it started at prom."

I knew it.

"At least that's when I started seeing her as more than a friend."

I couldn't believe I was sitting here, at Tuck's house, talking about Grace. As casually as if she were in the next room. And yet maybe this was what I needed, had needed, for years—to have someone I could talk to about Grace. Someone who perhaps loved her as much as I did.

Tuck was quiet for a moment, then got up. "I'm going to get another beer. Sure you don't want one?"

If I was going to talk about Grace, I needed a shot of courage.

"No but I'll take a glass of wine after all."

He returned, and I wrapped my hands around the goblet. Tom's face hovered in my mind, but I pushed it back. *You walked out on me*, I thought. *You left*. The crickets were screeching, and the fireflies lit up the deck. For the first time in how many months, I felt like myself. Like Jo Wilson.

Screw you, Tom Rivers.

"We never kissed, never dated, until college though. Freshman year we would run in to each other, but, you know, we had different majors. She was taking all those math classes, and I was history all the way. Just no overlap."

I took a big gulp and waited.

"And then she showed up in the ATO house in September sophomore year, and it was like we were meeting for the first time. She had died her hair red that year; do you remember?"

I did. Once I was at Georgia, and Grace and Tuck were at Sewanee, it was harder to keep in touch. Or perhaps it just began to feel that way. The girl who called me her sister had blossomed into a social butterfly. Gradually more time ebbed between our letters and phone calls. Finally we just saw each other at holidays. In the summers Grace continued to help Doro at the Inn, while I did a writing internship in Georgia. In a way, she became more Doro's daughter than I was.

She had sent me a picture of the red tint she put on her hair.

"It looked awful," Tuck said. "But I guess that's because I knew her as the strawberry blonde who could beat me at ping pong when we were fourteen. My frat brothers saw her differently."

"And you did too."

"Yeah." Tuck drank down half the bottle and burped silently. "Sorry."

"A new Tuck. The old Tuck would have tried to belt one as loud as possible." My wine was almost gone, and I felt the tingling behind my eyes. The desire for another.

"Yeah, well, I guess law school and Debra civilized me a bit," Tuck chuckled.

Our conversation droned on, Tuck relaying the beginnings of his relationship with Grace. While I was reading *Adam Bede*, dating a boy named Jake, and jumping at the thought of a byline in the Georgia *Red and Black*, Grace was going to ATO parties, and my two friends were meeting for lunch every Thursday and dinner every Sunday. And, then, whole Saturdays.

"I've got something to tell you, Jo Jo," Grace had said on the Friday in June that she asked me to take a hike with her to The Point. Now I knew. Perhaps I had always suspected. She was in love with Tuck.

The truth was that the further we got into college, the more distant I became from Grace. My life was wrapped up in Georgia, in the heartbreak Jake caused me. Even when home on holidays, I felt shut off from Grace and Tuck—from what they obviously had become to each other. I told Tuck as much.

"Yeah, I know. Or I guess I knew. I sensed that." Tuck leaned back, and I saw him as he was in high school. Broad shoulders. Little bit of chest hair sneaking out above his shirt. That impossibly real tan and white blonde hair. Tuck had refilled my glass, and I knew it was a mistake.

"So let's change the conversation to you. What about you and Tom. Tell me about him."

Halfway through my second glass of wine, Chicago seemed as distant as Yemen.

"He's a very talented photographer," I said. "In fact, he just won an Addy." Tuck looked at me hard. "And he's good to you."

"Very."

At that moment, the awning dipped with the wind and a stream of stale rain water drenched my lap.

"Jesus. Sorry. Something else Coach T will want me to fix." Tuck ran into the house to grab some dishtowels.

I set my wine glass on the deck and wiped off my lap. "It's okay. I needed a wake-up call."

Tuck replenished my wine glass. Was this number two or three? I was relaxed, at peace. Must be glass three. *You left me, Tom,* I thought. *You walked out on me.*

The awning sent down another shower.

"Here, come sit with me. We can share," Tuck shifted in his chaise to make room for me. Nestled far beneath Tuck's arm against the back of the chair, I could smell a light scent of aftershave. His full lips curved around the bottle, and I felt an unfamiliar yearning.

Grace, is this the man you loved?

"So how is it in Chicago?' He asked, tipping his bottle to toast my glass.

"Big. And great. But I have to say that at first I felt a little lost and alone."

There was a pause, then, "On some forgotten highway?"

I giggled. "Travelled by many. Remembered by few."

"Were you looking for something you could believe in?"

"Looking for something I'd like to do with my life."

We dissolved into laughter, remembering Adam Garrett.

Adam Garrett was one of Doro's frequent guests in the early '80s. He carried a camouflage duffle on one shoulder and a Fender acoustic strapped over the other. John Denver was the lion's share of his repertoire. In the evenings he would delight Doro with everything from Annie's Song *to* Calypso. *Long after Denver's popularity had diminished, Adam carried on. Doro's favorite was* Sweet Surrender. *Adam never put away his guitar until that was sung.*

"I wish he'd add a little Stones to his mix," said Tuck.

Doro snapped the dishtowel at him. "Hey, you were supposed to quit an hour ago. You're off the clock. I'm not paying you to stand around looking pretty."

"Oh I know, the music was just too captivating to leave, ma'am." Tuck could accomplish more with a wink and a smile than any sixteen year old before or since. Silver-tongued sarcasm, Maddy said.

Adam was just one of many characters who passed through Mt. Moriah, endowing the Inn with anecdotes.

There was Marjorie Ruff who came through every November on her way to spend the holidays with her children. She carried a wicker purse that sprung open to resemble a box. And into that went her dinner. We watched her—Tuck, Grace, and I—from behind the swinging door. First, Mrs. Ruff carefully divided the food on her plate into two sections. The first she scraped off into the purse; the rest she ate. We learned to seat her at the end away from the other guests. She didn't care for small talk; rather she scowled through the dinner.

"I don't believe you guys," said Doro when we first saw Mrs. Ruff in action in the fall of 1989.

"Swear to God," said Tuck, raising one hand in the air.

"Don't swear in my presence."

"Okay, I promise."

Doro frowned. "Maybe she has financial troubles. Maybe she needs extra food."

"Maybe she has a crazy sister that is hidden in the room, and she has to bring her food," giggled Grace.

"Maybe she is the crazy sister," added Tuck.

"Well, tomorrow night is Salisbury steak. There's no way she can drop that in her purse," said Doro.

The next night, Doro and Maddy joined us at the swinging door. Across the plate went the knife, dividing the meal into two. Down into the purse went the Salisbury steak. Taking a quick glance around the room, Mrs. Ruff looked up and discretely reached for her teaspoon, to drop some gravy on top.

"She did not just put gravy in there," said Doro.

It became a quest, during the three days she was there, to watch her. More importantly, we wanted to see inside that purse.

"Tuck, offer her a to-go box," Doro said on the final night of Mrs. Ruff's stay.

Tuck, flashing his most winning smile, offered the Styrofoam box to her.

The woman, who sat four foot ten on a tall day, looked at him with a face that would scare a gargoyle.

"Why do I want that, boy? Don't you see that I clean my plate every night?"

"Yes ma'am." Tuck returned to the kitchen. We waited fifteen minutes and then, just as surely as the sun would rise, off went spaghetti and meatballs into the purse.

"I'll be damned," said Doro. In fact, she said that every year Mrs. Ruff stayed with us. When she stopped making reservations, we assumed she had died.

"Probably ingested too much wicker," said Maddy, laughing at his own joke.

The truth was that we never heard the whereabouts of our regular visitors once they stopped coming. When we waved goodbye, we didn't know if we'd see them again. They were character actors serving as extras on the set of our adolescence.

"Remember Clifford Means?" Tuck asked.

I almost choked. "Oh my gosh, the summer we made Doro watch *The Shining*?"

"You had a thing for Clifford."

"I did not."

But I did. Clifford Means rented the August room every June. September through May, he was a high school English teacher in New Jersey. In the summer he was an aspiring writer. I was fascinated. He was shy, almost reclusive, but in the early mornings he sat in one of the cane rockers on the front porch. Swaying back and forth, steaming cup of coffee in hand, he stared at the front lawn in front of him.

The summer I was fourteen, I was writing a series of short stories about a girl named Nan. I made it a habit to set my alarm early and casually wander out onto the porch by seven. Gradually, over the course of several mornings, I was able to engage Clifford in conversation.

"What is your book about?" I asked shyly.

He put down his coffee, a brown earthenware mug with a chip on the corner. He insisted on having his coffee in his own mug every morning. Doro catered to peculiarities like that; those were the reasons people wanted to return to the Inn.

"It's about a boy in the South."

"Is that why you like it here? It inspires you?"

He paused. "It reminds me of my grandfather's farm when I was growing up."

I was poised to leave if Clifford showed signs of being annoyed. But I think perhaps he enjoyed the little bit of companionship I offered. The next summer he smiled when he saw me. "Still writing about Nan?"

"No, I'm writing a new story, about a boy in college."

He chuckled. "Ever been to college?"

I shook my head.

"Ever been a boy?"

"No."

"Hard to write about what you don't know."

"Can I read your book?"

"It's not, eh, age appropriate for you."

I was indignant. "I read Erica Jong's Fear of Flying."

He was obviously surprised. "The zipless whatever, eh?"

I reddened. "Yes."

Clifford stretched his legs that morning and stood up. "Well, my book is not ready for reading. But I'll keep you in mind." He set a hand on my shoulder as he passed toward the doorway. "Keep writing, JoAnna. Practice is the only way."

Although I was inspired by Clifford, Grace was circumspect.

"He's creepy," she said one night as we were stacking the dinner dishes. It was 1992, and we had a full crowd, with a group of Floridians taking up almost the entire Inn on their way to the Democratic Convention in New York.

"He's a writer, Gracie." Sometimes Grace seemed so anti-intellectual.

Tuck agreed with Grace. "Yeah, The Shining all the way." Tuck was making a rare appearance on a Friday night, his t-shirt drenched in sweat. He was cutting off bites of uneaten key lime pie.

Doro swatted him with a towel. "I can't believe that you would eat off of someone else's plate, nor would I ever have believed it's possible to stink so much."

Maddy passed through the kitchen on the way to his study. He stole two rolls off a plate and wagged them in Doro's face. To Tuck, he said, "Yep, you're a bit ripe, son."

"So what is The Shining anyway?" asked Doro.

"Oh that's a scary movie, my dear. Too scary for you."

It was Tuck's idea that we have movie night and watch The Shining. Doro alternated hiding her head on Maddy's chest and behind a pillow. Grace and I sat on either sides of Tuck, ducking our heads under his armpits whenever Jack Nicholson appeared.

"Gaggle of scaredy cat women we got here, boy," Maddy said to Tuck.

"Good times," I said, resting my head back against the chaise.

"You wrote to Clifford for a while, didn't you?"

"Yeah, but at some point he stopped responding, and he stopped coming to the Inn."

"Maybe his fake book got finished." Tuck laughed.

"Shut up. He let me read the first page, and it was beautiful."

"Well, I still say he was a weirdo. And I'm willing to bet you publish your book before he does!"

My book about Jillsandra. The book about nothing.

I sighed. "I seem to have permanent writer's block."

Tuck leaned his head back so our heads were touching. "It'll happen for you, Jo Jo."

"Yeah?"

"Yeah. Everyone's always known you'd be a writer." He shifted his head so our eyes were close, so close that our mouths breathed in and out the same air.

"I always knew."

The wine had once again worked its magic on me. As the stars danced above, I felt calm, peaceful. The relaxed way you can only feel with an old friend.

"I like it here. It feels safe."

Tuck was quiet. I knew we were both thinking about Grace.

"You're safe here with me."

"I know that."

And I did. I felt secure with this boy who had known me through acne and heartbreak and braces and loss. I nuzzled my head against his and, once again, Tom's face pierced my thoughts. *You left me, Tom.*

"Tuck," I began. Could I trust myself? Could I trust Tuck who had known me most of my life? Could I share with him the secret Dr. Weisz said I needed to let go.

But to those searching eyes I could say nothing.

We lingered like that, our mouths dangerously close. The Woodbury High quarterback who had alternately invaded my adolescent fantasies and driven me crazy was a man now, and although in my heart I knew he was Grace's, Debra's, for a few hours he was mine. Filling my wine glass. Not judging.

The door opened and Debra stepped out in an open weave white robe. Her hair swept up and no makeup, she was stunning. She looked warily from me to Tuck. Her eyes on Tuck, she said, "JoAnna, your, uh, Mr. Blair called. He was concerned because it's so late. He wanted to make sure you're okay." Debra's eyes never moved from Tuck's.

I pushed myself up to a standing position and steadied myself on the nearby table. The effects of the wine had worn off, yet I still felt a bit light-headed and my stomach churned.

"I better go."

"You okay to drive?" Tuck was on his feet, slipping his flip flops back on. "Need me to run you home?' In my mind I saw images of Tuck running me home, running Grace home, running us both home, the windows rolled down in his Jeep, Bon Jovi blaring. *Yes, take me home,* I thought.

"No, I'm fine," I said. Debra smiled weakly at me, her face registering the empty bottle of wine on the deck. "Thank you for dinner, Debra. I really did enjoy meeting you." My tongue felt heavy, but I enunciated the words carefully.

"Anytime," she said, which I doubted she meant.

And then I was back in my Corolla, driving away from the couple standing in the doorway, arms around each other. Away from the shaky deck and the sturdy oak. Away from the memories of a Mt. Moriah that were, for better or worse, part of me. Away from the dreaming child and the cozy bed.

Back toward home. Wherever home was.

25

STILL SMALL VOICE

Taped to the April door was a note, scratched in Maddy's almost illegible script. *Tom called again.* The last word was underlined.

But my mind was miles away from Tom and Chicago. Bouncing in my mind were a million memories stirred up by my evening with Tuck. My eyes glanced at the stairs leading to the attic at the end of the hall: my room. I almost climbed up, but I couldn't. For it wasn't just my room: It felt like Grace's room too. I was not ready to open the door to those memories.

My stomach was doing flip flops, and I rushed to the bathroom. In my panties was the smallest spot of blood. I wiped myself, finding another trace on the toilet paper.

"Well, is that it then?" I asked to no one in particular. I washed myself and searched the cabinets for a maxi pad. Doro usually kept the bathrooms well equipped for guests. I found a small package and inserted a liner into my panties. Tossing my clothes on the floor, I pulled a t-shirt over my head, and climbed into bed.

I pulled the sheet and comforter up, smoothing them around my chin so that only my face was visible. My heart and mind were racing: What did the blood mean? I found myself whispering, "Please. Please."

But I didn't know what I was asking for, nor did I know whom I was asking.

Outside my window the sound of mewing, the scornful cat's outline punctuating the moonlight.

I was awakened at seven by Maddy's booming voice.

"Church, little thing. Wake up."

I was drifting through those last layers of sleep—the moments before you realize you're worried about something, before you remember where you are and even who you are. I floated to the top and opened my eyes. Tom was in Chicago. I was in Mt. Moriah. Doro was dead. And I didn't know what I wanted for the rest of my life.

"I think I'll sleep in today."

"Are you sick?" Maddy leaned against the doorframe, a cup of coffee in one hand. He suddenly looked old to me. Grey. Tired.

"No, I could just use the sleep."

"God doesn't sleep. Get up."

Maddy's "God doesn't sleep" adage, articulated in just the right tenor, worked when I was a teen. But I was an adult now and said as much.

The old man slurped his coffee. "Doesn't matter. You're home. House rules."

He rubbed his chest and continued. "I made bacon and eggs. They're waiting on you."

Starting to head downstairs, Maddy turned back. "By the way, I need you to read scripture today. My liturgist is sick."

"Maddy!" I cried out, just before a wave of bacon aroma-induced nausea hit me. I rushed to the bathroom but only had dry heaves.

And the pad was clean.

"I'm doing this under protest," I said, strapping my seat belt in Maddy's Ford Ranger.

Maddy smiled. "Hush. You're just doing an old reverend a favor."

Leaning my head against the car window, I counted the streetlights as we passed. I had a vague memory of doing this as a child from the middle seat of our family Oldsmobile, my head in my mother's lap. She smelled like Ivory soap and ran a soft palm across the top of my head, back and forth, back and forth. From my vantage point, I could see only the tops of the street lights and the greenest parts of the trees as the sun danced in and out of the foliage, playing hide and seek with me. Where was that girl?

Maddy hummed softly as he bounced us along, over the potholes that he either didn't see or care about. The banana I had eaten was salve to my stomach, and for the first time in many days I didn't feel sick. I didn't feel anything. I was drifting, sheltered by the forest canopy that had protected me as a child.

When we reached the church, Maddy pulled around back. It was almost eight o'clock, and Ronny Glaser was already there, opening the church as he did fifty-one Sundays of the year.

Before we got out, Maddy lay his hand on my arm. "I'm glad you're here with me, little thing."

And then I considered what I had been too self-absorbed to realize. This was Maddy's first Sunday without Doro. I leaned over and kissed him on the cheek.

"I wish I could believe, Maddy. I wish my faith hadn't left me."

"Did it leave you or did you leave it?" Reaching into his coat pocket, Maddy pulled out the day's scripture reading. "Don't just read it, Jo. Hear it."

Maddy stepped out of his truck, reaching inside for his Bible, torn, frayed, and stuffed full of notes.

I climbed the few steps into the chancel and took my seat on one of the ornate chairs, sheathed in red velvet. I unfolded the page Maddy had given me. 1 Kings.

As Lucie Leffler played the prelude, I watched the congregation trickle in. Someone had freshened the flowers from Doro's funeral. The gladiolas had sprung to life, the Asiatic lilies opening. I remembered the choir director complaining about the smell of lilies and what it does to the vocal chords. And I remember Doro rolling her eyes.

"God gave us beautiful flowers and beautiful music. Everyone just get along!" she scoffed. The thought brought a smile to my lips.

Although I had only been away for four years, the congregation seemed to have aged a decade. Mr. Willis now walked with a cane. The Anderson twins, once pudgy fourth graders, were on the cusp of being beautiful teens. The Drummonds, married the summer I moved to Chicago, were toting two toddlers. Eugenia Page, a member of Doro's bridge club for years, had lost thirty pounds.

The choir processed, singing the opening hymn, "Just as I Am." Many nodded to me as they took their place.

Throughout the service, I was swept up in memories. Looking toward the second row, I spotted Genia Collins. She smiled at me—a weak, sorrowful smile. As surely as if it was real, I could see myself and Grace sitting on her right, stealing offertory envelopes and passing Gra-Jo notes—kicking my white patent leather heels together under the seat, until Genia, her eyes not leaving the pulpit, placed a firm hand on my knee. Her head still focused on the altar, Genia extending her hand for Grace to spit her bubble gum into. Grace and I punting a ladybug back and forth on the cushioned pew between us. Grace leaning up to take the flame from her mother's "Silent Night" candle on Christmas Eve. Turning, those luminous cocoa eyes sparkling in the candlelight, Grace passing her light to me.

Closing my eyes, my throat knotted as scenes from my childhood played out in my head. Kelly Abernathy throwing the baby into the manger and stomping off stage during the Christmas Pageant when she was four. (She was now twenty and a religion major). Wilson Hobart, overheated, fainting in the choir and knocking out the baritones domino-style. The Furnesses, whose nasty divorce kept them at opposite sides of the church, their poor children divided, casting looks at each other. The Remrods, who on the Sunday after their house burned, assumed their usual stance as ushers.

As the Doxology concluded, I took my place at the pulpit and, clearing my throat, began to read. I was sixteen again and looking out at Grace.

"A reading from First Kings:

The Lord said, 'Go out and stand on the mountain in the presence of the Lord, for the Lord is about to pass by.' Then a great and powerful wind tore the mountains apart and shattered the rocks before the Lord, but the Lord was not in the wind. After the wind there was an earthquake, but the Lord was not in the earthquake. After the earthquake came a fire, but the Lord was not in the fire. And after the fire came a still small voice. When Elijah heard it, he pulled his cloak over his face and went out and stood at the mouth of the cave."

I paused, looking at the congregation before me: people who, through seconds or minutes or years of interaction, had formed me, loved me. Looking into the face of Genia Collins, I noticed her fighting back tears, the weight of time and grief bearing down upon her. Suddenly she was not the dominating, controlling figure of my childhood. She was an old woman who had lost too much.

She was a mother.

I look over to Maddy. *I know,* his eyes said as he nodded.

I put the paper aside and stepped down from the chancel, taking my place next to Genia. Maddy rose and, as was his habit, took his glasses off and prayed silently for a moment.

"Amen," he said. And then, looking directly at me, "Thank you for reading the Scripture, JoAnna."

Clearing his throat, Maddy launched into a story about a little boy hiding from his parents. As was Maddy's style, the story was riddled with punch lines and funny anecdotes. It was a simple story, the moral being that the boy's parents knew where he was all along.

"Now you'll notice there's no Gospel reading this week. I thought this verse from 1 Kings was an important one for us to hear—perhaps this week of all weeks." Maddy held his hand to his mouth for a moment before continuing. "Next Sunday we'll move on to the Good News. This week I want to speak from the heart, and share my favorite scripture.

"It's important to know the context here. At this point, Elijah had been speaking out about false prophets. He was fighting with the prophets of Baal and challenging the king's theology. This verse takes place after Elijah fled and took refuge in a cave.

"Earlier in the passage, God asks Elijah what he is doing there. We see an Elijah who is weary in the way that so many of us are. He feels alone, isolated, and discouraged.

"And God tells Elijah to go stand on the mountain, 'for the Lord is about to pass by.' And when Elijah does, what do you think he expects? He expects to find God in the powerful wind, in the earthquake, in the fire."

Maddy looked directly at me, those piercing blue eyes not leaving my face.

"My friends, how often do we seek God in the wind and the fire? On the mountain top? How often do we expect our faith to rumble in our heart and make our hair stand on end?"

Maddy patted down the few white strands that remained on the top of his head. "Of course, for some of us, that would take quite a miracle." The congregation laughed; I smiled. The buttery lilt in Maddy's voice was that of a Southern gentleman, a modern prophet. A calming force to the raucous questions ringing in my ears—and in my heart.

"But those many thousands of years ago, God instead spoke to Elijah through a still small voice. Just as today he speaks to us in the quiet of our hearts. Often that still small voice is hard to discern.

"Remember the father of Methodism, John Wesley, who describes his heart as *strangely warmed*. He didn't say he was bowled over. He didn't describe being swept away. Subtly and unexpectedly, his heart was touched, and he was changed.

"God still seeks to warm our hearts, to speak to us." Leaning his arms on the lectern, Maddy's voice softened, the threat of tears apparent. "Someone recently said to me that her faith had left her. Does it leave us? Or do we not know how to listen for that still small voice.

"Do we forget how to listen?"

Maddy continued with a story from Vietnam, a reading from Henry Nouwen, but I stopped hearing. I gazed up at the kaleidoscopic windows, at the brass plaques commemorating the people who had given them: people who died decades before I existed. Whose voice had they listened to? And had they heard?

Leaning back ever so slightly, I positioned myself in a beam of sunlight, tumbling through the olives and turquoises and auburns and ochres of the window panes. Was it possible that if I sat perfectly still, I could quiet my mind to the clamorous change overtaking my body? Quell my anger at Tom and allay my fear and my grief. Was it possible, at all possible, that there was a still, small voice inside me?

And therefore a God?

Yet I heard nothing.

Making my way outside after the service, I was hugged and patted and my hands shaken— extended the same kindnesses I had been shown at Doro's service. At the front door, Maddy was done shaking hands and stepped out of his robe in preparation for Sunday School. He held out his arms, and I moved into them.

"Good sermon, Maddy."

"Did you listen, little thing?"

"I did, Maddy."

He kissed me on my forehead. "I've got to teach a class. You staying for Sunday School?"

I rolled my eyes. "Sunday School too, Maddy?"

As a hand tapped my shoulder, a voice whispered in my ear.

"Wanna ditch Sunday School with us?"

Tuck looked so handsome in his seersucker suit. A young Atticus Finch, I thought.

I smiled at Debra who stood next to him holding Andy.

"Wouldn't be the first time," I said.

"That's what I've heard," Debra laughed.

Tuck and Debra were in Coach T's cherry red convertible—a mid-life crisis purchase—and I hopped into the back seat next to Andy. Eyes closed, the little boy sucked slowly on his pacifier. I watched the rubber "bubby" go back and forth, as he sunk deeper into sleep.

"Is this his nap time?" I whispered to the front seat. I had no idea at what time a nap might come.

"No, he just always falls asleep when we're driving," said Debra. "He'll come back raring to go. Just enjoy the peace."

Her hand was on the back of the headrest and sporadically she rubbed the back of Tuck's neck. I was enamored with this woman who seemed so at ease, so in control. Did she ever have nightmares? What did she fear?

"You hungry?" Tuck called back to me.

"Little bit. Where are you taking me?"

"Our favorite place, Art's Hardware."

"And then to breakfast? Or have you started biting on nails?"

Tuck laughed. "Actually, you'll be surprised. Investors are revitalizing the downtown."

He slid into a spot in front of what used to be Art's Hardware. The sign remained—an oversized black sign with bright red letters, with a hammer and paintbrush as logo accents. The sign was the only thing recognizable, though, as the interior had been converted to a pancake house.

"Does Art still own this?" I asked as a hostess led us to a window seat. A giant paint can was suspended above my head. Art Wallis had owned the hardware store for decades and his father before him.

"Nah, remember Jamie, his daughter?" Tuck fastened Andy in his high chair, wiping down the chair's arms with a wet wipe. My mind jumped to Tuck as a teenage jock, who dipped fingers dirty from football practice into Doro's cake batter and then double dipped.

"Art turned sixty-five and announced he was heading to the beach. Jamie convinced him to sell to her, and all this was her creativity."

Debra whispered. "Part of why we love it is that kids under two get free pancakes."

We lingered in Art's for almost two hours. I was surprised by how few people I knew.

"It's becoming trendier here," said Tuck. "Lots of young people moving in and buying up property."

"Not a bad life here." Debra reached across Tuck for a wipe and began to work on Andy's syrupy hair. "I told Chris I'd consider settling here."

The look on my face must have said it all.

"Really, Tuck? You'd consider moving here?"

Tuck and Debra exchanged glances.

"We've actually talked about it. I'd like to be back here."

"What kind of law would you practice here?"

"I'm actually interested in real estate law and contracts," explained Tuck. "As this area grows, it's going to need more lawyers—and Birmingham, Nashville, and Atlanta are just a few hours down the road.

"It'd be nice to raise Andy where I was raised."

Tuck took a final swig of coffee. "Do you think you'll ever be back, Jo Jo?"

"Funny you should ask. Doro left me the Inn." I paused, careful to choose my words so they wouldn't be offensive. "Mt. Moriah is just not for me— maybe it never was."

"Always wanted to be in the big city. I remember that."

"So Chicago feels like home?" Debra asked, fighting a losing battle on Andy's hair.

"I guess." I thought briefly of Tom, and then of Maddy. And finally of

Grace and Doro. Sadness and a dull ache crept back into my head. "Honestly, I don't know where home is right now."

Debra smiled. "It's a lot to take in, I'm sure. And then there's your husband. He's from Chicago, right?"

"Yes, Tom. He is from Chicago." My voice trailed off. What could I tell them? That I had hurt my husband? That he had left me? That I didn't know who and what and where I was to be?

Debra looked at Tuck, and I thought I saw one eyebrow go up.

"Well you should move back to Mt. Moriah and renovate the Inn, and we will move back and we can play bridge and drink martinis." Tuck pulled out his credit card. When I reached for my wallet, he waved me away. "Please. You may be a big city dweller, but I'm a soon to be rich-as-shit ambulance chaser."

I laughed. I found myself not wanting the morning with the Tucks to end. I felt at ease—something I had not felt in weeks. Months. Years?

As we approached the car, Tuck swung his arm around my shoulder. "Go on back to Chicago, then. Write that Great American Novel, and then you can come back and buy this whole flippin' mountain!"

"I wouldn't hold your breath. My writing is stalled."

Andy had started a low whine. "Uh oh, it's nap time. Drive fast, Chris!" Debra said, buckling herself.

"Do Mommy and Daddy get a nap too?" I asked.

"Well, Mommy does," Debra laughed. "I don't know about Daddy. He didn't get much studying done yesterday."

"I do need to get some hours in." Tuck saw me staring at Andy. "You can touch him, ya know. He won't break."

I took Andy's tiny hand in mine. "I've just never been around children," I said. "They are so mysterious."

My right hand moved to my stomach. Was this life possible for me? Eating pancakes and longing for naps, laughing carelessly and easily. Was this the kind of future that Tom could foresee that I could not?

Holding Andy's hand, I was almost lulled to sleep along with him. With my eyes at half- mast, I watched the couple in front of me as if cycling through the frames of a movie: the way Tuck groped around in the cup holder for a mint and Debra found it for him, knowing him like an old habit. The way she reached for his free hand and their fingers did acrobatics: a light touch signaling something much deeper.

Did Tom and I look like that? Did we make people smile when they watched us? Was happiness beyond my reach or did I just not know how to grasp it?

When we reached the Inn, I pried my finger loose from Andy and reached down to kiss the still syrupy crown of his head.

"So how long are you staying?" Debra asked.

"I really don't know. I only booked a one-way flight, but I was planning on leaving in the next couple of days." I pushed wind-blown curls out of my face. *"JoAnna, for goodness sake use a barrette!"* Doro's voice popped into my ears. "I need to get back to work."

"And to Tom." Tuck looked squarely at me.

"Yes. And to Tom." And to the calendar days propelling me further and further away from July 30, I thought.

"Can we have lunch before you go?" Tuck asked.

"I'll call you in the morning."

Inside, Maddy was stretched out on the sofa. Thinking him asleep, I tip-toed over. His eyes were open wide, staring at the ceiling.

"Hello, little thing."

"I thought you were napping."

"Well I'd like to be. I'm bone tired, but I can't sleep."

"Can I get you anything?" I smoothed out Doro's favorite afghan, knotted around Maddy's feet, and tucked it up under his chin.

Shaking his head, Maddy continued to stare straight ahead.

I sat for a second on the edge of the sofa. "You miss her, don't you, Maddy?"

"Like losing a limb," he said, turning his head then to look at me. "It's like I lost a limb."

Laying my head against his chest, I listened to the rhythm of his broken heart. I sat up and looked at him, ready for more conversation, ready for him to talk if he needed to, but Maddy was silent, continuing to stare at the plaster ceiling.

Planting a kiss on his cheek, I went to their bedroom and opened Doro's closet. I felt energized after the pancakes, and my stomach for once was at rest. Perhaps I could clean out her clothes. That would be probably the hardest thing for Maddy. I set about taking the dresses off hangers. Doro's habit was to choose appropriate costume jewelry for the outfit and drape it over the coat hanger. I went to her dressing table and rummaged around until I found some safety pins. I pinned the jewelry to each outfit, then folded the garments neatly.

Before I knew it, three hours had passed and the bed was stacked with outfits. I went to the kitchen to look for trash bags and peeked in on Maddy. He was sound asleep, snoring, one hand on his chest.

In two more hours I had the dresses, slacks, and blouses bagged up. I held up one of Doro's Vanity Fair DD bras and giggled at the memory of Grace and me stretching one of her bras around both of our nine year old bodies.

Grace. I pushed back the thought and continued working.

My back started to hurt from the bending, and I looked at the clock. Six o'clock. Maddy must be getting hungry. Was he still sleeping?

The snores answered my question, and I moved about the kitchen, opening the pantry and refrigerator, waiting for culinary inspiration. Finally I decided to make BLT sandwiches and pulled the ripest tomatoes from the window sill. I cut some apple slices and finished the plate off with one of the three congealed salads the congregation had brought.

Arranging the food on a tray, I added a class of milk and went to the den. Maddy was awake and looking at me.

"I made you dinner, sleeping beauty. Are you hungry?"

Raising one eyebrow, Maddy looked at me warily.

"Depends. Can you cook?"

Maddy and I watched football side by side on the sofa. I had little interest in football, but I knew it was something he and Doro had done together. He said little, just nibbled on the sandwich. I cleaned up the kitchen while he remained on the sofa, staring at the television as if seeing it for the first time. On his face was the blankest of expressions.

Soon darkness covered the house, and I went through the rooms turning on lamps. When I went back into the den, the TV was still on, but Maddy wasn't there.

I found him in his bedroom, staring at the piles on the bed.

"Oh, Maddy, is it okay that I did this? I thought it would help you to get Doro's clothes out."

Peering inside the bags, Maddy touched the garments as gingerly as if they were crystal. "Yes," he said. He looked up at me and those blue eyes were swimming pools. "I'm tired. I want to go to bed."

"Of course. I'll move these bags to the front hall."

Maddy perched on the edge of the bed and let me carry and drag the bags to the hallway. "Do you need me to help you?"

"No I got it. They're just bulky, not heavy."

After three trips with the bags, when I returned to the bedroom, Maddy had Doro's chenille bathrobe in his arms. It was cream with lilacs, the middle button was missing, and one cuff was frayed. I didn't have to hold it to know that it smelled like Oil of Olay. Maddy reached out his hand and took mine.

"I'm sorry, little thing. You feeling okay?"

I smiled. "I'm okay, Maddy."

"Please don't give this one away. This one I want to keep."

I nodded.

"I'm just so tired." His was the sigh of a man who had lost his wife, buried her, conducted a funeral service and a church service, and pretended to be a rock for the last seven days.

I kissed Maddy goodnight and pulled the door behind me. I looked at the clock: 9:30. I wasn't tired. I roamed through the house, looking at all the trinkets Doro had picked up over the years. I ran my fingers over the sterling silver tea set atop the Jackson press; it needed polish. Doro never let it tarnish, yet there it was, looking old and tired.

Had Doro felt old and tired?

I looked at the Christmas village houses inside the curio cabinet in the front hall, remembering the amount of time it took every year to arrange each house on the drop leaf table in the front hall, to connect and hide the cords. I remembered making fake snow with Doro, shredding cotton so it looked realistic.

What would become of these?

It struck me that they were now mine. All of this I would have to give away, sell, throw out. How to dispense of a life like Doro's?

I went outside to the front porch and climbed into the swing. With each movement I traveled back in time.

I was about five years old. The front lawn on Magnolia Drive was alive with lightning bugs and my hand was in my father's, a mason jar in his other.

Pipe in his mouth, Dad sat on the top step, holding the jar and waiting while I darted frenetic paths around the yard, catching one or two at a time. Each time I'd return, delighted to add to the jar. Eventually fatigue hit me and I plopped down beside my father. I lay my cheek on his bony knee and looked up into the jar he held in front of us.

"I don't think I'll be able to catch them all," I sighed.

"No, I wouldn't think so. There will always be more and more," my father said between pipe puffs.

"If I try really really hard?"

"Well, I do think you are a little girl who can do anything," he said, his large hand stroking my hair.

"Daddy, are they scared in there?"

"Maybe." He waited for a minute. "Do you want to set them free?"

I nodded, then asked. "Can we catch more tomorrow night?"

"Sure thing. There's always a tomorrow night and always more lightning bugs."

I can see myself setting the jar down and watching the bugs climb and fly for freedom. I vaguely remember how heavy my eyes felt as my dad carried me up the stairs: looking up and seeing my mom standing in the window.

I remember feeling safe.

I closed my eyes against the night, and interrupting that sweet memory was a vision of Tom with a little Andy. Or a little JoAnna. Carrying him or her on his shoulders. Enfolding them with those arms that blocked out everything.

Would it be like that for us? And what about me: Would I be standing in the window? Could I trust myself to love a child that much, and could I trust anyone else with my child? Did I have any faith in the world to which he or she would be born?

My mind continued to jump around like the fireflies themselves. Powerful were the memories of evenings on this porch with Maddy and Doro, visions of Grace and me throwing ourselves into the leaf pile the Robinson brothers collected. I could smell hot blueberry pies baking in the oven and hear Tuck's muddy cleats stomping through the hallway. Feel the heat of a bonfire after the football game and see the pear trees spring to life beneath my window.

The vignettes dancing in my head were not mere recollections. They were pieces and parts of what I had lost. Home. They were visions of home.

Having dozed off, I awoke feeling unsettled and cold. My watch said one in the morning. My sock feet made little sliding noises as I locked the door behind me and moved down the hall. I peeked in at Maddy, snoring softly, one hand on Doro's pillow.

Doro. Why did you leave me all this, Doro?

In the April room, I flipped on the light and saw the cat perched on the windowsill. I was unnerved every time I saw this feline.

"Scat!" I said, gesturing at the window. But the stubborn cat remained, watching.

I pulled my phone out of my pocket: a missed call from Tom. *You left me.* I hesitated, then dialed his number. Tom's voice told me I had awakened him.

"Jo, are you alright? What time is it?" I knew Tom was fumbling to see the alarm clock on his nightstand, the oblong walnut table that rocked back and forth because one leg was rickety. I knew he was sitting up, running his fingers through his hair. I knew his DePaul t-shirt smelled like sleep.

"Yes, I'm okay."

"I've tried to call several times."

"I know. I've been, uh, busy."

"Maddy said you were out with Tuck."

So he told him that. "Yes. And his wife."

Tom was quiet. The conversation that had always ebbed and flowed easily between us was tight and uncomfortable.

"I wanted to know you're alright. I wanted to know . . ."

"I know what you wanted to know. But I don't have an answer."

"You're my wife, Jo."

"You're the husband who walked out on me."

A pause. "And you're the love of my life. Who hurt me."

Again, an abyss we couldn't cross.

"Tom, I called to tell you I've decided to stay in Mt. Moriah for a little while. I'll call Candace tomorrow. I should have enough sick and vacation days built up.

"Tom?"

"I heard you. I wish you were back now."

His voice—tender, gentle, hurt—annoyed me. Did he want me back or did he want me back on his terms?

"Are you sure? I haven't changed how I feel about . . ." I didn't know how to say what I meant, what I felt. I didn't *know* what I felt. Part of me wanted to run into Tom's arms and part of me wanted to disappear. "I need to figure out who I am."

He cleared his throat. Was he staring at the Monet poster across from our bed? The one in the cheap metal frame that skewed every time the door shut?

"I hope I factor into that equation, Jo."

I looked up and the cat had left its post.

"I've got to go, Tom. It's late here."

"It's late here too." A smile was in his voice.

"Maddy needs me right now. I need to stay at least another week, maybe two."

"Okay."

"So that's it?"

"What else do you want me to say, Jo? You don't trust me enough to tell me what's going on with you," said Tom.

It was true, but I couldn't explain why. How could I make him understand the effect Grace's murder had on me. How could I tell him all he didn't know?

And then, before he hung up, "You know, Maddy's not the only one who needs you. I need you too."

26

ALONE

THE NEXT MORNING, Maddy was already outside weeding the vincas when I got up.

"Geez, Maddy, it's not even nine o'clock!"

"Gotta get on it before it gets too hot, little thing." Maddy's color was better, and he seemed to have recaptured his old energy level.

Sinking down beside him, I started to pull weeds. Doro was fastidious about alternating colors when she planted flowers—white, pink, purple, then back to white. A scene flashed into my mind: Doro and me retrieving discarded tulip bulbs from the Woodbury Golf Club when they expanded the course; the devastation on her face when we arrived home, and she realized we had forgotten to separate the colors. The next year—and every year after—the tulips were an abstraction of colors. Every spring, while others commented on the beauty of the tulip-lined pathway, Doro muttered in exasperation at what could have been.

Maddy leaned back, bottom on his heels, and wiped his forehead. "How ya feeling, little thing?"

"I'm okay, Maddy." There was no blood in my panties this morning, and my stomach was temporarily at peace. "Did you get a good night's sleep?"

Maddy sighed. "It's different, sleeping alone. I had slept alone for so long, and then Doro was there." Maddy wiped his forehead and rubbed his chest.

Side by side, we worked in silence for a while until Maddy spoke.

"You been to a doctor, Jo?"

"I have a doctor in Chicago. I haven't been to him yet." I stabbed the earth. There was a subtle rage behind my stabs—at Tom? At Doro? At Mt. Moriah?

"Shouldn't you go in, you know, your situation?"

I smiled at both his kindness and his obvious desire to stay away from the topic. "I'm okay, Maddy. I'm going back to Chicago soon, and I'll make an appointment."

Maddy frowned and sat back on his heels. "I know you need to get back, little thing. And you just go on whenever you need to." He paused, his heart in his voice. "I just want you to know how much I enjoy having you here.

"It feels like home when you're here, Jo."

I leaned over and kissed his sweaty cheek. It does feel like home, I thought. This. Right here with Maddy. We weeded for another hour until the humidity forced us inside for iced tea so sweet it coated my teeth.

"I'm going to head over to church for a little bit, then I need to go visit Ernie Dale in the hospital," said Maddy. "What are you going to do?"

"I think I'll just hang around here, Maddy. Is there anything you need me to do?"

I followed Maddy into his bedroom where a clean shirt and pants were laid out on his bed.

"I wouldn't mind at all if you picked up the groceries we need." He dug a wadded up envelope out of his pocket where an almost illegible list was scribbled. Then he reached for his wallet.

I pushed his wallet back toward him. "I got it, Maddy. I think I can even decipher your writing."

Smiling, Maddy took my face in his two oversized hands and kissed my forehead.

"You know what I think, little thing? I think you can do anything."

That week I worked like someone possessed. I cleaned out closets, creating piles to donate. Tuck stopped by every afternoon and together we took walks, made trips to Goodwill with boxes and bags. As we spent time together, I realized that no one in my life had ever made me laugh like Tuck. He had an almost pristine memory—of people and events that I hadn't thought of in years. Debra never came with Tuck, and soon it began to seem like neither she nor Tom existed: It was just Tuck and me, and I craved more time with him.

He set up an appointment for me to talk to a realtor about selling the Inn and offered to go with me. When I invited Maddy to come, he turned his mouth down. "I can't be part of that, Jo."

I sighed, climbing into Tuck's car. "Maddy doesn't want me to sell the Inn."

Tuck shifted into reverse and then reached over and squeezed my knee. "No one wants you to sell the Inn, Jo."

"What? You too? Then why did you set up a meeting with this realtor—what's his name?"

"George Mellsum." Tuck reached over and stuck in a Bon Jovi CD. "And I did it because my friend asked for help."

"What am I supposed to do with an Inn, Tuck? I have a life in Chicago."

"Hmmm, I guess."

"And that means?"

He tapped a drum beat on the steering wheel. "It means, Jo Jo, that there is not much evidence of that life here. You don't ever talk about Tom. We haven't seen him here."

"He's working," I said quietly.

"And the other day when we were eating lunch and he called and you asked Maddy to tell him you'd call him back?"

I reached over and stopped his incessant drumming. "What is this, the inquisition?"

"Not at all. This is your friend who knows you well enough to know something's going on. Something you somehow think you can't confide in me about."

I changed the CD to REO Speedwagon and looked out at the passing houses, the familiar landscape, thinking not for the first time that we do not travel on streets as much as they travel within us. I knew from instinct which house was coming up next. I saw the Hortense barn before we reached it. I knew the Lawrence's fish-shaped mailbox was on the left immediately after the dogleg on the highway. I knew the Johnsons' flower beds across the front of their house would be immaculate, and I knew that the Simpsons' yard next door would be anything but.

As we neared the downtown district, a low billboard advertised the annual tomato festival.

I pointed to the sign. "Reminds me of Doro. She went every year."

"Yeah, Debra was asking me about it. She wants to go, for some strange reason. It starts next Monday the thirteenth."

All at once the thought I had been suppressing, hiding in boxes of sheets and towels and knick knacks, throbbed in my head like a heartbeat.

August 13: the date of no return.

And my secret came tumbling out—like a slinky down a flight of stairs.

"August 13 is an important date," I said, the words hovering in the air like a word cloud.

Tuck looked at me. "Oh? Why's that? You into this tomato thing too?"

"August 13 is the day I'll be twelve weeks pregnant."

Fortunately, we were at a traffic light so Tuck's surprise didn't affect his driving.

"What the crap, Jo? You're pregnant?"

"Yes. I'm pregnant." Somehow naming it made it real.

The light changed, but it took a honk to get Tuck moving. "You blow me away, girl. Why didn't you say something? How do you feel? Are you excited?"

Somehow I knew I could be honest with Tuck.

"Scared to death. Curious. Anxious. Name the adjective and that's how I feel."

"But this is a good thing—for you and Tom? What does he say?"

"He's very happy. He wants the baby." I looked at Tuck to gauge his expression. No sign of judgement. Could I really be brutally honest with him? "Actually, the baby is something we fought over—right before I came here in fact."

"Let me guess: you like the name Mary and he likes Maude." Seeing my expression, Tuck shrugged. "Sorry, you know I make bad jokes when someone is telling me something important."

"I made an appointment at Planned Parenthood to, you know, understand all my options. Tom got angry, very angry, and walked out."

"Oh." Tuck was uncharacteristically quiet.

"You see his side?"

"Oh, Jo Jo, there's no side. The only side I'm on is the side of being happy, and I can tell you from experience that babies create a lot of happiness."

We drove in silence for the next few minutes.

"Are you seriously considering ending the pregnancy?"

And I was honest with Tuck, as I had not been to myself. I didn't want an abortion; perhaps I had known that all along. The thought of a child in my arms: I could not turn away from that. Deep down inside, what I wanted was a choice. What I wanted was to be able to control something in a world of tragedy. What I feared was my ability to bring a child into that world—to protect it.

Tuck slid into a parallel space near the realty office and turned off the engine. "It's not like you'll have to do it alone. You have Tom."

"Do I?" I undid my seatbelt and felt the familiar flipflop in my gut. "He walked out," I said quietly.

"People walk out. People get mad. But usually if they don't intend to stick around, they don't call." Tuck reached over and gingerly lifted the hem of my shirt. "There's something there, Jo Jo. Andy will have a friend!"

Again I tried to picture a baby: my baby, Tom's baby. It just didn't seem real. I said as much.

"It will, soon enough," said Tuck, nodding at the car seat in the back seat. "Come on, we're about five minutes late for George."

George Mellsum had probably looked fifty years old since he was in high school. His hair had been receding since the day it came in, strategic comb overs his form of denial.

"Ms. Wilson, is it?" He took my hand in his thick clammy one and pressed another, even more moist, on top, squeezing.

"Nice to meet you."

Tuck reached out his hand. "Hi, George. It's Mrs. Rivers, by the way. Wilson was a maiden name." His direct look at me spoke volumes.

"Oh, yes, sure. I apologize. Let's step into my office, shall we?"

This office looks like somewhere people go to die, I thought. It was a phrase Tom used, nodding at the hallway of offices so small, so nondescript, that their occupants must have to memorize the office number to find themselves. "Imagine a whole lifetime growing old in a crummy little office," he had said.

A smile crossed my lips at the thought of Tom, and then that familiar feeling of dread.

You left me, Tom.

George Mellsum's office was stacked with folders and Alabama football paraphernalia. On the credenza were pictures of little boys in baseball uniforms, waiting at the pitcher's mound for their hair to recede.

He smiled. "I understand you want to put the Inn on the market."

Nodding, "Yes."

I opened the file with the blueprints I had recovered in Doro's filing cabinet. I set them on the edge of the desk and flattened them with my hands. My fingers ran over the little lines and boxes and numbers—impersonal representations of the Inn.

"I brought these floor plans. Just so you could get an idea of the square footage." George continued to smile directly at me without looking at the plans. Unnerved, I continued, "I understand you'd have to do a formal appraisal."

Smiling, the realtor pulled the plans toward him, giving the stack a ten-second perusal.

"Well, you don't see old plans like these anymore." He looked up at me and then to Tuck and smiled. "These are very interesting." He pushed them back across the table to me and turned to his computer, starting a two-finger typing sequence. "Do you have an idea of what you want to get from the property?"

I looked at Tuck whose face registered nothing. "Well, that's partially why I brought the plans. I'm not sure what the house is worth—I figured that would be based on square footage."

George squinted at the computer screen, distractedly grabbing some dark rimmed readers from his desk drawer. "I've pulled up the county records with a plot of the land. That's what's important here." Staring at the monitor, he jotted down some numbers on a legal pad before turning back to me. "You understand that the value of this property is in the land."

I glanced over at Tuck whose gaze remained straight ahead. "Well I know it's a beautiful piece of land, but the house—I know it needs some repairs—my aunt has let a few things go the last few years or so, but it's a beautiful house. Someone—"

George's phone buzzed, and he held one hand up to pause me.

"Hold my calls please, Maureen." Lowering his hand, he spoke.

"Pardon me. It's a lovely old home, yes, but the parcel of land is what will interest a buyer. There are several developers who have been looking for property in this area."

"Developers? To build homes?" I pulled the blueprints back toward me, feeling as if they were suddenly vulnerable children. "You mean tear down the house?"

"Yes." George spoke slowly, obviously surprised at my surprise. "We are talking about $400,000 and up homes. One developer envisions a gated community—entering from the highway." He pivoted to his credenza and opened a file, extracting a subdivision drawing. In the rendering, I saw Birkham Road and could tell it was Doro's land.

I grabbed the paper from his hand, creasing the corner in the process. "This is already drawn up?" I looked from George to Tuck and then back. "Who did this?"

"It's just a diagram, Mrs. Rivers. Developers have been hungry to get their hands on that beautiful land for years." George paused before continuing. "The zoning board is ready to approve its development. Several people have approached your aunt in the past few years, but she was not ready to sell. Given that you now are, we may even see a bidding war."

He smiled, sure that I would be happy to hear that news. But I could only hear Doro's ancient ice cream grinder and see the porch swing where two little girls licked strawberry cones.

We remained in George Mellsum's office for another thirty minutes, Tuck and I, leaving with a paper estimate and a contract to sign Mellsum as listing agent. I saw that there were seven digits on the estimated sales price, but all I could really see was that swing.

Stepping out into the summer humidity, I felt temporarily weak in the knees, grabbing hold of Tuck's elbow to steady myself.

"Whoa, you okay?" He grabbed my hand and we began to walk.

"Tuck, you didn't say anything in there."

"What did you want me to say? It's not my land to sell. Not my deal."

Tuck didn't start the car. "Want to go get something to eat? Maybe you need to eat."

I shook my head. "No, I want to go . . ."

"Home?"

I let out a dramatic sigh. "Yes, home. To my gated estate."

We drove in silence for a moment, before Tuck spoke again.

"Lot of money George was talking about there."

"Yes."

"I take it you were surprised the land would be parceled off? Developed?"

Anger tickled the back of my throat. "Surprised puts it mildly. Why would someone not want to buy that beautiful old house? Run it as an inn? Live there with a bunch of kids? It's a great place to—"

"Raise a child?"

I was quiet, feeling tired and a bit embarrassed. Had I been so naïve as to think I could sell the Inn and it would continue as it had always been? I said as much to Tuck.

"No, I don't think you're naïve, Jo." He put his arm around the back of my shoulders and rubbed my neck. "I just think you've moved on, and you don't realize that not everyone loves the Inn like you and me—"

"And many other people! Many people loved the Inn." *People loved Doro*, I thought. And then, *What were you thinking, Doro?*

"Yes, lots of people. But there was only one Doro. I don't think you realize that."

"I don't realize how special my own aunt was?"

He stopped rubbing and took his hand down. "Yes, but I also think that you think you can have things both ways—sell the Inn and live your life in Chicago, but anytime you want to visit, it'll still be here waiting, just the same.

"Things change, Jo."

Change. Not until he said the word did I realize how much I hated it.

"What do I do, Tuck?"

"As your lawyer," he leaned over and smiled that impish smile. "I would advise you to consider your two options. Sell the land and buy a kick-ass dwelling in downtown Chicago. Or move back here and live in the Inn." His eyes moved to my stomach. "Raise a family as you were raised."

He pulled up in front of the Inn and put the gear into Park.

"You want to come in?"

"No, my books and my wife await me. Besides, I think you need some time to think."

"Thanks for going with me."

That smile again. "I'm happy about your news, Jo. And this real estate thing, it's a good problem to have. You wanted to get rid of Mt. Moriah. This is your ticket." He paused. "Or you could do what Doro thought you might do."

I leaned in the car window to hear.

"And what is that?"

"Write the Great American Novel from that porch swing."

That night I called Tom.

"I'm glad you called. I've been worried."

I told Tom about the visit to the realtor, about the amount that the Inn would fetch.

He whistled. "That's a lot of cannoli."

"I want the baby, Tom."

I could sense a smile in his voice. "I do too, Jo."

"But I don't know where I want to raise it."

Tom was quiet for a moment, and I sensed his smile had evaporated.

"I hear too many Is in your sentences and no we's. Where's the we, Jo?"

I was sitting on the swing, listening to the crickets, and watching June bugs slither across the porch. Maddy had gone to bed early, and Tuck was at his parents' house. For the first time in many weeks, months perhaps, Earth seemed to have righted itself.

"I honestly don't know, Tom."

"I said I was sorry for walking out. You hurt me. You have to own that."

"There are things you don't understand, Tom. Things I need to work through."

"I can help you work through them."

Closing my eyes, I saw the gravediggers shovel one, two, many clumps of soggy soil onto Doro's casket. I saw Grace's closed casket being carried out of the church where I hid behind sunglasses, behind Doro. Buried with them was a secret grief I could not explain, could barely name, even to myself. "No, these things you can't."

A sigh from Tom. "You won't let me try. You won't let me in."

I ran my finger across a rough spot on the wooden arm of the swing, back and forth until a splinter pierced my skin: a metaphor for my life. "You and I are different people, Tom. You're always happy, always ready to be happy. Me, I'm scared all the time."

"I'm not happy right now." A pause and then, "Scared of what?"

Of being murdered. Of dying. Of being a mother. Of being a wife.

Of myself.

"Just . . . scared, Tom. Overwhelmed. You take things—deaths, losses—and move on. I, I can't move on." I continued to talk against Tom's silence. "You don't understand how Grace's murder affected me—it changed me."

Finally he spoke. "You need someone you can talk to. I want to be that person." He cleared his throat. "I *expect* to be that person."

"I don't know if you can be. You weren't there; you didn't know Grace."

Tom was quiet again, measuring his words before his question. "And what about Tuck?"

"Tuck? What does he have to do with this?"

"Can you talk to him? Are you talking to him instead of your husband?"

Tuck. Those arms that made me feel like I could fall asleep and take the longest, sweetest nap. That mischievous grin. All the history, all the days we had spent together. He was my past; he was a part of my history, my foundation. I loved him like the good friend that he was, like a brother. Was there something more? Something I was hiding from myself? I knew the answer, and perhaps Tom could sense it.

"Tuck has been very supportive. He knows me well."

"I thought I knew you well. I know the girl I married."

I closed my eyes, wishing to be a cricket, chirping and bouncing through life. "I'm tired, Tom."

"Then you should go to bed." He paused. "I want to tell you I'll wait forever, Jo. But the truth is that I'm not sure I can."

"You're walking away again."

"Good luck with your decision, Jo. Keep me posted."

Never had I heard such thick sarcasm from the man with the sunny eyes and dimples.

"Don't be like that Tom. I, I just need some time."

Sighing, "I don't know how you want me to be." And then, "Goodbye, Jo."

The receiver went dead, and I sat perfectly still, staring at the obnoxious dial tone until an operator's tinny voice came on.

There amidst the night crawlers, under the crescent moon and surrounded by a million murmuring leaves, I realized I was totally alone.

27

THE STRANGER

I DIDN'T TALK TO TOM FOR ALMOST TWO WEEKS. Schools opened and stores posted their school supply sales. Outside the temperature dropped ten degrees—as if on cue—and the burgeoning fall sky painted itself the purest of blues.

Each time the phone rang, I imagined it to be Tom. With each passing day my flat stomach expanded and along with it my knowledge that I had pushed too far, had held Tom at arms' length for too long: I had lost him.

I stopped drinking and substituted chocolate as a new vice. I also made an appointment with Dr. Overby, the ob/gyn who had delivered most of Mt. Moriah and passed up retirement three years running.

It was looking into his cataracts that I heard the heartbeat for the first time. I began to cry.

Holding out a tissue, "JoAnna, are those tears of joy?"

"They are tears of I-can't-believe-this." I dabbed my eyes. "I guess I'm a little overwhelmed."

He held up my ring finger. "And your husband? What does he say?"

"He, he's in Chicago. He's very happy." I wondered how many pregnant women with their bellies exposed had lied to Dr. Overby. I wondered if seeing someone's vagina gave him the omniscience to read minds.

Dr. Overby smiled. "Good. Women with support often have easier pregnancies. From what I can see, all is well. Strong heartbeat. I'd like you to start pre-natal vitamins."

I took the prescription from his hand.

"Dr. Overby, I drank some—before I knew. Before I realized . . . I drank alcohol. Will that affect the baby?"

He sat on the stool, pushing his glasses to the top of his head and running his hands over his eyes.

"You're, what, twenty-four?"

"Twenty-six."

"Right. Well, I can tell you that your mother probably smoked when she was pregnant. And if she was a drinker, she probably drank. Most of that generation did. All that to say we have learned the best ways to make a healthy baby, but babies are very resilient. Chances are slim that you have damaged your baby," he paused and put his glasses back on his face. "Unless you have gotten drunk every day—really drank to excess."

A vision of myself in the mirror at the Addys flashed in my mind.

"No, not really," I said quietly.

"Good. Then let's concentrate on that February due date and on eating healthy from here on out."

When I got back to the Inn, I dialed Sandalwood & Harris and asked for Tom's extension. Heart pounding, I waited through the voice mail greeting that told me he would be out of the office for a week. A minute later, I redialed and pushed zero to be transferred to the operator—a plump Hispanic woman named Rita whose raspberry nails curled over at the tips. I knew that on Rita's desk sat a picture of her and her son Julio taken at Christmas. She was wearing a hot pink apron with "Kiss the Cook" stretching across her breasts, and the somewhat-hot Julio was planting a kiss on her cheek. I knew the pen cradled in her left hand had a sunflower on the cap, and that she was chewing on at least three sticks of gum.

"Sandalwood & Harris."

"Rita, hi, it's JoAnna Rivers."

"JoAnna, girl, how are you? We missing you around here. When you coming back?"

Her years in the US had not erased Rita's Puerto Rican accent, nor had her verb tenses improved. Closing my eyes, I could see myself walking through the glass lobby doors and greeting her. Rita smelled like vanilla. I knew little about her life, didn't see her outside of work. Yet she was a new definition of friend, a familiar face that greeted me on my comings and goings. I was suddenly homesick for Chicago.

"I'm not sure, Rita. I tried to call Tom but got his voice mail. Have you . . ." I paused, wondering how I could explain I didn't know where my own husband was. "Has he checked in today?"

"Yes, lucky dog. My Roberto always tell me we would go to River Walk and see the Alamo. I ask your Tom to bring me little statue. But when you coming back?" Her voice dropped to a whisper. "Cruella has been asking."

Like so many at S&H, Rita shared a contempt for Candace who clearly did not approve of Rita—her dress, her voice, the way she spilled coffee on phone messages. Often, as Candace walked away, barely acknowledging Rita's existence, Rita let loose with a litany of Spanish slang that made Tom chuckle. It made me wish I had studied Spanish, instead of French, in college.

"Well I speak enough Spanish to know what she's saying would curl your hair up a bit tighter," Tom once chuckled.

"I'm not sure, Rita. What's going on there?"

"Hold a minute, girl."

While I waited, I thought about Tom in San Antonio. Was this a big shoot? Was he excited? The thought that he had gone without telling me was an arrow to my heart. He truly had left me.

"Sorry, girl, this phone crazy today. JoAnna, I sorry about your aunt. You okay, girl? Tom tell me you not feeling good."

So Tom had not told her about the baby. He knew I would want to tell her that myself. At least that. Or maybe he didn't want anyone to know. Maybe he wanted to walk away and pretend like I didn't exist—like *we* didn't exist.

Rita told me what I had missed. Much of it I tuned out, although the names and stories were comforting in their familiarity. One detail I did note was the hiring of a second Copy Manager.

"Where is she sitting?" I asked.

"It's a him. And in your cubicle."

Closing my eyes, I pictured my work space at the back of the twelfth floor, positioned against the glass wall so that half a window was mine. Casting my eyes to the left, I could glimpse the Michigan Avenue Bridge. Across the cubicle was another desk where I stored file folders.

"Okay, girl, it almost noon so I need to go."

Noon was Rita's lunch break, when she could escape to the break room and watch *Days of Our Lives*. *"Ah, mierda! Susan Lucci que canalla!"* she would hiss at the nineteen-inch screen. I knew Rita would not miss a moment of her break.

"I'll let you go, Rita," I said, then, thinking I might never see her again, "take care of yourself."

"You too, girl. You want I transfer you somewhere?"

"Yeah, actually, can you transfer me to Candace?" I spoke quickly, getting the words out before my courage evaporated.

"Oh girl, I can't. She's in San Antonio too."

With Tom. With her pink bras and tight pencil skirts. With her ability to tie neckties and the delicate, polished fingertips that she used to flip lint off men's jackets. With that flirtatious giggle and fuck-me-pumps. With my husband.

After my conversation with Rita, I moved to the swing, swatting away mosquitos and watching Maddy on the lawn mower, riding around in circles until the high grass was all gone.

The phone rang, and I almost tripped myself running for it.

"Hi, Jo, you're out of breath."

Tuck's voice had never sounded so good to me. My lifeline.

"Hi yourself. I was just swinging on the porch and wishing you were here. I'd really like to talk to you."

"Everything okay?" Tuck sounded concerned.

"Yes, I just, I need to talk to someone."

"Well, it's going to have to wait two days. I'm headed to Birmingham to take the boards. Can it keep?"

"Of course, Tuck. Good luck on your boards. I'll be crossing my fingers."

"Toes too, please. Okay, see you Friday." And then, "Love ya."

"I love you too," I said to the dead phone line. And at that moment I knew I did. I had loved Tuck forever, and I wanted him back. I cherished the swing and the land the Inn sat on, treasured the creaking floorboards in the foyer and the magnolia trees that curled around themselves. I loved the fact there was no Thai food within thirty miles, and I coveted the predictability of life on the mountain. And suddenly I knew what I had to do. Quickly, before I lost my nerve, before I lost my way.

I logged on to Doro's computer and typed in Candace's email address. My resignation letter was polite but short: I hoped she'd understand and appreciated the opportunity. Ten minutes later her reply came through. It, too, was cordial and polite. So abbreviated that it told me the new copy manager was already sitting in my chair, craning his neck to see the Chicago River.

Candace didn't mention Tom. I wondered if they were sitting in a riverfront café, sipping wine. I wondered if my name ever came up. I wondered if Tom had ever existed at all . . . if any part of us had been real.

I wondered whether I had just said goodbye to Chicago forever.

The days passed in a haze. I was sure Tom had heard of my email to Candace, but he didn't call. He was gone, and if I stood still for too long, fear of the future clinched me like a vise. And so I didn't stop moving. Increasingly withdrawn, Maddy took more naps. I knew he was grieving but I had nothing to give. All I could do was clean. Putting order to the splendid chaos of Doro's things became my focus.

With the drop in humidity and passage of time, my energy level returned— to the point that one Tuesday I decided to walk the mile to the library with a satchel on my shoulders. The path I took was so familiar my feet seemed to move by instinct. It was the route we had taken weekly, Doro and I, when we first moved to Mt. Moriah. Down the Inn's long driveway, onto Birkham Street, crossing the bridge at Woodbury Avenue, and cutting across the Family Dollar parking lot. The library outpost was a small cottage wedged in between a bank and a Sonic that was new since my departure four years ago.

Mature white crepe myrtles flanked the narrow structure, and the building's mossy green shingles seemed incongruous with the elegant Palladium window in the front. I remembered that the children's section was in the front, with a maple table and coloring sheets in front of that window. I remember passing hours there, losing myself in a book as the world outside marched on.

A bell rang as I pulled the wooden door open. I immediately noticed that there was now a loveseat and two arm chairs in front of the window. The walls had been transformed from sunny yellow to soothing gray, and the card catalog files had acquiesced to two computer kiosks.

But the checkout desk greeting me was comforting in its sameness—same position, same blonde wood, even same dusty potted plant, or so it seemed. I set my satchel on the desk and waited as the librarian finished the last bite of a sesame bagel.

"I need to return these books for my aunt," I stammered. "I have a feeling they might be overdue."

The woman named Nanette excavated readers from atop a messy gray bun and pulled the books across the desk.

Scanning the top book, she peered at the screen and then looked directly at me and smiled sympathetically. "Mrs. Blair. I was so sorry to learn of her death; she was quite a woman."

"Yes, she was. Thank you." I pulled my wallet out of my satchel. "Do I owe anything to settle the bill?"

"Well it looks like they were all two months late, but how about we just erase that balance?"

"Are you sure? That's very nice." I put away my wallet and turned to leave, when Nanette put her hand on mine.

"You're Mrs. Blair's niece, right?"

I nodded.

"And you were friends with that girl Grace, right?"

My heart beating faster, I nodded again.

She took off her readers and leaned forward. "You don't know me; we never officially met. I'm Sam Snelling's sister."

Indeed I never met her, but I'll never forget the night Grace and I met Sam Snelling.

Grace and I were sixteen, and I was in my first month of driving alone. Doro's rule was that I had to drive with either her or Maddy for six months before I could venture out alone. And so Friday night, October 4 was a night I had looked forward to all summer, not for the reason that the rest of our high school did—because it was the football game with our rivals—but because I could drive myself and Grace there and back alone.

It didn't matter that our rival's Hail Mary pass knocked us out of championship contention. Keys in my jeans pocket pressed against my thigh. Our sweatshirts were not heavy enough against the chilly fall air, yet still we kept the windows down on the drive home, as Billy Joel belted his ballads in Doro's Chevrolet. The brisk breeze blew cherry-colored leaves across our path, and lighted pumpkins scowled from every house. We made the turn onto Birkham Road and sat idling at the bottom of the driveway, waiting for "She's Always a Woman" to end. Grace and I had not talked during the drive home, simply enjoying our independence.

Tuck and his friends were coming over after they showered. We knew they would be in bad moods from the loss, but also knew that Doro's brownies and pizza would bring them around. The air blowing through our car felt like Friday nights: youthful, free. Full of possibilities.

I started to continue up the driveway, when suddenly I saw lights behind me and heard an awful noise: the sick cymbal of steel against stone.

Birkham Road was bordered by a stone wall marking Doro's property. The wall continued for over a half mile before the sharp turn into the Inn driveway. The green Nissan had collided with the wall, compacting the hood almost to its windshield, a sizzling noise seeping from its engine.

Jumping from our car we ran toward the accident; pinned inside was a boy, blood caking the side of his face, windshield debris on the road.

"Is he, is he alive?" I was frozen at the sight. But not Grace.

"I don't know. Go get Doro and Maddy." Grace moved to the driver side window, cracked but not broken. She turned and yelled at me once more. "Go, Jo."

I got back into Doro's car to go up the drive, but Maddy's truck met me. Doro jumped from the truck, relief on her face that I was not the one in the wreck changing to horror as she saw the mangled car and the blood spattered window. She pulled me to her in a hug that told me what she had imagined in the moments since she and Maddy, watching from the kitchen window for my return, had seen a car airborne and heard the crash.

"Maddy's calling the ambulance," Doro called to Grace who was at the window, pulling on the door. "You should back up, Grace. That car might go up in flames."

"Is he dead?" My voice quivered.

"I don't know. He's not moving." Grace's voice was shrill with the tears. "Mister, can you hear me?"

Styx crooned from the radio, piercing the deadly silence of the night, as Grace continued to talk to the stranger.

"Help is on the way. Hang in there. Can you hear me?"

Billy Joel transitioned into Air Supply, but nothing from the driver. And then Air Supply changed to Aerosmith and to a weather report and then Kiss. And back to Air Supply. Over and over, a constant change. With only his fingers free, the stranger was pushing the radio buttons to tell us he was alive.

"You're alive! Keep pushing the buttons. My name is Grace. Don't be scared. We're here." Grace, who almost needed sedation to get a flu shot, seemed immune to the blood and the glass and the smell of anguish in the air. She continued a stream of conversation, as Tuck and his buddies arrived.

"What is she doing?" Tuck asked, the gravity of the situation shading his face.

"She's comforting a stranger, it seems," Maddy said softly.

The ambulance and firetruck arrived ten minutes later, and the team went to work prying open the car. Doro tried to coax Grace back from the car, but she flinched away. The radio station had played all the way through one song.

"Please, let me talk to him," she said to the crew manning the jaws of life.

A firefighter standing nearby put safety goggles on Grace and led her to a safe spot. "Keep talking. Keep him awake."

"Bohemian Rhapsody" droned on.

"Hey, the music stopped. Please keep changing the stations. Let us know you're okay." Grace's voice was loud and steady, even though her whole body trembled. "They're going to get you out, but please stay awake. Can you change the station?"

All we could hear was the whir of the tools trying to rescue the boy; the radio remained fixed.

"Please! Let me know you hear me!" Panic rose in Grace's voice, but she continued to talk, shouting above the machinery attempting to pry open the door.

And then Grace turned and faced us, a broad smile on her face: the radio stations were changing again.

It took ten more minutes before the crew was able to extract the stranger, his face bloody and swollen and his legs curled unnaturally away from his body. He had on a Doors sweatshirt and was about our age. As the medics gingerly placed him on the stretcher, he reached out a hand. We all knew he was reaching for Grace.

"Can I ride with him to the hospital?" she asked. "I don't want him to be alone."

The medics exchanged glances, then helped Grace into the back of the ambulance. We all piled into Doro's car and followed the ambulance the thirty minute drive to the hospital. Maddy kept pace with the ambulance driver.

"Way cool. I've never gotten to go this fast and miss lights," said Tuck's friend Joey.

"Epic," Tuck agreed.

Scrunched between the boys in the backseat, I thought of my parents, of the moments after the collision: Were they alive? Did they hear anyone's voice? I thought of my own paralysis that night and how Grace moved forward, doing what needed to be done. None of us were surprised by that. By Grace.

The stranger survived the accident but needed extensive rehab for his legs. He was moved to a hospital in Atlanta. Grace and I went to the hospital to tell him goodbye, but I hung back, sending Grace in by herself. To me, he was a stranger, but to Grace he was Sam Snelling.

My eyes misted at the memory of that night—the evening we all realized what Grace was capable of: her capacity to console.

"How is Sam?"

"He's living in Atlanta and has triplets," said Nanette, his sister. "He still walks with a limp and still talks about his angel—your Grace."

"Will you give him my regards?"

"Of course, honey, and again I'm sorry for your loss. For your losses."

I smiled and turned to go when Nanette called me back to the counter.

"Sorry, I just checked the record; there's still one book missing, if you could find that.

"It's *The Optimist's Daughter.*"

28

WELTY'S WAKE

The walk back to the inn was more exhausting than I expected, so I was happy to see Maddy's truck pull up alongside me.

"Pretty girl needing a ride today?" Maddy asked out the open window.

"You read my mind, Maddy."

"I need to stop at the hardware store to get a flapper. The downstairs commode is running."

After parking, he asked if I wanted to come in.

"I'm kinda tired, Maddy. I'll just wait here."

The minute in the store stretched to ten, undoubtedly due to Maddy's running into people he knew. It happened everywhere we went. I smiled at the thought of Maddy and Doro, of how loved they were, of the integral roles they played in the town. I watched as a crew took down the summer banners and raised the fall ones. The petunias in the hanging pots on the street lanterns looked old and tired. Signs in storefronts advertised back to school supplies, and a school bus rounded the corner. Mothers pushed babies in strollers, and squirrels raced across the telephone lines.

I felt suspended in time, not a part of Mt. Moriah, not a part of Chicago. Belonging only to myself. When Maddy returned to the truck, I told him of my resignation.

"Why, little thing, I have to say I'm surprised. I thought you loved that job."

"I love writing, but I wasn't doing writing." When I saw the concern on his face, I added, "I can find another job."

"And what did Tom say about your quitting?"

When I was quiet, he knew.

"Ah, my lord, Doro would have something wise to tell you, but I just don't know what to say." He removed his cap and scratched his head. "This business of you and Tom worries me."

"I can afford to take some time and think of what I want to do—"

Maddy cut me off. "What *you* want to do. You mean what you and your husband want to do. You're in a marriage, little thing."

"I think Tom's left me, Maddy," I said quietly, shocked to hear how the words sounded out loud.

"Now why do you think that?"

"I haven't talked to him in weeks, and he went to San Antonio on a business trip and didn't tell me." My voice quivered. "I think it's over, Maddy. I think I'm alone."

"Now listen here. I don't know Tom all that well, but I know enough to know he's not a man who walks out on his wife and baby." He paused before adding, "What did you say to him?"

Clearly Maddy sensed Tom's feelings toward me had changed because of something I had done. And that was true, wasn't it? I had shut him out. I had toyed with the idea of not keeping the baby. I had come to Mt. Moriah, and I had fallen for Tuck. I had myself to blame.

I sighed. "I need to talk to Tuck. He's only been away a day, but I miss him. He's been so great."

We were in front of the Inn, and, turning off the ignition, Maddy turned to face me. His look registered the same disappointment and anger as when I struck down his elephant ears.

"Now listen to me, Jo. You are a married woman, and Tuck is a married man. That's all I'm going to say about that, but I hope you are hearing me." His eyes sharpened. "Grow up. You are not a girl anymore, Jo."

And with that he slammed the door and left me in the truck, feeling like I had disappointed one of my last friends in the world.

He was right. I was not a girl, not a child, not carefree. My youth was over, had been since Grace was murdered, since I had moved to Chicago. Mt. Moriah was a lovely respite from my life, but I needed to move on. With or without Tom. I could support myself. And my baby.

I settled in Doro's recliner with my laptop. Maddy moved through the house, slamming doors, something very unlike him.

"Do you need help, Maddy?"

"No," was his brusque response.

I wanted a drink. I wanted to drink myself into a wine coma—to fall asleep pretending my life as a writer was not out of reach. "Grow up," I muttered to myself. I pulled up the *Chicago Tribune* online and scanned the jobs page. Restless, I turned to the want ads and looked for apartments. The writer in me imagined a world in which the baby and I rented an upstairs studio apartment in a brownstone near Logan Park. There would be built-in shelves and walnut plank floors, and the widow downstairs would care for the baby while I worked two jobs. I would come home exhausted at night, but together the baby and I would read books until bedtime. On the weekends we would stroll to Lake Michigan.

I would put the baby to bed in a bassinet set up beside my bed, and when she was asleep, I would write—pacing myself, forcing myself to take the Jillsandra saga just two pages further each night. In a year, I would have over 700 pages. I would find a good editor—perhaps I could become an editor: I should look for jobs in publishing.

Such were the ramblings of my mind as I whiled away the afternoon in an internet fog. The truth was I couldn't see beyond tomorrow and didn't know who I was. How could someone drifting through her life mother someone else?

When the panic turned my palms clammy, I got up and paced. I saw the end table stacked with Doro's papers and decided to look for the missing library book. I smiled at the thought of Doro reading the book I had recommended, probably thinking until the day she died that the author's name was Endora.

The Optimist's Daughter was nowhere in the den or the parlor. It soon became a quest, and I moved like a madwoman through the house. Maddy finished the toilet repair and, washing his hands, took eggs out of the refrigerator. The clock said six o'clock, and the sight of food made me realize how hungry I was.

"Want me to cook dinner, Maddy?"

"No. Thank you." Maddy pulled out a pound of bacon and soon the break-fast for dinner was ready. We sat at opposite ends of the dinette set in the breakfast room, the clinking of forks the only break in the silence. I knew Maddy was disappointed in me, knew it by the way he held the paper in front of his plate. Perhaps inane conversation would bring him back to me.

"Maddy, there's a missing library book of Doro's I can't find. Have you seen it?"

Shaking his head, he put the paper down. "But it might be in that lap desk she kept by her bed." A pause. "By our bed." The paper went up again.

I removed the plates and cleaned the kitchen. Maddy remained, nodding over his plate. Eventually I heard the shower start. Five minutes later, he was in pajamas, hair damp, ready for bed.

"Goodnight, Maddy," I said from the doorway.

"Night," he said, turning on his side.

I started to close the door when I saw the teal paisley lap desk on the floor beside Doro's side of the bed. Curling myself in a ball in Doro's recliner, I lifted the lid and found the missing library book. I smiled at the Post-it Notes peeking from the page edges.

In a Southern literature course in college, I got hooked on Eudora Welty. For high school graduation Grace had given me *One Writer's Beginnings*, the story of how Welty started writing. I was young and sure of my abilities, then, and the world seemed *possible*.

Over the course of the next two hours, as the light faded outside, I reread *The Optimist's Daughter* all the way through, one Post-it at a time.

I laughed out loud at Doro's notes about the McKelveys: *"How crass!"* and her Post-it about a loose bird in the house: *"I don't blame Laurel for locking herself in the bathroom!"*

In English class I wrote about a passage in which the protagonist, Laurel, "cages" herself in the bathroom while a bird flies loose in the house. I described the cages in which humans find themselves—in Laurel's case a cage constructed not of steel but of anger and resentment. While the paper garnered an A, it was a collection of naive words written by an ingenuous girl who at that point saw nothing but open doors: a girl who hadn't lost her best friend, or her aunt, who hadn't tied herself to a dead-end job or fallen in love with a man who walked out on her. A girl whose heart didn't lurch at footsteps and darkness.

A girl not yet caged by fear.

My eyes clouded, and I turned pages. Pulling off each Post-it, I set them on the arm of the recliner. They were Doro's last words to me.

On a note mid-way through the book, Doro wrote, *"That's love."* It was a passage I cherished, describing the life-changing love Laurel had shared with her deceased husband:

"And they themselves were a part of the confluence. Their own joint act of faith had brought them here at the very moment and matched its occurrence, and proceeded as it proceeded. Direction itself was made beautiful, momentous . . . It's our turn! she'd thought exultantly. And we're going to live forever."

I had experienced that kind of love, lived it—the feeling that tomorrow would beget a new tomorrow and that we'd live forever. Such was my friendship with Grace. Such was the way I felt standing on the Loyola courtyard, my hand in Tom's. But wasn't that what I also felt as my head rested against Tuck's on the chaise lounge? The magnetic draw of two men, each so distinctive. Was there a forever love for me? A forever?

Feeling a sting behind my eyes, I knew tears were taunting me. One Post-it remained, next to one of the book's most poignant sections:

". . . the guilt of outliving those you love is justly to be borne, she thought. Outliving is something we do to them. The fantasies of dying could be no stranger than the fantasies of living. Surviving is perhaps the strangest fantasy of them all."

On the note, I could hear Doro speaking to me. *"Is this how Jo feels? Why she won't come home? Does she know how much I love her?"*

Surviving is perhaps the strangest fantasy of them all.

Suddenly, my body was wracked with tears—millions and thousands and hundreds of them. Tears I had fought back in the last church pew at Grace's funeral, that threatened me in the night as I huddled in my bed in the corporate hotel. Sobs that teased at the edge of my mind as strangers danced too closely at Tony's. Sorrow eclipsed by anger when Tom walked out. Weeping that had barely come even as I listened to Maddy's broken voice and saw the shovels of dirt sprinkle atop Doro's casket. Tears spawned from a grief so deep inside me that they took my breath away. Clutching the Post-its to my chest, I sobbed the names on my heart. "Gracie. Doro." As if I cried hard enough, uttered their names with enough ache in my voice, they would return to me.

And then, "Tom. Tuck. Maddy." For they felt lost to me too.

Yet, at that moment, through the haze of my tears I could see clearly: I understood. I knew why Doro had left me the Inn. She wanted me to return—to face the good and the bad that was Mt. Moriah. Doro had sent me away not out of avoidance, but out of love. And she wanted me back, because this place of our yesterdays was the last and greatest gift she could bestow on me. This Inn was her life; it was our life together.

"Doro," I whispered. "Doro, I loved you too." For hours my sobs bounced against the ticking clock and around the room full of the life that Doro had built. For us. Until finally, shirt wet and chest sore from the weeping, silence absorbed my grief and I slept.

In my dream I was twelve years old, but Doro and I lived in her studio apartment, not the Inn. I was playing with Barbies on her Murphy bed, which didn't make sense given my age, but then nothing ever makes sense in dreams.

I started singing softly, and suddenly Doro came over and looked at me strangely.

"Stop singing that. Stop it."

"Why?"

"That was Grace's song, not yours. We can't sing that now." She looked down at my pants, covered in cat hair. "You know I don't like cats."

"Doro, what's wrong? Did I do something?"

"You know what you did." Her voice shook, heavy with disappointment.

"I don't know," I pleaded. I was suddenly eighteen years old and the Barbies were shards of glass. I was making a mosaic, aquamarines and violets and tiger eyes. I ran my hand across the pieces of glass—to cover them? To sweep them off the bed? My hand began to bleed.

"Now look what you did." Doro came over to the bed and shook me by the shoulders. "Careless. Why are you careless?"

"I don't know, Doro, I don't know." Then I was twenty-five, but Doro was the younger Doro who picked me up from the hospital waiting room in 1983. Her eyes were wild, darting back and forth, and I thought she might strike me. Suddenly afraid, I started running down a long hallway that grew longer the faster I ran. Without looking back, I sensed that Doro was following me. At the end the hallway turned sharply and I was at a dead end. With a door.

I opened the door and ran into Doro. In her hand was a jagged piece of glass.

"What have you done?" she asked. Stepping aside, she revealed a large mirror, shattered into a million pieces.

I awoke with a start. It wasn't a dream. It was a memory.

29

SHARDS OF GLASS

I SAT UP WITH A CLEAR SENSE of where I needed to go, what I needed to face: the attic, my old bedroom.

Slowly, deliberately, I climbed the steps to the top floor. In my head it was June 1, 1997 again, and darkness was creeping over the house. I hesitated at the top of the attic stairs. Opening the door, I felt stifling heat waft across my cheeks.

I crossed over to the window and turned the air conditioning unit on. It rattled and spit dust out at me, then settled into a loud hum. Outside the window, the crepe myrtle was a brilliant fuschia. When I was eight, that tree was so young that, peering down, I could view only its top. Now I had reached the top. Or it had reached me.

Nested on either side of the east window were the twin beds where Grace and I had spent so many nights. Sinking onto my bed, I ran my hand across the fabric. I knew exactly where to look for the quarter-sized ink dot—the casualty of a late night writing session. As surely as if it were a day ago, I could feel the pen sliding out of my hand as I settled into a delicious teenaged coma.

Doro purchased the twin quilts when I turned thirteen. She thought it was time to renovate my room as I transitioned into a teenager. One weekend we went to a crafts fair in Nashville—Doro, Grace, and me. Bored with the amount of time Doro spent looking at pottery, Grace and I wandered off on our own.

It was Grace who saw the quilts.

"*Look, Jo Jo, these would be pretty.*" Grace and I had been poring over magazines; she was my chief consultant when it came to decorating.

"*You think?*" I wasn't sold on quilts. "*Would I get two the same?*"

"*No, silly, we'll find one that's your personality and one that's mine. Ooh, I like this one.*" Grace held up a quilt with deep hues of green and blue.

"*Can I help you?*" The voice belonged to a short, pale woman named Sarah, as wide as she was tall.

Grace spoke up. She always spoke up for us. "*Yes ma'am, we're redecorating our bedroom and there are twin beds.*"

I giggled at her mention of "our room."

"*Well, now, how much do you girls know about quilts?*"

Exchanging glances, we shook our heads.

"*Let me tell you a little, then. All the patterns have names. Those you're holding are called Sister's Choice quilts, I'm not sure why.*"

Grace's eyes sparkled. "*Jo Jo, it's perfect for our room.*"

"*Oh, so you two are sisters?*"

Before I could speak, Grace put her arm around my waist. "*Yes ma'am we are!*"

Oh Grace, we were, weren't we? I thought.

We ended up purchasing two quilts—Grace's in sea foam green and navy and mine in yellow and red. "Different colors?" Doro had asked, scrunching up her forehead. As it turned out, Grace's was only available in a full size, so Doro, sighing, bought it anyway.

I crossed over to Grace's bed. I could tell the extra fabric had been tucked under the side that was against the wall. On the side facing my bed, the quilt looked exactly the right length.

And then I saw it.

Protruding from the corner of the bed was a long string. It looked like a mouse tail, but of course I knew better: I knew exactly what it was. Through the lens of my subconscious I could see Doro kick it under the bed— perhaps, probably, not even realizing what it was. But I knew what it was. And whose.

Grace's missing tennis shoe.

I had dropped it there. That day. The day Grace died.

The truth, then: I was there that day. With Grace.

I remember the light was sinking quickly that day in June when I hobbled up the steps of the Inn. Looking over my shoulder every few seconds, I felt my panting breaths pounding in my ears. But behind me were only shadows. My ankle hurt and blood trickled down my leg. Into the hallway. Shutting the door behind me, I leaned against it.

"Doro?" I whispered, my voice not sounding like mine. "Maddy?"

At that moment, had I been able to think clearly, I would have remembered that Doro had gone on a day long shopping trip, and Maddy had left that morning on his annual week-long fishing junket.

I ran to the front window and drew the drapes. Bile gathered at the back of my throat, and I thought I would be sick at any moment. The bathroom: I needed to make it to the bathroom. My heart thumping in my chest, I limped up the steps as quickly as I could. Then up the attic steps where I almost tripped on something white.

The cat.

Now I remember.

Those years ago, there had been a cat that would sneak in when the door was open. Doro cursed the cat but left it food and water on the back porch. That day I picked up the cat from the steps and found myself covered in white fur. The cat pressed itself to me, grazing my neck with its emery board tongue.

In the bathroom, I shut the door and wished for a lock. The cat jumped up on the window sill and watched me, amber eyes wise with the moment.

I ran scalding water in the bathtub and yet I could not get warm. I sank down under the water, staring at the film of soap left behind. Still I shook. Still I was cold. I don't know how much time passed before I heard Doro come in downstairs and call for me.

"Jo? Are you here?"

"Yes." How odd that my voice sounded like it always did.

I heard Doro's footsteps on the stairwell.

"I was getting worried. I came home from shopping, and you weren't here. I called Genia, and she said you and Grace were supposed to go for a walk at the Point, but that you had cancelled. I ran out to the grocery." Doro kept chattering as she climbed the steps. "It's getting dark. Why are you so late?"

"I'm taking a bath."

I thought I could hide in that water, that I could wash away the swollen eye, the areas on my inner thighs that tomorrow would awaken purple. The long gauges that tree branches had made on my shins, at the base of my neck. If the water were hot enough, the lather were thick enough, it would wash away all signs. I would emerge from the bathroom the person I was before four o'clock that afternoon.

"Jo?"

While the cat kept vigil from his window perch, I sat still in the water, hugging my knees to my chin. I wanted to cry, but there were no cleansing tears. I heard the door open, but kept my eyes pressed shut: I did not want to see the expression on Doro's face.

"Oh my dear God."

I remember feeling dizzy, and it seems that at some point I threw up. When the bath cooled Doro ran more hot water. I opened my good eye to see her scrubbing my dirty knee with a sponge. Her tears dripped onto my knee and mingled with the soapsuds. Atop my knee was a scar that I had gotten from a bicycle fall when I was eleven. Doro knew that scar. Once all the dirt was gone the mark was still there. She ran her fingertip over it and leaned to kiss it.

"I'll take care of everything, Jo. I'll make everything okay."

I loved her for those words. She meant them; she believed them. But I knew better. I knew Doro was powerless. I knew power was powerless.

When the phone rang downstairs, Doro handed me a towel and left the room.

"Stay in here," she said.

I stepped out of the tub, limbs still shaking, and began to gingerly pat myself dry. Was this my skin? My pain? Turning, I caught a glimpse of myself in the white wicker mirror above the sink. I didn't recognize the person I saw. A small corner of my lip was bleeding, and I leaned in close enough to see the little puddle of blood form. I collected a drop on my finger and then pressed it onto a tissue. A crimson streak fanned out like a sunray. A pink star on the snowy whiteness of the cotton.

Then I heard Doro's screams downstairs, crying into the phone words of disbelief. She knew now. About Grace.

I looked in the mirror. I projected a mouthful of blood onto the face of the woman staring back at me. She was helpless and weak and ugly. My bloody spit ran down her cheek, and I wished her dead. Picking up the porcelain vase Doro kept on the counter, I held it with two shaking hands and silently cursed at that reflection.

"I hate you."

With those words, I flung the vase at the glass, shattering the hideous girl into bits and pieces until she was no more.

Shaking now with the memory, I arose, Grace's shoe in my hand, and went to the bathroom. Above the sink was the white wicker frame where the mirror had been. I had been adamant that Maddy not hang a new one, resolute that I would only sleep downstairs, and all these years Doro had respected my wishes.

I looked up, and at the window sill, silent as a statue, he sat. I pushed and prodded until the window opened, reached out, and grabbed the cat.

"You remember me, don't you, kitty?" The cat's golden eyes said it all. He remembered the girl who left the house for a walk with her best friend, and he saw the girl who returned that night—broken into a million shards of glass like the mirror.

Perhaps he had been waiting all these years for her to come back home. To see if the girl had been put back together.

30

THE ELEVENTH COMMANDMENT

I REMEMBER THE SMELLS THAT DAY: the honeysuckle and freshly mowed grass that bespoke summer. The dreary winter, the damp spring were over, and June beckoned all of Mt. Moriah outdoors—including me and Grace.

Grace had called the day before. "Let's hike up to the Point, Jo Jo. I have something to tell!"

"I can't. I have to finish six more chapters." I had taken a summer job helping one of my college English professors transcribe his book.

"Well, if something changes and your fingers get speedy, call me."

Something did change. I found myself typing the last page just after two, the summer sun urging me outside. I called Grace.

"Hey I'm done! I'll meet you at the bottom of the path at four."

I started to leave Doro a note that I was joining Grace, but she had left before sunrise to drive to Atlanta to shop and I knew I'd be back before her. Maddy was on his annual week-long fishing junket.

And so it was that I met up with Grace on that bright, perfect June day.

Our college diplomas not yet framed, it was the start of summer and the beginning of our adult lives.

So we thought.

We started on the narrow gravel road up the side of the mountain—an ambitious path, mostly of rugged terrain. We had not hiked it in two years but in our memories we knew what was in store for us at the top: a breathtaking view of the town in its leafy splendor.

Soon we developed a rhythm: my size five feet double-stepping for every broad step that the size nine feet took. In our steps there was a syncopation, in the trees a bending and stooping, from the birds a happy purring.

"Gosh, slow down, Miss Elephant Foot," I said.

"We need to trim our winter thighs, Jo Jo. Besides, you'll lose weight, with your little jog there."

"And speaking of little jogs, I should've brought my jogging bra—not that there is much to bounce."

"You mean, nothing to bounce."

Ours was the casual, teasing banter of old friends. It seemed so long since we had been together, and longer still since we had laughed freely and easily. For the moment, as the sun burned in the periwinkle sky, we were girls again— with the beautiful uncertainty of life laid out before us on porcelain china.

"So what's your news, Gracie?"

"First you. Heard anything from the letters you sent out?"

I shook my head. "I had a second phone interview with the Chicago ad agency. But that was two weeks ago.

"Now, Gracie, what gives?"

Grace turned, back stepping in front of me. Afraid of tripping, she reached out to stop me. "This is something scary. Wonderful, but scary. But I need your support. You can't imagine how much."

"Alright, already. Just spill the beans." I was fully expecting Grace to tell me that she and Tuck were serious.

A quick glance around. The wind had picked up, and brittle leaves crunched as we walked.

"I just want you to know this is something I've planned." Grace grabbed my wrist. "I realized the one thing I want most in the world."

We rounded a bend where kudzu hung thick and low, draping us in shadowy coolness. Overhead the sun tried to penetrate the canopy, but the trees were too old and the leaves too thick. On my face was the impatience of waiting to hear Grace's news; on Grace's the impatience of a secret about to be divulged.

We stepped out from the mossy overhang, our winter eyes temporarily blinded.

Grace cleared her throat and started to speak.

"Stop," I said as something crossed my peripheral vision. "Gracie, I think I just saw a possum." I paused for effect, knowing possums had terrified Grace for years.

"If a possum runs across our path, I'm out of here."

"Like where would you go?" I saw the dogleg in the road ahead. "Hey, we'll never make it up and back before dark. Let's turn around, okay?"

I don't know exactly why I said it. Four miles roundtrip was nothing for us, even with winter thighs. Yet something told me the next bend should be the last.

"Finish your story, Gracie!" Suddenly anxious, but unsure why, I talked faster, like a nervous traveler on a turbulent plane.

"No wait. I hear something too," said Grace, extending her arm. "See—I've got the willies."

Indeed, the proverbial goosebumps were there: Had Grace ever survived a scary movie without her hair follicles standing on end?

"I don't think it's the boogeyman. C'mon, let's turn around."

After all, there was no boogeyman: He was the fantasy of childhood nightmares. Did we really believe that or just tell ourselves so?

I turned and looked. Of course there was nothing. Those suspicious ears of mine: When I was five, my mother swore I could hear a wasp six feet away. My mother. When was the last time she popped into my thoughts? Rubbing my calf, I resettled my petite foot in the new Nike. I was definitely getting a blister.

Grace stopped now. "Okay, I'm afraid that possum is going to run out."

Time for theatrics. "Maybe it's not a possum, Gracie. Maybe it's a crazed mental patient."

Grace stuck out her tongue. "Hold up," she said. "My shoelace broke!"

Hands on hips, leaning over to stretch, I watched Grace's tedious process of reallocating laces and holes. Closing my eyes, I felt the sun burning my back. Years later I would remember the rays and how warm I was: Warm to the touch like there was no way I could ever be chilled again.

It was only a moment before I opened my eyes. Right before the scream. Or maybe right after. Which came first?

Straightening, before I could reel around, I felt it. It was heavy and uncomfortable in my back. Was there any question it was a gun? I had never held a gun, never felt one, yet there was no question. I froze in place.

But Grace wasn't frozen. "Oh God, don't hurt us. Here. Take my wallet." Her shoe was still untied, the laces a loose mess of turns and loops. She pulled a red billfold from her shorts. It had been banging against her hip as she walked. It was going to set us free.

Grace pried dollars out, plastic cards, and flung them at the stranger. He ignored them. "Don't scream. Just walk. Do this or I'll kill you."

Dizzied, with adrenalin invading our every pore, we looked at each other. This was not happening.

But it was not a dream. Under hostile sun, six feet crunched and climbed through the brush. This was the place that looked so tranquil only minutes ago? Now the shrubbery, the swaying trees, gnawed at our legs, drawing bits of our blood while our minds raced and our eyes darted at each other.

Think, *think*, said the voice in my head. Grab the gun; it's probably not loaded. Criminals usually operate without bullets. Hadn't I read this in a magazine? Yes, it was on an airplane— a peaceful flight, dancing in the clouds with no hint of turbulence. I had drunk apple juice, the whole can.

I'm thirsty, I thought. *I can't think when my mouth is this dry. What's happening to me? My skin is wet. I'm cold. How can I be cold in this sun?*

We kept climbing. Gone were thoughts of summer, vanished were visions of trim thighs. Secrets never told lingered in the air we panted in and out. Higher and higher, we neared the top. The tree roots threatened to trip us. The metal was still pointed in my back.

Down below, had we turned to look, we would have seen Grace's dollar bills flying in the June breeze, along with the credit cards knocked from her hand with a smirk.

"Over there. Take everything off," he commanded me when we reached the top. And to Grace: "To the tree."

I'd always thought it such a strange tree: an ivory birch alone here anchoring the bluff at the top. There was the town, to our right. To our left, the river. I remembered the game we played as girls.

"Okay, find the Nelsons' house."

"Easy one. Two o'clock."

My mind, racing with survival strategies, was plagued by hints of what could be. Cluttering my mind. Preventing me from thinking clearly.

Think, *think.*

A thick rope was thrown around Grace's knee, and her untied shoe fell off and rolled towards me. In another instant, another rope: this time at Grace's arms.

Her hands flailed wildly behind her, trying to find their way under the rope. Grace's countenance was one of desperation as she gulped the oxygen that taunted her. The stranger moved swiftly to bind her arms to the tree. The rope was just tight enough: Grace could not move.

"Let her go! Why are you doing this?" I had an idea: "There are people waiting for us at the bottom, men. Our boyfriends."

Grunting, he moved away from the tree and toward me. "What's your name?"

The girl at the tree called an answer. *Did she really just give my actual name? Surely not! What was Grace thinking?* For a moment, we were back in class together, one giving a ludicrous answer to an easy question. Soon we'll be through this, and maybe we'll even laugh over such a silly response. Wouldn't we? Think, *think.*

His voice was mocking as he turned his head toward Grace. "I don't remember asking you. I asked your friend here." He kicked a large stick out of his way and moved closer to me. There was little left on me, and yet fear consumed my modesty. I backed up. Slowly, for I knew the edge was close behind.

"Shit, you don't have far to go." He was close enough to touch me now, the gun aimed at the damp ground below. Could I grab it? He smirked and through suntan pantyhose I glimpsed sallow teeth.

I knew how his hand would feel even before I felt it. Clay-like, a damp piece of Play-Doh against my breast. A pungent smell of liquor on his breath. I clutched my tank. Why did I wear that? Was I like those women in the articles, those women that no one believed? They asked for it; isn't that the way the story always went?

I took one more step backward, knowing that I could take no more. Below me was Mt. Moriah. Business people, mothers, babies awakening from naps. Flushed and clammy. The people I would leave behind.

I'm going to die, I thought. It was here: that unfathomable day that you don't anticipate. This is how it would happen. *They won't find me for a few days.*

Think. *Think.* I could hear Grace sobbing. Screams would not help, for they would be carried off by idiotic birds that continued their vapid songs. Chortling starlings that soared above as a pistol butt knocked me to the ground.

What people say is inaccurate. The truth is that the weight is crushing. They didn't ask for it, those women. They couldn't fight hard enough. I was the hardest fighter there was. That's what Maddy had always called me: a fighter.

Maddy. Doro. Tuck. Where are you?

Silence filled my ears as the sun spun in the sky. Had I been asleep? Where was I? Think, *think.* I had taken a seminar on self-defense in college. Three hours. Police Officer Myers was the teacher. Or was it Martin? Remember, *remember!* Go for the eyes—one finger on each side of the neck. But one hand was pinned.

Holding my breath against the smell of his tepid breath, I kept my eyes tightly shut and continued to kick. As. Hard. As. I. Could. As. Long. As. I. Could.

I felt his hands upon me: *both* his hands. *The gun: where was the gun?*

"If you let us go, we won't tell." *Where was that voice coming from? Was it really mine?* I thought. "Please stop!"

I shouted the words as fast as my brain thought them. He was smart, but I was smarter. I could say something; one of my words would make him stop and realize this was a mistake. Maybe my words could rehabilitate him.

Or I could kill him. I could jab. If I could move a shoulder, if I could free a hand, it would all be over. *I want you to die, you sick bastard. I live and you die. That's how it's going to be.* I had to open my eyes; I needed to see him. I didn't want to, those scornful eyes glaring through the nylon. The chafe of it against my cheek was bad enough.

Open your eyes. It'll help you think.

The pain in my pelvis, the pressure on my chest were so intense, I couldn't breathe. My temples tingled. *I'm so tired. Maybe it's time to stop kicking. If I stop, maybe it'll be over. Maybe it's time. Don't people say you feel ready when death comes? Maybe I'm ready.*

How did he know, without looking, that Grace had picked up the gun? Had he heard the rope snap free? Had he heard Grace struggling under that birch? But know he did and with one swift motion the gun was his again. Now he stumbled to his feet.

I could breathe again. There was no pressure, but instead pain from every part of me. And in my temples a warmness, a drowsiness: Blackness was coming.

Grace was crouched beside me now, holding on to me. Had she saved us? *That's what friends are for. Was that a song?* More black. There would soon be total darkness. Where had the sun gone?

Unable to open my eyes, I realized one was swollen shut. *I've got to help,* I thought. *How did Grace get untied?* Thoughts rolled around like pinballs in the dark caverns of my mind.

I struggled to sit up and eyed the figure looming overhead. He wiped his mouth, the pantyhose off now. His hand, big and clumsy, wiped back across his face. He took a step closer.

And that's when I saw his trembling hand: He was scared.

"I'll kill you. I swear I'll kill you. Is it your turn? Is that why you left that tree?"

He spit at Grace's feet, the big feet of a beautiful girl. Another step. "Answer me!"

In his hand the gun trembled.

"Please. Let us go. You don't want to do this. We won't tell," pleaded Grace. Her arms around me, I tried to pull myself into a sitting position, but the ground seemed unsteady.

"Shut up! I told you to mind me. I don't want to kill you. Just shut up." The gun was aimed directly at me. Think, *think.* Sit up. *Sit up.*

As he took another step, several things happened at once: His foot sank in a mole hole, a crow called overhead, and a squirrel darted under a nearby rock.

It was probably all three of those things together plus his shaking hands. All happening in a split second. In less time than it took me to draw in a breath, the stranger's hand moved twenty inches. In the years to come, I would be convinced it was twenty. Somehow it mattered that I knew how far the hand with the gun traveled.

It mattered, because in the space of that twenty inches, the gun moved from my face to Grace's.

As I heard the bullet, I felt our linked arms separate. I could feel myself rolling backwards. Then downwards. Smoke in the air above. Could I go any farther down?

Rolling with me, a size nine shoe, laces undone.

Besides my innocence, I lost many things that day at the Point. I lost the feeling of walking freely down a corridor, without turning at the slightest hint of footsteps. The ability to sleep without dreaming. The naïve confidence that people are basically good. The silly supposition of growing old. The beauty of closing my eyes to the tender kiss of a good man.

And something even more precious: I lost my faith.

Surviving is perhaps the strangest fantasy of them all.

Deep inside me—the part given to maddeningly maudlin acts of self-pity—I envied Grace that bullet. For it washed away the feel of his fingertips on her skin; that bullet separated Grace from the dirt and the fear and the blood. Spared the bullet, I was also denied its cleansing powers. My skin would continue to sear from his gritty touch, scorching through the dermal layers to the basement of my soul. Year after year, smoldering.

And this: the knowledge that the footsteps Grace took toward me were the ones that sealed her fate. In trying to save me, she lost herself. As surely as if I held the gun myself, I was responsible.

Fear became my constant companion. In a darkened corridor, in broad daylight and the draping of dusk, it was ever with me—like a playground bully, relentless in its pursuit. At times, I have wanted to surrender to that bully, be consumed by fear, pierced like a bullet, and thus able to move on to a new place: one without fear. That's why I linger on the train tracks, waiting for the bully, ready to succumb to the place where Grace had gone.

But I don't. I pick up my pace and run breathlessly toward light—toward what I perceive to be safety. I do this because I am human, and humans are built to survive. Perhaps God wants it that way. The eleventh commandment: Thou shalt survive. Maybe we ourselves want it that way. Perhaps it's a little of both. Death is a fantasy, but life—living— is the dream that makes us round dark corners and hide from bullies.

Come out into the light.

Once I reach the light, I know the bully has beaten me at his game. He has taunted me with death and forced me to accept survival. And for those of us who bury the dead and remain on earth, survival is probably the cruelest punishment of all.

An ironic term, survival. For there are no survivors.

31

ON THE MOUNTAIN

I MOVED DOWN THE ATTIC STEPS, into the April room, pulling on tennis shoes. A jarring pulse pounded in my temples and tears continued to flow, but no sound came out. My voice, like myself, was invisible. I knew what I had to do, knew with sparkling clarity how this would end.

The grandfather clock was chiming eleven when I grabbed the keys by the door. I paused, looking toward Maddy's room. Part of me wanted to kiss his cheek and say goodbye. But the darkness beckoned, and so I quietly let myself out into the inky air stinging my tear-stained face. I bumped my way down the driveway and turned onto Birkham Road, heading toward the wooden sign that Grace and I had passed that June day so many years ago. A car, passing me, flashed its lights and honked. I parked badly in one of the three parallel spaces. The sign at The Point warned me: Overlook closed from 10:00 p.m. to 7:00 a.m. The sheriff didn't want teenagers up here drinking or making out late at night. Ironic—no signs foretold of the dangers lurking on a bright summer afternoon.

Out of the car, I began to run. Run as I did by the shore of Lake Michigan, when the wind chapped my face and threatened to knock the breath out of me. Even pregnant, I had strong legs, and the fear, the rage, the hollowness inside propelled me up the hill.

I ran to escape the grief and the guilt, bottomless both of them. My breath came in gasps as I struggled up the mountainous path. I felt chased and yet knew I was the chaser. My heartbeat was frantic; would that be the way this would end? Would I simply be chased into arrhythmia? Silenced by a throbbing embolism? Or would I have the courage to do what needed to be done?

At last at the top, my inclination was to throw myself over my knees, to bend at the waist and suck in air, like the jogger I was. But instead I tilted backward, baring my neck to the sky—the broad, vapid sky.

I felt the first bullets of rain: tiny, cruel pellets dousing my weary limbs.

"I'm here!" I shouted. My arms flung wide and my eyes closed. "Come get me!"

Someone who happened upon me would have thought me insane, for there was no one with me on that cool night—only me and my memories.

"Come get me!" I bellowed again, turning in little circles, my arms pivoting me around.

I was a ready victim, ready to finally be relieved of the chase, the shadows, the pain. Prepared to see Grace, to accept the fate that should have been ours together, the one I was spared. The fate I had to live with every time the sun rose or set. Ready to see Doro and be consumed by those soft motherly arms.

I was ready to die.

Spinning, spinning, turning round and round, I dared my heart to stop. The rain was steady now, and my arms were soaked, my face smeared with sweat and tears and rain. My eyes were closed, sealed tight, not daring to open for dread of what I would see. Or wouldn't see.

For there was no one there: I was alone. And that was the scariest fact of all: knowing I was my own stalker. Knowing I would have to decide for myself what to do next. I looked ahead at the drop off.

"I'm ready!" My voice was filled with bravado and strength. Was it really mine? For I was weak, trembling, never the strong one. After all, I was not the one who had broken free of the tree.

"Are you listening? God, are you there?"

My shouts continued, agonizing cries choking my tears, until I could scream no more. That's when I sunk to my knees, slowly, for I was dizzy with the spinning and the shrieking. I sucked in shallow breaths and succumbed to sobbing.

"God, are you there?" I whispered now, desperate to return to the faith of my childhood, to the faith that was given to me.

I expected no answer.

Kneeling there in the mud, I knew I was faced with a decision: to go on or not. I looked around, my contacts clouded with mascara and moisture. There was no boogeyman, no strangers hiding. Skeletal against the stormy sky, taunting me with its height, was the bleached birch to which Grace had been tied. Somewhere in the recesses of its trunk was the fragile print of hands that had escaped; somewhere across the damp ground was the distant memory of legs that ran. Toward me. Legs that saved me.

Holding my breath, I closed my eyes and heard the shot again. Death hung around me, tempting me, daring me. No end to the memories, to the chase. No magic bullet for me, no end—unless by my own hand. I could almost hear God's laughter at the irony of it all: a survivor, fated to survive. Saved from a demon's gun—only to surrender at her own hands. I looked straight ahead. Thirty paces to the edge. Could I do it? Could I put an end to it all?

But I already knew the answer.

I knew that amidst the screaming and the crying, there was part of me aching to live. Like a lone red blood cell lost in a night sea of cancer, I had an instinct to go on. To fight. To outrace the phantom stalker.

I brushed a thick clump of dripping hair out of my eyes and, as I did, glimpsed a sparkle, ever so subtle, in the wet grass. Something that still remembered how to shine was protruding from the wormy ground.

Many people have said that their decision not to commit suicide was due to something mundane—like wanting to watch a movie, see how a book ends. One more this, one more that, finding bits and pieces of life that make you go on.

The shiny object was that for me. It made me focus, reach out. I pried it from the clammy clump of dirt and grass: a single gold band.

I knew whose it was before I read the inscription: "Grace from Tuck."

"I need to talk to you, Jo. I've got something big to tell you."

Something big. Those words had haunted me for four winters. The big something: This was it.

You could say that band saved my life. Or perhaps, probably, it was the hand I felt on my shoulder at that moment.

Without turning, I knew whose it was. Deep inside, I desperately wanted him to come.

"You were married." I whispered—not as much to him as to myself. "Married."

Tuck kneeled beside me, reached over and took the band from the tip of my thumb where it was perched. Grace had such thin fingers.

"It didn't fit her. It kept sliding off her finger, so she'd put it in her pocket. I kept nagging her to get it resized, telling her it would get lost." He gulped. "Guess I got the last word there."

I looked up at him. Tuck was not crying; he was calm as his thick fingers scraped caked mud from the metal.

"I didn't know," I whispered.

"We hadn't told anyone but our parents," he continued. "We were planning to, I wanted to." He looked up and into my eyes. "She didn't want to tell anyone else until she had told you."

"When . . ." I whispered over the mucous in my throat.

"Valentine's Day." Tuck settled himself on the wet grass, still fixated on the ring that he turned over and over, rubbing it as though it would bring a magic genie to him. "It's funny, she agreed to elope but wanted it to be on Valentine's Day. Hopeless romantic through and through."

And so neither of us had the weddings of our childhood fantasies.

"Tuck, how many people know now?"

He smiled—a sad, deflated smile. "Our parents. And now you." He looked up from the ring and pushed my hair out of my eyes. "Doro knew. I told her a couple of months ago. I told her I wanted to tell you myself one day." He smiled again—no longer his youthful grin but the half smile of someone who has suffered so intently that smiles become but nervous facial tics.

A long silence hung between us. The rain was not as petulant; it had settled into a rhythmic soaking of the land, the trees, the hillside. Us.

I spoke first.

"Tuck, I have to tell you something . . . " I stopped. Could I let it go? My secret? Could I really let it go?

He looked at me, his eyes dry, unblinking. His hand moved to my lips.

"You were here. With Grace."

I'm sure my eyes revealed my shock.

"I knew your plans had changed, and that you were going for a walk with her that day. She called and told me. Grace was so happy she was going to get to tell you our news," Tuck said. "When the police . . ." his voice was choked now, almost hushed, "told me, I thought of you. I even asked. Later I went to your house, knocked and knocked . . ."

I heard those knocks, echoing up the stairwell as I lay in bed, shivering beneath stacks of blankets, Doro sitting on the edge of the bed rubbing my hair. Over and over. The hand on my head. The knocks below. "Let them knock, doll. We're not here. You don't need to see anyone right now."

Tuck continued. "I tried to see you at the funeral. I tried to talk to you. Your sunglasses were on; I think everyone thought your eyes were swollen from crying." He paused. "There was a distance to you—a pain I could sense."

"I knew it wasn't all about losing Grace."

I could feel those large red-rimmed glasses pushing against my cheekbones, pressing on the tenderness and the swelling. I could smell the concealer—what a word—that Doro had applied to my cheek. I could see Doro sitting beside me, protecting me, her hand on my back, moving me through the crowd, away, away. A quick moment with Genia, my hand on hers, and then the hand in the back propelling me forward. Hiding me.

"Doro didn't want anyone to know. She didn't want them to know that I was there, that I was—"

"I know, I know." Tuck's voice was stronger now, anger running across the words as they came from his lips. Did he really understand? Did he *know* what happened?

"Another confession. A couple of months ago, Doro asked to see me. She said it was important that she tell me something."

"And that something was about me."

"Yes," Tuck said quietly, his voice steady even as his eyes clouded. "That's when I told her about me and Grace. Doro said she was feeling old lately. I think she must have had an intuition that she could die, and she wanted someone else to know what happened to you on this mountain. Someone else to be able to help you."

I laughed, a bitter little screech. "To help me," I muttered.

"Yes, to help you." Tuck reached out and took my hand. "She was an old woman, Jo; she was faced with this unspeakable crime that she could barely say—"

"And so she didn't. Doro sent me away like a child, like the dirty secret I was—to what, to *protect* me? I don't think so." My acidic words were pungent from being locked inside me for too long.

"To protect you and, yes, to protect herself," he said softly. "I think that if she had admitted what had happened—if she allowed herself to imagine that such a heinous crime could happen—it, well it would have killed her, Jo Jo."

I dropped his hand and wiped at my eyes.

"It almost killed me, Tuck. Damned Doro! There was no room in her goddam faith for a tragedy like this, was there?"

He gave no answer so I continued.

"There's no room in her stained-glass sanctuary for words like rape. Or murder." I was crying again, my voice coming out in raspy whispers.

Again, silence from Tuck.

"I heard the shot, Tuck. It was so close I *felt* it." My words could barely emerge over the tears, and Tuck reached out his hand to steady mine. I drew back. "At the end I envied Grace."

His eyes searched mine then, wild with emotion.

"I envied Grace because I wanted to die. But I survived. I survived so that I could remember and remember and remember." My fists, clenched, beat on my kneecaps. Sounds as hollow as myself.

I hugged my arms around my chest now and sobbed. Tuck neither touched me nor spoke for a long time. When he did his voice was heavy with angry tears.

"We both survived, Jo. You and I. We both lost something. Don't forget that I lost something too."

Looking up, I saw that Tuck was transfixed by the gold ring. His nails had scratched off all the mud so that it looked almost new.

For the first time in the hour that we had been crouching there on the soggy earth, I saw him as a widower. There was a dimension to his grief that was his alone. That I could never know. Grace was his wife. My *friend*. But his *wife*.

Tuck spoke softly, still staring at the ring in his hand. "The police said that according to the bullet entry, it was quick. For Grace." Tears slipped down his cheeks and his voice was a scratchy whisper. "Was it quick, Jo?"

I nodded. I had no idea but knew my affirmation would bring him some comfort.

Then he looked up and cupped my chin in his hand.

"You got a raw deal, Jo Jo. And maybe what Doro did wasn't right. You've been suffering alone and no one could reach you in the place where you are." He pulled a twig of hair from across my mouth. "I wasn't there. But you know what? I'm thankful I wasn't there. I'm glad there's no memory of a gunshot ringing in my ears when I sleep.

"But that doesn't mean I don't have memories too. That I'm not haunted."

Tuck continued, moving in closer, "You see, I lost three people that day. Not only Grace but my best friend." His intensity now was that of a man throwing a life jacket to a drowning friend. Only I was too far away to reach.

"I lost you that day as surely as if the bastard had shot you too. I've known it every day since you've been back—every time I saw you, every time I put my arm around you. Every smile you smile gives it away."

I was crying harder now. My arms hugging my knees, I rocked back and forth in Tuck's arms, to his words.

"I know that part of you died that day, Jo. I don't understand it; I can't understand what happened to you, but I know there's part of you—a big part of you—that died with Grace."

Tuck pulled me more tightly against him, and I continued my steady rocking, as if the motion would still my heart, my brain, stifle my sobs. Stop everything.

"That's not the end of the story, though, Jo Jo." That high school nickname. Who was that girl, that Jo Jo? Hadn't she died here on the mountain? Hadn't she disappeared?

"The fact is that you're the strongest person I know. Look at your life and what you've survived. You're alive, and you get to go on living. And now someone is living inside you."

"I don't want to live." Mine was the small whine of a young child, rocking against my mother, my toes chafing the ends of footie pajamas.

"Don't say that. That's not fair. That's not fair to Grace." Tuck clutched me more tightly, squeezing the sobs that shook my chest. "I don't believe you want to die." He paused. "You're alive for a reason, Jo Jo. For some crazy, wonderful, unexplainable reason, you're alive." He drew my hair back from my face and kissed my forehead, my cheek. "And I'm glad you're alive."

And then he said the words that perhaps I had been waiting years to hear, needing most to hear. Words that pulled me up, up, upwards, through guilt and confusion and self-pity. Toward the shallow water. The words that sucked me toward light and life.

"You're being alive doesn't betray Grace. She would want you to live, Jo Jo."

I stopped rocking then and looked up at the man whom I left as a boy and who had miraculously aged into someone I did not know, but deeply respected. And loved.

"I want you back, Jo Jo. I want my old friend back." Tuck's face was damp, whether from my own tears or his I didn't know. "I don't want to lose you too."

All at once I remembered something he had said.

"Tuck, you said you lost *three* people. Grace and me and . . . yourself? You're saying you lost yourself?"

Tuck put the ring to his mouth and kissed it gently. We both knew whose face he was touching as his lips grazed the metal, shiny now from tears and rubbing.

"No, Jo. There's something else. Something else you don't know." He cleared his throat before continuing. Suddenly I knew what he was going to say, and I felt vomit rise in the back of my throat. The words that fell from his mouth were arrows piercing my skin.

"She was going to tell you. Man, Grace was so excited about telling you that day."

"God, no, Tuck."

His tears flowed freely then, a release of the secret that had been locked between husband and wife. One living, the other dead.

He nodded at me.

"I lost my baby too."

32

SUNRISE

FOR HOURS TUCK AND I SAT still together on that hillside, drifting to sleep and then waking. The rain dissipated and the first rays of sun appeared. We didn't talk, no longer cried. We simply sat, huddling against each other in the dampness, blocking out time and motion with our composite grief.

It was me who finally broke the silence.

"How were your boards?

"Tough in spots. I guess we'll know in a month."

I shivered, and Tuck drew me into his arms, so close we were almost one mass in the trembling light.

"What would Debra say if she saw us sitting this way?"

"Who do you think sent me up here?"

"Really?"

"She called me. She was on an emergency run to the store to get diapers. She passed you and said you were driving fast and looked distraught.

"Debra said she thought you needed me."

Without thinking, I spoke the truth. "What a woman."

Tuck smiled. "I know how to pick 'em, don't I?" He squeezed my hand and kissed it. "Do you like Debra, Jo?"

Liking Debra meant turning my back on my past, on what Tuck and I were, on what we might be. It meant turning my back on the union that had made Grace happier than anything else.

"It's hard for a woman like me to like a woman with big boobs like those," I said.

That impish high school grin was back. "Those girls are pretty great, I can't lie."

"I do like Debra." I traced the lifelines on Tuck's palm. "Somehow it's easier, now that I know about you and Grace."

Tuck looked puzzled. "Easier?"

"I guess I wanted you to love Grace as much as I did. And now I know you did.

"I know now just what you've lost."

Leaning back, Tuck stretched out his long legs before speaking.

"I shut down when Grace died. I didn't think I could love anyone else. I had, for a brief time, a wife and child." His voice broke on the last word. "Nothing could replace that."

He looked at me, waiting intently for him to continue.

"And Debra doesn't replace Grace. She can't. Neither can Andy. But Debra was my friend and loved me when I was unlovable, when I couldn't love back.

"One day she and I had been out for pizza. We were just friends. Great conversations, a little laughter. Someone to pass the time with, ya know?" I nodded; I did know. "Anyway, I drove Deb home and before she got out of the car she reached over and kissed me on the cheek. And it was so sweet. I liked it.

"The next time I saw her I thought maybe I could kiss her just once, hold her hand. Maybe I could like her just a little more. And before long, you know what?"

I shook my head.

"Before long, I was able to love Deb. One day at a time. A little bit at first, then more deeply. So slowly. It was like learning to walk again.

"It was falling in love with Debra that restored my faith."

I winced at the word. "My faith could use some restoring."

Tuck frowned at me. "I probably felt that way too for a while. But one weekend, Deb came home with me. We were having a picnic in the meadow behind the cemetery. There we were, not a hundred yards from where Grace was buried, and the sun was out and I didn't think of Grace at all.

"I almost started crying when I realized that not once had I thought of Grace. And in that setting! How could I forget? How could I have been so caught up with another person?"

My mind flashed to those Saturdays in Tom's house: dry walling, steaming wallpaper, music drifting over us and bits of conversations happening in comfortable stops and starts. I thought of our picnics at Loyola, of the quick kisses in the elevator at S&H. Deep down inside, that's exactly how I had felt: *How dare I be happy?*

Tuck continued to talk slowly, deliberately.

"Once I realized that, I made a lame excuse and took Debra home. Then I went back to the cemetery—oh it was eight at night or so—and I sat with Grace, by her grave all night. I didn't sleep, barely blinked. My guilt kept me awake.

"And then the sun rose and I thought, this is it. This is the way the rest of my life will go—talking to a grave and remembering not to forget her.

"So here I am, on this insane morning when I've had no sleep and all of a sudden I hear this thud nearby. The wind had knocked this cute little nest down, and there was the mother robin. I swear she shook her feathers like, 'What the crap!' and then here comes a big maple leaf, plop! Smack dab on top of the nest, covering it like a bedspread.

"That robin walked up to that leaf like, 'What the hell happened here?' and it was all just so comical."

He paused, noting my countenance.

"Okay, clearly you had to be there. I'd had no sleep, remember? But here's the point. I had seen this cute, funny thing—it made me laugh out loud—and I wanted to tell someone. And guess who I thought of?"

Silence from me. I knew.

"I had this strong, powerful urge to see Deb, and I felt no remorse about getting up from Grace's grave and driving straight back to Deb. I loved Grace, and she loved me. Debra loved me, and I was loving her. I realized then that our hearts aren't so easily destroyed—that they're stronger than we know."

Tuck leaned forward and put his hands on my cheeks. "We are stronger than we know. And I believe that we're made to love again."

He wiped away traces of dried tears, smoothed down my wild hair and kissed my forehead. "Those curls of yours," he smiled.

"Think of it, Jo Jo. I was as unlovable and shut down as anyone can be, and yet Debra broke through. Doesn't that tell you that someone is watching over us, helping us survive the unsurvivable and love the unlovable?"

I thought then of Tom, of the remote, godless me who brought a host of demons into every embrace, every conversation. I thought of the secret I could not share—*chose* not to share with him. I thought of the nights he woke me from nightmares, holding me when I could not voice my fears. Just holding me and expecting nothing more.

"I think I've been unlovable. I know it. I've pushed Tom away." There. I had said it out loud.

Tuck was quiet for a minute, then, "Is he really pushed away? Or is he there waiting for you?" Another pause. "Maybe he's like Debra, refusing to be pushed away. She did all the loving for both of us for a while. Maybe Tom's doing that now."

I'm right here. I could hear Tom's voice. *I got you.* And then, *I have to walk away.*

"You've heard my story. What brought you and Tom together anyway?"

"Well, we sort of lived in sin for a while, unknowingly."

Tuck's eyebrows went up, and I told him our story—tales of the hotel room, of Candace, work at the agency, the house we never seemed to stop renovating. As I talked I realized I was telling stories of the best friend I had known since Grace. In a sense, Tom had filled Grace's void, filling my days with conversation, with laughter, with insight. Is that why I married him?

"No."

I startled at Tuck's response to my thoughts and then realized I had spoken aloud.

"You asked if it sounded like you had married a replacement friend, and I said no. It sounds to me like you married someone you could spend the rest of your life with." Tuck recrossed his legs and played with the gold band. All night he had been doing this, on one finger, off and onto another. Over and over.

"Do you ever wonder if Debra is who you're meant to be with forever? That there will never be anyone else?"

I knew my question was treading into dangerous waters.

"Anyone else like a writer who's moved on to the big city?"

I blushed.

"Tuck, did you want to kiss me the other night on your deck?"

Tuck's face told me he was being absolutely truthful.

"Yes. I did. And I don't feel guilty about that. There will probably be other women I'll want to kiss." His hand clutched his heart theatrically. "Miss Connie with the sagging knee-his, now she makes me warm all over."

He noticed his joke fell on deaf ears. "So did you want to kiss me?"

I nodded. "I think at that moment I thought I could go back to our old life—that I could be with someone who knows all about me."

Grow up, Maddy had said.

"Tom doesn't know all about you?"

"He knows me, yes. But he doesn't know everything . . . well, he doesn't know the whole story about Grace's murder, about my . . ." I paused. "I guess I left here with the idea that I could be someone new."

"Sometimes new is not better. It's just new." We both smiled. Tuck was quoting a line Doro said constantly as we urged her to replace her old car, to replace the Kitchen Aid mixer circa 1960.

"It's hard to build a future without all the story, Jo Jo. I think at some point you're going to have to let Tom in. If you want a future, that is."

My expression voiced what I could not articulate: the fear, the confusion.

"You can't continue to lead two lives, Jo Jo. They have to collide. Tom has to know all of you—the good as well as the, well the unthinkable. He's your husband, and he loves you."

"How do you know he does?" I whispered.

"Because he'd be crazy not to. Because you're lovable. Because you're you. Because I love you."

My tears started again, tears of sorrow and fatigue. My heart sighed with the knowledge that Tuck spoke the truth. My old friend telling me the truth. And now softly asking the question that I had been burying for months.

"Do you love Tom back, Jo Jo?"

A warm stream running down my dirty cheeks, my answer was barely audible.

"I don't know, Tuck. I love—I love being with him. I love who he is, what he does. I respect him. But there's part of me that feels I'm hovering above us when we're together—that I'm playing at love, at marriage . . . like I'm not really there."

Tuck was quiet and still, eyes closed. He sat that way for a full minute or two before speaking.

"I think you're *not* really there. There's a big part of you that's still here, on this mountain. Blaming yourself. Not loving yourself."

He opened his eyes and looked at me, wiping my cheeks with his finger-tips, ever so gently, lamb's wool against my burning skin.

"You have to decide whether to stay here—to keep this girl on the moun-tain—or bring her back with you to Tom. And only one of those options will keep Tom in your life." Tuck rolled the ring over each knuckle in succession, a mesmerizing glimmer before my eyes. "Can you imagine Tom not being in your life? Not knowing him when you're seventy? Not ever knowing what he became, what he did? I couldn't imagine not knowing Debra, and so I had to leave Grace behind.

"I had to move on."

With Tuck's words, pictures of Tom came to mind—bending over his light board, slinging his Nikon over his shoulder before boarding a canoe, watch-ing baseball with a beer and a can of peanut butter, smoothing down unruly gray tendons above his ear.

I could not imagine Tom not being in my future. Not smelling his musky scent or feeling his arms around me. Not waking up to those dimples.

I looked squarely at Tuck. Perhaps the love danced from my eyes.

"You have to take the girl down from the mountain, Jo Jo. You have to let her meet her husband." Tuck leaned over and kissed me then, full on the lips. It was a warm, long kiss. Neither sexual nor platonic, it was rather a kiss of closure, of redemption. A kiss that said so much that needed to be said. That told me it was the kiss of my past but not my future.

"Now neither of us has to wonder or wish," Tuck said. "Tom's a lucky man, and he's going to love the woman who comes home to him."

I clasped my arms around Tuck's neck and, as I did, imagined it was Tom whom I was embracing. Imagined his hair against my nose, his hands rubbing my shoulder blades.

"I do love him," I whispered into the shirt of the man whom I didn't love.

At least not in the way I loved Tom. Tuck held a piece of my heart, but not the part that made me want to arise from the ground and continue to live. That man was far away, and I needed to get back to him. Get him back to me.

We pulled apart from our embrace and minutes later frantic footsteps overtook us. Debra was panting.

"Thank goodness I found you." Debra's eyes shifted from Tuck's to mine. "Maddy called looking for you, JoAnna. He dropped the phone, and I called 911. He's had a heart attack."

33

SIGNS OF LIFE

TUCK AND DEBRA FOLLOWED ME back to the Inn and pulled up next to me, one car on each side. Debra leaned out the car window. "I checked with the hospital. Maddy's in surgery. It will be a few hours."

"We'll wait for you to change clothes," Tuck said. "We'll ride together."

But I shook my head. There was something I needed to do first, and I needed to do it alone.

"I'll meet you at the hospital." And then, seeing the concern on their faces, "I'm okay. I'll be right there."

Inside the April bedroom I stepped out of the mud-caked jeans still drenched around the hem. I pulled on a dry pair and an old Georgia sweatshirt from the drawer. As it fell down around my neck, I caught a whiff of one of Doro's cachets. Lilac. I hated it as a teenager. Now it only made me want to cry.

I drew my hair up into a ponytail and, tugging on shoes as I went, hobbled downstairs to Doro's Dell computer. A few seconds later I was connected.

My hands sat poised over the keyboard. I waited to hear that familiar voice: "You've got mail." But there was no noise except the hard knocking of my heart. I glanced at the clock. It had been over an hour since Debra first got the call. Maddy would be coming out of surgery in three more hours. An emergency bypass. I rolled the words around on my tongue. Stupid terminology: There was no way to bypass a heart like Maddy's.

The cursor clicked at me, impatient. I took a deep breath and began to type. My fingers flew faster and faster across the keyboard, tripping over themselves. If I could just get the words out, I wouldn't have to see them again. Words I could never say out loud looked almost elegant on the cyber page.

I did a word count for no apparent reason: two hundred and seventy-seven words. Not even three hundred words had stood as a chaperone between me and Tom. How few words it took to bring a girl down from a mountain, as Tuck said. How few words and yet how many.

I didn't read what I had typed; I didn't dare. I directed the mouse to send the message and immediately a window zapped open with a little noise: No Subject Given. Do You Wish to Send the Message With No Subject?

After only a moment's hesitation, I highlighted the space beside the RE: and typed "Why I don't close my eyes." And then SEND.

The horizontal bar at the bottom gradually changed from gray to blue and then disappeared altogether, as my message sat on Tom's computer, waiting to be read. *Being* read? When would he log on?

Come back to me, I thought.

I glanced at my watch; fifteen more minutes had passed. It was time to go. I reached to shut down the computer and then impulsively typed a new email. I wrote the words that were perhaps more important than the previous message. The words that Tom had probably been waiting for years to hear: words that came directly from my heart.

"I need you."

As Windows was shutting down, I walked out to my car, my mind now focused on a seventy-nine-year old man with garden dirt under his nails.

Debra and Tuck had gotten there before me and gone to the cafeteria for a snack. I spoke with the nurse. The operation would take longer—until afternoon. There were some complications with the bleeding. The nurse, who looked like she didn't smile very often, smiled. "Dr. Burns is an excellent surgeon. Mr. Blair is in good hands."

And with that, her crispy white Reeboks squeaked away, leaving me alone in the waiting room where time stood still.

I sank into one of the rust vinyl chairs that made a little cushion fart every time I moved around. I stared at the green cinder box walls and news magazines scattered around the tables. This is what there will be if Maddy dies, I thought. This is what I will have to come back to. The world. Walls and news and traffic and people.

My eyes burned from the night of sleeplessness and weeping. I found myself talking—to whom? It was a quiet voice, one that had not been used since . . . since when? It was the voice of prayer. And my prayers were for Maddy.

"I can't lose him, God." My mouth moved and possibly my words were even audible. "I lost Grace, I lost Doro, I can't lose him too." And then the word *if*. "Just a little more time with Maddy. Please. If you bring him back to me, I'll believe. I'll know you're there."

The day dragged on in this manner, me making deals with a God that I doubted.

"Maddy believes in you. Isn't it enough that *he* believes? Don't you want to save one of your own?" Over and over, my lips whispered what my mind screamed. "Don't you need him here? I need him here."

In the end it was all about me. I knew that. I also knew not to bargain with God. But what I wanted at that moment was a reason to believe. I wanted proof I wasn't alone.

My eyes drifted to a floor lamp in the corner, its polished brass shell shade shielding the forty watt bulb. I thought back to that March 15 night so many years ago. When I entered the waiting room that night, escorted by Mrs. Webber, Doro's hand clutched the pole of a lamp in a different hospital, a different city, as if for support. I remember Mrs. Webber's words echoing my thoughts.

"Miss Wilson, you're all alone here." And Doro's response: "I'm not alone."

What assurance, what confidence. What *faith*. "But I am alone, Doro. I don't have your faith," I whispered. "I don't know your . . . I don't know your God."

And, at that moment, sitting all alone in that hospital as morning drifted toward afternoon, I knew what I wanted. Perhaps I had known it for some time; maybe I had just realized it. Yet staring at the empty walls, there was no question in my mind. I wanted Tom, and I wanted home.

Two months ago, if asked the question, I would have had to admit that it wasn't love that had brought Tom and me together, but infatuation. Common ground, friendship. But throughout the time we had been together, through the days when I whispered "Love you" on the telephone at work before hanging up, the nights in bed when I whispered it in response to his kisses, I wanted to mean it. But something held me back. Perhaps before I could mean it I had to understand it.

Who could explain the nuances of love? In my life, each instance of love had been so distinctive. It was passionate and impulsive, like my recent days with Tuck. It was protective in Doro's case and possessive, as with Genia. It was innocent and simple, like my parents. With Grace it was painful, horribly painful. And now, this was a tender and all-consuming love for an old man in surgery. It was roses and thorns and birds of paradise and elephant ears—yes, elephant ears—all bound up in one swollen heart.

With Tom, for the first time in my life, love was easy and undemanding and perhaps that's why it was unrecognizable to me. But as I sat in the hospital I yearned for the simplicity of our relationship in a way that I had wanted few other things before. Closing my eyes, I didn't imagine kissing Tom or daydream about lovemaking—didn't think about his voice or his touch.

What I wanted was the one thing that Tom alone could give me. He had restored equilibrium to my life. With him I felt something that had been stolen from me on that mountain with Grace: With Tom I felt secure. Loved, yes, and wanted and special. But most importantly, I felt assurance—like I could bury my head in his arms, and he would swell around me like a dark, sweet smelling quilt. As if I could get lost a thousand times, but he would always find me.

Find me now, I thought. No, not a thought. It was a prayer.

And as much as I wanted Tom, I wanted Mt. Moriah. I craved the place that was more a part of me than I had ever realized. I wanted to tend the land that had tended me. Mt. Moriah had not forsaken me; rather it was the other way around. Or perhaps I had forsaken myself.

I wanted to drive down streets I knew by heart, to hear the tinny music on Woodbury Avenue at Christmastime and get goosebumps from the familiarity. I yearned to watch the pumpkin patch come to life behind the church, to turn onto Walker Drive and instinctively slow down because so many children live on that street. I longed to stroll alongside the small man-made lake and feel suddenly as if my feet had springs—and to sip coffee on the square outside Town Hall and watch autumn leaves swirling at my feet. To know that the trees, and the seasons that changed them, had born silent witness to my seasons. To drive down Chapel Avenue and immediately be immersed in the vista in front of me—the magnolia marquis that had been alive before me and would be living here long after I was gone. To travel down that road and feel the sunlight seeping through the leaves. To remember that very sunlight from a place deep down inside where my memories lived. To sit in that white frame sanctuary and feel at home. Loved.

To know that all of it is a part of me and me of it.

Tuck and Debra interrupted my thoughts. "What do you need, Jo?"

I shook my head.

"Chris, I'm going home to check on Andy," Debra said. Turning to me, "He's with our neighbor."

"No," I said. "Take Tuck with you. I'm okay. I'll let you know when the surgery is over."

Tuck looked worried. "You don't need to be alone."

I smiled wearily, trying to reassure him. I knew he would stay, and I knew Debra would be fine with that. But I knew Tuck's place was with his family, not me.

"Go," I said, and after we hugged, I was alone again.

Muttering quietly, I prayed to a tile ceiling that held no answers. In my solitude, my prayers bounced around like gnats drawn to and from a light-bulb. And I finally brought myself to say what I feared most. "I don't want to be alone!"

Rubbing my eyes with both fists, I stared at a plant, long abandoned on a high table in the corner. Numb with fatigue, I could no longer think, no longer cry. Could not pray. The air in the room seemed to stop moving and hover around me, waiting for me to move, to feel. But I could not: I was lost in darkness.

And that's when it happened.

It felt like a tiny hiccup erupting from deep within me. Or a paintbrush lightly sweeping the inside of my stomach. People liken a baby's first kick to butterflies. They call it quickening. To me, it was a paintbrush.

I changed my position and sat poised, waiting for the brush. Had I imagined it?

There, again. The tiniest bristles sweeping across my womb with pastel colors. A speck of color here, there. In spite of myself, I laughed out loud and threw my hand over my mouth at the very moment the surgeon walked into the room.

"The surgery went well. The next hours and days will be critical, but Mr. Blair's chances look really good. He'll be in recovery for a little while, but the nurse will come get you as soon as he's in his room."

His hand gripped mine briefly and then he was gone and I was alone again. And yet not. I had just received two signs of life. Two gifts. Two answers.

An hour later the nurse directed me to Maddy's room where he had just been wheeled in. His chins spread out under those thin lips. He looked so very old. But his chest rose and fell in what seemed to me a beautiful dance. Gently, I lay my cheek against his hand and fell fast asleep, my hand resting on my stomach.

Alive, Jo Jo, you are alive!

It was Tuck's voice in my ear.

And Grace's.

I wiped at the little spot of drool at the corner of my lips and opened my eyes. The clock on the wall said 5:00. The sun was teasing its descent. Maddy was staring at me. How long had he been awake?

"I hurt like hell, little thing. Why are you smiling so big?"

Indeed I was smiling. "You're going to be okay, Maddy. The doctor said he opened the blockage. No more bacon for you, mister." My words toppled over each other to get out as I fought back tears. *Thank you, God. Thank you for bringing him back.*

"Are you okay, Jo?"

I cleared my throat. "Yes, why? I'm just so glad . . ."

"You look different."

He knew me so well. He loved and knew me so well.

I pushed his pillow into the crook of his neck, and Maddy smiled in appreciation. One tear seeped from the corner of my eye. "I prayed for you, Maddy. God heard my prayer."

Those blue eyes stared hard at me, daring me to drop our gaze.

"There was never any doubt He heard your prayer, little thing. What I wondered was if you could hear His answer."

His eyes closed then and he turned his head away for sleep.

"I heard this time, Maddy," I whispered to his light snore.

I prodded my stomach, anxious for the flutter. That feeling of life. Unexpected, undeserved. A shadow inside me stirred from the womb that I thought had been destroyed. I was not only alive but endowing life. The magical, mystical brush—with all its varying hues— would paint my life back. After all those years of searching, I had found God in a hospital waiting room and inside my own body.

Although all my questions weren't answered that day—weren't even all asked—at last, I thought I knew Doro's Big Secret. It was not that the world was full of all things good. Rather, the Big Secret lay in the fact that there was a bit of God in *everything*—in things both wonderful and wicked—in anything that had life to it: everything human, every struggle, every celebration. That's what Doro and Maddy understood that I did not.

I understood finally that God is not only in a church sanctuary. He is also in the blood-spattered operating room as surgeons try to save a little girl's grandmother.

God is in the perfect ascent of a golf swing on a bright spring afternoon. And just as surely he's in the ferocious lightning bolt that downs a stately timber.

He resides in the timid, wet goodnight kiss of a senior prom date, and in the tear-soaked pillow of an eight-year-old orphan. In the delight of shared French fries and the odious tenor of a bully's mocking.

God lives in the highest trumpet notes of Beethoven's Ninth Symphony and in the smelly sweat of a front line soldier. He floats in the cool stillness beneath the surface of a summer lake and in the cries of a mother whose baby lies blue and lifeless. In the late-night telephone call of two lovers and the silent phone of an old widow. In the crash that took my parents. And the aunt who called me hers.

God is in the warm careless hug of two lifelong friends.

And God was in the bullet that tore one from the other.

God is in life *only* because He is also in death. Finally I saw the challenge: to find Him in both. Maybe doing that means finding the part of us—however veiled—that is Him.

Our still small voice.

That was my myopia: While I had searched for a God who was separate from me, all the time, He was within me.

Perhaps before you find God, you have to find yourself.

I ate dinner with Tuck and Debra when they returned, and then I settled into the recliner next to Maddy. Despite its discomfort, I slept deeply and well. When the nurses came in to bring Maddy some breakfast, I saw that the sun was high in the sky, a new day.

"Time for a bath, Mr. Blair."

Maddy groaned and muttered.

"I should've gone toward the light, little thing."

I moved toward the bed. "Behave. I'm going home for a while." I kissed the groggy old man goodbye as the nurses poked and prodded him. I pushed open the door and took in a deep, deliberate breath. From my womb, that desolate homestead of memories deep inside me, stirred the little piece of life—a mere cluster of cells—that would lead me back to where I needed to be. The piece of Creation that would make me arise each day and give thanks for the dawn.

Although tired to my very core, I didn't think about going to bed.

There was somewhere I needed to go first.

34

ALIVE

Stopping by the inn to brush my teeth and wash my face, I stepped into Maddy's room and saw that the bed had been slept in. Had the heart attack come in the middle of the night? I noted the bedside phone off the hook. Had he tried to call me? How long had he been by himself? And was he worried where I was?

I had to push these thoughts out of my mind. Grabbing Maddy's toothbrush and robe to take to the hospital, I was back in my car and headed down the mountain. The cottony clouds were puffs created by an artist's feathery strokes.

Alive!

The flutters continued in my stomach. I found myself eagerly awaiting the next one.

"Are you real in there?" I spoke softly. I began to hum and then sing "Bye Bye Blackbird." To the car next to me at the stoplight, I was singing and talking to myself. But I knew better.

Twenty minutes later, I found Genia Collins on her knees pulling weeds. Her back was hunched over, and I watched as she paused to wipe her cheek with the back side of her gardening glove.

She was a woman I had hated all my life. And loved.

"Mrs. Collins. Genia."

She turned then and arose carefully, one hand in the small of her back.

"JoAnna, dear." She moved four paces toward me, then frowned ever so slightly. "What's wrong?"

"Everything's okay, but Maddy had a heart attack. It happened night before last. They did surgery and it went well."

Genia covered her mouth with her muddy glove—not thinking or, it seemed, caring about the smear on her lips.

"Thank the Lord."

"Yes." Genia moved to hug me—timidly, perhaps afraid I would push her away. I didn't. We stood there amongst the dahlias and the peonies and hugged, neither lightly nor clinging. A simple falling into each other's arms.

A jab of nausea hit me. "Genia, could I come inside and talk for a minute?"

She led the way, holding the screen door open for me to pass through. Inside I could smell cinnamon and hear the loud ticking of her mantel clock.

I sniffed dramatically. "Coffee cake?"

She smiled. "You remember my coffee cake?" Genia went to the sink, washing first her hands and then her face. "It's for Circle meeting tomorrow.

"JoAnna, you look pale. Are you alright?"

I nodded. And then I told her my news that Doro had never gotten to hear. It was right that Genia Collins should hear it. She was now the closest thing to a mother I had. And I was finally mature enough to know I needed one. An imperfect one, but yet a mother.

Tears welled up in her eyes. "Oh, this would make Doro so very happy." Genia's voice quieted. "And Grace."

I squeezed her hand and we sat quietly for a minute. I knew what I wanted to tell her—what I needed to tell her, about Grace, about me, about that day on the mountain. But where to start?

"Did you know that Grace was pregnant?" she asked suddenly.

"I just found that out last night. Tuck and I talked for a long time. I just don't know," and I didn't know, "how you have managed your grief."

"It never goes away," said Genia. "I never stop thinking about Grace— something I want to say to her, something I think she'd like. I make her favorite desserts. You know what a sweet tooth she had, amazing she didn't have every tooth in her head filled—but then you know I can't take a bite. Those beautiful pies and cakes just sit on the counter and rot."

She searched my eyes—for understanding? For sympathy? Perhaps just for companionship.

"But what can I do? I have to go on."

"Yes. We all do." *How could I tell her?*

"You know, I have a CD Grace made me years ago; I guess she was seventeen or so. I've listened to that lovely voice so many times I'm surprised the CD still plays."

"She was very talented, you know."

"I know that, JoAnna. And sometimes—you know, those days when it hits me so hard, I almost can't get out of bed—I wonder what would have happened if she had taken that scholarship and gone to Georgia and pursued her music."

I bristled. "Genia, she didn't know that was an option!" I immediately regretted the words. I was here to make peace, not argue.

"What in the world, JoAnna? What makes you say that?"

I was past the point of no return.

"I know you loved Grace, Genia. But she knew you wanted her to be an accountant—to have a dependable career." My voice quieted almost to a whisper. "And you didn't want her to leave home."

Genia cast her eyes down to her folded hands in her lap. I detected a slight tremble. She was so still, so quiet that I wondered if she had fallen asleep. Or was just terribly hurt.

But when she looked up at me, there was a fire in those tiny eyeballs that I hadn't seen in a long time.

"Is that what Grace said?" Her voice shook. "Is that what you think?"

I wanted out. I imagined myself rising and walking out that screen door—away from Genia, away from Mt. Moriah. But I came with a purpose. Courage, I told myself. *"You're the strongest person I know,"* Tuck had said.

"I didn't mean to upset you. Perhaps that's just what Grace thought."

Genia smoothed her apron, picking at a piece of red rick rack that had escaped its seam. Sighing loudly, she sat up straight, and I was reminded of her tapping Grace and me lightly on the back with a broom handle. *Posture, girls!*

"JoAnna, I would have been so proud for her to pursue her music. I know you were her best friend. I know you were encouraging her to go on and do something with her music . . . to go away like you did." Her voice rose, but it had not the timbre of anger, but rather of a voice finally being heard.

"And yes I encouraged the accounting field, but you have to know where I was, at that point in my life, JoAnna." Genia stood and paced in front of me. "I was left with nothing when Grace's father left me. I just wanted Grace to be able to take care of herself."

The little gasping sobs began, and I started to move toward Genia—across the history that lay wide open between us.

"And you need to know, JoAnna, that Grace wasn't you. She was scared to go. She wanted to stay close to home. That's what she couldn't tell you." She sat next to me on the sofa and tucked my hair behind my ears. "She wanted you to be proud of her."

"Aren't you scared to go away to school, Jo Jo?"

"Scared? Nervous maybe but excited." We were on my twin beds, and I was making my tenth list of what I was packing. University of Georgia brochures and paraphernalia had overtaken my room. "You need to see if you can still take that scholarship and come with me. We could be roommates!"

Grace was quiet. "No, I just don't think singing is for me."

"Because your mom said it wasn't?"

She was defensive. "It's so hard to make a living as a singer, Jo. You know that. I'm okay but not that good." She swallowed hard. "And I, well, I can't imagine what Mom would do."

"You can't live your life for your mother, Gracie."

"I'm not, Jo. That's not it. I just, well I just can't go."

Years later, that conversation rolled around in my head like pearls.

I can't go. Did she mean she didn't have it in her? Was she trying to say *I won't go?* Had I blamed Genia Collins for a fear that was her daughter's alone?

"I just didn't know she didn't want that," I said quietly. Had I imagined Grace's excitement over each new piece of mail from Georgia? Was she just being who she thought I wanted her to be?

"I thought maybe Tuck would give her the push she needed—or the confidence, you might say." Genia sat, leaning back against the tufted cushion, sighing her fatigue. "She had done such a good job in college, working part-time at the accounting firm, and she was saving money. It seemed, well, it seemed that . . ."

Her voice cracked. "It seemed she had her whole life ahead of her."

I cleared my throat. It was time.

"Genia, I want to tell you something about the day that Grace died. Something I need you to know." A pause. "I think it might be hard to hear. It's about, it's about Grace and me that day."

Genia put sandpaper fingers to my lips. "Hush, JoAnna, don't say it. Doro told me everything."

Phlegm rose in my throat, and the fluttering in my stomach quickened.

"She told you?" My voice was barely a whisper. "*Everything?*"

"Everything. And JoAnna, it's not your fault—what happened to Grace. I can't imagine how you've been suffering."

"I've, I've felt—"

"Guilty? JoAnna, I was worried you would feel guilty when Doro told me what happened." She clasped my hands in hers. "But JoAnna, darling, it's not your fault. You couldn't have prevented it."

She drew my head to her shoulder.

"Maddy and I have said many times that we're so glad you weren't able to go on the walk with Grace that day. You might have been hurt too."

The room began to spin then, and little black dots danced in front of my eyes, and before I could catch myself, I was on the floor.

Genia was kneeling over me, mopping my face with a wet dishcloth.

"Poor girl," she said calmly. "How far along again?"

I sat up, leaning back against the sofa, rubbing my tailbone.

"You know, I suspected this when I first saw you a few weeks ago. A mother knows the signs. I guess you could say we have wise wombs." She smiled gently. She tucked a pillow behind my back and then went to the kitchen, returning with a bag of Lay's.

"I'm not sure why, but grease works wonders on nausea."

I smiled weakly and began to chew. My mind was racing with what Genia had said. So Doro had not told her anything. Genia and Maddy—and the rest of the town—still thought I had cancelled my walk with Grace. It was Doro trying to erase the past by keeping it a secret between us. Even from her husband she had spared the horror.

And I saw, finally, that Doro did it not out of pride, control, or fear. She did it out of love—misguided, flawed, imperfect love. For me. And I saw, also, that I had to extend that same love to Genia. I had come to tell her my story, but I knew it would cause only more pain.

It was to stay my story, my secret. Mine and that of the dead.

I stayed at Genia's for another hour, telling her my plans to convert the side porch to a bakery—her bakery.

"And what of the Inn, dear? Are you going to reopen the Inn to guests?"

I told her I didn't know. And I didn't. *We* didn't. There were three of us to consider now. There was still a nagging fear that Tom had left me forever, that my words would not bring him back. But then I fantasized about Tom taking to mountain life—just as surely as I had discovered that mountain life was in me. I knew that I wanted to raise my child—our child—on Mt. Moriah. To wake to the snowy pear trees and the hummingbirds, to climb the oaks and spend hours gazing into the sky.

Tom. Had he read my email? Would he come? Would he take me back?

After I had eaten a pimento cheese sandwich and forced down a glass of milk, I drove back to the Inn. My mind was awhirl with the voices of Tuck and Genia. Of what I had learned. Of the secrets I now possessed.

Making the final turn up the driveway, I saw the figure sitting there, on the concrete steps of the front porch. When he saw the car, he arose. I slammed the car into park and darted across the lawn. My legs were quick. Strong. Powerful. I was no less.

The September sun silhouetted him so I could not see his face or his eyes. But I felt Tom's arms as they closed around me. When he released me, holding me at arms' length, he surveyed my blossoming belly before searching my eyes.

"Maddy?"

"He's going to be ok. The surgery went well."

"And you?"

"I think I'm going to be okay too."

"Don't leave me again."

"Don't *you* leave me again."

"Never." Tom pulled me to him and whispered into my hair. "I got you, Jo. We got this."

I began to cry then, tears of raw happiness. Tears that bespoke how over-whelmed I felt. And with each grateful sob I leaned farther into the arms of the man who was my future: the man with whom I would spend the rest of my days. Thankful and alive.

"Welcome to Mt. Moriah," I murmured.

"Close your eyes," Tom said, moving his mouth close to mine.

And I did.

35

STILL HERE

THE NEXT TUESDAY, two days after we brought Maddy home from the hospital, on a perfect autumn morning, Maddy, Tom, and I watched the television in horror as the Twin Towers fell. Members of the congregation organized an impromptu late afternoon service at the church, and we wheeled Maddy in the side door. Although too weak to preach a sermon, he delivered a beautiful prayer from the first row—one of redemption and forgiveness and loss. Even as daylight faded from the stained glass windows, we sat still, the community of Mt. Moriah, singing hymns and crying together. Tom shook hands and exchanged hugs as if he had known these people all his life. And in a way, he had. For the faces of Mt. Moriah were part of me, and me of them. And for all the time I had refused to believe it, my husband knew me well.

Knew my very soul.

Two weeks later, Tom and I made a final trip back to Chicago—to the house on Hudson Street. As we packed our things in boxes, we worked in silence. We would find each other pausing now and then, as we found a stray Christmas tag or movie ticket stub, or simply to watch the morning light gleaming on the hardwood floors. The day after we put a FOR SALE BY OWNER sign in the yard, we received two offers. "That's a good omen," said Tom. "Maddy would say God's hand is in this." I smiled. The weeks he had spent with Maddy had forged a special friendship between the two.

We packed a special bag that we referred to as Renovation Duds. Upon our return to Mt. Moriah, we set about immediately redecorating the upstairs rooms. Down came the tulips, the tartan plaid. Hormones raging, I alternately laughed and cried as my memories flooded each room.

We left the August room alone. White would be the perfect blank slate for our baby.

One morning, I awoke with a distinct feeling, a memory. I padded in Doro's thick pink slippers—she called them her marshmallows—to the June room. That bedroom was the only one with an unusually large walk-in closet tucked under the eaves of the house. Grace and I used it as a clubhouse when guests were not there. We would lug a basket of toys and papers into the clubhouse, only to be told the next day, "Girls, clean out that closet! Room's rented!"

I tugged open the door of the closet. Beneath a piece of torn wallpaper at the back corner—original wallpaper that Doro had never seen fit to replace—I found what I was looking for. With hearts dotting the I's were the words "Grace loves Will Simmons." A catch in my throat, I closed my eyes and could feel the pen passing from Grace's hand to mine. I could recall the momentary discomfort of not knowing what to write, Grace's impatient foot tapping. Opening my eyes, I saw the flowery script of a novice writer. "JoAnna Wilson was here," the words read.

I'm still here, I whispered to the ghost of that little girl.

Many evenings, as I sat on the floor in the den, sorting through Doro's sideboard and trying to discern trash from treasure, I heard sounds below me and knew Tom was in the basement. For reasons I couldn't understand, he was thrilled with the idea of a basement. "It's a guy thing," Tom explained. So he spent evenings tinkering around down there, planning for the darkroom he was going to build. Often I tiptoed down the basement stairs, holding carefully to the railing to protect my off-balanced body. Halfway down, I paused, watching Tom move, the way he twisted his head from side to side to pop his neck, run his fingers through his hair first one way, then another. The soft, off-pitch humming that accompanied his pacing.

I knew not to intrude. I knew he was finding his way—trying to discern how to take the world of Mt. Moriah and make it his own. How to reconcile my past and build our future. How to be a husband, a father.

I'm not sure why it became my nightly ritual to spy on Tom. I guess part of me wanted to make sure he was still there—always there. After a few minutes of watching him, I would retreat to the bedroom and soon enough Tom joined me, patting me lightly on the shoulder as he passed and leaning down to coo at my bulging stomach. His smiles had changed since those early days of our relationship. They now held the burden of the world's evils—knowledge I had forced upon him in that email the day of Maddy's heart attack. Tom had joined in my resignation to the reality of fear. In doing this, he took some of my own fear away.

But Tom's smiles voiced something else. They said he was happy, content with our plans, satisfied to be on the mountain, with all that entailed. In the early mornings I awoke to find him already out on the lawn, seeing through his lens the majesty of the land. Once I found him on the branch below Grace's and my oak treehouse, teetering on unsteady feet. He settled himself, wedged in between two strong limbs. He took his camera out, focused, set and reset the aperture several times, clicked and then gave a satisfied smile.

I never asked to see that photograph. I knew from my heart, from my memories, what it showed: Now Tom saw through my lens.

While we did the renovations, Maddy was a daily inspector. He gave advice freely, and Tom took to calling him Reverend Contractor.

"Jesus was a carpenter, wasn't he, Reverend Contractor?" Tom would jest.

"You betcha, buddy. Darn sight better than you, too," Maddy would chuckle.

Standing back, I watched them together, these two men who were worlds apart, and yet not. They redeemed my faith in the gentleness of mankind. I bathed in their love and care that enveloped me and enjoyed their doting attention.

Upwards. Ever upwards toward light.

Maddy never fully got his strength back. He was frail and would tire easily. His bright blue eyes still sparkled, but his deep voice was softer, and frequently we would find him napping on the porch, wrapped in Doro's favorite afghan.

Although we never said it out loud, we both knew we would lose him. A few years perhaps, or a few months. Still, armed with that knowledge, I was strangely serene. For this time my grief would not be born alone.

As I moved through the rooms of the Inn, as I cooked in her kitchen and trimmed her rose bushes, Doro's spirit moved with me. I played Bach every afternoon, as the sun was sinking over the hillside. Sometimes I roused Tom out of bed with Vivaldi. I lingered at Doro's bookshelf and sorted through and organized her photo albums. Gradually I realized that I had forgiven her. What was there, after all, to resent? The crime of deep, selfless love? The sin of knowing me better than I knew myself?

One day, after carting away some old linens from the August room, I caught a glimpse of myself in the floor length mirror attached to the door. The image startled me. How long had it been since I had seen myself in a mirror? Since I had *looked*? I leaned in closely and examined my close-set eyes, my wild hair cascading around my face. My broad lips and hips and the protruding belly. I spent countless minutes this way, just staring.

And gradually it happened.

The image changed. I saw for the first time what I imagined Tom saw when he looked at me: eyes not close-set but deep and piercing, hair not wild but thick and luscious. And my body: not wide but warm. Welcoming. For the first time in so many, many years I felt pretty. Every day I lingered in front of the mirror and whispered to the alien love inside me.

"Pretty inside makes pretty outside," I said, reciting something Doro told me when I was an awkward eleven year old. I knew she was right. And I knew the baby would be born knowing that beauty. Knowing the prettiness that came from strength that I did not know myself.

She alone would know me from the inside out.

Through all of these months, the baby kicked wildly inside me. I knew she was a girl even before Dr. Overby told us, and I knew her name. We bought a maple rocker for the August room, and I sat there, looking out upon the driveway, rocking back and forth. Hours would pass like that, with a spirit of calm and happiness descending on me like a benediction.

Tom and I joked about the baby—how beautiful, smart and kind she would be. Perfect in every way with, of course, an acute affinity for Cheerios. But I knew there was only one thing I really wanted her to be: happy. To *create* happiness. I wanted her to be the kind of person who could find the blessing in every loss, the laughter hiding at the edge of every tear. I wanted her to be like Tom. Like Doro.

Like Grace.

And, yes, like me. For although I could never protect my child from darkness and loss, I knew I could lead her toward light, toward happiness. I could love her in ways she could never imagine and would often resent. I could teach her to cling to laughter.

The week after we finished stripping all the wallpaper and did all the painting, I began to write again. "Find your voice," Doro had said once, and at last I did. I knew finally the story I was to tell. It was not the voice of Jillsandra, not the tale of a stranger. It was *my* story, and so the words flowed and the pages filled easily. Each word was cleansing, redeeming. Perhaps one day my daughter would read the story. Perhaps no one would ever read it. But I wasn't writing for readers.

I was writing for myself.

Each day that I set out to write, I picked up page one and reread it, reminding myself of how it started, of how far I had gone the day before. All the days before.

The story's beginning was simple:

For every person there is a place.

EPILOGUE

A YEAR LATER, I took baby Grace for a walk through the neighborhood. It was that quintessential autumn day for which watercolors were made. The sky had played its annual trick, turning into a deep, soulful indigo that we had forgotten in the hazy summer heat. And the leaves: scarlet, golden, umber.

A lone mosquito, misplaced after the summer vacations, had bitten my left calf and, turning to scratch, I almost missed the next moment. A few more calculated gouges by my nails, and my head would not have turned in time to catch the moment, to preserve it in the annals of my brain. And my heart.

But turn back I did, in time to see a leaf winding its way toward baby Grace's head. It could not have caused any wind on her, buoyed as it was by the magical fall air that tripped through the trees. And yet Grace seemed to feel it before its touch. Her head fell back and her pudgy, sticky hand reached up as if to catch it. As she did, she grinned to reveal those miraculous two razors of enamel in her delicious gum.

I watched as the leaf did back flips down toward my daughter. I saw Grace's eyes sparkle with infantile magic. A lock of auburn hair, the only one she possessed, blew against her eye and she giggled as the leaf drifted against the collar that was smeared with her sweet potato lunch.

The moment stood still for me. Grace was frozen in her two toothed smile; the leaf was frozen against cottony warmth. Years later I would be able to close my eyes and see the very point on the exact street at that precise moment in time. I would be able to return—retreat—to that memory, tracing the leaf's downward spiral against the sky.

I know with certainty that that leaf did not fall but was sent. And I know from Whom it was sent. At that moment I felt more alive than ever before. I felt the soles of my feet, the hangnail tearing at my thumb, the ventricles swelling in my lungs, and the cartilage releasing and expanding in my knee.

I knew at that moment that my top was spinning, sometimes wildly, sometimes cautiously, but spinning, spinning, spinning. I realized that the beauty of tops lies not as much in where and how they spin, but in the fact that they do spin: day upon day, movement upon fluid movement. I saw with unimaginable clarity that endings are sometimes beginnings.

On that day, I knew that I had done nothing in my life to deserve such a trivial delight as an autumn leaf or such a precious gift as Grace. And yet both were mine, given from a Love that paints our worlds a mirage of brilliant hues.

And smiles back when we notice.

AUTHOR'S NOTE

AT MY CHILDHOOD DINNER TABLE, suppers were anything but sedate. Sometimes lively from teasing and laughter, other times loud from arguments over religion and politics, the family table fed not only our bodies, but our souls and our minds.

I remember discussing religion at that Formica table of my childhood and volleying questions back and forth across the lazy Susan. As I grew, so did my faith, and it was one that did not preclude questions. As an adult, I have lost and found faith; I have raged at God; I have wept for His forgiveness. All of these I have done as my parents' child. They consumed my rantings without regurgitating pat answers. Rather, they answered with a silence that said, "We know. But still. We believe."

Many years have passed since our nuclear family of five gathered at 6:00 p.m. sharp. It has been decades since we clamored for the last butterscotch brownie and made up rhymes about the rutabagas. My brothers and I have founded our own families and our own dinner tables, over which noisy chatter and discussion hover like a blessing. Around each of these, I believe my parents are silent, smiling guests.

Like most others, our imperfect family was perfected by love. In days of celebration, in times of angst, we gather because we are family. I am thankful for brothers who teased me so mercilessly that I learned not to take myself too seriously. I am thankful for parents who set the table and called us to it. And I am thankful for sharing my life now with a man who knows of no better place to be at six o'clock than at our family table.

306

My faith journey is not unlike Jo's. We are all prone to be boisterously thankful when good things happen to us. And so it is only natural that our sorrows carry shouts of why, and—for us believers—why, God? If we view the good, the joyous as *gifts* from God, does logic not compel us to therefore define bad things that befall us as His *absence*?

How easy to focus on that which we don't have, rather than our blessings—to view ourselves as victims rather than survivors. And it's that type of glass-half-empty thinking that makes life pass us by. For me, my faith gelled—and, in many ways my life began—when I was able to see God in all things good and bad, as a constant in the human continuum that knows the highest highs and the lowest lows. When I learned to listen to my still, small voice.

Many thanks to Brooke Warner and Shannon Green of She Writes Press and the community of talented female writers they represent. Thanks also to Julie Powers Gallagher for her early advice and encouragement, and to Books Forward for championing this novel. I appreciate Jenn Kimble's generational input as an alumna of the Class of 1993. Finally, special thanks to my early readers: Vicki, Kim, Anna, Susan, Lydia, Nancy, and Elena. Entrusting someone with your manuscript is only slightly less terrifying than handing over a newborn infant, and I appreciate their tender care.

If you are a person of faith, it is my hope that you will see some of your own journeys and questionings in these pages. If you are not a believer, then you are still a child of Creation and hopefully this story will touch the humanity in you—the part of us that asks why and struggles to find hope and happiness in a world where sometimes it seems all is for naught.

As a parent myself, I wonder if my own parents knew, at that nightly dinner, that they were sowing seeds of faith and hope. I wonder if they saw their three children of faith, with voices loud and questions louder, and knew that they did something really important.

I hope so.

MNC

ABOUT THE AUTHOR

© Meredith James

A NATIVE SOUTHERNER, Melissa Norton Carro has over twenty years of experience in marketing and communications, including her own business, Norton Carro Communications. She has edited textbooks and been a non-fiction ghostwriter, as well as a regular copyeditor for Gannett Publishing. She received her Bachelor of Arts, with Honors, from Vanderbilt University, where she currently works. Carro was a closet fiction writer for years while raising three daughters, and *Mt. Moriah's Wake* is her first novel. She writes a weekly blog, *In the Middle*, about life in the sandwich generation and is currently working on another novel, *Bagels at Nine*. She lives in Nashville with her husband and blue heeler mutt. Learn more at melissacarro.com.

SELECTED TITLES FROM SHE WRITES PRESS

She Writes Press is an independent publishing company founded to serve women writers everywhere. Visit us at www.shewritespress.com.

Magic Flute by Patricia Minger
$16.95, 978-1-63152-093-8
When a car accident puts an end to ambitious flutist Liz Morgan's dreams, she returns to her childhood hometown in Wales in an effort to reinvent her path.

The Fourteenth of September by Rita Dragonette
$16.95, 978-1-63152-453-0
In 1969, as mounting tensions over the Vietnam War are dividing America, a young woman in college on an Army scholarship risks future and family to go undercover in the anti-war counterculture when she begins to doubt her convictions—and is ultimately forced to make a life-altering choice as fateful as that of any Lottery draftee.

The Rooms Are Filled by Jessica Null Vealitzek
$16.95, 978-1-938314-58-2
The coming-of-age story of two outcasts—a nine-year-old boy who just lost his father, and a closeted young woman—brought together by circumstance.

Profound and Perfect Things by Maribel Garcia
$16.95, 978-1631525414
When Isa, a closeted lesbian with conservative Mexican parents, has a one-night stand that results in an unwanted pregnancy, her sister, Cristina adopts the baby—but twelve years later, Isa, who regrets giving up her child, threatens to spill the secret of her daughter's true parentage.

Beautiful Garbage by Jill DiDonato
$16.95, 978-1-938314-01-8
Talented but troubled young artist Jodi Plum leaves suburbia for the excitement of the city—and is soon swept up in the sexual politics and downtown art scene of 1980s New York.

The Wiregrass by Pam Webber
$16.95, 978-1-63152-943-6
A story about a summer of discontent, change, and dangerous mysteries in a small Southern Wiregrass town.